POWERLESS . . .

"You will be glad to know that I will not make you suffer any longer," Valerian said.

Bjorn's head fell against his chest. "Thank . . . the gods . . ." he whispered.

Valerian grabbed Bjorn's hair and forced the mage to look at him. Bjorn's heart pounded in his chest in sudden fear. "The gods have nothing to do with it, Bjorn," Valerian hissed at him. "You can thank *me*."

"Please, let me die," Bjorn begged.

"No," Valerian said. "I need you—I need you to watch your common worm friends for me and report to me."

Bjorn's heart fell. He knew that his next words would send him back to the rats.

"I . . . I cannot," he whispered.

"But Bjorn," Valerian replied, also whispering, "you have no choice . . .".

Ace Books by Thomas K. Martin

A TWO-EDGED SWORD
A MATTER OF HONOR
A CALL TO ARMS
MAGELORD: THE AWAKENING
MAGELORD: THE TIME OF MADNESS

Coming in May 1999
MAGELORD: THE HOUSE OF BAIRN

MAGELORD: THE AWAKENING

THOMAS K. MARTIN

ACE BOOKS, NEW YORK

This book is an Ace original edition,
and has never been previously published.

MAGELORD: THE AWAKENING

An Ace Book / published by arrangement with
the author

PRINTING HISTORY
Ace edition / April 1997

The Penguin Putnam Inc. World Wide Web site address is
http://www.penguinputnam.com

ISBN: 0-441-00435-0

ACE®
Ace Books are published by The Berkley Publishing Group,
a member of Penguin Putnam Inc.,
375 Hudson Street, New York, New York 10014.
ACE and the "A" design are trademarks
belonging to Charter Communications, Inc.

PRINTED IN THE UNITED STATES OF AMERICA

10 9 8 7 6 5 4 3 2

This book is dedicated to my new family, who were very understanding when we were trying to move and I had to finish this first. Many thanks and all my love to Mary, Autumn, April, Michael, Alicia and, of course, to my son Jonathan who has been there since it all began.

Chapter
-------- **One** -----------

BJORN WARILY PARTED the bushes with a gentle hand, lest he be seen. He cautiously examined the tiny clearing ahead of him—empty. *Damn!*

He rose to his feet from behind the bushes, walking out into the clearing to better examine the homemade trap he had left there. This was the fourth trap he had found empty—not so much as a baby hare for dinner. He knelt to examine the bait. The greens had been untouched, save for a caterpillar gnawing on one of the leaves.

Bjorn rose. He would leave the trap overnight. It was more likely that something would take the bait after nightfall—although nothing had last night. Bjorn sighed. There were three other traps to be checked. Perhaps they had fared better.

He adjusted the bow on his shoulder as he walked. Game had seemed scarce today. Even with his Art, he had not felt the presence of a single deer nearby. Bjorn closed his eyes, took a deep breath and let it sigh slowly out, frosting on the crisp autumn air.

Slowly, the scrub and tundra of the Wastes yielded its secrets to him. There was game here—families of hares hiding deep in their burrows, not out foraging as they should. Overhead a hawk cried, it too complaining at the lack of small game.

It had been thus all day. The large game not to be found and the common, small game hiding in their lairs. Something was amiss. . . .

Bjorn's mind finally touched something, though. Large, grazing—seeking out grass and leaves with flat teeth—snorting in anger as its head was pulled away from its prize by the heavy weight it bore on its back. . . .

1

Bjorn's eyes snapped open. *Horses! Horses with riders!*

His traps forgotten, Bjorn ran back down the trail toward home. The only horses in Hunter's Glen were the four dray horses that Lief the lumberer used to haul timber. They were not broken to the saddle.

Bjorn was over two hours from home, and he had sensed the riders almost halfway there. They would arrive long before he did.

Bandits, almost certainly, Bjorn thought. The nearest chieftain's hall was over two weeks' travel away on horseback.

Bjorn summoned what Power he could and thought a warning homeward. Hopefully, his aged father would sense it. Bjorn slowed to a jog. Home was a long way off. It wouldn't do him any good to exhaust himself before he arrived.

Bjorn approached the small cabin cautiously. His heart pounded in his chest. With the Power, he could sense more than a score of men near his home. Thankfully, he could also sense his father's living presence.

Bjorn peered toward the front of the house from underneath a bush, and his heart fell. Eight and ten men loitered around their horses in front of his home. All wore identical armor, carried identical weapons and bore the identical sign of a golden eagle painted on their shields. These men were *not* bandits.

Bjorn counted a score and one horses. Three men were inside—with his father. He closed his eyes and reached out with his Art. His father was definitely alive—even seemed calm, or at least calmer than Bjorn would have expected, given the situation.

He touched his father's mind, sending a wordless question. Calm reassurance reached him in reply. What was happening? Bjorn watched and waited.

Soon, the door opened and his father stepped out. Beside him was a young man, fair of face and with chestnut hair tied back into a horse's tail. He did not look to be much older than Bjorn, if at all. His build was slightly heavier than Bjorn's, with more bulk in the shoulders.

The young man was dressed much like the others, save for the quality of his armor. Where the soldiers were clad in leather reinforced with strips of bronze, this one wore a breastplate, bracers and greaves of gleaming bronze.

The shields of the soldiers were wooden, with bronze rims, but the young man's shield was fully plated in bronze. The rich leather underneath his armor and the violet mantle, emblazoned with the same eagle that the others carried on their shields, identified him as their chief.

These men were not from this area. No local chieftain held such wealth—the land was just too poor. No, this must be a young clan chieftain from the warmer lands to the south. Why were they here? And what business did this alien chieftain have with Bjorn's father?

"Bjorn!" his father called, cupping his hands around his mouth. "Bjorn, come here! We have guests!"

Apparently he was about to find out. If his father had instead said "visitors," that would have been Bjorn's signal to cut and run—warn the other members of the Circle. As it was. . . .

Bjorn gathered his feet under him and stood up from beneath the bush less than ten hands from one of the soldiers.

"Gods!" the soldier cried in alarm at Bjorn's sudden appearance so close to him. The soldier hastily backed away a step, gesturing with the sign of the hammer to ward himself. Bjorn glanced at the man—there was no power in his ward.

"Yes, father?" Bjorn asked suspiciously.

"Come inside," his father replied. "It is all right."

"Yes, father," he replied. As he walked past, he could hear the soldiers muttering under their breath.

"Damned hedge wizards," said the one he'd startled. Well, obviously they at least *suspected* who Bjorn and Rolf were. . . .

". . . should burn the lot of 'em," agreed another. Typical.

"Prince 'as gone mad," another offered. Prince? Not a chieftain, then, but a chieftain's son.

"What's going on, father?" Bjorn asked. "Why are the other two still inside?"

"How did you know that?" the chieftain's son interrupted. His voice was heavy with suspicion.

"I counted your horses, *lord*," Bjorn replied sarcastically.

"Oh," the young prince replied, glancing back toward his men. "I . . . see."

"Prince Gavin has come to us with an . . . interesting problem," Rolf told his son. "Please, join us inside."

Bjorn hesitated. Problem? What did they care about some southern clan's problems? The problem was that they were here and that Bjorn and his father had been discovered. Would the stake be much further behind?

Still, his father did not seem to be concerned. Bjorn crossed his threshold and glanced about the small main room.

Two older men waited inside, both more richly dressed than the soldiers. Neither wore the purple mantle with the golden eagle, however.

One, black-haired and bearded, carried a silver wolf on a black field as his insignia. The other, red of hair and fair of skin, wore a burning sword on cloth of white. Neither of the blazons was a local clan marking. Both men were large of build, and their eyes held the look of seasoned warriors.

"What do these men want with us?" he asked his father.

"I shall let them tell you," Rolf replied. "Your highness . . ."

"I am Prince Gavin of Reykvid," Gavin said. "This is William, chief of the Gray Wolf clan and Ivanel, chief of the Fire Sword clan. We desperately require the services of a mage."

"There are no such people in this area," Bjorn interrupted. "My father and I are simple trappers. . . ."

"They *know* who you and I are, Bjorn," Rolf interrupted. His phrasing told Bjorn that these men did not know the identities of the other members of the Circle.

"I . . . see," Bjorn replied, after a moment. He turned to the young prince. "Why should we help you, Gavin? What are the concerns of a southern clan, even three southern clans, to us? Do you seek to lure my father and I southward so that you can burn us publicly?"

"If that were my desire," Gavin replied, ignoring Bjorn's omission of his title, "you would both now be without your tongues and bound over two of our horses."

That was true enough. There was no way that Bjorn and his aged father could overcome a score of soldiers.

"We need your help," Gavin concluded.

"And we need our seclusion," Bjorn replied. "Your problems are of no concern to us."

"This problem concerns all men," Gavin replied. "Especially you and your father."

"How could . . . ?" Bjorn began.

"Hear me out," Gavin interrupted. "Once I am finished, if you still feel that this is not your concern, I and my men shall depart without malice."

"Very well," Bjorn agreed, hoping that the prince was a man of his word. Once they had left, Bjorn and his father would have to move on—find another place to live.

"My father is Magnus Urqhart," Gavin began, "king of Reykvid."

"Reykvid?" Bjorn asked. "I am not familiar with that clan. . . ."

"Reykvid is no clan," Gavin explained. "Reykvid is a kingdom ruling many clans." The prince gestured toward the two men with him.

"Both the Gray Wolf clan and the Fire Sword clan have sworn allegiance to my father, as have others," he finished.

Bjorn glanced over at Rolf, who nodded to him.

"I had heard of a great kingdom to the south," Bjorn began, "but I did not believe . . ."

"That kingdom is Reykvid," Gavin assured him.

"Magnus Urqhart is a man of honor and vision," William added. "Or at least . . . he was. . . ."

"And you call him king?" Bjorn asked.

"Yes, I do," the black-haired man replied fervently.

"As do I," Ivanel agreed. "My clansmen have swelled the ranks of King Magnus's army on many campaigns. He is a great man."

"A conqueror," Bjorn replied with a trace of contempt in his voice.

"My father is no conqueror!" Gavin objected. "Most of the clans have joined him willingly. Of those that have not, Reykvid has never dealt the first blow."

"Not before now," the chief of the Gray Wolf clan corrected softly.

"Yes," Gavin agreed sadly. "Not before now."

"What do you mean?" Bjorn asked.

"Three months ago, my father was travelling to negotiate the annexation of the Raven clan," Gavin explained. "We made camp in some barren hills. That night our scouts found a small cave at the base of one of the hills . . ."

Bjorn listened as the prince recounted the events of that night. The guards had explored the cave and had discovered a sealed door—apparently a burial vault of some kind.

Upon forcing the door, the searchers found the perfectly preserved body of a man laid upon a stone bier. He was dark-haired and beardless, wearing fine garments. The chamber was devoid of the normal treasures that such a man might have been buried with, however.

"And then," Gavin continued, "within moments of our entry, he awoke."

A chill passed across Bjorn's shoulders.

"Awoke?" he asked.

"Aye," William replied quietly.

"We were frightened, to say the least," Gavin continued, "but a strange calm came over us. The man attempted to speak, but we could not understand his words. When he next spoke, it was in our own tongue."

"What . . . did he say?" Bjorn asked.

"That his name was Valerian and that he had been travelling and had found the tomb empty two days before," Chief Ivanel replied. "He claimed that the tomb had sealed itself and that he had been trapped inside. He had thought his fate sealed until we opened the tomb."

"A . . . reasonable explanation," Bjorn observed.

"We found no evidence of occupation for those two days," Gavin countered. "Surely he would have found it necessary to . . . relieve himself during that time."

Bjorn nodded. That was true—if a man spent two days locked in a room, he would certainly leave something behind.

"Not only that," William said angrily. "The man has bespelled the king!"

"How so?" Bjorn asked. He doubted that Chief William

would know an enchantment from a lullaby. Even so, Bjorn found himself becoming interested.

"By morning," Gavin explained, "Valerian had won his way onto my father's council. By the time we had returned to Reykvid, Valerian had become my father's most trusted advisor."

Bjorn said nothing. The chill returned to the back of his neck and, this time, did not depart. He looked toward his father, who simply nodded at him.

"We believe," Gavin concluded, echoing Bjorn's own thoughts, "that we awoke a MageLord."

"Could it truly be a MageLord?" Bjorn asked his father. Outside, Gavin and his men made camp in the tiny clearing occupied by their cabin. Bjorn closed the shutter and turned back to his father.

"I can think of no other explanation," Rolf replied, easing himself down onto their only padded chair. "I pray you can find another."

Bjorn nodded. Gavin and his kind would never believe it, but Bjorn's people had always opposed the MageLords. Over a thousand years ago, it was the common mages, such as themselves, who had enabled humanity to survive the Time of Madness. Now, they were repaid with fear, hatred and the fire. . . .

"Bjorn?" Rolf asked, interrupting the young mage's thoughts.

"Yes, father?" Bjorn answered, pulling himself from his reverie.

"Why did you return here?"

"I . . . I feared for your life," Bjorn replied, bowing his head in shame.

"You should not have returned!" Rolf told him sternly. "Your first duty was to warn the Circle. You *know* this!"

"Yes, father," Bjorn agreed.

"Regardless, we will both be barred from the Circle," Rolf added. "Once you have left with Prince Gavin, I shall tell them of what has happened here. When you return, we shall move on."

Bjorn nodded. Now that they were known, Rolf and Bjorn could not risk exposing the rest of the Circle. They would be barred from the Circle and would have to disappear into another remote corner of the Wastes and try to rebuild their lives.

He thought of Helga, and Freida, and tears came to his eyes. Freida had practically been his mother since his own had died in childbirth. Now he would have to leave and never see her, or her family, again. And Helga, his betrothed—would she abandon him as well?

"Bjorn," Rolf said, more gently. "What's done is done. We will find another Circle—new friends to replace those we must leave behind. And, perhaps, some of our old friends will choose to travel with us."

Bjorn nodded, blinking back the tears that had not quite fallen. Rolf rose from his chair with some difficulty and walked over to put his hands on Bjorn's shoulders.

"Perhaps," Bjorn said in a thick voice.

"I will be here when you return," Rolf said. "Come, it is time for you to sleep. Your journey will begin early tomorrow."

"Yes, father," Bjorn agreed.

Sleep did not come easily for Prince Gavin. They had spent three weeks travelling the Wastes in search of a practitioner of the Forbidden Arts to help them. When they had finally managed to uncover one, they had found only a decrepit old man and his son.

What could either of these two hope to accomplish against someone of Valerian's power? Against a MageLord?

On the one hand, Gavin felt they should continue searching until they found someone of greater power. On the other hand, he suspected that such a person did not exist. It had taken three sevennights just to find these two. He could search the Wastes for another year and not find any better.

No, time was short. Gavin would have to return with what he had managed to find. Bjorn Rolfson would have to suffice.

Sleep eluded Bjorn as well. Could Gavin be trusted? Or would more of his men circle back and burn Rolf and the cabin to ashes after Bjorn had left with him on the morrow? What awaited Bjorn in Reykvid? The stake? Or a MageLord?

Bjorn would almost rather face the stake. The MageLords had been nothing short of gods and had persecuted Bjorn's people as fervently as any did today.

Actually, that was not quite true. According to legend, the MageLords had not actively hunted the common mages down. It was more like what Gavin would do if he happened across a roach in their home. Step on it and go about his way.

And Bjorn was that roach, boldly going forth to stick his tongue out at the man who could crush him. Nevertheless, he had to go. If a MageLord did indeed walk the earth, it was vital that they know for certain.

Chapter
-------- Two ------------

BJORN SHIFTED HIS weight in the saddle. One of Gavin's retainers had been ordered to walk so that Bjorn could ride alongside the prince. Bjorn would rather have walked. His feet had been toughened by years of travelling on foot. His backside did not have that advantage.

"You are unaccustomed to riding," Gavin observed as Bjorn once again shifted in the saddle.

"Yes, highness," Bjorn replied. "My father and I are too poor to own horses, as are most who live in Hunter's Glen."

"Are there others of your kind here?" Gavin asked.

"Not to my knowledge, highness," Bjorn lied. "Only I, and my father who trained me."

"I presume his father taught him," Gavin mused.

"Yes, highness," Bjorn confirmed.

"Will you be able to tell if Valerian is who we fear him to be?" Chief Ivanel of the Fire Sword clan asked.

"Not directly," Bjorn lied. Those with the Talent could sense the Power in another. It could be hidden by conscious effort, but not easily and not for long. If Valerian were indeed a MageLord, Bjorn would know at a glance. It would not do for normal men to know that one mage could sniff out another, though.

"But you *can* tell," Gavin stated. "Your father led me to believe that it *was* possible."

"If he has bespelled your father, I should be able to sense the Power that he is using to do so," Bjorn replied. "However, if he is not actively using his Art, I will be able to sense nothing."

The riders fell silent. Bjorn shifted again in the saddle. Gavin had told him that they would ride southward for ten

10

days until they arrived at a small river town. There they would take ship down the river to Reykvid itself. The trip down the river should take approximately a sevennight—the equivalent of a score of days on horseback.

Gavin would have been gone from Reykvid for almost a full season. If Valerian were indeed a MageLord, there was no telling what they would find waiting for them. Bjorn was not comfortable with this thought.

"Highness?" Bjorn said.

"Yes, mage?" the prince replied.

"Please, don't refer to me that way," Bjorn said. "It would be a shame if your subjects in Reykvid burned me before I had the time to examine Valerian."

Gavin chuckled in response, although Bjorn was certain he had said nothing at all humorous.

"It would indeed," the prince agreed.

"Highness, where do those back at Reykvid believe you are?"

"In other words," Gavin said, "is Valerian going to know that something is amiss and be waiting for us with an army?"

"Something like that, yes," Bjorn said.

"Not to worry, Bjorn," Gavin said. "I told my father that I was going to spend the harvest in my uncle Ivanel's hall."

"I told my clansmen," Ivanel added, "that my nephew and I were going on a long hunting trip. Suitable trophies should be waiting for us when we take ship."

"A full season is rather long to be away hunting," Bjorn observed.

"Not when one is hunting wyvern," Ivanel countered.

"That *would* explain a trip to the Wastes," Bjorn agreed. Wyverns were poor cousins to the dragons of legend, but still a foe to be wary of. A nest of wyverns could devastate the livestock of a large region. No doubt several herdsmen were going to be grateful to Gavin and Ivanel's men this winter.

The important thing, however, was that Gavin's absence would be adequately explained. A nest of wyverns was not a simple afternoon's hunt. The MageLord, if such he were, should not be suspicious of the prince's absence.

*   *   *

Gavin watched the blond-haired, bearded young man who rode beside him. He was not small of frame, but neither was his build that of a warrior. His blue eyes constantly scanned their surroundings like a trapped animal looking for an avenue of escape or for the direction of an impending attack.

He was not what Gavin had expected. Of course, what Gavin had expected had been derived from childhood stories about monstrous people who stole and devoured children.

The old man and his son had been nothing of the sort. It had actually been a stab in the dark that uncovered them. They were known by the locals as trappers and healers. Herbalists and apothecaries—not mages. Rolf had been well spoken of by his neighbors, such as there were.

Outwardly there was nothing, nothing whatsoever that marked them as anything but the trappers and hunters they claimed to be. Bjorn had startled several of his men by appearing in their midst yesterday, but that had merely been woodsmanship, not sorcery. Gavin had seen the young man stand up from beneath the brush surrounding the cabin. No doubt Bjorn was an excellent hunter. That gave him an idea.

"When we arrive at Reykvid," Gavin said, breaking the silence, "you will be introduced as the local guide who helped us to find the nest of wyverns. That is in keeping with your appearance."

Bjorn simply glanced over and nodded in reply. Gavin continued to study the young man in short, side glances.

It was only in their speech that one would suspect that Rolf and Bjorn were more than what they claimed to be. Both were far too well spoken to be simple trappers. They were obviously far more educated than their neighbors.

There were more questions here than answers. Gavin would have to find some of the answers before he trusted this man further. . . .

Bjorn was grateful when Prince Gavin called a halt to make camp for the night. The prince was setting a hard pace—he was obviously anxious to return home.

Bjorn climbed down from the saddle, wincing at the ache in his thighs and buttocks. The soldier whose horse he had ridden was waiting to take the reins. The man glared at him.

"I'll walk tomorrow," Bjorn said. "We'll both be more comfortable." The man said nothing in reply, just led the horse away after Bjorn reclaimed his pack.

Bjorn knelt and unlaced the thongs that held his bedroll to the bottom of his pack. Sleep would not come easy tonight— not among so many who would just as soon slip a knife into his ribs as travel with him.

It had been thus ever since the fall of the MageLords. Men had forgotten the common mages. Even though it was the common mages who had foreseen the Time of Madness and had led the bulk of humanity to the caves that had sheltered them from it.

Men had remembered only the evil of the MageLords. Not even a generation had passed before the common mages were driven from the shelter of the caves or slain outright. Even now, centuries later, they burned those who had saved them, fearful that the common mages would one day take that place held by the MageLords of old.

Bjorn gathered several armfuls of fir needles to spread under his bedroll. Not only would they help to soften the hard ground, they would keep the cold earth from stealing his precious warmth during the night.

The worst part, Bjorn supposed, was that it made no difference what good his people still did. If their neighbors ever learned the truth about them, Rolf and Bjorn would die at the hands of the very people whose lives they had saved from fever and injury. Little or no consideration would be given to the fact that, without the past help of the two mages, their executioners would not be alive to kill them.

Bjorn spread his bedroll out on the makeshift mat of fir needles. Things were not likely to change in Bjorn's lifetime— especially if Valerian were indeed a MageLord. The old fears would be rekindled even brighter than before. If anything, the common mages would be hunted even more vigorously.

"Why do you prepare your bed so?" Prince Gavin asked. Bjorn started at the unexpected voice so close behind him.

"I did not mean to startle you," Gavin apologized.

"How do you move so quietly in all that metal?" Bjorn asked.

"I don't," Gavin replied. "You were deep in thought. Also,

there are sounds of armor throughout the camp." Bjorn nodded in agreement.

"The fir needles keep the ground from chilling you as you sleep," he said in answer to the prince's question. "Your men would be well advised to do the same. It also makes for a softer bed."

"Perhaps you could demonstrate for them," Gavin suggested.

"I . . . suppose I could . . ." Bjorn agreed grudgingly.

"It could not hurt your . . . popularity in the camp," Gavin pointed out. Bjorn snorted in amusement.

"You can't hurt what isn't there," he replied. "And I think it will take more than a simple woodsman's trick to help my standing with your men."

"Nevertheless, it could not hurt," Gavin repeated. "Dinner will be ready soon. Will you join us at the fire?"

"Yes, highness," Bjorn replied.

"Good," Gavin said. "Now come, and you can show the others how to prepare their bedding." Bjorn sighed in resignation. Apparently he wasn't going to be allowed to separate himself from the camp.

"Yes, highness."

Dinner consisted of a stew made from jerked beef and a few potatoes and onions. Bjorn thought that it was probably only slightly more edible than the horses' saddles would have been. Still, it was better than what his traps had provided the last few days.

That thought made Bjorn think of his father. Who would tend the traps while Bjorn was away? His father was too old. . . .

One of their neighbors would probably help out. Bjorn had been away before—when Lief's mare had borne her colt, for instance. Before, it would have been one of the Circle, but now that could not be. Not now that he and Bjorn had been discovered.

"A copper for your thoughts, Bjorn," Gavin said. Conversation around the fire died. Why was the prince doing this?

"I was merely wondering who would tend the traps while I was away," Bjorn replied. "My father is too old."

"Surely one of your clansmen will help him," Gavin replied.

"There are few clans in the Wastes, highness," Bjorn said. "A man has only himself and those few friends he may happen to make near him. I am certain one of our neighbors will help—my father and I have tended many of the sick in our area."

"Yes, of course," Gavin agreed. "Still, I would have expected your thoughts to be on what lies ahead of us."

"Actually, I have been trying *not* to think of that," Bjorn replied.

There were a few muttered agreements around the fire. That much they all held in common—no one wanted to face a MageLord.

"Still," Gavin continued, "it is something we must consider. After dinner, the four of us shall gather in my tent to discuss plans."

"Yes, highness," Bjorn agreed.

"Wine?" Prince Gavin asked.

"Thank you, no," Bjorn replied. The tent barely held the four of them, seated on bedrolls. A makeshift table had been fashioned from a small barrel and a round shield. It was surprisingly stable.

"Do you fear poison?" Ivanel asked. Bjorn shifted his gaze from the prince to the chief of the Fire Sword clan.

"No," he replied. "Should I?"

"Indeed not!" Gavin answered, obviously insulted.

"It was not I who raised the question," Bjorn pointed out. "I only drink with family."

"Why is that?"

"Wine loosens the tongue," Bjorn replied. "That can be fatal to a practitioner of the Art."

"A wise precaution," Gavin observed, calming from his initial outrage.

"A necessary one," Bjorn replied.

"On to the matter at hand," Gavin announced. "What action can we take once you have determined that Valerian is what we fear?"

"*If* I determine that Valerian is what you fear he is," Bjorn said.

"Granted," Gavin agreed. "What can we do?"

"Nothing," Bjorn replied.

"Nothing?" Chief William objected. "Is there nothing you can do to free the king from his enchantment?"

"I highly doubt it," Bjorn said. "If your king were under the influence of some rogue mage, I could *possibly* do something about it. If Valerian is a MageLord, I might as well try to break an oak with my bow."

"Can he be killed?" Prince Gavin asked.

"All men can be killed," Bjorn replied. "However, I don't know that a MageLord could be killed by anyone other than another MageLord."

"So, you can only tell us whether or not Valerian truly is a MageLord," Ivanel concluded. "You cannot fight him."

"You do not fight an avalanche, Chief Ivanel," Bjorn replied. "You run before it."

"That is not an option, I fear," Prince Gavin said.

"No, it is not," Bjorn agreed. "If Valerian is indeed a MageLord, and I suspect he is nothing of the sort, your best strategy would be to catch him off guard and kill him."

"Assassination," Gavin replied softly.

"Precisely," Bjorn agreed.

"I am curious," Ivanel said. "Why do you believe that Valerian is not a MageLord?"

"Because I would rather believe that than believe that the world has ended."

"That seems rather fatalistic," Chief William said derisively.

"If he is a MageLord," Bjorn replied, "and you fail to assassinate him, what can you do against him? Can you battle a god, Chief William? Will you pit your sword against his Power? You would be ashes before you completed your swing."

"That is not a contest which *I* would care to enter," Ivanel agreed.

"Then the plan is begun," Gavin said. "If Valerian is what we fear him to be, we take him by surprise and murder him .... somehow."

"And if he is not?" Bjorn asked. The three warriors were silent for a while.

"If he is not," Gavin finally answered, "then we must come to terms with the fact that my father has violated our trust in him and act accordingly."

"That is treason!" Chief William objected.

"This is *all* treason, William," Gavin said.

"What if Valerian is simply what Bjorn suggested?" William asked. "A rogue mage who has bespelled the king."

"Then I shall kill Valerian myself," Bjorn replied acidly. "And then you can hang me for murder if you like." There was a short, surprised silence.

"That is a . . . vehement statement," Prince Gavin observed.

"If Valerian is a rogue mage," Bjorn explained, "then he has violated every belief that my father and I hold. If that is the case, I claim the right to kill him."

"It shall be yours," Gavin agreed.

Bjorn watched as William and Ivanel left the tent. Gavin closed the flap behind them and returned to the table.

"Wine?" Gavin asked. He held up his hand when Bjorn started to respond.

"Only a small amount," he insisted. "Not enough to 'loosen your tongue,' as you put it."

"Very well," Bjorn agreed reluctantly. True to his word, the prince only poured a little over a mouthful into Bjorn's goblet.

The prince studied him for a moment, not speaking. Bjorn felt a little uncomfortable. What did the prince want of him? He had been acting strangely all day.

"You are not what I expected," Gavin finally said, breaking the silence.

"Oh?" Bjorn replied, taking a small sip of his wine.

"No," Gavin affirmed. "Not at all."

"What were you expecting?" Bjorn asked. "Someone who lived alone in a hovel, covered in filth and keeping small children chained up in the cellar for dinner?"

"Not hardly," Gavin replied indignantly. "I'm not some superstitious peasant."

"I see," Bjorn said. "In that case, you were expecting some

haughty and aloof recluse, living in a tower surrounded by shelves of books and strange creatures."

"Uh . . . something more along those lines, yes," Gavin agreed.

"You are confusing us with the MageLords, Prince Gavin," Bjorn said. "However, as you say, you are *not* a superstitious peasant. You are a superstitious high-born."

"You have a sharp tongue, Bjorn," Prince Gavin said. "If someone spoke to me in that manner in court, they would find themselves in the dungeon."

"And which of us do you say hungers for the Power of the MageLords, highness? I would never imprison a man merely for being unpleasant to me. My ego is not that fragile."

For a moment Gavin only stared at Bjorn in surprise. Bjorn returned the prince's gaze evenly.

"I shall . . . remember that," Gavin finally said.

"My . . . apologies, highness," Bjorn said quietly. "I shall . . . go." He had probably gone too far. Still, it was hard, now that he was known, to contain all of the old anger. Even so, it was not this man who was at fault.

"No," Gavin said. "Please, stay. It is I who must apologize. You make an excellent . . . conscience, mage. And that is truly what I did not expect to find—a man of courage and conviction."

"Conviction I shall grant," Bjorn agreed. "Courage? No, I am no hero."

"Perhaps not," Gavin said. "However, it takes courage to ride with us to face what awaits us."

"I see that I have little choice in the matter," Bjorn said. "If a MageLord again walks the earth, we *must* know of it. I would be a liar if I said I felt no fear. A grand liar."

"A man without fear is a fool, not a hero," Gavin said. "A man who acts in spite of his fear is truly courageous."

"You must have wished to speak to me about something other than the strength of my character," Bjorn said, feeling more than a little embarrassed by the unexpected praise.

"Yes," Gavin said. "I do not understand you, Bjorn."

"There is little to understand, highness."

"I think there is more than you let on," Gavin said. "Bjorn, if you do not hunger for their power, as you put it, why do you, and your father, strive for it?"

"We don't," Bjorn replied.

"Do you mean to tell me that you don't practice the Forbidden Arts?"

"As you understand them, yes."

"I am becoming . . . confused," Gavin said.

"Highness, to understand me you must understand who we are," Bjorn explained.

"Then help me to understand," Gavin said. Bjorn took a deep breath.

"The explanation begins centuries ago, highness," Bjorn explained.

"Then begin," Gavin insisted.

"Very well," Bjorn agreed. "Centuries ago, as you know, the world was ruled by the MageLords."

"Indeed."

"What you do not know is that the MageLords were not the only mages who lived during that time. The common mages lived among the bulk of humanity—in hiding from the MageLords."

"Why?"

"Because we did not hold the Power that the MageLords held," Bjorn explained. "But they feared some of us might achieve it. If they found a child among us with sufficient Talent, they took it and either killed it, or raised it as one of their apprentices."

"How do you know all of this?" Gavin asked. "These things occurred over a thousand years ago, if the legends are correct."

"Because the common mages passed their history down," Bjorn explained. "We recorded it for future generations because, like you, we are determined that the MageLords shall never return."

"I see. Please, go on."

"The common mages served the common good," Bjorn continued. "We were the healers and teachers—trying desperately to ease the suffering the MageLords left behind them."

"The most powerful of the common mages, Bairn, foresaw

the coming of the Time of Madness. Under his direction, the common mages prepared deep places with supplies and even weapons. When the war began, we led humanity to these refuges beneath the earth."

"Are you telling me that mankind owes its survival to the mages?" Gavin asked incredulously.

"Yes, highness," Bjorn confirmed. "I am. And we were repaid with fear and the hatred born of fear. In less than a generation we were driven from the caverns *we* had prepared. The war of the MageLords had depleted all of the Power—we could not have defended ourselves had we wanted to."

"Even so, we did not condemn those who persecuted us. After all, it was only the fear of the MageLords that made them fear us and we understood that fear all too well. So, once more, we were forced into hiding."

"And you have been in hiding ever since," Gavin concluded.

"No," Bjorn said. "When mankind emerged from the caverns, we met them and once again led them to places that we had prepared for them. We taught them how to better survive in the harsh world that waited for them outside the caverns. And, once again, we were rewarded with fear and suspicion. Once again, we were forced into hiding, and we have been forced to hide ever since."

"It is no wonder that you are so bitter," Gavin said, "if this be the truth."

"It is," Bjorn assured him. "And that is also why I claim the right to kill Valerian if he is merely a rogue mage. Not only has he endangered all mages by his actions, but he *is* striving for the Power of the MageLords whose return I am sworn to prevent."

Gavin sipped at his wine long after he had dismissed Bjorn Rolfson. Could it be true? Could mankind truly owe its survival to the people it most feared?

Gavin shook his head. In the end, it did not matter if Bjorn's version of history was correct or not. What mattered was whether or not Bjorn himself believed it to be true. The prince was inclined to believe that he did.

That would certainly explain many things about Bjorn. The

basic decency he seemed to possess which was contradicted by a distrustful and suspicious nature. That nature would be necessary to survive in a world where one slip of the tongue could place one on the stake.

And the secrecy that one learned would not only apply to oneself. It would be necessary to maintain a tight lip about any others of his kind he knew of. A conspiracy of survival.

Bjorn did know of other mages, Gavin was certain. The type of historical recording he spoke of could not be accomplished by one line of fathers and sons.

There was also the matter of Valerian. Bjorn had spoken of a rogue mage violating their beliefs. Gavin could see how such a code would be created, once again for survival. Any rogue mage with aspirations of power could bring the wrath of humanity down on all of them, indiscriminately. Such a person would have to be killed quickly.

However, the existence of such a code still spoke of a society rather than isolated pockets of practitioners. Perhaps a loose society, and certainly a secret one, but a society nonetheless.

And therein lay the danger. True, most of these mages were probably good people—using their knowledge and power secretly to help their neighbors as Bjorn and Rolf did. However, it would take only one—one who strayed from those beliefs and achieved the power he sought—to bring the MageLords back into existence.

That was why, even after this was over and humanity once again owed its survival to the mages, they all had to die.

Chapter
-------- Three -----------

BJORN LOOKED ABOUT aimlessly at the forest. Just three days south of Hunter's Glen the nature of the landscape had changed considerably. The thin, scrubby forests of Hunter's Glen gave way to lush pine forests. Bjorn knew that Lief did much of his lumbering in these woods, but he had never seen them for himself.

The weather seemed considerably warmer, as well. Of course, the weather in Hunter's Glen could have warmed also. It was still very early autumn, and the last few days before Gavin's arrival had been unusually cool.

"We should arrive in Pine Grove by nightfall," Gavin said.

"Pine Grove?" Bjorn asked.

"Yes, it's a small village," Gavin replied. "Do you know it?"

"I have heard of it," Bjorn answered. "One of our neighbors cuts lumber in these woods. Lief says that it is a lawless place and that many bandits take refuge in the surrounding forests."

"That is not an inaccurate assessment," Ivanel said. "We are well armed, however, and not carrying anything particularly worth stealing."

"Same watches as before?" William asked.

"Yes," Gavin replied. "Three watches, six men per watch as well as one of us. We will maintain these night watches until we reach Nalur's Ridge."

Pine Grove was every bit as lawless as Lief had described. As far as Bjorn could tell, no one actually lived here on a permanent basis except, perhaps, for the innkeepers.

Bjorn revised that estimate when Gavin's party entered one

of the inns. The raucous laughter and conversation that had been in process stopped the moment Prince Gavin stepped through the door. He was followed by William, Ivanel, and Bjorn.

All eyes in the establishment turned toward them. Bjorn was decidedly less than comfortable under such scrutiny. Gavin, William and Ivanel returned the stares evenly.

It was apparent that many of the women in the room were permanent . . . residents of the inn. Bjorn imagined that the large, armed men sitting by the fire were also employed here. This place was only four days' travel from Hunter's Glen? For some reason, that thought troubled Bjorn.

"Innkeeper!" Gavin shouted. *"Innkeeper!"*

A large, dirty man stepped through a doorway and looked toward them. His features visibly brightened at the sight of Prince Gavin.

"Ah, m'lord!" he said, hurrying up to them. "''Tis good to see ye again. Will ye be wanting the, ah . . . same lodging as last time?"

"Yes," Gavin replied. Bjorn noticed that the attention of the other patrons was turning away from them as they spoke with the innkeeper. Soon the conversation had risen to its original, boisterous level.

"Good, good," the innkeeper said. "Shall I 'ave dinner sent out for your men?"

"No, thank you," Gavin replied. Bjorn agreed. For some reason, jerky and potato stew sounded like a much better option tonight.

"But have a small keg of ale sent out," Gavin continued. "A *small* keg—untapped."

"Yes, m'lord," the innkeeper replied. Gavin surreptitiously handed the innkeeper a small, gold coin.

"Let's go," Gavin said to them, turning to leave the inn. Whereas everyone had noticed their arrival, no one seemed overly interested in their departure.

"Where are we going?" Bjorn asked once they had gotten outside.

"The stable," Gavin replied.

"The stable?" Bjorn said.

"Don't complain," Chief William advised. "It's cleaner."

"And we can guard our horses," Ivanel added, "as well as ourselves."

"I see your point," Bjorn agreed.

Bjorn had been very glad to leave Pine Grove. The evening had been uneventful, if noisy. However, Bjorn was half convinced that that was only true because Gavin had maintained his camp watches inside the stable. The sentries had once challenged someone who had approached too close to the stable for their liking. That had not happened again.

Now it was nearing sunset. Gavin had seemed to want to put as much distance as possible between his party and the logging town, setting a hard pace for the horses and men to follow.

Bjorn rode his own steed now. Somehow, Gavin had found a suitable horse to purchase for the newest member of his entourage. Although not the heavy beast he and his guard rode, it was more than enough to carry one unarmored man.

"Shall we stop to make camp, highness?" Ivanel asked.

"No," Gavin replied, to Bjorn's surprise.

"We shall follow the trail for another hour or so," Gavin continued, "and then make camp. I want the first watch established as soon as we stop."

"Yes, highness," William and Ivanel replied almost in unison.

"Is it wise to ride in the dark?" Bjorn asked.

"I would rather ride in the dark than be ambushed in camp," Gavin replied. "Any bandits seeking to waylay us will be looking for us an hour further back."

"Good point," Bjorn said.

"These woods need to be cleaned out," William grumbled.

"Perhaps we will, someday," Gavin replied.

"Not . . ." William began. Before he could finish, an arrow flew past Gavin to strike the gruff chieftain in the shoulder.

"Bandits!" Gavin shouted. The cry was taken up by the men as arrows flew at them from the forest. The orderly troop scattered along the road. Gavin's warriors dismounted to attack the enemy in the forest. Bjorn unslung his bow from his shoulder and nocked an arrow.

The fading sunlight made it almost impossible to see back among the trees. Fortunately, the bandits either could not see either, or were terrible shots—or both.

Bjorn slid from the saddle and landed on the balls of his feet. He focused on the shadows, raising the Power around him. The sounds of battle around him faded as Bjorn concentrated on his sight. The shadows slowly yielded their secrets to him. He was barely aware of the shouts and screams of battle.

There! A dim silhouette stepping out from behind a tree to fire at them! Bjorn raised his bow and let fly. The bandit cried out and staggered back, a feathered shaft protruding from his chest.

Bjorn nocked another arrow and fired at another bandit who believed himself hidden in the shadows of the forest. He almost missed, but the shaft penetrated completely through the bandit's neck. The silhouette dropped its weapon and fell, clawing at its throat.

Bjorn was able to fire twice more before Gavin's men reached the bandits hiding in the woods. He put away his bow—it would not do to shoot one of Gavin's men. Their trust of him was not the best as it was.

Soon, the battle was over. The remaining bandits fled deeper into the woods. From what Bjorn could see, not many survived to flee. Gavin's men returned to the road. Bjorn met them to help with the wounded.

"You have a good eye, Bjorn," Gavin said upon his return. "We found four bandits dead by your arrows."

"Thank you," Bjorn replied distractedly.

One of Gavin's men was dead, shot through the heart with a bandit's arrow. Several others had sustained minor wounds in the infighting, and William had an arrowhead buried in his shoulder.

"We have to make camp here," Bjorn told Gavin. "I have to get that arrow out of William's shoulder before he can travel further."

"I can . . . ride," William insisted.

"Of course you can—now," Bjorn retorted. "In less than another hour, you'll be unconscious. Or dead. Highness, we *must* make camp!"

"Spread out in twos!" Gavin ordered the men. "Find us a place to camp. *Go!*"

"Help me get his breastplate off," Bjorn told Ivanel. Ivanel did not argue. He and Bjorn unfastened the straps and lifted the heavy bronze armor off William.

"Somebody get a fire going!" Bjorn ordered as he began to examine the wound. The prince himself began gathering up wood. Soon a small fire was crackling in the middle of the road.

The wound looked clean. The arrow had missed the major vessel of the arm. Bjorn laid his knife on a rock near the fire, with the tip in the flame itself.

"What are you doing?" Ivanel asked.

"The flame will cleanse the knife," Bjorn replied, using a cloth to sop the blood from William's shoulder.

"Do you have any drink stronger than wine?" Bjorn asked.

"Aye," William said. "I could use . . . a little."

"It's not for your belly, fool," Bjorn said. "I need it to clean the wound."

"Here," Ivanel said, handing Bjorn a small flask. Bjorn removed the stopper from the flask and smelled—potato whiskey. That would certainly do. He poured some on the cloth.

"Waste of . . . good . . . drink," William complained.

"It won't be a waste if it saves your life," Bjorn quipped. "Now hush." William winced as the strong liquor burned his shoulder.

"Will he be all right?" Gavin asked.

"If I can get the head out, yes," Bjorn replied. "It's a nasty one—multiple barbs. But it missed the large vessels. Hold him."

Gavin and Ivanel each pinned William's arms. Bjorn made a small cut and William cried out as the hot metal sliced his flesh. Bjorn spread the wound open and reached in, carefully drawing out the arrowhead.

"Got it!" he said. "Hold him."

Bjorn poured more whiskey into the wound. William cried out and briefly lifted his arms against Gavin's and Ivanel's weight. The two armored men struggled to keep him down.

Bjorn folded a clean cloth from his pack and pressed it against the wound.

"Hold that," he told Gavin. "Press hard while I bandage it."

"Right," Gavin said. Bjorn cut large strips of cloth from the dead guard's cloak to hold the bandage in place.

Soon, Bjorn was tying the last knot in William's bandages.

"There," Bjorn said. "He ought to be able to ride after a good night's sleep."

"Highness," William croaked.

"Yes, old friend?"

"Can I . . . have a drink of . . . what's left of my . . . whiskey now?" William asked. Gavin looked to Bjorn.

"A small one," Bjorn said, handing the flask to the prince. "It's not good after losing this much blood." William took the flask and drank deeply.

"That's enough!" Bjorn said, pulling the flask from William's hand. "I said a *small* drink!"

"Highness?" William said. His voice sounded a little stronger.

"Yes, William?"

"When we get back to Reykvid?"

"Yes?"

"Either make him," William said, pointing at Bjorn, "your physician or your torturer."

Gavin laughed.

Gavin's party left what passed for the main road to the village a quarter day's ride to the north. In the sevennight since the bandit attack, William's shoulder had begun to heal nicely. Enough so that it could be passed off as a hunting injury—especially when wyverns were involved.

"We shall circle the village," Gavin explained, "and rejoin our hunting party a half day to the south. On the morrow we shall ride into town with our trophies."

"Makes sense," Bjorn said.

"Tonight you shall have to speak with the scout," Gavin continued. "You must gather all of the details of the hunt that you can if you are to pose as our guide. We can test your performance in the village tomorrow."

"Highness!" Bjorn objected. "These villagers will be much more difficult to convince than your subjects in Reykvid.

They are much more familiar with this area than Valerian or anyone else will be."

"Then you had best question the scout thoroughly," Gavin said.

"Indeed," Bjorn replied sullenly. In all likelihood, he would never make it to Reykvid. The villagers would burn him themselves, tomorrow.

Bjorn rode passively, allowing his horse to pick its own trail through the darkness. The sun had set some time ago. Ahead, the lights of campfires and watch torches illuminated the darkness. Gavin's camp, he hoped.

Bjorn shifted in the saddle. The days of riding had toughened his muscles to the saddle, but today had taxed them beyond their limits. He was road weary and dirty.

Instead of a hot meal and his bedroll, however, a long session of questioning Gavin's scout about the hunt awaited Bjorn. Even so, Bjorn did not see how one night's questions would give him enough information to convince the locals that he had been the one to lead Gavin's hunters.

They were hailed at the camp perimeter by the sentries— more men in Gavin's colors. They quickly parted to allow the prince and his party to pass. A huge pavilion stood in the center of the camp, surrounded by a dozen smaller tents.

Bjorn, Prince Gavin, and the two chieftains rode to this tent. Guards took their horses as they dismounted. At least they wouldn't have to tend to their own horses tonight. Bjorn reclaimed his pack before the guard led his borrowed mount away.

"Summon the scout," Gavin ordered one of the guards. "And rouse the camp. There is much to be done before morning."

"Yes, highness," the guard replied.

"The men will be exhausted," Ivanel cautioned once the guard had departed. Bjorn listened idly as he gazed around at the interior of the pavilion. This was obviously only one of many rooms within the massive tent. If this one room were any indication, this southern prince travelled in more luxury than many northern chieftains enjoyed in their own halls.

A table, large enough for six to eat at comfortably, sat in

the center of the room. Six wooden chairs sat around it. Against the cloth walls sat three lounge chairs, cushioned and carved of walnut. Small tables sat next to each of the lounge chairs. Oil lanterns, with real glass chimneys, filled the room with light.

"As they should be," the prince replied to Ivanel's previous comment. "We should not return from a wyvern hunt fresh and well rested."

"Aye, that is true," Ivanel agreed.

"Do you like my father's pavilion, Bjorn?" Gavin asked, having noticed Bjorn's silent inspection of his surroundings.

"It is certainly . . . pretentious," Bjorn commented.

"Pretentious!" Chief William objected. His shout was followed by Gavin's laughter. Ivanel and William both looked at Gavin in confusion.

"I like you, Bjorn," the prince said. "You have a unique way of putting things in perspective. Yes, it *is* pompous and arrogant to travel in this type of splendor. However, it is also necessary when negotiating with the neighboring clans. I assure you, my father's war pavilion is much more . . . austere."

"Then why did you not bring the war pavilion?" Bjorn asked. "It would have seemed more appropriate for a wyvern hunt."

"Well . . ." Gavin began, "that is, I . . . that is a good point, Bjorn. My father suggested that I take the grand pavilion instead. I didn't question his decision at the time."

"It would certainly slow you down on the march," Bjorn noted.

"Aye," Ivanel agreed. "And make our little expedition take that much longer."

"And it left the war pavilion at the king's disposal," William observed.

"Perhaps it was not your father's idea, after all," Bjorn suggested.

"Valerian . . ." Gavin mused aloud.

"Highness," a guard interrupted, entering the tent. "The scout is here in answer to your summons."

"Good," Gavin replied. "Send him in."

The prince turned to Bjorn after the guard had left the room.

"Learn your part well, mage," he said. "Our success against Valerian depends upon it. He is more devious than we realized."

The scout, whose name was Johann, was atypical for the region. His black hair and beard was marked with gray, and his dark brown eyes seemed almost black themselves. His leathery skin was bronzed from long hours outdoors. More surprising, however, was the fact that he possessed the Talent.

Still, there were many who held the Talent who were not Circle. Bjorn allowed his right hand to rest on his leg with the fingers splayed. Casually, he placed his middle finger atop the index finger in the Sign.

Prince Gavin had bid them retire to one of the back rooms in the pavilion to discuss the details of the hunt while he met with his officers in the main room. Muffled voices carried through the tent walls. Bjorn was pleased with how much of the sound was blocked—it would make his conversation with Johann more private.

"So," Johann observed, "they found one o' the Circle, after all." The scout held up his hand, returning Bjorn's sign.

"You knew of their plan?" Bjorn asked.

"Aye," Johann replied. "Fortunately, when they found me, they were lookin' for a scout—not a mage. They asked me not a few questions about findin' one, howe'er."

"Do you know why they wanted one?"

"Nay," Johann said. "I was tae busy coverin' my tail. Yet, ye still live."

"Yes," Bjorn agreed. "For now. Gavin fears that he and his father have woken a MageLord from magical slumber."

"Bairn protect us!" Johann hissed. "Do ye believe them?"

Bjorn shook his head in response.

"That Valerian is a MageLord?" he said. "No, I do not. I do suspect that he is a rogue mage, though."

Johann spat in contempt.

"That is almost as bad," he said. "Ye *will* kill him?"

"If he is a rogue? Of course."

"And if he *is* a Lord?"

"We shall . . . try," Bjorn conceded.

"Aye," Johann agreed. "That is all ye can promise. So, his high-and-mightyness wants ye tae pose as the scout who led them on their wyvern hunt?"

"Yes," Bjorn replied. "He wants to test my guise on the villagers in the morning."

"Ye don't know this area!"

"I am aware of that."

"We'll have tae commune . . ." Johann mused.

"Are you willing?"

"If a MageLord walks the earth?" Johann asked. "Aye, I will do aught that I can tae help ye."

"My thanks, Johann," Bjorn said.

"Enough," Johann said. "Raise the Circle and let's be aboot our business."

Bjorn nodded. He gathered the Power and spun it in a protective circle about them, calling on the spirit of Bairn to protect and guide them. The Circle formed, stronger than any Bjorn had raised before. Fear was a powerful motivator.

"Impressive," Johann breathed as he joined his own consciousness with the Circle. Bjorn felt Johann's Power flow into the Circle he had raised. He reached for Johann's hands with his own as his mind reached to Johann's through the Circle.

"Now," Bjorn said, releasing Johann's hands but not his mind, "tell me about the hunt."

"We began trackin' the beasts at Nalur's Ridge," Johann began. As he spoke, the images and memories of the events he described flowed through the Circle into Bjorn's mind. Nalur's Ridge was not a geographical feature so much as it was a farming community.

"Cattle and sheep had been comin' up missin' for months," Johann continued. Images of a council of frightened and angry farmers flowed into Bjorn's mind.

Thus it was throughout the entire tale. Johann would verbally relate the events of the last few weeks to Bjorn and the sights, sounds and smells of those events came to Bjorn through the Circle. Occasionally Bjorn would question some detail, and the answer would come to him before he had finished the question.

It had been a phenomenal stroke of luck that Gavin's scout was of the mages. Now Bjorn actually had a chance of playing his part not only at the village, but also in Reykvid.

Still, he had best concentrate on Johann's tale, lest some precious detail be lost. The two of them would likely be at this for several hours.

Prince Gavin dismissed the last of his officers with praise. The camp had been prepared for tomorrow's trip into the village. The hunting trophies had indeed been impressive. Three adult wyverns, eight fledglings and over a dozen hatchlings.

As he retired toward his bedchamber, Gavin heard muffled voices from back in the tent. Were Bjorn and Johann still discussing the hunt? The mage needed *some* rest before morning.

Gavin turned and reached out toward the flap to the room in which they were talking. His hand stopped on the flap.

No, he thought, not feeling the gentle Power that turned him aside. *Best not to disturb them.*

Bjorn climbed into the saddle, blinking against the morning light. He had managed to get perhaps one or two hours of sleep before dawn.

The village ahead of them was Nalur's Ridge, he now knew. His tired eyes looked on their surroundings with new familiarity. He knew that to the east, across the river, lay the stony ridge that gave the village its name. An old tower on that ridge now served as feed storage for the small community. He could picture both the ridge and the tower that sat on it in his mind.

"You look tired," Prince Gavin observed, riding up alongside him.

"As I should, returning from a wyvern hunt," Bjorn said, quoting Gavin's remarks of last night. The prince chuckled.

"Indeed," he agreed. "Do you feel confident with what you learned from the scout?"

"Yes, highness," Bjorn replied. "I am curious how you are going to explain the change in scouts to the council of farmers, however."

"I'm not," Gavin replied.

"But . . ." Bjorn began.

"You are not going to speak with them," the prince interrupted. "Johann will address them with me."

"But you said . . . ?" Bjorn said.

"I felt that you would work harder to remember his stories if you believed that you had to convince the locals," Gavin explained.

"And you call *Valerian* devious," Bjorn grumbled.

"Yes," Gavin agreed. "I do. And the only way to defeat him, if he is a MageLord, is to be more devious than he is. Now, shall we ride?"

Bjorn watched as Gavin's men loaded the trophies into the hold of the longboat. Fortunately, the cargo was separated to the fore of the hold. The only thing worse than the stench of wyvern was the stench of rotting wyvern.

The crew would sleep belowdecks in the aft section of the hold. A small cabin aft of the mast was the only private area aboard the longboat. Bjorn had first assumed that this was Gavin's cabin. He learned, instead, that Gavin and the two chieftains both made use of it.

Bjorn would probably sleep abovedecks. The thought of crowding in with the crew made him uneasy. It would be far too easy for him to wake up with a knife in his ribs.

"A fine ship, is she not?" Gavin asked, walking up beside him.

"I suppose so," Bjorn agreed. "I fear that I am not much of a seafaring man."

"Not surprising, considering that the nearest sea is more than two fortnights' travel from here on foot," Gavin observed wryly.

"With your permission," Bjorn said, "I would like to sleep on deck rather than below with the crew."

"Denied," Gavin replied.

"Highness . . ." Bjorn began.

"You shall sleep in the cabin," Gavin interrupted. "There is an empty bunk since only myself, Ivanel, and William are aboard. I do not want to find you with a knife in your back one morning." Bjorn turned and eyed the small cabin suspiciously.

"How did you manage to fit four bunks into that?" he asked. The prince laughed.

"There is a table in there, as well," the prince replied, laughing again at the surprise on Bjorn's face.

"'Tis a ship," Gavin explained. "You *find* the space."

"And you call *me* a wizard," Bjorn grumbled.

Chapter
-------- **Four** -----------

BJORN LEANED ON the side of the longboat near one of the unmanned oar stations. The oars had not been manned for the entire trip. Rather, a northern wind had sprung up soon after they departed the village and had persisted for the last three days of their trip. The sail had been deployed, saving the men from the labor of propelling the longboat downriver.

Bjorn had heard whispered mutterings from the crew that perhaps *he* was responsible for the fair weather. He did not disillusion them. If they thought him the bringer of their good fortune, perhaps they would not blame him for their bad.

The trip had been swift, far swifter than travelling by horse had been, and pleasant. Bjorn watched the forest on the far bank flow by at the speed of a brisk run. A deer, drinking at the riverbank, glanced up as the longboat approached. From the corner of his eye Bjorn saw one of Gavin's men raise a crossbow.

Flee! he thought angrily, reaching out and touching the mind of the buck. It turned, flashing its white tail as it disappeared into the brush. The bolt flew wide of its mark as the soldier cursed.

Bjorn clenched his teeth in anger. The arrogance! To kill an animal one had no use for, merely for sport. Or, even worse, to *fail* to kill it. To only wound it and leave it to die slowly as the ship sailed on. Bjorn would have to speak to the prince about this . . .

"Hunt master," someone said behind him. Bjorn turned at the sound of his new title, careful to veil his anger. One of the prince's men stood behind him.

"His highness wishes to see you in the cabin," the guard explained.

"Thank you," Bjorn replied. Bjorn walked around to the back of the cabin, opening the door. The bottom bunks served as chairs for the small table in the room. Prince Gavin was seated in the only chair. William and Ivanel were also seated at the table, intent in discussion.

"Your highness," Bjorn said, a touch of anger creeping into his voice.

"Thank you for joining us, hunt master," Gavin said.

"Highness, I must speak with you," Bjorn insisted.

"Is something amiss?"

"One of your men just attempted to shoot a deer drinking by the river," Bjorn explained. "An animal he had no use for! I . . ."

"Guard!" Gavin shouted, interrupting Bjorn.

"Yes, highness!" a guard replied, opening the door to the cabin.

"Tell the men that they are not to fire on game along the river," Gavin ordered. "Any man who does so shall be lashed to the mast and flogged!"

"At once, highness!" the guard replied, closing the door.

"Thank you, highness," Bjorn said.

"Of course," Gavin replied. "Now if you would please join us . . ."

"Yes, highness," Bjorn replied. As he took a seat on the bunk next to Ivanel, he noticed Chief William observing him intently.

"What?" Bjorn asked. William smiled.

"You can tell a lot about a man by what makes him angry," William explained. "Until now, I have not seen you angry. I am glad you are with us, hunt master."

"If we may continue . . . ?" Gavin asked. When there was no response, he continued.

"This weather has taken a full day off our journey," Gavin explained, probably for Bjorn's benefit. "We should arrive in Reykvid by midday after tomorrow."

"When will we meet Valerian?" Bjorn asked.

"Almost immediately," Gavin replied. "He will probably meet us with my father on our return. Are you prepared?"

Bjorn laughed—a single, short bark of derision.

"Prepared?" he asked. "How does one prepare to meet a MageLord?"

"Prayer," Ivanel replied quietly.

After another day and a half the prince's longboat arrived at Reykvid. Nestled by the mouth of the river, the city sat at the base of a deep fjord. The palace itself sat atop the steep cliffs, overlooking the city from its nearly impregnable position.

Bjorn could easily believe that this was the center of the newly forming kingdom. The palace was huge, constructed of heavy stone. It was surrounded by two stone walls. Both were battlemented and pierced with arrow slits.

Even the city itself boasted a stone wall, although smaller. It wove along the beach like a snake at the high tide level. Several longships sailed into or out of the fjord, returning from or bound for unknown destinations. To Bjorn's magical senses, the city teemed with the power of Life.

Gavin's longship sailed out of the river and into the fjord, maneuvering to an empty pier. Several other longships, all bearing the colors of Reykvid, were docked nearby. Separated from the other docks and well guarded, Bjorn concluded that these must be the royal longships.

Bjorn's eye followed the narrow trail up the side of the fjord to the palace. He would not want to lead an attack up that face. No, any attack would have to come from atop the cliffs.

"Beautiful, is it not, hunt master?" Gavin asked, walking up beside him as the oars were deployed to guide them into dock.

"Beautiful?" Bjorn replied. "Perhaps. Impressive? Absolutely. All of these stone walls must have cost . . . more than I can imagine."

"Taxes from our loyal barons," Gavin replied.

"Bairns?" Bjorn asked, in surprise. Bairn was a figure of legend among the mages. Why had Gavin used it as a title?

"Bar*ons*," Gavin corrected. "A title granted to those next in line for the throne after myself and my as yet unborn heirs. William and Ivanel are both barons. Beneath them rule the chieftains. The barons tax the chieftains and then pass a portion on to the king."

"The chieftains pay this tribute willingly?" Bjorn asked.

"Yes," Gavin replied. "In exchange they gain the protection of an army larger than any of them could raise alone. Not to mention roads, guaranteed safe trade and countless other boons. All paid for by their taxes."

"It seems well planned," Bjorn said. "And if a chieftain does not join willingly . . . ?"

"They do," Gavin said. "Eventually. A few do not wish to swear on from time to time. They soon find that they can no longer raid their neighbors who have, however. One clan went to war against us. They were conquered. Most have joined willingly over time."

"I see. Your father is indeed a man of vision."

"Was," Gavin replied, somberly. "Two clans, the Badger and Elk clans, were taken by force before I left. Clans that would have joined of their own will, given time."

"And you think this is because of Valerian?"

"It was Valerian that counseled war," Gavin explained. "No other opinion was considered. That is not the king I know."

"We should know, soon enough," Bjorn replied.

"Aye," the prince said. "Come, we have docked. Remember our role, hunt master. We return triumphant from a great hunt!"

The trail up to the palace was steep, with many switchbacks as the stairs carved into the cliff face wound their way to the top. Carrying supplies up to the palace must be a constant chore. Just transporting the hunting trophies up required ten mules.

Bjorn looked up at the stone walls looming over them. One stone dropped from those walls could clear the entire trail. Hopefully Valerian was not preparing just such a welcome for them.

They reached the palace gate without incident. The guards beside the open gate came to attention, bringing their spears upright before them as Gavin passed. So far, so good.

They passed through a tunnel in the wall. To either side deep, narrow slits lined the walls of the tunnel. Bjorn glanced up. Similar openings pierced the ceiling of the gate. He had never seen such construction before—the gate was a death trap.

They emerged into the field between the two walls. Bjorn blinked. There was no gate in the wall before them, and the inner wall was a good ten feet higher than the outer wall. The prince turned to the left, and Bjorn followed.

Halfway around the side of the palace the inner gate stood, just as forbidding as the outer. An invader would have to traverse several hundred feet to reach the second gate, presumably under fire. If any fortress in the world were impregnable, it was this one.

Inside the inner wall was a veritable village of buildings. Stables and smithies, kennels, storehouses and barracks—all built into the wall itself. A large, open ground surrounded the palace.

And the people! Hundreds of people milled about within and without the palace proper. Bjorn could only stare at the subdued chaos in awe. He had never seen so many people in one place.

"Can you sense anything?" Gavin whispered to him. Bjorn shook his head.

"I will not know until I see Valerian," he explained.

"That should be soon," Gavin replied.

The palace was an immense hall of stone. Four huge, round towers flanked the corners and two more stood guard by the main gate. Only a few narrow windows, slits really, pierced the wall. It did not look like a pleasant place to live.

"This is your home?" Bjorn asked. His tone betrayed his distaste.

"It is more pleasant than it appears," Gavin assured him. "This used to be the outer wall in my grandfather's day. My father tore down the central hall and rebuilt the palace around the inside of the wall after he added the two outer walls. There is a large courtyard and garden inside which is much less . . . defensible."

As they passed through the final gate into the palace, Gavin's words proved to be truthful. They emerged into a large entrance foyer, larger than many chieftains' halls. Most of the opposite wall was open archways onto what was, even in late autumn, a beautifully lush garden.

Had the weather been more harsh, Bjorn was certain the archway doors would be closed. Even so, glass windows (glass!) in those doors would still permit a pleasant view of the garden from the foyer. Draped tapestries were tied back between the archways. Apparently the entire wall could be draped against the cold.

"This *is* beautiful," Bjorn conceded. "I am . . . impressed, Prince Gavin."

"Just when I was beginning to think that nothing could," Baron William grumbled behind them.

"Smile, barons," Gavin admonished them. "'Tis all right for Bjorn to look awed, but we've just had a victorious hunt!"

"Aye," Ivanel agreed, getting into the spirit of his role. "And what a hunt it was, too!"

As Prince Gavin led his retinue toward the throne room, the palace staff gathered behind them. All were impressed by the sight of the prince's trophies. The prince smiled and waved to them all—called many by name when they welcomed him home or offered him their congratulations.

And then they were through the massive double doors and into the throne room. If the foyer had been impressive, the throne room was nothing less than magnificent. Marble columns supported the ceiling.

Along the left wall were the same archways leading into the garden that Bjorn had seen in the foyer. Rich tapestries adorned the opposite wall, hiding the bare stone of the outer wall. Ornately carved walnut benches faced the even more elaborately carved pair of thrones at the end of the long hall.

Despite the extravagance of the throne room, Bjorn did not notice it. His eyes had locked on a tall, slender figure standing behind and to the right of the king's throne. Valerian—it had to be.

Bairn protect us, he thought, stopping in the doorway. Gavin had been right. One mage could discern the aura of Power surrounding another, like a faint, ghostly glow around the person. Valerian wore his aura like a mantle—thick and radiant. It burned around him like the noonday sun, leaving no doubt in Bjorn's mind.

Valerian was a MageLord.

"Come, hunt master," Gavin admonished him. "You can gawk later." Bjorn took a step forward, and then another, his eyes never leaving Valerian's form.

Bairn help us, he thought. *We are all dead men.*

"Bjorn?" Gavin whispered.

"Gods help us," Bjorn whispered in reply.

"Valerian? Is he . . . ?"

"Yes," Bjorn replied, slowly regaining his composure. "Gods help us, yes."

"Bjorn!" Gavin growled in a harsh whisper. "Pull yourself together before you give us away! You've hidden all your life. Do it now!"

Bjorn swallowed. Gavin was right; he must not let fear overcome his training. He must hide, as if from a mage hunter. He was Bjorn, the hunt master from Nalur's Ridge. He did not know that Valerian was a MageLord. He had nothing to fear, for, if he feared, the smell of it would betray him.

Years of training came to his rescue, evening his steps and his breath—calming his jangled nerves. He was innocent. He was Bjorn, the hunt master. He had nothing to fear.

"Greetings, father!" Gavin called to the man seated on the throne. "We bring trophies to adorn the Grand Hall."

"So you do," the king replied. Now that they were closer, Bjorn could see that King Magnus was an older, more powerful version of his son. His hair was slightly redder, and his beard was beginning to gray.

Valerian was another matter. He seemed quite young, although, if the stories of the MageLords' powers were true, he could be centuries old. Beardless and black of hair, he appeared dangerous even without his aura.

As his eyes met Valerian's, Bjorn was surprised to see a look of recognition and fear cross Valerian's face. The expression was quickly replaced by puzzlement and then by nothing at all. What had Valerian seen? Or thought he had seen?

"And fine trophies they are, too," the king's voice said almost next to Bjorn. Bjorn turned his attention back to Gavin and his father. King Magnus had descended from the dais to join his son. "Three adults! That was no mean battle!" The king turned to his son.

"I am proud of you, Gavin," he said.

"Thank you, father," Gavin said. "We could not have succeeded without the aid of Bjorn, the hunt master, however." The prince gestured toward Bjorn by way of introduction.

"Indeed?" Magnus said, turning his attention to Bjorn.

Bjorn knelt, as before a clan chieftain in his hall.

"Your majesty," he said.

"Rise and be welcome, Bjorn . . . ?"

"Bjorn Rolfson, of Nalur's Ridge, majesty," Bjorn replied, rising to his feet. "Your welcome honors me."

"Your majesty," Valerian said, stepping forward. His voice was as soft and smooth as a snake's might be. "Perhaps the royal artisans could have the trophies mounted in time to adorn the hall for tomorrow night's banquet."

"Banquet?" Gavin asked.

"In honor of your return, highness," Valerian explained.

"An excellent idea, Valerian!" Magnus agreed. "Have the castellan see to it."

"And quarters for the . . . hunt master?" Valerian asked, pausing significantly before pronouncing Bjorn's false title.

He knows! Bjorn thought.

"Of course," the king replied. "Gavin, you must be tired. We can talk more at the banquet. And I want to hear the tales of your hunt!"

"Yes, father."

Bjorn walked through the garden. As afternoon crept toward evening, the air had begun to chill. The garden was filled with late-blooming flowers as well as the summer plants that now slept, awaiting the coming of next spring. When the autumn flowers also fell to the coming snows, evergreen bushes and trees would still give the garden color.

For now, however, Bjorn sought only a little solitude away from the sterile isolation of his quarters. Meeting Valerian had been a shock. He had thought himself prepared for that meeting, but nothing could prepare one for the wreath of Power that surrounded the MageLord.

MageLord. That word alone was enough to summon fear in both commoner and mage alike. Bjorn sat on a bench in a secluded pocket of the garden and allowed his head to fall back. He closed his eyes and exhaled a deep breath in a long sigh, allowing some of the tension to ease from his body.

MageLord. One of the godlike tyrants who had crushed humanity beneath their heels for uncounted thousands of years. Alive and, apparently, in the full of his Power. How could Gavin, or anyone for that matter, have even the faintest hope of opposing someone like that?

"Enjoying the garden, hunt master Bairn?" Valerian's voice said from before him. Bjorn's eyes snapped open as he gasped in surprise. There had been absolutely no sound, or other sense, of the MageLord's presence. Yet there he stood, smiling down at Bjorn.

"Your pardon, m'lord," Bjorn stammered, rising to his feet. "You startled me."

"My apologies," Valerian replied. "So, master Bairn, are you enjoying the garden?"

"Yes, m'lord," Bjorn replied, attempting to regain his role as a simple huntsman. "But my name is Bjorn, m'lord—not Bairn."

"Oh, my mistake," Valerian apologized. For some reason Bjorn doubted that it had been a mistake at all. Bairn was a figure of renown to the magi—almost a god. Was Valerian trying to bait him?

"I look forward to hearing your stories of the hunt during the banquet tomorrow night," Valerian continued.

"Thank you, m'lord," Bjorn replied.

"Good afternoon to you then, master Bjorn." Valerian nodded his head in farewell, an amused twinkle in his eye. He then turned and walked away. Bjorn waited until the MageLord was lost from sight amid the foliage before collapsing back onto the bench.

Gods! he thought, trembling as his stomach knotted in reaction to the encounter. There had been no hint of Valerian's approach. The MageLord had slipped past Bjorn's senses without so much as a ripple.

It was certain now, however. Valerian knew quite well who

Bjorn was—or at least suspected it strongly. Bjorn would have to let Prince Gavin know of this tonight.

Bjorn rapped lightly on the door to the prince's chambers. Gavin had ordered a meeting in his chambers an hour after sunset.

Bjorn glanced nervously down the hall and then back toward the large foyer outside the king's chambers. After his garden encounter with Valerian, Bjorn was practically jumping at shadows. The prince's door opened and Bjorn started in surprise.

"My apologies, Bjorn," Prince Gavin said. "I did not mean to startle you."

"Not your fault," Bjorn said, quickly ducking into the prince's anteroom. Gavin glanced up and down the hall before closing the door. William and Ivanel looked at Bjorn with expressions of puzzled concern.

The prince's quarters were richly furnished. Comfortable chairs were drawn into a half-circle in front of the fireplace against the outer wall. Bookshelves lined the walls, filled with books. Handmade rugs covered the floors, and tapestries flanked the fireplace. Bjorn barely noticed, claiming a seat against the wall, near the fire.

"Are you well?" Gavin asked.

"Considering that I was just cornered by Valerian in the garden!" Bjorn replied. "After that I would say that being alive is sufficient to qualify as 'being well.'"

"What happened?" William asked.

"Nothing, really," Bjorn replied. "He merely asked if I was enjoying the garden and said that he was looking forward to hearing the stories of the hunt at tonight's banquet."

"Seems innocent enough . . ." Gavin mused.

"He sought me out, highness!" Bjorn insisted. "I believe that he knows I am not your hunt master."

"Have some wine," Gavin said, offering him a goblet. "It will help to calm your nerves."

"Thank you, highness," Bjorn said, taking the goblet.

"Gavin tells us that you have confirmed that Valerian truly is a MageLord," Ivanel said as Bjorn took a sip from the goblet. The wine was mulled—heated and spiced with cinnamon. As the prince had promised, its warmth helped to calm him.

"There is no doubt," Bjorn replied.

"How can you be certain?" William asked.

"When a mage is working his craft," Bjorn explained, "another mage can . . . see the Power he calls. It surrounds the other like a pale haze."

"But only when he is practicing his Art?" Ivanel asked.

"Normally," Bjorn lied.

"And Valerian has this . . . haze surrounding him?" Gavin asked.

"Yes," Bjorn replied. "But with Valerian it is no pale aura. When I look at Valerian, it is like looking into the noonday sun."

There was a moment of silence as the prince, William, and Ivanel exchanged somber glances. Finally, Gavin broke the silence.

"Then it is as we feared," he said. "Has he bespelled my father?"

"I cannot tell," Bjorn replied. "However, from what you have told me, it certainly seems likely."

"So," William said with false confidence, "what shall we do about Valerian?"

Bjorn laughed shrilly.

"Do?" Bjorn asked. "Do? What *can* we do? The man is a *MageLord*. There is nothing we can *do*!"

"He is *still* a man," Gavin said. "And men can be killed."

"Exactly," William agreed.

"You would all be dead before you could raise a blade against him," Bjorn objected.

"Perhaps not, if we place it in his back as you suggested," Ivanel countered.

"Poison," Gavin said.

"Yes!" William agreed. "Poison his wine at the banquet tomorrow night."

"What shall we use?" Ivanel asked. "Nightshade?"

"Certainly not!" Bjorn objected. "Have you ever tasted belladonna?"

"I . . . cannot say that I have," Ivanel replied.

"One sip, and he would know that his wine had been poisoned."

"Well then, apothecary," Gavin said, "what *shall* we use?"

"In wine?"

"Mulled wine, much like what you are drinking now." Bjorn looked down at his goblet and then took a sip. He held it in his mouth a moment, savoring the flavor.

"Mandrake root," he finally announced. "It has a wooden taste, but this wine has been stored in casks, has it not?"

"Can you obtain it?" Gavin asked.

"Probably," Bjorn replied. "A well-stocked apothecary should have the root. It is used to force vomiting and to thin the blood. It is very expensive, however."

"As if that mattered," William muttered.

"How quickly will it kill him?" Gavin asked.

"It will take the better part of an hour," Bjorn replied. "However, his mind will be gone long before his death. In this case, that is an important consideration."

"How long will the poison take to prepare?"

"An hour at most," Bjorn replied.

"How much gold will you need to purchase it?"

"That is difficult to say," Bjorn replied. "One, perhaps two measures. I will also need a small phial and two pots to prepare the potion."

"Give him five royals," Gavin told Ivanel. "That should be more than enough."

"I presume there are apothecaries in the city?" Bjorn asked.

"Any number of them," Gavin confirmed.

"Will I have any difficulty entering the palace once I have purchased the root?"

"No," Gavin replied. "People pass into and out of the palace all through the day. The guard will allow you to pass freely before nightfall."

"Good," Bjorn said. "Then I should have plenty of time to purchase the root and brew the poison before tomorrow's banquet."

"So," Ivanel noted glumly, "we are reduced to assassins."

"Better to be reduced to assassins," Bjorn replied, "than to ashes."

Chapter
------- **Five** -----------

REYKVID WAS ALMOST overwhelming. Before today, Nalur's Ridge had been the largest community that Bjorn had ever seen. Here, there were more people merely in sight than actually lived in the entire village of Hunter's Glen.

The crowd made Bjorn more than a little nervous. However, the people who jostled past him did not even look at him as they passed. There was little danger of discovery here.

The smell was almost as overwhelming as the crowd. Reykvid smelled like a fishing village that Bjorn had visited once as a child, only more so. Even though he was almost a mile from the docks, Bjorn could still smell the fisheries. It was no wonder that Magnus's grandfather had built his hall atop the fjord—he had been fleeing the smell.

The street that Bjorn had been following opened up into a small square lined with shops. The city was filled with such clearings. Unfortunately, the extra space did not alleviate the crowding—it just meant there were more people. If anything, the squares were even *more* crowded than the streets.

Street vendors sold their wares from carts and pavilions, hawking at the crowd that their wares were, of course, the best in Reykvid. People talked, argued, traded or just tried to push their way through the press. Bjorn found an eddy in the human current and stopped to scan the shops.

As were most of the buildings in the city, the bottom half of the first floors were fashioned of stone. The second floor and the top half of the first floor were built of wood. A few buildings, not many, rose up to a third floor before ending in some sort of tiled roof.

Bjorn finally found what he was looking for. Above one shop was a wooden sign emblazoned with a mortar and pestle. That seemed to be the universal sign for an apothecary in Reykvid. Hopefully, this one, the fifth he had checked this morning, would have what he sought.

Bjorn maneuvered around a knot of women surrounding the obligatory fishmonger. That was why, the smell of fish permeated the entire city. Every square had at least a cartful sitting in it.

"Eight pennies!" one woman cried in dismay. "I bought one for five yesterday two squares north of 'ere!"

"But, m'lady," the fishmonger began. The crowd swept Bjorn out of earshot toward the apothecary. A sudden clanging sound caught Bjorn's attention. A tinker was banging on a pot with a ladle. Behind him was a cart loaded with various pots and utensils.

"Pots!" he cried. "Finest pots in the city! Small pots, big pots!"

Bjorn made a mental note to look over the tinker's wares once he got through with the apothecary. He would need a medium and a small caldron to prepare the mandrake extract. He would also need a phial in which to place the finished extract. He could undoubtedly get that from the apothecary.

Bjorn stepped out of the crowd into the relative silence of the apothecary. He deeply inhaled the sweet-bitter-musty odor of the shop, letting the tension of being surrounded by so many people slip away from him.

"A bit crowded out there, eh?" an old man's voice asked.

Bjorn opened his eyes, assessing the shopkeeper. The man was near his father's age—perhaps a little older. His hair and beard were mostly silver with just a hint of the deep red they must have once been. His blue eyes were keen and sharp, however.

"More people than I'm used to seeing," Bjorn replied honestly. This man would be able to tell instantly that Bjorn was not a local—there was no point in trying to hide the fact.

"Where are you from?" the old man asked.

"North," Bjorn replied, stepping up to the counter that blocked the front of the shop from the apothecary's workroom. "Nalur's Ridge."

"Hmm," the apothecary said. "I'm not familiar with that one. 'Tis in the Wastes?"

"That's right."

"Chieftain?"

"None," Bjorn replied. "We've a town council."

"You must be from a ways north," the apothecary said. "Say, you didn't come in with the prince's party, did you?"

"I was his hunt master while he was in our village," Bjorn said. He was almost relieved to know that, even in a city the size of Reykvid, gossip still travelled quickly.

"Why didn't you say so, lad?"

"Why?" Bjorn asked. The apothecary nodded.

"I like a man who doesn't crow too much about himself," the old man said. "What can I get you?"

"I picked up a bit of a wheeze on the trail," Bjorn replied. "And it seems to be getting worse. Do you have comfrey, coltsfoot and mandrake?"

Bjorn had told the truth, except for the part about his condition becoming worse. In actuality, it was clearing, but the apothecary would not know that if he decided to examine Bjorn.

"Mandrake is a bit hard to come by," the apothecary said. "Comes from far to the south, you know. However, I happen to have one root."

"I presume you also have the comfrey and coltsfoot?" Bjorn asked.

"Of course!" the man replied. "What kind of apothecary would I be if I didn't? Mind if I ask a question?"

"Not at all," Bjorn replied.

"Why don't you have the palace physician look at you? He wouldn't take your money, and he probably has the root on hand."

"Physician?" Bjorn asked, honestly surprised. He hadn't even know that a physician lived in the palace. It made sense, though. . . . The apothecary laughed.

"You didn't know, that's why," he said.

"Anyway, I've been brewing my own teas for too long to start letting someone else do it for me," Bjorn added. "Would you go to the physician?"

"Hell, no," the apothecary agreed.

"How much do you want for the root?"

"Four sovereigns—that is, measures." Each Reykvid sovereign was one measure of gold.

"Four measures!" Bjorn said. "I was expecting to pay a little over one! I'll give you one and a half for the root."

The apothecary shook his head. . . .

Bjorn hung the larger of the two pots from the hook in the fireplace. He had negotiated the apothecary down to two and a half measures—sovereigns, actually. One small caldron and an even smaller caldron from the tinker had only cost him half a measure total in comparison.

Four crystal phials from a different apothecary had cost him another measure. Gavin would probably not be pleased with the amount Bjorn had been forced to spend.

Once the water started to boil, he would place the mandrake root in the pot and allow it to boil for an hour. He could use the tiny pot to heat water and refill the large one as it boiled down. Once the root had boiled long enough, he would take it from the pot and allow the extract to boil down.

A soft knock sounded at the door. Bjorn quickly glanced around the room. This was *not* a good time for visitors. He removed the larger pot from the fire and hid both behind his bed. Fortunately, the pot had not gotten too hot yet.

The knock sounded again. Bjorn walked over to the door.

"Who is it?" he asked in as normal a tone of voice as possible.

"Gavin," someone whispered on the other side of the door. Bjorn opened the door.

"Did you get it?" the prince asked once Bjorn had closed the door behind him.

"Yes," Bjorn replied. "I was beginning to think I was not going to be able to find it."

"How long before it is ready?" Gavin asked.

"I suppose that depends on how often I am interrupted," Bjorn said. Gavin smiled at the mild rebuke.

"I shall see that you are not," Gavin assured him.

"About two hours," Bjorn told him.

"Good; bring it to my chambers when you are finished," Gavin told him.

"Yes, highness," Bjorn replied.

*   *   *

Bjorn lifted the larger caldron from the fire with a rag and set it down on the hearth. The poison had cooked down to approximately a third of the pot. The originally thin brown liquid had gotten darker as the water had boiled away.

He poured the remainder into the small pot, almost filling it. Bjorn lifted the smaller caldron and hung it on the fireplace hook. Another half hour and he would be able to set it aside to cool.

He set the phials on the hearth to begin warming. It would not do for them to shatter when he poured the hot broth into them.

Bjorn went and sat in the room's only chair. There were no guarantees that this would work. In fact, it was not even likely that it would. If poison had been sufficient to kill the MageLords, they would not have ruled the world for all the millennia that they had.

Still, that and knives in the back were their best options. Bjorn rose and checked the pot. Once this smaller pot cooked down about halfway, he would set it aside to cool. Each phial would hold enough extract to kill two men at this concentration. Hopefully, it would be enough to kill Valerian.

Bjorn casually knocked on the door to Gavin's chambers. He smiled and nodded at the few who passed by. Most did not respond—the castle staff was harried in preparation for tonight's banquet. The door opened.

"Ready for the banquet, highness?" Bjorn asked pleasantly.

"Almost," Gavin replied. "Come in, hunt master." Bjorn stepped inside, and Gavin closed the door. William and Ivanel were already here.

"Is it ready?" William asked.

"Yes," Bjorn replied. He pulled three phials from his pouch.

"I have a phial for each of us," he said. "Each phial contains enough poison to kill two men, let alone one."

"So, any one of us will be able to . . ." Ivanel began, his words trailing off.

"Poison the bastard," William finished.

"I know it's distasteful, uncle," Gavin said to Ivanel. "But we have no choice. We all know what Valerian is. This is the only chance we have. The only chance Reykvid has."

"I know," Ivanel replied, looking through his phial at the dark brown liquid. "But I do not have to like it."

"We have to be careful not to double dose a single goblet of wine," Bjorn interrupted. "The taste of the mandrake would be too powerful if that happened."

"And we would all be dead men," William concluded.

"Precisely," Bjorn agreed.

"Well, then," Gavin said. "We have a banquet to attend in our honor, gentle sirs. Shall we?"

Bjorn applauded with the rest of the hall as the jugglers concluded their performance. It was difficult to appear festive, however, with the presence of the MageLord.

Valerian was seated at the king's left, wearing his aura like a mantle of office. Gavin was seated on the king's right. William sat next to Valerian, and Ivanel was seated next to Gavin. Bjorn sat next to Ivanel at the prince's request.

"William is prepared," Ivanel whispered to Gavin and Bjorn. With the seating arrangements what they were, William was in the best position to poison Valerian's wine. Gavin nodded and turned toward the MageLord.

"Valerian!" he called.

"Yes, highness?" Valerian replied.

"Where are the trophies? I thought you were going to have them mounted before the banquet." As Gavin distracted the MageLord, Bjorn saw William covertly empty the brown liquid into Valerian's goblet just before the wine steward arrived to refill it. Good—the pouring would stir the contents.

". . . shall arrive shortly," Valerian was saying in response to the prince's question.

"Excellent," Gavin replied. Bjorn watched aside as Valerian picked up his goblet and drew a long draught from it. Valerian set the goblet down, apparently unalarmed.

It begins, Bjorn thought. In a few minutes, they would know if the poison was effective.

Valerian continued to drink from the goblet throughout the

banquet. The next troupe of entertainers were almost finished with their short play and yet there seemed to be no effect.

Had the poison been ruined? Bjorn had been extremely careful in its extraction. Perhaps the root had been old. Even so, there had been enough extract to have *some* effect even if the root had been dug up last year.

Bjorn caught Gavin's eye as the actors completed their play. The prince, too, looked concerned. Something was amiss.

The sound of conversation in the great hall began to die. Bjorn glanced away from Gavin to watch as the revelers fell asleep at their plates, one by one until only those at the high table were awake.

Bjorn glanced over toward Valerian to find the MageLord looking him directly in the eye. Valerian took another drink of his wine.

"An excellent vintage, don't you think, hunt master?" Valerian asked. "I found that the mandrake extract added a unique flavor to the wine."

Gods help us! Bjorn thought as panic tightened his chest. He attempted to rise and flee only to find himself unable to move in the slightest. It was then that he noticed the small tendrils of Power that extruded from Valerian's aura to engulf all of them.

"Whom did you fools think you were treating with?" Valerian asked. Frozen as they were, it was obvious that the question was rhetorical.

"Did you honestly believe that I did not know of your little plan tonight?" Valerian continued. "I am Lord Valerian, of the House of Rylur—and you thought that you could poison *me*?"

Valerian rose from his seat and took the phials from Gavin and Ivanel's pouches. The anger in his face was replaced by a pleasant expression. Only his eyes betrayed the anger he still felt.

"Still, it is convenient for me that you decided to use poison," he added. "That fact alone will be enough to get you burned at the stake, hunt master. Once the prince and his two coconspirators die of poisoning, that is. And once it is discovered that you are in possession of the very poison used to kill them."

Bjorn's eyes moved from Valerian to the prince as Valerian poured the brown liquid into Gavin's drink.

"Did your little hedge wizard explain the manner of death you attempted to inflict on me?" the MageLord asked. "The poison will set fire to your mind long before you die. You will see all of the demons of every Hell you have ever imagined. And you will feel them ripping out your bowels as the poison burns through you."

Bjorn glanced over to the king, who sat staring at Valerian. Tears gathered at the corners of the old warrior's eyes as he glared in anger.

Valerian was oblivious to Magnus's rage. He held him as motionless as the others. Still, even the MageLord's Power must be strained, at least a little, by the effort of holding five men against their will and that of keeping the entire hall asleep.

Bjorn summoned the Power as Valerian continued to poison the drinks and describe, in gruesome detail, the horrors of the poison. He focused on the king, ignored by Valerian. Bjorn tried to reach past Valerian's control, to form a wall around the king's soul.

Bairn, aid me now! he prayed as he poured more Power into the ward he was building around Magnus's mind. Seemingly from nowhere, Bjorn once again felt the rush of Power flow into him as he had when casting the circle around himself and Johann. The ward suddenly crystallized into solidity around the bespelled king's mind.

"*Demon!*" Magnus shouted as he leapt to his feet.

Valerian whirled in surprise just in time for the dagger in Magnus's hand to drive upward into his stomach.

Bjorn was knocked to the floor as a sound like a thunder-clap echoed through the hall. As he fell, Bjorn saw Magnus hurled away from the MageLord as if struck by a giant hand. Then his head struck the floor and dancing lights filled his vision. Bjorn shook his head to clear it, and found that he could move again. Where was Valerian?

Slowly rising to his knees, Bjorn found the MageLord slumped against the wall, clutching at the dagger in his belly.

Valerian gingerly pulled the blade from his stomach, covering the wound with his fist. Then he looked directly at Bjorn.

"This is *not* finished, little mage," Valerian said, his voice strained with pain.

"Finish him!" Gavin shouted, drawing the ceremonial sword at his side. Ivanel and William did likewise. Shouts and screams sounded behind Bjorn as the guests awoke from the magical slumber Valerian had cast on them.

Before the prince and the barons could close on the wounded MageLord, a flash of light preceded another thunderclap, smaller than the first. When the spots cleared from Bjorn's eyes, Valerian was gone.

"Guards!" Gavin shouted. "*Guards!* Search the palace! Find Valerian. Do not attempt to capture him—*kill* him!"

"Highness!" William shouted. "The king!"

"Father?" Gavin said, turning toward the sound of William's voice.

William knelt by the king, cradling Magnus's form in his arms. Pink froth bubbled at the king's lips. Bjorn looked away—if the king was not dead, he soon would be.

"Father?" Gavin said again, kneeling by his father.

"Physician!" he shouted. "Physician, attend the king!" Bjorn saw an elderly man make his way through the crowd to kneel by Magnus's side. His examination was brief.

"There is naught I can do, highness," the physician said. "His ribs have torn through his lungs. He will be dead very soon."

"No!" Gavin shouted. "Father!"

"G-Gavin," Magnus said. His voice was so weak he could barely be heard.

"I am here, father," Gavin replied. Silence fell on the crowd as the king spoke.

"That m-monster . . . played me like . . . a puppet," Magnus said. "You must . . . kill him. Promise me. Swear it."

"I swear it," Gavin said. "I swear it on Hrothgar's name. I will kill the MageLord." A gasp from the onlookers greeted Gavin's use of that title.

"Hunt . . . master," Magnus called weakly.

"Yes, majesty?" Bjorn replied. What did the king want with

him? Had Magnus heard Valerian call *him* a mage as well? Was he bound for the fire?

"Thank you for . . . your help," Magnus said. "I fear my . . . boon to you will not be . . . welcome, however."

"Majesty, I ask nothing . . ." Bjorn began.

"I lay my . . . death charge . . . at your feet," Magnus said. "Stay with my son—aid him until this . . . demon is slain."

"That has always been my intent, majesty," Bjorn replied. "I accept your charge."

"You are . . . a good . . . man, hunt master," Magnus said. "I wish . . . I could have . . . known you . . . better. . . ."

The king's last words trailed off as his head slumped against his son's shoulder.

"Father?" Gavin said, his voice trembling. "Father?" He held his father tightly and began to weep, ignoring the blood that stained his tunic.

"The king is dead!" William shouted. "Long live the king! All hail, King Gavin Urqhart!"

"All hail King Gavin!" echoed the crowd.

Bjorn looked down at the young man crying over his father. Somehow, he doubted that the new king even heard them.

Bjorn sat, uncomfortably, on the back pew in the temple of Hrothgar. Whatever else Magnus may have been, he had been a pious man. The chapel was larger than the king's throne room. Of course, as Bjorn examined the mural that took up the entire wall behind the altar, piety was not always a good thing depending on one's point of view.

The mural showed Hrothgar in combat with a MageLord. Dragons and demons reached for him from the earth itself, but still the hammer-bearing hero pressed on toward his true enemy—the MageLord.

The version of history that Bjorn had been taught spoke differently of Hrothgar, however. Hrothgar had faced no MageLord—all of them had died during the Great War before the Time of Madness. All save Valerian, that was.

No, the MageLord that Hrothgar had faced had truly been

nothing more than a Circle of the mages. Nor had he defeated them valiantly in battle. Rather he had befriended them, made use of them against his enemies and then betrayed them.

And when his mother, Hela, had killed him and then herself it was not because she had been bespelled by the nonexistent MageLord before he died. It had been because she was also a member of the Circle. She had carried out the Circle's final punishment before turning the knife on herself in grief.

Still, these facts were not known to most, and the values that the priests of Hrothgar taught were mostly valid, except where they concerned Bjorn's people. The ideal had become more than the man. In the face of that, the truth was not as important as the ideal.

Even so, Bjorn did not understand why Gavin put this funeral before pursuing Valerian. The guards had reported seeing the former counselor fleeing to the east on horseback. How the MageLord had been able to ride after the wound he had received was beyond Bjorn.

Nevertheless, here they were rather than pursuing the Mage-Lord. Every moment they delayed was that much more time for Valerian to regather his Power. That much more time for Valerian to prepare his revenge. That much more time to seal their doom.

". . . as Hrothgar himself," the priest droned on, "in battle with a MageLord of old." Yes, Magnus had earned himself a place in the myths of coming generations. Perhaps Gavin, too. As usual, the mage who had also helped to make it possible would be left out.

Finally, the last prayer was uttered over the corpse—the candles surrounding him were extinguished. Slowly, the heavy wooden casket was removed from the chapel by an honor guard clad in bronze. King Magnus would be laid to rest with his ancestors in the crypts beneath the garden.

Gavin motioned for Bjorn to follow him out of the chapel as he passed. Bjorn rose quietly and followed the king from the chapel.

"My scouts have been tracking Valerian all day," he whispered. "The troops are prepared to march. We ride as soon as my father is interred."

Gavin's voice held a quiet anger that Bjorn could sense was barely held at bay by the king's will.

"Yes, majesty" was his only reply.

"Go and prepare for travel, yourself," Gavin ordered. "We will be on the trail within the hour."

"Yes, majesty," Bjorn replied. At last! Hopefully Valerian's wounds had prevented him from mustering his resources against them. Now that the MageLord had been unveiled, he was even more dangerous than before. . . .

Chapter
──── Six ───────

BJORN SAT EASILY in the saddle. His horsemanship had improved considerably since he had first met Gavin. They had ridden all afternoon, following the trail blazed by King Gavin's scouts. Now the sun was setting, and Bjorn still felt as though he could ride for a while longer.

"We shall make camp here," Gavin announced once they had left the patch of forest they had been riding through.

"Majesty," Bjorn said, riding up alongside the king, "we should press on."

"In the dark we risk laming the horses," Gavin replied.

"Every moment we delay . . ." Bjorn began.

"Is more time for Valerian to recover his strength," Gavin concluded for him. "My scouts are following him closely. If they intercept him, they are ordered to kill him, if possible. If a dozen men cannot kill Valerian, we shall need our rest."

"You *know* where he's heading," Baron William said. It was a statement—not a question. Bjorn looked to Gavin, waiting for more information.

"Yes," the young king replied. "He runs for the tomb in which we found him."

"We will need sapping and mining tools if he seals himself within," Ivanel concluded. Bjorn dismounted with the others. Gavin's men came to take the horses.

"Yes," Gavin agreed. "Ivanel, send a scout back to Reykvid. Have them send a team of sappers behind us—just in case. You might also order them to send engines. He could conceivably take over Chief Balder's hall. If he does, we will need them."

"Yes, majesty," Ivanel replied, bowing before taking his leave.

"William, send a scout ahead," Gavin ordered. "Send him

two hours out, and then have him return. I want to know if there is any further sign of our vanguard. With luck, they will have killed him and we can all go home on the morrow."

"With luck, majesty," William agreed. "Although, somehow, I doubt it."

"As do I," Gavin agreed. "Bjorn, what can you tell me?"

"Nothing," Bjorn replied, shaking his head. "I have no sense of Valerian, but he shields himself well."

"And my scouts?"

"I can tell nothing of them," Bjorn replied. "Although that may be good of itself. If Valerian had used the Power against them nearby, I would almost certainly have some sense of that."

"Then we shall hope for the best," Gavin said. "Sleep well, hunt master."

"Thank you, majesty," Bjorn replied. Somehow, though, he doubted that he would be able to comply with the king's request.

Bjorn rolled over in his bedroll for probably the thousandth time. Apparently he was not the only person with difficulty sleeping. A small group of men was gathered around the camp's central fire. They appeared intent on conversation.

Some sense of foreboding teased his mind. Bjorn closed his eyes and gathered the Power. Once, he had been proud of his command of Nature's energies. Now, having seen the overwhelming strength at Valerian's disposal, he felt impotent.

Still, his Power, and King Magnus's strong will, had overcome Valerian's Art. Bjorn might not be Valerian's equal, but neither was he completely helpless.

Bjorn forced his breathing to shallow into a slow, steady rhythm. Focusing, he channeled the Power into his physical senses. Sight faded until he could barely see the flickering campfire through his eyelids. His body numbed until it felt as though he were floating, disembodied in darkness.

As each of his other senses faded, however, his hearing sharpened. He could hear the snap and pop of the campfires— the footsteps of the sentries watching the perimeter of the camp, and, most important, the whispered conversation of the men at the fire.

". . . mad, I tell you," one man was saying. "We cannot fight a MageLord."

"He didn't seem too hard to cut to me," another said. "The king got a knife in his belly."

"Only by surprise," the first man objected. "Now he'll be ready for us. Do you want to face an army of demons, Barik?"

Bjorn opened his eyes. He was going to have to join this conversation. Not that he blamed the men for fearing Valerian. After all, he himself had wanted nothing more than to flee when he first encountered the MageLord.

"We should get out now while we still can," the first man was saying as Bjorn walked up behind him.

"And where shall you go?" Bjorn asked. The man turned and glared at him.

"Anywhere!" he said. "Anywhere but Reykvid."

"Do you have a family?" Bjorn asked.

"Aye," the soldier replied. "I just had a son last spring."

"This is a *MageLord*!" Bjorn said. "Do you think your son will grow up to be a freeman if we don't kill this man now?"

"I . . . that is . . ."

"If we don't kill Valerian now," Bjorn continued, "he will be openly ruling Reykvid by the end of the winter. From there, he will continue until the entire world is in his grip, and then it will be far too late to think about killing him. Your son will be his slave and your wife will be his concubine. And you will probably be dead. Nowhere you can run will make you, or your family, safe from him."

"What can *we* do?" the first man shouted, forgetting his earlier stealth.

"You can fight," Bjorn replied. "You can kill him or you can be killed by him. The question that you have to ask yourself is, are you willing to die so that your son may live as a freeman?"

"That is right," a familiar voice said from Bjorn's left. All eyes turned to King Gavin.

"Majesty!" the guards said, dropping to their knees.

"I hold here a dagger," Gavin said, "covered in this worm's blood. Valerian is a *man*! He bleeds, eats, drinks and sleeps.

He may be powerful, but he is a man, and men can be killed. My father proved that. He died for the sake of his son—will you do less?"

"No, majesty," the soldiers replied.

"Forgive me, majesty," the first added.

"Forgiven," Gavin replied, placing a hand on the man's shoulder. "Fear is understandable. We fight a legend. But it is a legend that bleeds, and we shall spill his blood on this land. Now, all of those not on watch, return to bed. We move out at dawn."

The men moved away from the fire as Gavin and Bjorn watched.

"My thanks, hunt master," Gavin said once the men had left. "You had best return to bed as well."

"Yes, majesty," Bjorn replied. As he returned to his bedroll, he wondered just how far Gavin could convince his men to follow him.

Early on the morning of the second day they met Chief Balder. He was a smallish man, but he seemed to hold the respect of his men.

"What is going on?" Balder asked Gavin as soon as he rode up. "Why do you march a small army through my lands?"

"*Whose* lands?" Gavin asked coldly.

"Have you forgotten how to address your king, Balder?" Ivanel asked.

"Magnus is my king," Balder replied. "And these *are* my lands to govern in his name."

"My father is dead," Gavin said. "We pursue his killer. *I* am your king now." Balder paled visibly.

"Then . . . it's true?" he said. "What your scouts told me is true?"

"If you mean that we hunt a MageLord, yes," Gavin confirmed.

"It cannot be . . ." Balder whispered.

"It is," Gavin said. "I myself have felt his power. He tried to kill all of us, but my father wounded him at the cost of his own life. He flees now, and we pursue."

"Majesty, forgive me," Balder said. "I took the message of your scouts as ravings. I didn't know . . . I apologize."

"Of course you are forgiven," Gavin replied. "I doubt that I would have believed such a report myself. Ride with us back to your hall, Balder."

"Yes, majesty."

"I am going to need sappers and engines," Gavin told him. "I have sent for them from Reykvid, but they are two days behind us."

"Anything I have is yours, majesty," Balder replied.

"Good," Gavin said. "Without your support we are *all* doomed."

Halfway through the third day they met the scouts. The small band rode as if the Devil himself were after them. The lead scout was brought to King Gavin as the small force continued to march eastward. His report was astonishing.

"A tower?" Gavin asked incredulously.

"Yes, majesty," the lead scout, Arik, replied. "We found it shortly after morning yesterday."

"That would put it near the tomb," William noted.

"Within an arrowshot," the scout confirmed.

"There was no tower within miles of there!" Gavin objected.

"There is now, majesty," Arik insisted. "It almost seems to have grown from the rock itself. There are no seams of stonework. The tower is fashioned from a single piece of stone."

"Defenders?" Gavin asked.

"None that we could see," Arik replied.

"Valerian is desperate if he thinks an unmanned tower will do more than slow us," Ivanel said. "We should be able to easily break down the door."

"There are two doors near the top of the tower," Arik replied. "With no way to get to them."

"Windows?" Gavin asked.

"Also near the top," Arik replied.

"Without defenders, we could still scale the walls and gain entry through the windows," William suggested.

"There is at least *one* defender," Bjorn pointed out. "Who wants to be the first in the tower alone with Valerian?"

"I will," Gavin replied firmly.

"No, majesty!" William objected. "I shall lead the men up

the walls. We have lost one king already and, as yet, you have no heir."

"We shall discuss that once we see this tower," Gavin replied.

"Yes, majesty," William agreed. Bjorn's feelings echoed the baron's solemn tone, albeit for different reasons. If Valerian was recovered enough to grow castles from living rock, it was already too late.

The tower rose from the morning mists like a black finger pointed accusingly toward the sky. It was exactly as the scouts had described it. No seams or tool marks marred its surface. It was as if, indeed, the forty-foot-tall tower had grown from the very stone that supported it.

What the scouts could not have seen was the aura of Power that enveloped the entire structure. How could one man command such Power?

"How long ere the sappers arrive?" Gavin asked quietly. Even he was subdued by this sight.

"Two days, majesty," William replied. "They travel more slowly. . . ."

Bjorn's eye travelled up the seamless stone walls. The design of the tower was odd. On the north and west sides a short wall extended no more than a man's length from the tower. At the top of each wall was a door leading into the tower.

"We cannot wait . . ." Gavin began.

"This tower is part of a larger castle!" Bjorn exclaimed, as the realization came to him.

"What?" Gavin asked.

"Look!" Bjorn said. "The two short walls have parts of the battlements attached. But there are no such structures on the ends. It is as if someone sawed a corner tower loose from a castle wall and set it down here!"

"He is right," William agreed, absently scratching at his black beard.

"Also, the arrow slits and windows do not open on those sides," Ivanel noted. "The tower's defenses are designed for those two walls to be present."

"And those walls, if extended, would also enclose the tomb in which you found Valerian," Bjorn pointed out.

"I fail to see how this matters. . . ." Gavin said.

"Majesty," Bjorn explained, "this tower was probably once a part of Valerian's castle before the Time of Madness. If so, it is possible that the spell which formed it was already in place. Valerian may have merely awakened magic that was already here. If so, it may mean that he is still too wounded to use his own Power."

"If that is correct . . ." Ivanel began.

"Then we can scale the tower and attack him with impunity!" Gavin concluded.

"There may be other, magical, defenses," Bjorn objected. "I would recommend caution, majesty."

"Prepare siege ladders," Gavin ordered. "Baron William, do you still wish to lead the assault?"

"I would be honored, majesty!" William replied.

"Good. Once the ladders are finished, you may lead a score of your men to scale the tower."

"Yes, majesty!" William said. Within moments, Gavin's men were busily cutting down the few small trees that grew from the heather.

Bjorn frowned. William seemed honestly eager to drive the attack. Was the baron hungry for the fame of slaying the MageLord? Or for revenge against the slayer of his king?

As the morning warmed, the mists rose and dissipated until the tower stood plainly before them. Bjorn scanned the battlements. There was still no sign of Valerian. Was the MageLord unconscious within his ancient tower? Or dead?

No, that was too much to hope for. Valerian had travelled this far with the wound from Magnus's knife in his belly. Bjorn doubted that it had been only to die. Still, if the MageLord had been in full possession of his strength, then Gavin and his entire force would already be dead.

Hopefully, he was depleted—desperately attempting to delay them while he healed. If so, Gavin was correct to press his attack, before the MageLord could regain his strength. If not, it would not matter if the attack was pressed or not. They would all die, regardless.

By midmorning, the two ladders were finished. Rough-hewn and lashed together with cords of woven bark, they were not pretty. Still, they did not have to be. They only needed hold the weight of several men long enough to reach the short walls.

"Come on, men!" William ordered his small force. Ten men carried each ladder to the tower. Bjorn watched as the ladders were placed at the ends of the walls and men began to climb up them. There was no response from the tower.

"Has anyone checked the tomb?" Bjorn asked.

"Yes," Gavin replied. "It was empty. Why?"

"It just occurred to me that we would feel very foolish if the tower were empty," Bjorn explained.

"Indeed," Gavin agreed.

The first man was about a third of the way up the ladder when the end slipped off the wall. To the north, the other ladder also began to fall.

"What is this?" Gavin asked. Fortunately, none of the soldiers seemed to be injured by the fall. They replaced the ladders and started back up the wall. Again, about a third of the way up, the ladders slipped from the end of the wall.

"Move to the corners!" Gavin shouted. The ladders were replaced again, this time in the corners between the walls and the tower itself. Again the ladders slipped, sliding around the sides of the round tower to topple into each other before striking the ground.

"What deviltry is this?" Gavin shouted.

"There is Power at work, here," Bjorn replied. "I warned there might be defenses."

"They seem harmless," Ivanel noted, "albeit frustrating."

"Permanent defenses would be, I suppose," Bjorn said. "You wouldn't want to fry normal visitors, after all."

"What do you suggest?" Gavin asked.

"The tower seems to repel anything that touches it," Bjorn replied. "Perhaps a freestanding structure built next to it . . ."

"Yes," Gavin agreed. "A siege tower. We shall need more wood."

"I shall put the men to work immediately," Ivanel replied.

"How long will this thing take to build?" Bjorn asked.

"All night," Gavin replied sourly.

* * *

All throughout the day and into the night there was no sign of activity from the tower. The siege tower slowly climbed beside Valerian's tower until it was almost halfway to the top of the wall.

Bjorn probed the MageLord's tower with his sense of the Power to no avail. The entire tower was saturated with more Power than any mage Bjorn knew had ever seen. Trying to find some sign of Valerian within was like trying to find a torch in a bonfire.

The search for wood to build the siege tower had expanded to the point that it was necessary to use the horses to transport it. Still, the structure should be ready by sunset tomorrow.

"Any news, Bjorn?" Gavin's voice asked from behind him.

"None, majesty," Bjorn replied. "I can sense nothing beyond the tower itself. It is like searching for a firefly against the full moon. If Valerian is within, I cannot distinguish his Power from that of the tower itself."

"He *must* be in there!" Gavin objected. Before Bjorn could reply, the earth beneath his feet began to tremble. Barely noticeable at first, the trembling grew until all within the camp could clearly feel it.

Shouts drew Bjorn's attention back to the siege tower. The wooden tower shook and trembled visibly atop the bucking earth. As he watched, its movements became more violent and the sound of splintering wood reached his ears.

The bottom half of the siege tower crumbled beneath its own weight. As Bjorn watched, the wooden tower fell like a house of cards. Men screamed and shouted.

As suddenly as it had begun, the trembling passed. Bjorn was already running toward the siege tower. How many men had been inside when it had collapsed? There had been over a score on the work crew.

Flames began to lick among the collapsed lumber as torches and lamps that had been used by the workers caught the wood. Bjorn hefted a burning plank and tossed it free of the wreckage. The fires had barely started—the burning wood could be cleared away.

Others joined him, digging silently through the splintered wood. A hand reached up from beneath the pile of wood.

Bjorn grabbed the hand, and it gripped his with the strength of panic.

Others began removing the lumber from around him. They uncovered a man who was fortunate enough to be almost uninjured. Next to him lay one less fortunate with a splintered post driven through his eye.

Bjorn glanced up at the tower, burning with anger. Had Valerian even noticed them? Or was he within, paying no more attention to them than King Gavin would to an anthill against the side of his castle?

Do you see us, MageLord? he thought. *Or are our pathetic struggles and lives beneath your almighty notice?*

Bjorn lifted a smoldering plank and tossed it over onto the pile of burning lumber. The dead man's body had already been carried to the makeshift pyre. How many more would join him?

Bjorn struggled to lift a fallen beam that pinned another survivor in the wreckage. Gauntleted hands joined his, and together they levered the beam off the man while another dragged him from the ruins of the tower.

With surprise, Bjorn realized that the man helping him was the king. They carried the beam away and dropped it beside the tower before returning to search for more survivors. Neither spoke, but Bjorn saw the hatred burning in Gavin's eyes. Bjorn was very glad that *he* was not Valerian right now. He also hoped that Gavin remembered that. . . .

"Three dead," King Gavin said quietly. "And eight sorely wounded."

"It could have been worse, majesty," Bjorn observed.

"Aye," Gavin agreed. "It could have. Do you still think these are ancient spells and that Valerian is not guiding them?"

"That is still a possibility," Bjorn agreed.

"What do we attempt now?" Ivanel asked.

"I can't think of anything else," Bjorn replied. "Unless you want to try taking hammers and axes to the tower itself."

"We wait for the sappers," Gavin replied. "They have the tools for that work."

Chapter
------- **Seven** -----------

THROUGHOUT THE NEXT morning a pall hung over the silent camp. The tower loomed above the tents, an ominous reminder of what they faced. Still, there was no sign of life from within. No enemy was visible, no attack came.

Bjorn could imagine Valerian within—healing, recovering his strength. Soon—very soon, Bjorn felt—the MageLord would come forth to dispose of this nuisance on his doorstep.

Spirits lifted somewhat when the sappers arrived at midday, a full half day early. Apparently Gavin had dispatched Arik to order the sappers to separate from the rest of their convoy and travel ahead to arrive early. The brawny miners carried only their picks and hammers.

"There are no defenders," Gavin told them. "I want a door there." He pointed to the base of the tower.

"Aye, majesty," Pol, the commander of the engineers replied. "Should take a couple o' hours with all o' us workin'."

"Then begin." Bjorn watched nervously as the sappers approached the tower. The king seemed apprehensive as well. What new defense would manifest itself against them now?

Nothing seemed to happen, however. Soon the steady ring of steel against stone echoed across the hilltops.

"A lovely melody," William said.

"The best I think I've ever heard," Gavin agreed.

Bjorn was not so optimistic, however. Valerian's defenses had proven their worth against all other attacks. Surely the MageLord had defended his tower against something so obvious as sapping.

The ring of steel continued unbroken for some time. Abruptly, the sound of mining stopped, however. Still, nothing seemed to be amiss—the sappers were simply talking among themselves. After a moment the ring of steel began anew.

It ended after only a moment this time. Pol could be seen walking back toward camp.

"Majesty," he said when he had returned, "I think ye should see this."

"What is it?"

"I don't exactly know," Pol replied. "I think ye'll have to see for yourself."

"Very well," Gavin agreed. Intrigued by the engineer's manner—more confused than alarmed, Bjorn followed.

The surface of the tower where the sappers had been working was unmarred. Bjorn and Gavin both stared silently for a moment.

"The tools have no effect?" King Gavin finally asked.

"Not exactly," Pol replied. "Watch this. Heave to, men!"

The sappers stood and lifted their picks to let fly at the tower wall. Chips of stone flew from the wall with each blow. However, the small gouges filled almost as quickly as the sappers could dig. Stone simply flowed into the chinks like water filling a leaking boat.

After a few moments, Pol ordered the sappers to stop. They were obviously having no effect. And that was not all.

"Look about, majesty," Pol said. "Where are the chips we've been cuttin'?"

Bjorn glanced downward, as did Gavin. True enough, there was no sign of any of the stone that had been chiseled from the tower wall. The bare ground of the hilltop was just that—bare.

"Damn!" Gavin shouted, striking the wall of the tower with a gauntleted fist. "Damn him! Damn him to *Hell*! I would rather face an army of his demons than this . . . this . . . *indifference*!"

"It does grate on one," Bjorn agreed.

"We should be a foot or two into that wall by now," Pol said. "This is just not natural, majesty."

"Obviously not," Gavin agreed. "When will the rest of your people arrive?"

"By nightfall, majesty," Pol replied.

"Including the catapults?"

"Aye, majesty."

"Let us hope that *they* are more effective."

"Somehow," Bjorn said, "I doubt it."

The sun had almost kissed the horizon when the sentries announced the arrival of the catapults. Unlike when the sappers had arrived earlier, there was no enthusiasm in the announcement. The camp's spirits did not rouse at the news.

"Get moving!" the king bellowed. "I want those catapults in position to fire before sunset! Any man slacking off will be flogged!"

That, and years of discipline, got the men moving. Bjorn would not have thought it possible, but the catapults were in firing position before the sun had sunk below the horizon. He watched as the two massive arms were winched back.

Massive stones were laid into the bowls. The engineers made final adjustments to the positioning of the engines before the last light of day faded from the sky.

The command to fire was given, and both engines let fly with their massive cargo. In the fading twilight Bjorn watched as the boulders flew toward the tower. The boulders struck the tower and, without a sound, the massive stones disappeared into the wall like pebbles vanishing beneath the surface of a pond.

Bjorn nodded. He had expected something like this when he had seen the sappers' strokes fade from the tower walls. The stone walls of Valerian's tower housed an elemental of Earth.

The only visible signs of their attack were two discolored patches where the stone of the missiles had been blended with that of the tower. It was difficult to tell in the rapidly fading light, but even that sign seemed to be fading. One by one, the men turned to return to camp. No orders were given to stop them.

"We have lost," Gavin said quietly. "Not once did the enemy show himself—and yet we have lost."

"We are not lost yet, majesty," Bjorn said. "We yet live."

"How can we fight this?" Gavin objected.

"Fire," Bjorn replied.

"Fire?"

"Yes, majesty," Bjorn replied. "Valerian has housed the power of Earth in his tower. We cannot attack him with tools of Earth. That leaves us Air, Water or Fire. Of those, Fire is the only element we can use as a weapon against him."

"What do you suggest?"

"Gather as much wood, heather and anything else you can find that will burn and pile it around the base of the tower," Bjorn said. "Did your engineers bring oil to hurl with the catapults?"

"I doubt it," Gavin replied.

"They did," Ivanel interrupted from behind them. "Although but a wagonload."

"We can try to smash a few barrels against those windows," Bjorn replied. "And we must hasten. Valerian has had three days to rest now."

"Ivanel, see to it," Gavin ordered. "Unload the wagons and use them for wood."

"Yes, majesty," Ivanel replied. "We'll put this MageLord to the fire!"

Bjorn flinched a bit at the tone in Ivanel's voice. If the baron noticed, he gave no sign as he quickly turned to carry out the king's orders.

"He meant nothing, Bjorn," Gavin said by way of apology. "You must admit, Valerian deserves such a fate."

"Yes, majesty," Bjorn agreed. "I just pray that it stops with Valerian."

The sun rose on their third morning in camp about the tower. The guard woke Gavin at the first sign of dawn as he had ordered.

There was no morning mist today. As far as Gavin could see, the hills had been cleared of heather. All of this vegetation had been piled around the base of the tower in a mound eight feet tall and twelve feet out. The men had worked hard through the night.

Today! he thought. *Today we will make this demon pay for the death of my father.*

"Are the engineers ready?" he asked his uncle.

"Yes," Ivanel replied. "They are about to take their first test shot."

"Test shot?"

"Yes," Ivanel explained. "We have cut some of the stones to the same weight as the barrels. They will have no effect on the tower, but we will know our shots are true before we start. We have no oil to waste."

"No, we do not," Gavin agreed.

One catapult fired and then another. One stone flew wide of the tower. Another struck just below one of the windows. The engineers began repositioning their engines.

Today! Gavin thought.

The sound of the catapults woke Bjorn. Had the attack begun? He climbed from his bedroll. Surely the king would have woken him for the attack.

The sight that met his eyes shocked him. For almost a mile around their camp, the hills had been stripped bare. Bjorn looked to the tower. A huge mound of vegetation surrounded the base of the tower. Just outside the camp, scores more bales of heather waited to be placed on the mound.

"Sweet mother of life," he whispered. "What have we done to you?" When the spring rains came, these hills would be washed away. It would be years before this one night's damage was undone, if ever. Bjorn looked back toward the tower.

"Forgive us, Mother," he said. "But it had to be done. Valerian is an even greater threat to you than this."

The catapults fired again. Bjorn watched as two stones flew toward the tower. One stone struck a window squarely, only to be absorbed into the tower. The second struck to the left of another window. Bjorn nodded. The engineers were getting their range before using the oil.

"Hunt master," a guard walked up and said to him. "His majesty wishes you to join him by the engines."

"Thank you," Bjorn replied. So, they were ready. What defense would Valerian have prepared against this?

Bjorn followed the guard to where King Gavin watched. One catapult sat to the south of the tower and the other sat to the east, covering the tower's only two windows. The king, Ivanel and William watched with a score of guards from between the catapults, southeast of the tower.

"Good morrow, hunt master," Gavin said in greeting.

"Let us hope so, majesty," Bjorn replied.

"Oh, it will be," Gavin assured him. "It will be."

Bjorn glanced over to the king. Bjorn could feel the doubt that lay behind the confidence in the king's eyes and words. How many more disappointments could he withstand? How many could they all withstand? If this did not work, Bjorn certainly did not know what to try next.

"It should be quite a blaze," Ivanel observed.

"Aye," William agreed. "If this doesn't flush out our prey, nothing shall."

Exactly, Bjorn thought.

A flare of flame to his left caught Bjorn's eye. The siege crew had set fire to the barrel in the catapult. As the man bearing the torch leaped to the ground, the crew fired. Before the first barrel could strike the tower, the second catapult fired as well.

Without realizing it, Bjorn stopped breathing as he watched the flaming barrels arc toward the tower. Would this work, or would the tower's defenses be proof against even this? At this point, Bjorn would hardly be surprised to see water flow from the stone walls of the tower to douse the flames.

The first barrel shattered against the narrow window. Burning oil spewed into the window or poured down the sides of the tower. Flames licked along the stone walls.

The second barrel struck mere heartbeats after the first. More flames crawled down the walls of the tower. The oil was beginning to ignite the mound of brush at the base of the tower. Gray smoke crawled up the walls of the tower from the smoldering heather.

A cheer rose up from the camp. A bit premature, perhaps, but at least the men's spirits were on the rise. This was the most noticeable effect they had managed against the MageLord's tower.

"How long before the engines can fire again?" Bjorn asked.

"Not long," Gavin replied. "They should almost be ready now."

True enough. The crew of the southern catapult was already loading their missile into the bowl. Soon another barrel of oil was flying toward the tower window. The barrel burst, releasing its fiery cargo into the narrow opening.

"Go tell the crew of the eastern engine to put their cursed backs into it!" Ivanel told a guard. "Or I shall have the pleasure of taking a lash to them!"

"At once, your grace!" the guard replied, hurrying off—no doubt to avoid inclusion in the threatened lashing. The eastern crew's second missile was under way before he got there.

Open flames were now visible on the mound of heather. Smoke threatened to obscure the tower from sight. Soldiers waited to throw more bales on the blaze. It was beginning to look like this might actually work.

Both catapults fired simultaneously. Apparently the guard had delivered his message. More oil poured down the sides of the tower. Bjorn thought he could see flames flickering through the windows of the tower, but it was difficult to be certain. Was Valerian dead? Had they slain the MageLord?

Another pair of shots were fired, and the tower was drenched with yet more oil. It was obvious that Gavin was not going to stop the attack until his supply of oil was exhausted. Again the catapults fired.

"How much oil do we have?" Bjorn asked.

"A total of forty casks," Ivanel replied. "Hopefully . . ."

"The MageLord!" someone shouted. "The MageLord!" It was difficult to tell from whom or from where the shout came. Bjorn's eyes and, indeed, all eyes in the camp turned to the tower windows. There was no one there.

Bjorn raised his gaze to the battlements. There, silhouetted against the sky, was the figure of a man.

"Raise your shot!" Ivanel shouted to the southern crew. *"Raise your shot!"*

He needn't have bothered. The southern catapult let fly, and it was obvious, even to Bjorn, that their target was the battlements. The eastern catapult followed suit.

Both barrels were true. Burning oil sprayed over the top of the tower. The figure standing atop the tower did not even flinch. Panic squeezed Bjorn's chest.

Bairn help us, we took too long, he thought. Of course, they could not have attacked any earlier. The catapults had arrived only last night. Whatever the reasons, though, they had taken too long and now they would die because of it.

A flight of arrows flew toward the tower battlements as the archers joined the attack. Before the arrows could find their mark, they veered left of their target to fly harmlessly past the tower. Another flight followed close behind the first.

One man against an army, Bjorn thought, *and it is the army which is outnumbered.*

The catapults fired again. Before the barrels could reach the tower, the figure atop raised his hands. Twin bolts of lightning flew from his hands and both barrels exploded in midair, raining their burning contents on the bare ground below.

As Bjorn watched, Valerian raised his arms. The flames of the pyre built around his tower suddenly roared up, engulfing the tower and soaring far above it. With horror, Bjorn watched as the column of flame split and began to arc back down toward the catapults.

The siege crews tried to flee, but there was no time. Catapults and men were all incinerated instantly. Bjorn could feel the heat of the burning even though he was almost a hundred yards from each engine.

The men, including their own guards, routed in panic. Gavin did not flee, however. Neither did Ivanel or William. Indeed, where could they run? The four of them simply stood and stared blankly at the tower.

Goodbye, father, Bjorn thought. *I've failed us. I've failed us all. Please forgive me.*

The fires were gone from the tower. Only a lingering haze of smoke and the charred catapults and corpses surrounding it gave any sign of the battle that had raged here less than a moment before. For a moment Valerian, visible now that the flames had cleared, simply stood and watched as Gavin's army fled from before him. Then the MageLord turned and descended out of sight.

Bjorn was confused. Why did Valerian not finish them? Surely he wasn't simply going to let them live.

No, Bjorn realized. *He's not simply going to let us* die.

With a shaking hand, Bjorn drew his hunting knife from his belt. Better to die cleanly and by his own hand than by whatever means Valerian had in mind for them. He closed his eyes and placed the point against his own chest.

Gauntleted hands grabbed his wrists.

"Bjorn!" Gavin shouted. "Fight him!" Bjorn opened his eyes.

"I am in my own mind, Gavin," he said, dropping all pretense of station. "I have no desire to fall alive into Valerian's hands."

Gavin looked stunned at first. Then understanding filled his eyes. He released Bjorn's hands and then drew his own sword.

"I suggest we follow him, gentle sirs," Gavin said to his barons. "I will not be Valerian's puppet as my father was."

"But you already are, highness," a silken voice said from behind them. "You all are."

Bjorn found that, just as in the hall of Reykvid, he could not move. He could not drive the knife into his chest. Bjorn desperately tried to strengthen the defenses of his mind, and Valerian turned toward him and shook his head, smiling.

"No, little mage," he said. "You are no match for me. Do not even bother to try. I have special plans for you."

"As for the rest of you," Valerian continued, "surely you don't think that I would allow you to dispose of yourselves before I am finished with you. I insist that you be my guests for the next few nights. We have *much* to discuss."

Valerian turned and walked back toward his tower. Bjorn found himself following placidly behind the MageLord along with the others.

Bjorn screamed as the rats chewed at his flesh. He was bound in chains both hand and foot in a stone pit of ravenous rats. A large rat ran up his chest to his face. Bjorn screamed and turned his face away.

The rat settled for his ear, ripping most of it away with its needle-sharp teeth. Another scream ripped from his hoarse throat.

His genitals and most of his legs had already been devoured. The rats were beginning to dig their way into his bowels. Bjorn screamed and sobbed in agony. How could he still live?

Bairn, let me die! he prayed.

"Please!" he screamed. "Oh, gods—let me . . . AAAAHH!"

A rat had dropped onto his head and snapped at his eyes. Bjorn closed his eyes and threw his head to the side. The rat's teeth bit into his eyelid and ripped it open as it fell from its perch. Blood poured into his eye.

"Noooo!" he screamed. "Let me *die*!"

The pain was gone.

Bjorn collapsed against his chains, sobbing. This was it. He was dying now. Thank the gods.

"Do not worry, little mage," Valerian's voice said. "I will let you die—eventually."

Bjorn's eyes snapped open. Eyes? But how . . . ? Valerian stood before him. Bjorn looked around. He was chained to the wall in a small room—naked but whole. He struggled to regain his feet, looking frantically about the room. There was no sign of the rats.

"The mind is an amazing thing, is it not?" Valerian asked. Bjorn just looked at him in confusion.

"I do not even know what horrors you have been experiencing for the last hour," Valerian continued. "I *could* have, had I wished to, but your screams were entertainment enough."

At that moment another hoarse scream sounded in the distance somewhere. Valerian cocked his head to listen.

"I wonder what horrors the king's mind is creating for him?" Valerian said once the scream had shuddered away.

"You . . . monster," Bjorn croaked. Valerian drew back his arm and backhanded him. The pain was nothing compared to what Bjorn had just experienced. Neither was the pain of his throat, hoarse from screaming, nor the pain of his scraped and bleeding wrists. These had been so minor that he had not even noticed them once the rats were gone.

"Be careful, little mage," Valerian said. "Or I will let your mind have you again."

"Why not just kill me?" Bjorn asked. "Why waste your time on me?"

"Because I still have need of you, little mage," Valerian

replied. "Apparently you common worms have outlived us. I need to know about your people."

"I will tell you nothing," Bjorn said, as resolutely as he could manage.

"I'm afraid you do not have a choice," Valerian said. "I intend to take the knowledge from you, not ask you to reveal it."

Bjorn tried to summon the Power, but was still too weak from the imagined torment. He felt Valerian's Power slide into his mind and begin sifting through his memories.

Oddly enough, he was able to tell which memories Valerian took interest in. As the MageLord travelled through his mind, Bjorn relived those times that Valerian focused on. There was also a vague sense of the MageLord's mood regarding each event.

The stories Bjorn's father had told him regarding the history of the MageLords seemed of particular interest to Valerian—especially those of Bairn's role in their downfall. Those stories seemed to provide Valerian with some sense of understanding, although Bjorn could not say of what.

Valerian seemed to be very amused by Rolf's amulet, which marked Bjorn's father as the head of their Circle. Valerian also took special note of the identities of those within the Circle. No doubt Valerian intended to hunt them all down and kill them.

Aunt Freida, I'm sorry, Bjorn thought.

Then something happened which surprised Bjorn. A small memory of one of his father's possessions. A large, silver book, unopened and unopenable, supposedly left from before the Time of Madness.

As soon as Valerian came across this memory, Bjorn could feel the MageLord's excitement. Bjorn found himself remembering every detail of the book—every instance where he had seen or touched it in vivid detail. There was no doubt— Valerian wanted that book desperately. Why?

Bjorn felt Valerian withdraw from his mind.

"Well, little mage," Valerian said. "It seems I cannot afford to let you die, just yet. I shall have to think on how to put you to use. In the meantime . . ."

Valerian reached out and gently stroked Bjorn's hair. Bjorn recoiled from the touch.

". . . I wouldn't want you to get bored while I think things over."

Valerian was gone. Bjorn found himself chained, sitting against the wall of a small pit. Something landed in the pit next to him and scampered up his naked leg to sink its needle-sharp teeth into his thigh.

"*Nooooo!*" Bjorn screamed.

The rats had not yet made it to his face by the time Valerian returned. In spite of himself, Bjorn could not stop the shuddering sobs that racked him once the hallucination had fled.

"Is it that bad?" Valerian asked.

Bjorn nodded. He had soiled himself this last time. It had been even worse, knowing that he could not die. And now, to hang before the MageLord, enfeebled and befouled, was humiliating.

"Then you will be glad to know that I will not make you suffer any longer," Valerian said. Bjorn said nothing. He only looked up at the MageLord, ashamed of the hope that he knew must be in his eyes.

"It's true," Valerian assured him. "You can trust me—I have no reason to lie to you." Bjorn's head fell against his chest.

"Thank . . . the gods . . ." he whispered. Valerian grabbed Bjorn's hair and forced the mage to look at him. Bjorn's heart pounded in his chest in sudden fear.

"The gods have nothing to do with it, Bjorn," Valerian hissed at him. "You can thank *me*."

"Please, let me die," Bjorn begged.

"No, Bjorn," Valerian said, shaking his head. "That cannot be. I need you—I need you to watch your common worm friends for me and report to me." Bjorn's heart fell. He knew that his next words would send him back to the rats.

"I . . . I cannot," he whispered.

"But, Bjorn," Valerian replied, also whispering, "you have no choice."

Chapter
-------- **Eight** -----------

A SCURRYING SOUND startled Bjorn awake. Frantically, he looked around the cell—nothing.

He was lying on a straw mat. Other than that, this appeared to be the same cell in which Valerian had questioned him. In fact, the chains were still hanging from the wall.

Bjorn's stomach protested its emptiness. How long had he been here? His hunger suggested that a day might have passed. Beyond that, it was impossible to tell. It could not be too long, however. Valerian would, no doubt, be in a hurry to return to Reykvid.

He struggled to his feet. Dizziness blurred his vision, and Bjorn reached out to the wall to avoid falling. All right, perhaps more than a day.

"Feeling better?" Bjorn heard Valerian ask. He opened his eyes.

"A little," Bjorn replied suspiciously.

"Good," Valerian replied. "Come."

"Where?" Bjorn asked. Valerian frowned, and his eyes met Bjorn's.

Bjorn was in a small pit, chained naked to the wall. Scurrying and chittering sounds came from above.

"*Nooooo!*" Bjorn screamed.

The pit was gone. Bjorn was, once again, lying in a heap on the straw mat. He looked up at the MageLord.

"*You* do not question," Valerian said coldly. "You *obey.*"

Bjorn nodded in response, hating himself for the fear that gripped him.

"I cannot hear you," Valerian said softly.

"I obey," Bjorn replied.

"You obey *what?*"

Bjorn's eyes widened. What did Valerian want him to say?

"You obey *what*!" Valerian said, raising his voice.

"I obey, m-master," Bjorn replied. His stomach knotted in revulsion. He could hardly believe that he had actually spoken those words.

"Close enough—this time," Valerian said. "In the future you will refer to me as 'Lord.'" Again, Bjorn nodded in response.

"I did not hear that," Valerian objected.

"Yes, Lord," Bjorn said, despising his own weakness.

"You learn quickly, Bjorn," Valerian said in mock praise. "Now, come."

"Yes, Lord," Bjorn said weakly. The MageLord turned to leave the room. Bjorn followed him from the small cell into a narrow hallway. The hallway was lit although there were no lanterns or windows. Bjorn could not tell where the light was coming from—it was simply there.

Valerian led him to a flight of stairs. Bjorn followed him. They emerged into a large foyer. To the right were a pair of double doors. To the left an archway led to another, larger room. Another flight of stairs continued upward across the foyer.

Valerian passed through the archway into the room beyond. A great hall, at least that is what Bjorn assumed it to be, stretched at least twenty feet ahead of him. He had to guess at its function since the room was completely devoid of furniture save for a single, stone throne against one wall.

Even so, something was not right here. Bjorn glanced about the room and then back toward the foyer, mentally estimating the dimensions of the rooms.

"What puzzles you?" Valerian asked.

"The tower . . . wasn't this large," Bjorn replied.

"I have expanded it," Valerian replied smugly. "It occurred to me that I should maintain an impregnable fortress."

"Seems rather . . . empty," Bjorn noted.

"Once furnished, it will be quite comfortable," Valerian assured him.

"If you want furniture," Bjorn said, "why don't you have it?"

"I choose not to squander the Power on frivolities when a

little patience will serve," Valerian explained, frowning. "Your questions are becoming bothersome."

"Forgive me, Lord," Bjorn replied.

So, Bjorn thought. *There* are *limits!*

"No matter," Valerian said. "Now it is time for you to be sent back to your fellow worms as my agent."

"I cannot betray my people," Bjorn replied. "Not even if it means my death—or worse."

"Your objections are irrelevant," Valerian said, smiling. Something about his smile sent a chill down Bjorn's spine. Valerian clapped his hands together twice.

From a side room, Gavin, Ivanel and William emerged.

"Be so kind, your majesty," Valerian said, "to explain my plans to Bjorn."

"We shall return to Reykvid with Lord Valerian," Gavin said as conversationally as if they were discussing the weather. Bjorn's heart fell. He, himself, would betray those of his Circle as casually as Gavin now betrayed Reykvid. Valerian's Power would see to that.

"Once there," Gavin continued, "we shall explain that it was *you* who were practicing the Forbidden Arts. You turned us against Valerian and, indeed, tried to poison all three of us."

Bjorn lowered his head. This would work—there were enough who knew the truth to give this story the credibility it needed. Valerian would resume his position as counselor to the crown of Reykvid almost without pause.

"We will claim to have broken free of your control," Ivanel added, "and to have slain you. You will actually return to the Wastes."

"Precisely," Gavin agreed. "After a time, Lord Valerian will be named the Lord Chancellor of Reykvid. This tower will be made the center of his palace."

"Once the king and his barons have been eliminated," William added as though he weren't one of those barons himself, "Lord Valerian will be able to take his rightful place as king of Reykvid."

"Thank you, gentlemen," Valerian said. "You may return to your cells."

"Yes, Lord," they all replied. Without so much as a backward glance they turned and left the hall.

"You see?" Valerian asked once they had left. "You *can* betray your friends."

Several hours later Bjorn stepped out onto the roof of the tower. The sun had almost set, and a chill was settling into the air. The tower had indeed been changed. From what little Bjorn was able to see, it had been broadened to almost forty feet across and the two side walls no longer existed.

"Come," Valerian commanded, and Bjorn hastened to comply. Not out of fear or any other motivation—he was simply unable to do otherwise.

Over the last few hours, Valerian had laid enchantment upon enchantment onto Bjorn's mind. Now Bjorn was a passenger in his own head, unable to do more than watch as another, with all his memories and manner, performed Valerian's will.

"You have your story?" Valerian asked.

"Yes, Lord," Bjorn heard himself reply. "Valerian was neither MageLord nor rogue. Gavin and the barons simply wanted to discredit the king so that they could have him killed and seize power."

No! Bjorn thought. *No! I cannot do this!*

"Immediately upon my arrival," his voice continued, "the king was assassinated. I was blamed for the assassination and exposed as a practitioner of the Forbidden Arts. I broke free during my execution and dove from the precipice into the fjord. King Gavin and everyone in Reykvid believes me to be dead. Indeed, they were almost correct—I barely survived the fall."

"Very good," Valerian said, more in praise of his own work than of Bjorn's performance.

"Now," Valerian said, "you must be on your way. I will check on your progress as you return home."

"Yes, Lord," Bjorn replied. He turned to go back down the stairs.

"No," Valerian told him. "That way." The MageLord pointed over the battlements.

"You must have appropriate injuries when you return home," he explained. "Jump."

"Yes, Lord," Bjorn replied.

With luck, Bjorn thought, *I will die.* It was not likely, however. It was only a thirty-foot drop to the mound of burned heather. Bjorn watched as his body climbed atop the battlements and jumped.

The wind whistled past his ears for a few short seconds and then he was crashing through the charred remains of the bales of heather. Pain flared across his right shin as he struck the ground. The breath was knocked from his lungs and, for a moment, he just lay there catching his breath.

His right leg burned like fire. Broken, no doubt. Well, he would certainly have "appropriate injuries," as Valerian had said. Slowly, Bjorn's body began to crawl out from underneath the heather as he watched, helpless within.

Bjorn glanced up at the tower as he emerged from beneath the heather. It was definitely larger than he had remembered.

Then his eyes turned away from the tower and his body began crawling the long, painful trip home.

"It is time, majesty," Valerian said in that falsely sycophantic tone of his. "We must return to Reykvid."

"Yes, Lord," Gavin replied.

"Oh, and we will have to drop that title at this point," Valerian added. "After all, *you* are the king."

Yes, I am, Gavin thought. *And somehow, I will find a way to stop you.*

"Yes, Valerian," his voice replied. Then his body turned to face his uncle Ivanel and Baron William.

"Come," he said. "We must ride to Reykvid and tell them of what has transpired."

"Yes, majesty," William and Ivanel replied.

If only they *could* tell the people what had truly transpired and have Valerian skewered on a stake for the burning. That would not happen, however. The MageLord's control was too absolute.

They left the tower and mounted the horses that Ivanel had gathered for them. Most of the horses from the army were still nearby, grazing on the heather that had not been cut for the fire. Gavin mounted his roan stallion. Sadly, he remembered that it had been a gift from his father on his Day of Manhood.

On my father's grave, he swore, *somehow I will find a way.*

As they began to ride toward Reykvid, Gavin spied a small figure crawling along the ground ahead of them. As they approached, he could see that it was Bjorn. His right leg was twisted behind him, obviously broken. Valerian called a halt as they rode up beside the mage.

"Make haste, Bjorn," Valerian called. "And have a pleasant journey."

"Yes, Lord," Bjorn replied, his voice pained. "Thank you, Lord."

Gavin fumed in anger, since it was all that he could do. Obviously Bjorn was as thoroughly in Valerian's power as they were.

I'll exact vengeance for you, Bjorn, Gavin thought. *Somehow. I promise you.*

Valerian rode off and Gavin and the others followed, leaving behind the pathetic sight of Bjorn dragging himself home on a broken leg.

Bjorn readjusted the makeshift crutch underneath his arm. Or, more accurately, his body readjusted the crutch while he watched.

He had been travelling for almost three weeks now. After the first two days, Bjorn had crawled into a wooded area. There Bjorn had watched while the one controlling his body set and splinted his leg and then fashioned the crutch. Ever since then he had made fairly good time. He had even caught rides on wagons a couple of times.

He did not look forward to arriving home, however. Twice during his journey Valerian had appeared to check on his progress. No doubt, as soon as he arrived home, the MageLord would put whatever sinister plan he had for the mages into motion.

A day ago, Bjorn had finally arrived in familiar territory. Now he was actually within a day of home. That is, a day if he hadn't been hobbling along on a broken leg. As it was, it would be two or possibly even three before he saw home.

He heard the clatter of a wagon behind him. His body turned to see Lief the woodcutter driving a brace of felled trees down the trail.

"Bjorn!" Lief called as he pulled up beside him. "What happened to ye? I heard ye were away!"

"Bandits," Bjorn's voice lied. "They attacked the party I was with. I fell down a small cliff and got a broken leg out of the deal. I guess everyone else thought I was dead or kidnapped. I've been hobbling home ever since."

"Not while I'm around, ye're not!" Lief protested. "Here—let me help ye up. I'll drop ye right on ye're father's doorstep. Have ye there by midday tomorrow."

"How is my father?" Bjorn asked as the brawny woodsman practically lifted him into the wagon.

"He's doing well," Lief replied, nodding. "He's a bit worried about ye, of course. He's like to have a fit when he sees ye like this."

Not as bad as he would have if I could tell him the truth, Bjorn thought.

"Thank you, Lief," Bjorn said. "I appreciate this."

"Nonsense," Lief replied. "Ye and ye're father have helped me enough." He waggled a gnarled left hand at Bjorn in reminder.

Lief had smashed his hand once beneath a timber. Bjorn and Rolf had worked on that hand for weeks with herbs and wrappings and even a bit of the Power, although Lief didn't know that.

"That's what neighbors are for, Lief," Bjorn replied.

"Exac'ly," Lief agreed. "And so is this."

Bjorn felt himself smile in response. They both fell silent for a time, watching the road pass as Lief's horses slowly but steadily pulled their load toward home.

The pain in Bjorn's leg slowly faded to a gentle ache. He absently massaged the leg. It was healing nicely. It was good to know that Valerian's enchantment hadn't impaired his skill as a healer. Lief glanced over at him occasionally as they rode along.

"So, ye've been on the road how long?" the woodsman asked, finally breaking the silence.

"About . . . four weeks," Bjorn overestimated. "Alone, that is. Almost a season all total."

"Did you see Reykvid?"

"No," Bjorn's voice lied again. "Never made it that far. Spent a week laid up while the leg healed enough to hobble on. It was a good thing I had food in my pack when I went over that cliff."

"Aye," Lief agreed.

"So, the news has spread this far, has it?" Bjorn asked. He had heard from others along the road about Reykvid's sudden expansion into several neighboring clans. Of course, that was old news to Bjorn. Those clans had been taken by Magnus before Gavin had left to find Bjorn.

"About Reykvid?" Lief asked in reply. "Aye. 'Tis all anyone speaks of anymore."

If Bjorn had been in control of his actions, he might have shaken his head. When Reykvid had been growing under King Magnus by peaceful means, no one here had even heard of the kingdom. Now that Magnus, and later Gavin, had become conquerors under Valerian's control, everyone seemed to know of the kingdom.

"I guess nothing travels like bad news," Bjorn noted.

"'Tis the truth," Lief agreed.

Rolf came out at the sound of Lief's wagon pulling up. His eyes widened when he saw Bjorn.

"Bjorn!" he exclaimed. "What happened?"

"Bandits," Bjorn explained. "I'll explain more when we're inside, father. Right now, though, I would very much like to see my bed. I've missed it terribly."

"Yes, of course," Rolf agreed. "Lief, could you . . . ?"

"Already there, Rolf," Lief replied. Bjorn reached to accept Lief's help down and yelped in surprise when the woodsman, instead, hoisted him like a new bride.

"I *can* walk," Bjorn objected.

"Aye," Lief agreed. "I've seen what ye call walkin'. Where to, Rolf?"

"Follow me," Rolf replied, smiling.

"This is embarrassing," Bjorn objected.

"I'll not tell anyone if you won't," Lief assured him. "Now quit fussin' or I'll be sure an' bump that leg on somethin'."

Bjorn was grateful that he fell silent. It was maddening to listen to oneself carry on a conversation without the ability to direct it. Lief carried him into the shack and laid Bjorn on his bed in the room he shared with his father.

"Do ye need me for anythin' else, Rolf?" Lief asked.

"No," Rolf replied. "I can handle this from here. Thank you, Lief."

"No trouble," Lief assured him. "I'll stop by tomorrow to see if ye need anythin'."

"Thank you," Rolf said again. "Now you had best be getting those logs to whoever wanted them."

"Aye," Lief agreed. "I'll be a half day late as 'tis. Take care, Bjorn. And don't give your father no trouble."

"I'll behave," Bjorn assured him tiredly. "Thank you."

"'Tis what neighbors are for," Lief replied. "Goodbye."

Rolf did not say anything as Lief left the room. He simply began removing the splint from Bjorn's leg. Finally, they heard the clatter of Lief's wagon leaving the clearing.

"Father," Bjorn began.

"Hush, Bjorn," Rolf interrupted. "Let me look at this. You can tell me what happened later."

I wish I could, Bjorn thought. *Bairn help me, I wish I could.*

"Did you set this yourself?" Rolf asked.

"I certainly didn't have anyone to help me," Bjorn replied testily. "Hurt like hell, too."

"I don't doubt it," Rolf agreed. "You did an excellent job. How old is the break?"

"About three weeks," Bjorn replied.

"You've used the Power to speed the healing," Rolf observed. "Well done. It should heal as good as new, once I resplint it."

"Father," Bjorn began again.

"Wait until I've splinted your leg, Bjorn," Rolf scolded. "This won't take long."

Bjorn waited while his father's expert hands built a splint that would be much easier to walk in. This late in the healing, Bjorn would probably not need the crutch any longer. That would be nice.

"There," Rolf finally announced. "Now, tell me how this happened."

"Father," Bjorn heard himself reply, "we were terribly wrong about Gavin. . . ."

"So," Rolf said, "you leaped off the cliff into the fjord?"

"Yes, father," Bjorn replied.

"If all you got out of it was a broken leg, you can thank Bairn for watching over you."

"Aside from a few cuts, scrapes and bruises and some sore ribs, that was it," Bjorn agreed. "I expected to die, but it was still better than the fire."

"Almost anything is better than the fire," Rolf agreed.

I don't know, Bjorn thought. *You should try being eaten alive by rats sometime.*

"Father, we have to move on," Bjorn said. "Word is spreading about the mage from the Wastes who killed the king. Eventually, people are going to connect me with those stories."

"Yes," Rolf agreed. "We shall move on in a day or two. The Circle will have to be told. That won't be easy. Although several have expressed the desire to move with us."

"Helga?" Bjorn asked. Would his betrothed go with them?

"Yes, she is one of those," Rolf confirmed. "Of course, Freida and Theodr are among the others."

Bjorn felt himself smile. Freida had all but been his mother during his childhood. She wasn't going to let him out of her sight that easy.

"Brand has replaced me as High Magus," Rolf added. "Most of the others are staying. Helga's parents will also travel with us."

"Of course," Bjorn replied. "Angus and Hilda would not let their daughter travel into the Wastes alone." Rolf sighed.

"I would have sworn Gavin could be trusted," he said, shaking his head. "His aura matched his words."

"Father," Bjorn chided, "we've both known those who can lie sincerely. Gavin projects what he wants you to think he feels. He may even have a touch of the Power."

"Well, the best thing we can do is avoid anyone from Reykvid," Rolf decided.

"I agree," Bjorn said. "Further north?"

"I think so," Rolf agreed. "Fewer people, more removed. I think it fits our needs for now. In the meantime, you need to rest."

"Yes, father," Bjorn agreed.

"Are you hungry?" Rolf asked. "You don't look as though you've been eating well."

"No, Lief fed me last night and today."

"Yes, of course," Rolf said. "Get some rest. I'll wake you for dinner."

"Thank you," Bjorn replied. He was asleep before his father left the room.

Valerian came that night. Bjorn simply awoke and the MageLord was standing over his bed.

"Show me the book, Bjorn," he commanded.

"Which book, Lord?" Bjorn whispered in reply.

"No need to whisper," Valerian assured him. "Remember the night in the great hall when you tried to poison me? Your father sleeps most soundly. I want you to show me the Silver Book."

"Yes, Lord," Bjorn replied normally. He got up from the bed and walked over to his father's bed. He slid out a large, locked trunk from beneath the bed. A key from beneath his father's pillow opened the chest.

From the trunk he removed a large rectangular object, wrapped in oilcloth. He handed it to the MageLord. Valerian practically snatched the book from Bjorn's hands.

No one had ever been able to open the Silver Book. There was some debate among the Circle as to whether or not it was truly a book at all, or just some type of ornament made to resemble a book. Tonight Bjorn learned that it was, indeed, a book.

Valerian's fingers touched the surface of the book, and Bjorn felt the flow of Power as the MageLord broke the spell on the book. Spreading outward from his fingertips, the silver sheen of the book became the brown of leather.

Eagerly, Valerian's fingers unfastened the latches that bound the ancient tome closed. He opened the cover and examined the first page of the book. Confusion crossed his features.

He flipped a few pages further into the book, and then a few more. Each time he stopped, the consternation in his expression increased.

"What fool would bother to preserve *this*?" he shouted, throwing the ancient tome to the floor. "This is nothing more than the rites to be taught a raw novice!"

"I don't know, Lord," Bjorn replied.

"I was not speaking to you," Valerian snapped as he picked up the book and flipped through a few more pages.

"Forgive me, Lord," Bjorn said.

"Silence!"

"Yes, Lord," Bjorn replied. Valerian studied the book. From what little Bjorn could see, the last half of the book was blank.

"Replace it," Valerian ordered, handing the book back to Bjorn. "I doubt you could even read it. It is worthless to me."

"Yes, Lord," Bjorn agreed. Bjorn was consumed with curiosity. Instruction for novices? That could be useful, if Bjorn were in his own mind.

Thank Bairn he did not ask me if I could read it, Bjorn thought. All of the Circle could read the ancient script of the MageLords and even speak the language to a degree.

Bjorn placed the oilcloth wrapped book back into its place in the trunk and slid the trunk back under his father's bed.

"I will check back with you in a few days," Valerian told him. "I will expect full reports on the members of your pathetic little circle."

"Yes, Lord," Bjorn acknowledged. With no farewells, Valerian was gone. Rolf stirred in his sleep, and Bjorn knew that Valerian's slumber no longer held him.

Father, forgive me, Bjorn thought as he returned to bed.

Chapter
------- Nine -----------

"Go to war?" General Hans asked. "Over two dozen cattle?"

"It is not the cattle, general," Valerian explained. "The Fox clan has attacked our border, stolen our property and murdered our citizens."

"Three men," Hans replied derisively.

"Would you care to explain to the widows of those three men why their husbands are not worth protecting?" Valerian asked.

As if you gave a damn, King Gavin thought.

"Or would you prefer to wait until the next time, when they steal twice as many cattle and murder a dozen men?" Valerian asked. "Or perhaps the time after that, when they occupy one of the border villages and claim the land as their own. Majesty, we must respond and we must respond firmly."

"Majesty, I agree," Hans said. "But all-out war? No! We should plunder one of their border villages and send a message that any future raids will yield the same results."

"I tend to agree with Valerian," Gavin replied. "Your course would only create more animosity."

"Invading them certainly will!"

"Yes, Hans, but not while leaving them with an intact army," Gavin pointed out.

"Majesty, winter is but a month away, two at best," Hans said. "'Tis not a good time to begin a war."

"Perhaps not," Gavin said. "But we must strike while this incident is yet fresh. If we wait, it will tell the Fox clan, and the other clans, that they have only to wait until near winter to raid us without reprisal."

"As you wish, majesty," Hans agreed. "I shall mobilize the army."

"Thank you, general," Gavin replied. "You are dismissed."

"Majesty," Hans said, rising to bow before leaving. Gavin could tell that Hans was almost as displeased as he was.

"Well played, majesty," Valerian said once the council room was clear.

Curse you to Hell, Gavin thought.

"Thank you, Lord," he said instead.

Things were settling down for winter in Hunter's Glen. With the false news that there was no MageLord to be feared, Angus and Hilda had decided to travel with Rolf and Bjorn. Brand had settled into his new role as High Magus better than Rolf had feared he would. Apparently, the actual responsibility of his new post had helped to curb his ambition.

Bjorn had been very relieved to discover that Helga had waited for him. Part of him wished that she hadn't, however. It would have been better, for her sake, if she and her family had fled. Still, he was glad to still be with her and, now, the seven of them prepared for travel.

"How are we going to explain our departure?" Bjorn asked.

"Bandits," Rolf replied.

"Bandits?" Bjorn asked.

"It worked with Lief," Rolf replied. "Brand has agreed to track up the clearing with horses and burn the house on the night we leave. Living out from town as we do, people will think that we fell prey to bandits."

"That explains you and me," Bjorn said. "What about everyone else?"

"Everyone knows they've been out here helping me," Rolf explained. "People will assume they were with us when the attack came."

"Where are we going?" Helga asked.

"North," Rolf replied. "A few weeks' travel and we should still have time to build a small cabin before winter sets in to stay."

"It's a bad time to travel northward," Bjorn noted.

"We've had to wait here far too long already," Rolf said. "I've had more than one person in town ask about you in connection with Reykvid. We dare not go south."

"How will we survive?" Helga asked. Bjorn shrugged.

"Same as we do now," he replied. "Trapping."

"Yes," Rolf agreed. "Further north, more valuable pelts are available. We can fill our pots and our purses at the same time. We'll do fine."

I doubt that, Bjorn thought. *Not with Valerian watching our every move.*

"Yes," Bjorn said. "We'll do fine."

King Gavin rode in his battle armor at the head of his men. That would change when they neared their border with the Fox clan. Scouts would be sent ahead followed by a vanguard of cavalry, and then the main body of the army would follow that.

The army would pass through the village that had been raided, as a show of support. According to Valerian, this was to let all loyal clansmen see the benefits of unity with the kingdom. Gavin suspected that it was, instead, to let everyone see the price of defiance.

It was madness to start a war one month, possibly two, before winter set in. Still, most armies did not have the advantage of riding with a MageLord. It would, more than likely, be a short war.

Gavin studied the Fox clan village from a distant hilltop. Obviously the villagers had been preparing for their arrival for some time. A dry moat had been dug around the town—no small feat in the cold earth. The earth from the moat had been piled on the inside into a rampart about the town.

The moat and rampart even cut across the two roads leading into the village. Obviously the villagers were more concerned with defense than supplies. Given what they faced, their concerns were valid.

Just surrender, Gavin thought. *You don't know what you face.*

"We should march around," Ivanel said. "If we delay here, that will give Marik's main forces time to intercept us."

"Are you suggesting that we leave an enemy behind us?" Valerian asked.

"They are mere villagers," Gavin said. "Outside of their makeshift fortress they are of little concern."

"The mere fact that they have this fortress would seem to me proof that they are not 'mere' villagers," Valerian objected.

"All that means is that they can dig," General Hans quipped. "I see no regular troops. Scouts report few true weapons. A few spears and crossbows. Most carry simple farming tools. I see no threat here, majesty. I say we march the army around before Marik has a chance to intercept us."

"Majesty, it is precisely this type of defiance that we must be concerned with," Valerian said. *"This* is more of a threat to the kingdom than Marik's armies in the long run."

Only for a tyrant, Gavin thought. *But then, that's what I have become.*

"I agree," Gavin heard himself say. "Razing these impudent farmers should not take long."

Gavin sat and watched the glow on the horizon that used to be a farming village. He gathered his cloak tighter around the unseasonably cold wind that was blowing through the camp tonight. The farmers had given Gavin's army stiffer resistance than Gavin would have thought.

Never underestimate the people, his father had told him. *The only thing which fights more viciously than a cornered animal is a cornered animal protecting its young.*

Magnus had loved the people—all people. Gavin recalled once, as a very young man, having seen his father weeping. With the love and innocence of youth, he had boldly approached his father to ask what was wrong, rather than leave him alone with his grief.

A border village had been destroyed—one in which his father had once spent a short stay. Every man in the village had been killed and the village itself burned. Many of the homes had still had women and children inside when they burned. His father had wept at the loss and then led his armies forth to exact vengeance.

Gavin's father did not wreak his vengeance on the people of the Star clan, though. He pressed through, past the border villages and on to Chief Harold's castle. When Magnus had finished with that battle, not one stone of Harold's castle was left standing on another. The next chieftain, Balder, later swore fealty to Magnus willingly, solely because Magnus *had* spared the people.

Today, however, Gavin had committed the same atrocity that had driven his father to tears. Every able-bodied man in the village had been put to the sword. Then the village had been burned to the ground with no regard for who might have taken refuge in the buildings. Gavin could almost feel Magnus glaring down on him from above.

Forgive me father, he thought. *Thanks to Valerian, I cannot even weep for them.*

"Both strongholds are unreachable?" Gavin asked the scout leader.

"Yes, majesty," Arik replied. "The snow is so heavy that one cannot see beyond five feet. We were almost lost."

"And you saw no troops?" Valerian asked.

"None, Lord Chancellor," Arik replied.

"Thank you, Arik," Gavin said. "That will be all."

"Yes, majesty," Arik said, bowing and then walking from the war pavilion.

"This is an unexpected boon," Gavin said.

Like hell, he thought. No doubt, this bizarre weather was Valerian's doing. The MageLord had effectively sealed Marik's army behind its walls.

"With those two holdouts clear," Valerian said, "our path to Foxmire Castle is unhindered."

It certainly is, Gavin thought.

"You don't mean to march past and simply ignore two castles full of troops?" General Hans asked incredulously. "We cannot plan a war on the weather! Those blizzards could lift at any moment—they may have already. We would be caught between Foxmire Castle and an army equal in size to our own forces!"

Oh, I suspect the weather will hold, Hans, Gavin thought.

"Majesty, winter is at hand," Valerian said. "We must strike quickly and pull out. Even if the blizzards were to end tonight, it would take some time for those troops to move out. *This* is our opportunity."

"I agree," Gavin said.

"Majesty!" Hans objected.

"We will keep our scouts out," Gavin interrupted. "Hans, at the first sign of reinforcement, we will withdraw."

"Very well, majesty," Hans grudgingly agreed.

"Hrothgar has handed us a valuable opportunity," Ivanel added. "We should not ignore it."

Hrothgar has little to do with this, Gavin thought.

The town of Foxmire sat on a marshy plain. Melting snow covered the plain and coated the city wall in white. Apparently Foxmire had been trapped in the blizzards as well. Now, however, the weather was returning to a more seasonable level and the snow was melting quickly.

How convenient, Gavin thought snidely. No doubt this was why they had not encountered resistance on the road here. Still, the muddy roads played hell with the wagons and catapults.

"Concentrate on the catapults," Gavin ordered. "Take the horses from the wagons. We can pull them up later. I want those catapults in range within the hour!"

"Yes, majesty," Hans replied.

"I want two hundred infantry to guard the wagons," Gavin ordered Ivanel.

"Yes, majesty," Gavin's uncle replied.

"Baron William, deploy two hundred infantry outside of each of the city gates," Gavin ordered. "I want that town sealed while we move the engines into position!"

"Yes, majesty!" William replied.

"General Hans, the remaining thousand infantry will wait with us," Gavin ordered. "I want the archers flanking us on the right and left. Once the wall is breached, the infantry will charge under archer support. Once the men have opened the nearest gate, we shall ride in with the cavalry. Move it, men!"

There had been little response from the town to Gavin's maneuvering. The townsmen had gathered on the walls to defend their city. These men were not Marik's castle troops. These were bakers, butchers, innkeepers and so on—the town militia.

They were little better armed than the farmers at the village Gavin had sacked. Spears and crossbows were the main weapons evident. Some few carried shields. All were unarmored.

The wall they defended was a scant twelve feet in height with twenty-foot-tall towers every hundred yards. Gavin knew from earlier visits that the wall was only a man's armspan in thickness. While battlemented, the wall was not machicolated, making it difficult for those on the walls to drop oil or stones on attackers.

This wall would not slow them much. The castle at the center of town would be the challenge. First, however, they had to control the town.

"Catapults are in position, majesty," Ivanel reported. "Shall we wait for the wagons to arrive?"

"No," Gavin replied. "Begin the attack!"

And may the gods have mercy on my soul, Gavin thought as the trumpets relayed his orders.

One catapult fired and the stone missile flew wildly over the wall, taking one of the townsmen with it. The man did not even have the opportunity to scream as he was smashed from the top of the wall.

Another missile struck the battlements, spraying the defenders with stone fragments. The townsmen fled the section of wall which Gavin's engineers had targeted, falling back to the towers.

The third missile fell short, sending a spray of dirt and snow against the wall. The missile from the fourth catapult struck squarely in the center of the wall. Stone flew from the wall, leaving a shallow depression where it had struck. A few more of those and the wall would be breached.

"A good first volley," Hans noted.

"Order catapults five and six to attack the towers flanking our target area," Gavin ordered. "Tell catapult three to reload with five loose barrels of oil and aim for the base of the wall. They are to hold their fire."

"Yes, majesty," Hans replied. He passed Gavin's orders to runners which he then dispatched to the engineers.

Catapults five and six fired before the others could reload.

Both missiles struck their targets. The engineers were getting the range. The townsmen retreated further down the walls.

Three more stones were hurled at the wall. All three struck squarely. A portion of the top of the wall collapsed, exposing the timbers within—another blow should breach it.

"Reload number four, five and six with oil," Gavin ordered. "Same orders as three. One and two, target the base of the wall."

"Yes, majesty," Hans replied. Again, Gavin's orders were relayed to the engineers by runner. Gavin waited while the catapults were reloaded.

Catapults one and two fired simultaneously.

"Reload one and two with water!" Gavin ordered before the missiles had even struck.

Both missiles struck the base of the city wall. The tortured section of wall groaned, collapsing from the center outward. Finally, in a roar of crumbling masonry, the two supporting towers were pulled down into the breach. Armed townsmen climbed atop the mound of rubble before the dust had settled, intent on holding the breach.

"Launch the oil!" Gavin ordered. Flames sprouted in the four catapult bowls as the engineers set torch to the oil-soaked barrels.

The townsmen fled as the flaming barrels scattered in flight toward the breach. The barrels shattered on the mound of rubble, coating it in flames.

"Archers, advance and fire," Gavin ordered. The archers would lay down covering fire against the sections of wall still standing. Gavin watched as the engineers began to load barrels of water into the two catapults as he had ordered.

"Sound the charge!" Gavin ordered. The trumpets blared and a thousand men charged the burning breach. Gavin waited until the men were over halfway to the breach.

"Fire one and two!" Gavin ordered. Again the trumpets sounded. The catapults fired. Gavin watched as the barrels of water flew over the charging infantry.

The aim was true. The barrels of water shattered on the burning mound. The remaining oil was washed away, and the flames were mostly extinguished. Gavin's men charged up the steaming mound of rubble before the townsmen could regroup.

Soon the shouts and screams of men and the ring of steel reached their ears. Gavin watched as his men gained the wall and began fighting toward the gate. Doubtless, more at the street level were doing the same. Gavin drew his sword and held it aloft.

"To the gate!" he shouted, spurring his horse. The roan stallion trotted down the road toward the gate. Two hundred cavalry followed.

Gavin pulled up, just beyond arrowshot of the gate, and waited. His men atop the wall had almost reached the towers flanking the gate. Gavin watched and waited.

Several of his men attempted to scale the short towers, only to be repelled. Finally, one made the tower. He died quickly, but held his place long enough for two more to scale the wall behind him. Soon, the towers were taken.

The heavy oaken doors of the gate began to swing inward. The town gate was simply that—two heavy doors barred on the inside. Gavin raised his sword aloft.

"Charge!" he shouted, spurring his horse to a gallop. In a thunder of hooves, two hundred horsemen entered the town of Foxmire.

Bodies lay all around the gate. Most were townsmen, but a few wore Gavin's colors. Shouts, screams and the ring of steel could be heard in the distance as Gavin's men pressed the townsmen back.

"Hans, stay with the men!" Gavin ordered.

He spurred his mount into the narrow streets. The cavalry's goal, for the moment, was the east gate. The townsmen were rallying to the south wall, where the fighting was heaviest. Gavin hoped to have the east gate open before they could fall back to defend it.

The cavalry followed him, two abreast, down the narrow streets. Gavin rounded a corner, and an arrow glanced from his shield. He reined his mount to a halt. Apparently there were some defenders secreted within the town itself. He took his crossbow from its hook on his saddle and looked to see whence the arrow had come.

Before he could find the source of the attack, he heard a

crossbow fire from beside him, and then several others. A man's cry from above told him the attacker had been found. No other arrows followed.

"On to the gate!" Gavin ordered, wheeling his mount and charging ahead. The sounds of combat receded far behind them as the swift-moving cavalry left the main knot of the battle behind. Soon they had caught sight of the southernmost of the two gates on the east side of the city.

"Uncle," Gavin ordered. "Have the men cover us while William and I open that gate!"

"Yes, majesty," Ivanel replied. "Crossbows!"

Gavin and William charged the gate behind a flight of arrows. A few cries came from above as the deadly missiles found human flesh.

One arrow glanced from Gavin's shield, and another fouled in his cloak. Thank Hrothgar the townsmen hadn't thought to shoot the horse. Another round of quarrels flew from behind. A townsman cried out and fell from one of the towers.

Then they were at the gate. Gavin dismounted, placing his mount between himself and the town. William did likewise, and the two of them strained to lift the heavy oaken beam from the gate.

With a crash, they dropped the bar to the ground and took hold of the gate handles, pulling as hard as they could. Slowly the massive doors of the gate swung inward. With a cry of victory, two hundred infantry charged the gate. Gavin and William remounted and rode to rejoin the cavalry as the cavalry let fly with another volley from the crossbows.

"To the northeastern gate!" Gavin shouted. The cavalry wheeled and retreated from the gate as Gavin's infantry swarmed through.

The battle had caught up to them. A band of over three hundred townsmen were slowly regaining ground against less than a hundred of Gavin's infantry. The cavalry was approaching from the flank. Gavin raised his sword in the air and swept it forward, signaling a charge.

Infantry and townsmen alike turned at the sound of clattering hooves. The infantry fell back, out of the path of the charge, and the townsmen turned to flee. It was far too late. The charge slammed into the panicked townsmen, scattering them like chaff. Gavin leaned over and decapitated a fleeing townsman. His head bounced on the cobblestones as his body stumbled a few more steps before falling.

Gavin wheeled his mount, surveying the battle as he raised his sword aloft. The townsmen had been scattered. The infantry could carry on from here.

"To the gate!" he shouted, turning to gallop down another street. The cheers of the rescued infantry rang hollowly in his ears. There was no honor in this war—not for him.

Chapter
------- Ten -----------

BY SUNSET, THE town had been secured. Of Gavin's original two thousand five hundred infantry, only a little over two thousand were in combat form. Almost two hundred were dead and over three hundred were wounded.

The infantry patrolled through the darkened streets, searching out and destroying pockets of resistance. Fires burned out of control here and there throughout the city. Gavin ignored the sights and sounds of the city as he studied the castle that stood before him.

Marik had added an outer wall since Gavin had last seen Foxmire Castle. Formerly the blocky keep had stood alone, nestled atop a low mound in the center of town. Now another wall surrounded it, a hundred feet out. Gavin estimated it at twenty feet with thirty-foot towers at regular intervals, surrounded by a dry moat ten feet deep and twenty feet across.

A gatehouse sat in the center of the east wall. The gatehouse was similar in design to those of Reykvid. Gavin had known of no other fortress to use that design. The gatehouse with its tunnel of death had been his father's inspiration. Prior to its design, fortresses simply relied on heavy doors, iron portcullises and drawbridges.

"Chief Marik has been busy these last few years," Hans observed.

"I had heard that he was expanding his hall," Gavin said. "However, neither father nor I suspected that he was fortifying it in this manner."

"I would say that Chief Marik has been expecting a war," Valerian said. "Preparing for it, even."

"If so, it is a good thing that we struck first," Gavin noted.

"How shall we proceed, majesty?" Ivanel asked.

"Empty the wagons," Gavin ordered. "I want them to start hauling rubble from the breach. Set the catapults up south of the castle, out of their range. We will use the catapults to fill the moat with rubble. Once we have a path across, we will lay siege to the castle itself."

Gavin lay awake in his bed in the war pavilion. The flickering lights of the watch fires shone through the walls of the tent.

Thrmm-chnk! The deep voices of the firing catapults throbbed through the night like a giant's heartbeat—pulsing through the constant creak of the wagons. Each firing delivered another load of rubble onto the slowly growing bridge across the dry moat.

Thrmmm-chnk! Gavin could almost imagine that it was the beating of the combined hearts of all the men who had been unjustly slain here today. Slain by his order.

Thrmmm-chnk! No—slain by Valerian's order. Gavin was nothing more than the MageLord's pawn. These deaths were not his doing—this war was not his desire.

Thrmmm-chnk! Gavin buried his head under the pillow, trying to muffle the sound. Anything not to hear that constant reminder of where he was—what he was doing.

Thrmmm-chnk! It was no use. The deep sound penetrated even the pillow—was felt as much as it was heard. Nothing would block it from his ears.

Thrmmm-chnk!

"Majesty," Valerian's voice said softly to him. Gavin sat up to see Valerian standing in the opening to his chamber. Gavin rose from his bed.

"Yes, Lord?" he asked.

"You need your sleep," Valerian said. "We attack the castle on the morrow. Lie down."

Thrmmm-chnk!

"Yes, Lord," Gavin replied. He lay down on his bed and Valerian walked over beside him. The MageLord reached down to place his hands on either side of Gavin's head. Fatigue and exhaustion washed over him, and darkness swirled across his vision. Sleep! At last!

Thrmmm-chnk!

* * *

Marik watched from the battlements of Foxmire Castle as King Gavin's catapults hurled rubble into the dry moat. An interesting tactic. Marik would have to remember it when he sacked Reykvid.

How dare this upstart whelp invade my lands! he thought, clenching and unclenching his gauntleted fists.

Magnus had been a pompous ass, but at least he had been honorable. Gavin, on the other hand, had burned an entire farming village to the ground, killing every man, woman and child within. Marik would make him pay for that tomorrow.

Another catapult fired a load of rubble into the moat. Marik's own engines were silent. Gavin's larger catapults were out of his range. He would see if that would be true tomorrow when Gavin had to pull them up to attack the wall itself.

Tomorrow, young king, he thought. *Tomorrow!*

The bridge across the moat was complete by sunrise. Almost all of the rubble from the breach had gone into building it. Now, however, Gavin had another problem.

"Our scouts report that the troops from the outer strongholds are finally on the march," Gavin told his council. "In two days we will be facing over a thousand fresh troops. So, as we thought, we do not have time for an extended siege."

"Aye," William said, "but we knew that."

"True," Gavin agreed. "We did *not* know about this outer wall, however. Marik has engines on the towers. We cannot move our catapults in range of the wall without putting them in range of Marik's engines."

"It will take them some time to get our range," William advised. "We can probably move the catapults into position and breach the wall before Marik can destroy them."

"Yes, but we may need them to attack the keep as well," Gavin said.

"It's quite simple," Valerian suggested. "We have to destroy his engines before he has a chance to use them against ours."

"I'm glad you think it's so simple," Hans retorted. "His

engines are atop thirty foot towers. We would be in his range long before we were in range to attack his catapults."

"I have noticed that the catapults cannot fire on moving targets," Valerian said.

"Not effectively," Hans agreed. "I don't see how that can help us . . ."

"If you will allow me, I will explain how," Valerian said.

Marik watched from the battlements. Two of Gavin's catapults had now fired three volleys of stones. However, not one of these volleys had even made it halfway to the outer wall. Marik's catapult crews were ready. As soon as Gavin moved his engines into position, they would be destroyed.

A brave scout had managed to get word into the castle at the cost of his life. Marik's forces from Foxwood and Heathton were on the march and should arrive within two days. Marik's brother should arrive with forces from Foxdale about the same time. If Foxmire could hold out until then, Marik could crush Gavin between the castle and the army.

Marik returned his attention to Gavin's engines. They had not fired for some time now. A small knot of men were in animated discussion at the base of each catapult. Probably the engineers.

A small group of armed men joined the engineers at each of the two catapults. What was this insane prince planning?

Suddenly the soldiers, and the engineers, charged toward the walls. Surely they weren't attacking? There were barely twenty men in each of the two groups. The engineers trailed a rope behind them.

The groups stopped briefly a little less than halfway toward the wall before turning and retreating. Marik watched. What in Friga's Hell was Gavin doing?

A team of horses was brought up and hitched to each of the two catapults. Gavin was only going to bring two catapults forward?

"Sound the alarm!" Marik ordered. Oh, well; if Gavin wanted to make it easy for Marik to destroy his engines, who was he to complain?

More of Gavin's men gathered behind the catapults.

Apparently they were going to push while the team pulled. Something was just not right here.

Marik could barely hear the orders of the drovers as the catapults began to move—slowly at first, but quickly picking up speed. Marik had never seen catapults moved into position so quickly. If Gavin was not careful, he would send them toppling into the ditch.

Flames flared in the bowls of the catapults as their contents were ignited. Oil. Gavin was going to fire oil without ranging first?

But he has ranged already, Marik suddenly realized. That was what the engineers had been doing when they charged the wall. They had fired their ranging shots from a safe distance and then calculated where the catapults had to be in order to fire. No doubt they had marked the positions on the cobblestones. Gavin was going to fire his engines on the move!

"Engineers!" Marik shouted, even though he knew it was already too late, even if they *could* hear him. "Target those engines and fire! Fire! *Fire!*"

The instant the catapults reached the location which Gavin's engineers had marked, they fired. With the wheels unlocked, the firing arm acted as a brake, slowing the catapults. Marik watched as the flaming barrels arced up high and down toward the towers where his own engines sat. He could already tell that the shots were true. . . .

A great cheer rose up as the fiery missiles landed squarely atop the towers of the outer wall. In seconds, Marik's engines were burning furiously.

"Move the other engines into position!" Gavin ordered. "Hurry, before Marik can bring other engines to bear!"

In spite of himself, Gavin was impressed. Valerian's plan had worked. Gavin would have never thought of firing catapults on the move. The MageLord had even assured them that firing the catapults would slow them so that they did not topple into the moat.

With most of Gavin's army pushing them, the other catapults were positioned quickly. Soon, the engineers were firing their first ranging shots.

"Well done, Lord Chancellor," Gavin heard himself say.

"Indeed," General Hans said. "Had I not seen it with my own eyes, I would never have believed it."

"You see, General?" Valerian said, smiling. "I am not completely useless in the field."

"Get those catapults into position!" Marik shouted. With the two nearest catapults destroyed, Gavin could assault the wall with impunity.

Marik's men had already toppled the burning engines over the battlements. Now his engineers were hoisting two catapults from the opposite side of the outer wall up into position. Hopefully the wall would withstand Gavin's attack long enough to bring them to bear.

Marik watched as the catapults made their way up the side of the wall, one painful foot at a time. A series of impacts shook the wall. Gavin's engines had gotten the range.

"Order the flanking catapults to range just in front of the section of wall under attack," Marik ordered. "Once they have the range, load them with oil and stand by."

"Yes, my lord," one of his men replied. If Gavin's engines breached the wall, Marik would be prepared to fire on his charge.

"Marik is ranging to fire on our charge," Ivanel observed.

"I noticed," Gavin replied. "He should almost have new engines in place atop those towers as well. How much longer until we breach the wall?"

"Hard to say," Ivanel replied. "We've fired two effective volleys. There doesn't seem to have been much damage."

"Can we fire a third volley before Marik gets those catapults in position?" William said.

"Easily," Ivanel replied.

"I think we can breach the wall," Gavin said. "The problem is going to be those flank engines."

"Aye," William agreed. "With oil or flechettes he can slaughter our men as they charge."

"Dismount the cavalry and send them to the rooftops across from those towers," Gavin ordered. "Have them lay down covering fire with their crossbows—perhaps we can kill the crews. Also, pick one man in ten to fire pitched bolts. If Marik has oil in those engines, we might get lucky and set the barrels afire."

"Yes, majesty," General Hans replied.

"Be sure and tell them to stay behind the peak of the roofs," Gavin ordered. "They're going to need the cover."

"Yes, majesty."

"Retarget catapults one and six on the nearest towers," Gavin ordered. "We have to keep him from getting engines up there."

"Yes, majesty."

Marik watched as another flight of arrows fell short of the towers. Gavin had divined his intent, and had placed archers on the rooftops in a desperate attempt to silence his flank engines.

Another volley from Gavin's catapults shook the wall. Only four of Gavin's engines had fired, however. The northernmost and southernmost engines were being retargeted. Marik watched as they let fly.

One missile struck the base of the northern tower where Marik's engineers were laboring to hoist the replacement engine. The engineers fell prone on the tower roof at the impact. The second missile, from Gavin's southern catapult, struck halfway up the southern tower.

Marik watched as the engine his men were lifting up the side of the tower swung out and back. The small catapult smashed against the side of the tower. Pieces of broken timber rained down on the ground below. *Damn!*

Gavin had just ensured that he would successfully breach the wall. With only one engine to bring to bear, Marik could not destroy Gavin's catapults quickly enough.

"Have the flanking engines stand ready!" Marik ordered. "We're going to be facing a charge soon."

"Y-yes, my lord," one of his men replied. Marik turned to scowl at the man. He was only a lad, barely sixteen summers old. He was already hurrying off to deliver Marik's orders. Marik turned back to the battle.

Another flight of arrows lifted up from the rooftops to the west. Marik smiled—they were far too short to be a threat.

A breath of wind touched his face, quickly rising into a strong gust from the west. Marik's smile vanished as the wind caught the arrows. Mostly spent, they landed on the tower roof with little effect—save for the burning ones.

Flames spouted from the bowls of both catapults as the oil-soaked barrels ignited. The engineers reacted quickly. Marik watched as his catapults fired, discarding the oil before the barrels could rupture.

Good, men, he thought. *Now get those damned things reset!* As he watched, the barrels landed on the very spot through which Gavin's army would have to charge when the wall was breached. Unfortunately, the fire would burn out quickly on the cobblestone plaza.

Gavin's catapults fired again. By the second impact, Marik knew the wall would no longer stand. The third missile came completely through the wall in a spray of shattered masonry. The battlements shuddered. Fortunately, Marik's men had already abandoned the besieged section of wall.

On the fourth impact, the wall gave. It rocked back and forth for a moment as the lower half crumbled away. Then, unable to support itself any longer, the upper half collapsed.

The two towers to either side were still standing, undamaged by the collapse. Ten feet or so from the towers, the breach began, sloping down steeply to a mound of rubble. Marik looked to the north.

The flank engines were not ready. *Curse the luck!* Marik heard Gavin's trumpets sound the charge. . . .

"That wind came along at a fortunate time," Hans observed.

"Indeed," Gavin agreed. "Sound the charge!"

Fortune had little to do with it, Gavin thought as the trumpets relayed his orders. The early blizzards, the wind— none of it had to do with fortune.

"Advance the archers!" Gavin ordered. "I want covering fire on those walls!"

"Yes, majesty," General Hans replied.

"Lord Chancellor," Gavin ordered, "you will wait with the supply train."

"Yes, majesty," Valerian replied.

"Hans, reassemble the cavalry," Gavin said. "We shall lead

them on foot through the breach once the men have secured it. Have the sappers follow us with the ram and the turtle."

"Yes, majesty." Runners were dispatched to retrieve the cavalry. Gavin watched as the archers advanced behind their mantlets. Soon they were laying down heavy fire on the sections of the outer wall adjacent to the breach.

The cavalry reformed around them, on foot. Gavin glanced behind and saw the sappers waiting inside the turtle. The leather-covered, peaked wooden roof had been liberally soaked with water to protect the sappers while they used the rams.

Gavin raised his sword high and slashed forward to signal the charge. Gavin's two thousand infantry had already taken the breach and the adjacent towers. Under the protective fire of the archers, men were advancing further along the wall. The cavalry and the sappers met no resistance through the breach.

Inside the wall was another matter. Foxmire had originally held a garrison of two hundred. With the addition of the outer wall, Marik had added additional outbuildings. There were easily three hundred men in the courtyard, in addition to the two hundred who held the castle.

Without Valerian we would never have taken this fortress, Gavin thought. *Not with* this *force*.

And then there was no time to think. The mission of the infantry had been to secure the courtyard. The mission of the cavalry and sappers was to gain entry to Foxmire itself.

The main gate lay on the east side of the keep. Gavin led his men to the right, directly into a fierce battle. The heavily armored cavalrymen quickly tipped the balance in that battle, killing and scattering the defenders. Gavin himself split a man's skull with his heavy sword.

Forgive me, father, he thought.

The turtle and the rams drew the attention of Marik's troops. Soon Gavin's force was surrounded by frantic defenders.

Gavin caught a spear thrust on his shield, forcing the tip upward, over his head. As the man's momentum carried him forward, Gavin stepped forward and thrust his blade into the man's armpit. Blood spewed over his arm as he pulled the sword free. Another soul on his hands. . . .

"Protect the sappers!" Gavin shouted. "Form up!" The cavalrymen formed a barrier around the turtle. For now, their advance was halted, but at least the sappers and their tools were safe.

Two more spears were aimed at Gavin. He caught one on his shield and slapped the other aside with the edge of his sword. The spears were larger and slower. While his attackers were recovering from their strokes, Gavin snapped his sword around, down, up and over to smash down on the helmet of the man to his right.

The wooden helmet shattered, but the blade did not penetrate the outer layer of leather. Even so, the man went down, possibly with a shattered skull. Gavin stepped back in time to deflect his first attacker's next thrust downward.

The spearhead buried itself in the ground. For just a moment, the man tried to retrieve it. Gavin sliced horizontally, drawing his blade across the man's throat. The spearman fell back, clutching at his throat as if he could stop the red flood with his hands.

Gavin's infantry rallied to the defense of their king. Two hundred men rushed to aid the cavalry. With the pressure off their rear, the cavalry were once again free to concentrate on the advance.

Soon they had fought their way to the castle gate. Now the turtle was brought forward. Gavin, William, Ivanel and Hans waited in the rear of the turtle as the sappers lifted the heavy ram. A hissing and pounding began on the roof of the turtle as stones and boiling oil were dropped from above.

The brawny sappers swung the ram back and forth, building up momentum. *Kthoom!* The heavy stone head slammed into the oaken door with no visible effect.

Kthoom! The second blow seemed to rock the doors more, but it was difficult to be certain.

Kthoom! The blows were picking up speed as the sappers got their rhythm down. The doors of the gate shuddered noticeably.

Kthoom! The first sound of splintering wood reached Gavin's ears. Hopefully, it was the gate beginning to give way and not the roof of the turtle. Gavin glanced up—he saw no cracked timbers.

Kthoom! The sound of splintering wood was louder and had definitely come from the gate. It rocked in almost far enough for a man to slip between the doors. Gavin could see men on the other side pushing the gate back closed again. The set of the sappers' faces told Gavin that they were increasing their efforts.

KTHOOM! With a loud crack, the bar gave. The sappers dropped the ram and threw their shoulders against the doors, forcing them open against the strength of the defenders inside.

"*Charge!*" Gavin shouted as he leaped forward into the narrow opening. Gavin thrust around his shield, disembowelling a man who was attempting to close the gate. The cavalry followed. Soon the gate of Foxmire Castle was opened wide as the mass of cavalrymen forced their way through.

The main hall of the castle was filled with defenders. There were easily a hundred men arrayed against Gavin's cavalrymen. If none had come down from the walls, that raised Foxmire's defenders to seven hundred total. Almost three times what Marik had maintained here two years ago.

Gavin's cavalry hopelessly outnumbered the defenders in the hall. Soon the stone floor was slippery with blood and bile. More defenders were streaming into the battle from the stairs above, but Foxmire Castle had already fallen. Gavin thrust his sword into the chest of a disembowelled man lying on the floor, ending his misery.

Hrothgar forgive me, he thought.

"*Gavin!*" a voice shouted. Gavin looked up to meet the ice-blue eyes of Chief Marik glaring down at him from a balcony.

"Do you have the courage to face me, you cowardly murderer of farmers and children?" Marik shouted at him. The sounds of battle in the hall fell silent. "Or is the son of Magnus Urqhart completely without honor?"

So long as he is Valerian's puppet, yes, Gavin thought.

"I will face you, Marik!" Gavin shouted. "If I defeat you, will your men lay down their arms? Or must there be more bloodshed?"

"I offer no concessions to cowards and murderers!" Marik

replied. "If you defeat me, you have my life. Nothing more."

"So be it," Gavin agreed. This was a wise ploy on Marik's part. Gavin had been embattled for the better part of an hour, while Marik was yet fresh. If Gavin was felled here, Marik could possibly rout Gavin's troops.

Perhaps I will die, Gavin thought. That would do little good, however. Ivanel would become king, and he was as much Valerian's puppet as Gavin. No, Gavin must live to exact his vengeance on the MageLord.

The forces parted to make room for the two combatants. Gavin's forces retreated toward the gate, while Marik's men fell back toward the stairs. Marik came down the stairs, and his men parted to let him through.

This was no unseasoned spearman that Gavin faced now. Marik was a bear of a man, with reddish blond hair and ice blue eyes. He stood almost half a head taller than Gavin and was easily half again as wide. His bronze armor gleamed in sharp contrast to Gavin's blood-soaked form.

He carried no shield. Instead, in both hands, he carried a large, double-headed axe. It was a slower, clumsier weapon, but Marik had the strength and the weight to make up for that.

Marik opened his attack with an overhead swing toward Gavin's head. Gavin sidestepped, slapping the side of the axe with his shield. He dared not try to block that massive weapon—a direct blow would shatter both his shield and the arm that bore it.

Even the glancing blow knocked Gavin off balance, giving Marik the time to recover from his swing and aim a horizontal slash at Gavin's bowels. Gavin leaped backwards, out of the vicious blade's arc. He landed nimbly on the balls of his feet.

The heat of battle washed away his fatigue. Marik had size and strength as his allies. Gavin had only speed and agility.

Gavin stepped forward to thrust his sword into Marik's side as the swing of the axe turned it toward him. Marik raised his leg and landed an armored kick on Gavin's shield, sending the young king sprawling.

Gavin desperately rolled away as the heavy axe came down. Stone chips flew over Gavin as the massive steel head slammed into the floor. Gavin thrust from one knee, but only succeeded in forcing Marik to back away, giving Gavin time to regain his feet.

Gavin's breath came in ragged gasps. He was overmatched—badly. It was time to try something different. Gavin waited.

Marik stepped forward, swinging flat at Gavin's side. Gavin stepped forward, inside the arc of the axe, thrusting toward the opening at the neck of Marik's breastplate.

Marik's eyes widened with alarm, and he·ducked to the side, narrowly avoiding Gavin's thrust. The haft of the axe slammed into Gavin's shield, knocking him to the floor for the second time. Marik's men cheered.

Gavin looked up to see Marik looming over him, his axe raised high. There was no time to dodge or to roll. Gavin raised his shield to meet the plummeting axe head.

Gavin felt the bones of his arm break as the axe shattered the wood of his shield. Fortunately, the bronze outer layer prevented the axe from shearing through his arm. Gavin collapsed on the floor as his vision blurred with pain.

Half conscious, Gavin felt Marik contemptuously kick his sword away. His vision cleared in time to see Marik raise the axe over him.

"Die, murderer!" Marik said.

Before Marik could bring the axe down, Gavin rolled forward, drawing the dagger at his belt. From his knees, he plunged the dagger upward, underneath Marik's breastplate.

The giant roared, dropping his axe and backhanding Gavin. The force of his blow knocked Gavin several feet. Gavin felt hands lift him from under the arms and drag him away. He remained conscious just long enough to see Marik on his knees, clutching at the dagger buried in his stomach. Then the darkness claimed him.

Chapter
-------- Eleven ------------

GAVIN AWOKE TO see the faces of the physician, his uncle and Valerian standing over him. His arm throbbed in agony.

"Majesty," the physician said. "Drink this."

Valerian lifted him so that he could put his lips to the cup the physician offered. He spit out the first, acidly bitter sip.

"What *is* this?" he said.

"Belladonna, majesty," the physician said. "It will help the pain. Please, drink."

"That's poison!"

"Only in large doses," the physician assured him. "In small doses, it relieves pain. Drink."

"Please drink, majesty," Valerian said. Coming from the MageLord, it was the same as a command.

Gavin forced down a mouthful of the horribly bitter tea. The physician took the cup away.

"That's good, majesty," he said. "The pain will ease in a moment."

"Foxmire?" Gavin asked.

"Taken," Ivanel assured him. "We took the castle shortly after you killed Marik. We have his widow and son hostage."

"Good," Gavin said, lying back on his pillow. He felt light-headed, and the pain in his arm had indeed lessened.

"Majesty," Ivanel said, "the men must see you. There are rumors that you are dead."

"My armor?" Gavin asked. His tongue felt thick. Had the physician poisoned him after all?

"Cleaned and ready, majesty," Ivanel replied. Gavin tried to sit up and found that he lacked the strength. Ivanel caught his shoulders before he could fall.

"Help me up," Gavin slurred.

The physician reached under Gavin's nose and crushed something. A pungent smell burned his nose. Gavin coughed and knocked the physician's hand away. A few more coughs racked his body. Once the fit had passed, however, his head felt much clearer.

"Is that better, majesty?" the physician asked.

"Yes," Gavin said. "My apologies."

"Of course, majesty," the physician replied.

"Ivanel, attend me," Gavin said.

"Yes, majesty," Ivanel replied.

Gavin strode through the gates of Foxmire Castle surrounded by his honor guard to meet the cheers of his men. It was hard to believe that the war was almost over. The Fox clan had been virtually defeated in only three weeks.

Valerian could claim credit for most of that. If he had not caused the blizzards to trap the forces of Foxwood and Heathton, Gavin would never have made it to Foxmire. Without his interventions during the siege of the castle, Foxmire would still be held by Marik and his men.

Now, however, Ivanel had informed Gavin that the forces of Foxwood and Heathton were on the march here, as well as forces from Foxdale. Almost four thousand men in all, including militia.

Of Gavin's original two thousand five hundred infantry, only twelve hundred remained. Only two hundred of the original two hundred fifty cavalry remained. The archers had taken few casualties, leaving Gavin with over four hundred. They would be seriously outnumbered when those forces arrived.

Still, he had Marik's son and widow hostage, and the castle to occupy as a defensible site. With those factors on his side, and reinforcements hopefully on the way, he should be able to withstand the remnants of Marik's army.

"Have the runners been dispatched?" Gavin asked.

"Yes, majesty," Ivanel informed him. Gavin nodded. In a few days, another five thousand men would enter the lands of the Fox clan. Now that Gavin had drawn the forces of Marik's three lesser holdings to Foxmire, it should be an easy matter for Gavin's troops to occupy those strongholds.

Gavin's guards led him into the great hall. There, his men had gathered the survivors of the siege.

"You pig!" a woman shouted at him. Gavin recognized her as Marik's widow, Alyssa. A soldier raised his hand to strike her. Gavin stepped forward and caught the man's wrist.

"Words will not harm me," he said. "You do not strike defenseless women in my service."

"Give me a knife and I'll show you who's defenseless," she spat, "Your father would never have committed this atrocity."

No, he would not have, Gavin agreed.

"My father would have responded just as severely to your murderous raids on our border!" Gavin said. "Did you think we would let you steal our property and kill our citizens with impunity? Your clan will never do so again."

"My clansmen are on their way here, butcher," the woman said. "You will pay for this outrage and I will see your head on a pike atop the walls of my husband's castle."

"I doubt that," Gavin replied.

Hrothgar forgive me, I doubt that, he thought.

Bjorn climbed down the makeshift ladder.

"'Tis done," Theodr said, with relief.

"Thank the gods," Angus replied.

"Yes," Bjorn agreed, looking up at the master chimney. "Now we just have to get a house up around it." The chimney served a four-sided fireplace. The main room and three smaller bedrooms would attach to that.

Another chimney served a two-sided fireplace that warmed two other rooms. It was going to be a grand cabin—almost a hall.

"I don't see how," Theodr said.

"One plank at a time," Bjorn replied.

"We'll never make it before winter," Theodr objected.

"We don't have to," Bjorn said. "The cave is comfortable enough until we finish."

The seven of them had been fortunate to find the cave. It was small, barely large enough for all of them, but it was comfortable. That find alone had decided their choice of a building site.

"We can't cut planks once winter sets in," Theodr pointed out.

"So we cut all the planks first," Bjorn said.

"We have to set the beams before the ground freezes," Theodr added.

"Theodr," Bjorn asked, "do you always have a problem for every answer?"

"I'm just trying to figure out how we're going to get the work done," he replied. "I don't see how."

"Faith," Bjorn said. "We will manage."

"With one or perhaps two more able-bodied men, I would say yes," he said. "But I don't see how the three of us can do it."

"We'll manage," Bjorn replied. "There are only ten main beams to set. We do that first and then we start cutting planks. Father and the women can start laying the floor as we cut planks."

"Perhaps," Theodr grudgingly agreed. "What do we do for a roof?"

"Let's worry about that when we have walls," Bjorn suggested.

"Has that breach been cleared yet?" Gavin asked.

"Almost, majesty," Ivanel told him. "Six feet of the wall still remains standing beneath the rubble."

"Good. And the moat?"

"Cleared, majesty," Ivanel replied.

"I want that palisade erected by dawn," Gavin said. "On the outer edge of the wall."

"Yes, majesty."

"Where is William?"

"Gathering supplies from the town," Ivanel replied. "Many of the castle's supplies were destroyed in the battle."

"How much do we have?" Gavin asked.

"A sevennight at best, plus our own supplies," General Hans replied. "My hopes are that Baron William can at least double our supplies."

Gavin nodded. It would be almost a sevennight before the occupational forces could take Heathton, the stronghold nearest the border. Foxmire needed supplies for at least three times that long.

"Keep me advised," Gavin ordered.

"Yes, majesty," Ivanel and Hans replied.

The palisade was completed well before dawn. Ivanel ordered Gavin roused from his bed to inspect the work.

"Very good," Gavin said, looking over the top of the palisade from the catwalk. "Do the approaching forces have any catapults?"

"Yes, majesty," Ivanel replied. "But those are a full week away, according to the scouts. The infantry is proceeding ahead."

"Indeed?" Gavin said.

"Yes, majesty," Ivanel assured him.

"Is it too late for a small force to escape the city?" Gavin asked.

"You intend to attack the supply trains?" Ivanel asked.

"Yes," Gavin replied. "Can you take the cavalry and the scouts and destroy those engines?"

"I believe so, majesty," Ivanel replied. "But that will reduce your strength here."

"Without those engines, we can easily withstand a force five times our size in Foxmire," Gavin assured his uncle. "Plus, it will extend our supplies here if we do not have the cavalry to feed. Go—rouse the cavalry and depart before dawn."

"Yes, majesty," Ivanel replied, bowing. He turned to depart.

"Uncle?" Gavin said. Ivanel turned back to face him.

"Yes, majesty?"

"Be careful."

"Yes, majesty."

The first of the Fox clan's forces arrived less than an hour after sunrise. Foxwood had sent three hundred regular infantry, one hundred cavalry and a thousand militia. They camped outside the gate, beyond archer and engine range.

Gavin frowned—Foxwood's entire garrison was only supposed to be about two hundred strong, with barely a score of cavalry. If he assumed that they had left a small force behind to guard the stronghold, that meant that Foxwood's standing garrison had more than doubled.

Gavin watched as the garrison's captain and a standard-bearer approached the walls bearing a white banner.

"Hail Foxmire!" he called.

"What do you want?" Gavin shouted down to him.

"I am Talhaern, Captain of the Guard at Foxwood," the man replied. "I wish to speak with King Gavin."

"*I* am King Gavin," Gavin replied. "What do you want?"

"Your majesty," Captain Talhaern began, "if you will surrender Foxmire Castle to me, as well as our chief's son and his widow, I am willing to guarantee you safe passage from our lands."

"That's very generous of you, Captain," Gavin replied. "But I really don't like the idea of being caught between your forces and the forces from Heathton once I'm away from the city."

"Your majesty, I assure you that is not my intent," Talhaern said. "I will personally travel alone with your army to insure your safe passage, if I have your word that you will release me at the border."

He actually means it, Gavin thought. *Gods, I wish I could accept.*

"I believe you, Captain," Gavin said. "However, I have no intention of surrendering either this castle or the lands of the Fox clan to you. It is my intention to occupy your lands and to take your chief's son and widow back to Reykvid to insure your clan's future good behavior."

"I cannot allow that, your majesty," Talhaern said. "My offer stands. You have until dawn tomorrow to reconsider."

With that, Captain Talhaern turned and rode back to his men.

"For the god's sake, majesty, accept their offer!" Hans implored. "We have sacked and plundered their chieftain's hall, widowed his wife and orphaned his son. The Fox clan will think twice, nay *thrice*, before they offend us again!"

"Until the day that orphaned son takes his father's hall," Valerian countered. "And then, we will be facing their entire clan at the gates of Reykvid. We can hold here, majesty, and await our reinforcements. Now that we have drawn Marik's garrisons to Foxmire, the outer holdings will fall quickly. No doubt they will retreat to Foxdale and we can starve them out there."

"Who *are* you?" Hans asked. Gavin's stomach tightened— was Hans about to expose the MageLord in council?

"I beg your pardon?" Valerian asked.

"Who *are* you?" Hans repeated. "You've come from nowhere and are leading us into one war after another. First against the Badger and Elk clans under Magnus and now here. Who *are* you?"

"I am Valerian," the MageLord replied, "Lord of the ancient House of Rylur. Gavin, would you and William leave us, please?"

"Yes, Lord," Gavin replied. Hans did not move—did not speak.

"We do not wish to be interrupted until dawn tomorrow," Valerian added, "unless our enemies break their word and attack before then."

"Yes, Lord," Gavin replied.

Forgive me, Hans, Gavin thought. *Please forgive me.*

The forces from Foxdale arrived that afternoon. Gavin counted five hundred regular infantry, two hundred archers and almost two thousand militia. This was not looking good. Foxdale's garrison had originally consisted of three hundred plus a hundred cavalry. There was no sign of Foxdale's cavalry.

The forces from Foxdale took up positions north and west of the castle. Apparently they were reserving south of the castle for the forces from Heathton.

Captain Talhaern once again approached the gate under a white banner. This time, the captain from Foxdale approached with him. The man looked disturbingly familiar. . . .

"What do you want, Captain?" Gavin called down, once they were within earshot.

"Have you reconsidered my offer of safe passage, your majesty?" Talhaern asked.

"It has been discussed in council," Gavin assured him. "There is still some debate."

"Debate it quickly, your majesty," the second captain advised. "After dawn tomorrow, the offer will be withdrawn and we will settle for nothing less than your head on a pike."

"That would certainly please Lady Marik," Gavin noted. "And you are?"

"I am Valther, Marik's brother, murderer," the second captain replied. That was undeniable. The captain could be a younger image of his brother.

"I personally hope that you refuse our offer," Valther added.

No, you don't, Gavin thought. *You don't know what you're facing here.*

"We will have an answer for you by dawn," Gavin told him.

"Yes," Marik's brother assured him. "You will."

Gavin watched the sun rise from the battlements. He had been wakened at first twilight as he had ordered. Now he waited, but not for the enemy. He waited to see what fate had befallen his general.

"Good morrow, majesty," Valerian's voice said to him. Gavin turned to see Valerian and Hans emerge from the stairs below onto the top of the gatehouse. He was glad to see Hans alive, although he knew that the stocky warrior was now under Valerian's control as thoroughly as the rest of them.

"Good morrow, Lord Chancellor," he said. "General."

"Majesty," Hans replied calmly.

Is there no end? Gavin wondered. *Can nothing stop this man?*

"What is the situation, majesty?" Valerian asked.

"The forces from Foxdale arrived yesterday," Gavin reported. "Their leader is Marik's brother, Valther. He will not be drawn away from here easily."

"So much the better," the MageLord replied. "When the occupational forces arrive in Foxmire, we shall crush him."

"Yes," Gavin agreed. "That will be easier than besieging him at Foxdale. The enemy forces from Heathton should arrive shortly after dawn."

"Any word from Ivanel?" Valerian asked.

"No," Gavin replied. "I would not expect to hear anything.

We will know if he was successful when the catapults fail to arrive."

"*I* will get word from Ivanel," Valerian replied. "What are their numbers thus far?"

"Eight hundred regular infantry," Gavin said. "Two hundred archers, one hundred cavalry and three thousand militia. It is a sizeable force."

"Yes, but the occupational force should be four thousand strong when they arrive," Valerian noted. "And they are *all* regulars."

Not to mention, we have a MageLord, Gavin thought. Even so, the force arrayed against them was much larger than had been expected, and the forces from Heathton had yet to arrive. Unless Valerian decided to overtly display his power, the outcome would be far from certain.

"Yes," Gavin replied.

"Someone approaches," the MageLord said. Gavin looked over the wall. Valther and Talhaern approached the gate under a flag of truce.

"That is Valther and Talhaern," Gavin explained. "They are probably going to tell us that we have overstayed our welcome."

"I see," Valerian said.

"King Gavin!" Valther shouted. "It is dawn! What is your answer? For your sake, I hope you have decided to accept our offer. For *my* sake, I hope you have not."

"I would hate to disappoint you, Captain Valther," Gavin called down. "Therefore, we have decided to continue to enjoy your gracious hospitality."

"You will be enjoying our hospitality for some time," Valther replied. "Your head, and those of your men, will sit atop our walls until they are picked clean by the crows!"

"I knew you would be pleased," Gavin replied.

"You have no idea," Valther replied. "Our offer of safe passage is withdrawn. I am looking forward to taking your head from your shoulders."

"Don't look too far, Valther," Gavin advised. "You might not like what you see."

Without another word, Valther and Talhaern turned to ride from the gate.

"Order them killed," Valerian commanded.

"Lord Chancellor, that would outrage their men," Gavin objected. "Angry men are much harder to kill."

"Very well," Valerian said. "But when this is over, I want *his* head on a pike. And it will still live while the crows feed on it."

Gavin felt the hairs on the back of his neck rise. He had no doubt that Valerian spoke the truth. No doubt at all.

"Yes, Lord," Gavin replied quietly.

The forces from Heathton finally arrived just before noon. Three hundred regular infantry, a hundred cavalry and fifteen hundred militia. That brought the opposing forces to over a thousand infantry and almost five thousand militia. Now, cook fires began to light the besiegers' camp as the sun set.

Gavin glanced over to the breach where the sappers worked. In the last two days they had brought the lowest point of the wall back up to nine feet. The work had slowed considerably as they proceeded up the breach, however. Gavin doubted that they had gained another foot of wall today.

Even so, every inch of wall strengthened the palisade on the other side. By the time the catapults arrived, the wall should be at twelve feet or so. That was, *if* the catapults arrived. If Ivanel was successful, that event should at least be delayed.

"The catapults and supplies are just beyond the horizon," Arik reported. Ivanel nodded.

"How many soldiers travel with them?" he asked.

"Roughly one hundred militia," Arik replied.

"Militia?" Ivanel asked.

"Yes, your grace," Arik assured him. "There are no regulars with the caravan."

"Is there anywhere from which we can lay an ambush?" Ivanel asked. On this accursed flat ground, the supply train would see them coming from over a mile away.

"No, your grace," Arik said. "All in between is flat farmland."

"Then how did you get close enough to count their noses?" Ivanel asked.

"A man can lie down in tall grass," Arik replied, smiling. "Horses are more difficult to hide."

"Indeed," Ivanel noted. He looked around at the fields of winter wheat waving in the wind. "Only a hundred infantry, you say?"

"A hundred militia," Arik corrected. "I would not call that rabble infantry."

"Captain!" Ivanel called.

"Your grace!" Captain Alhric replied, stepping forward.

"Dismount your best hundred crossbowmen," Ivanel commanded. "Have the other hundred surrender their crossbows to them. You and the scouts will lead the remaining hundred, along with the extra horses, out of sight down the road. Quickly!"

"At once, your grace!" Alhric replied.

"Well planned, your grace," Arik said.

"Just because we are cavalry does not mean that we *have* to fight from horseback," he replied.

Ivanel lay in the tall wheat. It had been over an hour since he had positioned his men in the wheat fields on either side of the road. The ground was still wet and muddy from the melted snows. The cavalry would not look very dignified after this exercise.

Ivanel looked up at the wheat that concealed them. The early snows did not seem to have damaged the crop too much. That was good—at least the people of the Fox clan would not starve for the sake of Valerian's ambitions.

Not that he *would care*, Ivanel thought. This thralldom chafed at him. Still, he felt worse for Gavin. He was the king—how must he feel at being forced to blindly obey the MageLord's bidding?

Finally, the tramp of feet and the creaking of wagon wheels reached them. It was time.

Ivanel peered through the wheat. He could see movement, but that was all. The front of the supply train passed his position. He released the guard on his crossbow. Another lay next to him on the ground. His men would fire two quick shots and then draw and charge.

Ivanel waited until he supposed the leading edge of the

caravan had almost reached the last man along the road. He rose from the wheat and raised the crossbow to his shoulder.

"*Fire!*" he shouted, letting his arrow fly.

His command was echoed up and down the fields as his men loosed their volley against the caravan. Ivanel stooped and grabbed his second crossbow from the ground. He hefted it to his shoulder and fired, almost without aiming.

The supply train was in chaos. Panicked horses were overturning wagons—men were shouting, or dying. Ivanel lifted his shield from the ground and drew his sword. The blade left its scabbard with a ring.

"*Charge!*" he shouted. Again his command was echoed up and down the fields as his men complied.

The chaos of the supply train was not indicative of the amount of damage that had been done. Ivanel's double volley had not been as effective as he had hoped it would be. Over half of the militia remained in fighting form.

Still, these were militia, not regular troops. The first man Ivanel encountered was quickly dispatched with a cut across his belly followed by a thrust through the chest. Ivanel stepped over the corpse to his next opponent.

There was not a third. Ivanel glanced around the field to see his men dispatch the few remaining enemy.

"Cut the horses loose!" Ivanel ordered. "I want these catapults burned! Forage through the wagons for food we can carry and then burn the remainder of the supplies. Leave *nothing* for the enemy to use against us!"

"Yes, your grace," the men replied.

Ivanel sighed. Another battle won for that demon Valerian. Would that he could take his sword to *him* instead of these innocent men.

Chapter
------- Twelve -----------

"IVANEL HAS DESTROYED the artillery from both Foxwood and Heathton," Valerian told them. "He is currently marching to intercept the siege train from Foxdale."

"What of casualties, Lord?" Hans asked.

"Minimal," Valerian replied. "Our occupational troops should arrive at Heathton in four days. From there, they will move on to Foxwood. If the siege persists until then, they will move to Foxmire and liberate us. Otherwise, we will join forces and move on to Foxdale."

"Lord, I doubt that Valther will withdraw to Foxdale," Gavin said. "With no reinforcements to hope for, he knows that we could simply starve him out."

"You believe he will maintain the siege?"

"No, Lord," Gavin replied. "If I were Valther, I would march out and meet the invaders on the field, perhaps a day away from the city."

"Our occupational troops would only number four thousand at that point," Valerian noted.

"That assumes few casualties, Lord," Gavin replied. "It would be safer to assume that there will only be three thousand."

"And Valther has over six thousand men in his command," Hans added.

"How has this happened?" Valerian asked.

Don't you already know? Gavin thought. Apparently, for all of his power, Valerian was not much of a tactician.

"Our estimates of the sizes of the Fox clan garrisons were incorrect, Lord," Hans replied. "Obviously, Chief Marik has been gathering his forces without our knowledge for some time."

"So, your neighbor has been planning to attack *you*,

129

Gavin," Valerian noted. "And apparently for some time now."

"I doubt that, Lord," Gavin replied. "The Foxmire militia numbered only three thousand or so. An army of ten thousand could not hope to take Reykvid. I would suppose that Marik intended to march against one of the other clans."

"Possibly the Bear clan," Hans suggested. "They have ports and the Fox clan does not."

"If Valther does march out to attack our forces, we should pursue and catch him between us," Valerian said.

"There would be nothing to prevent him from turning back on us, Lord," Gavin pointed out. "He could attack us long before we joined with our other forces, and we would be even more heavily outnumbered than they."

"We need more men," Hans said.

"Or we need for Valther to have less," Valerian suggested. "How far would his numbers have to drop to even the odds?"

"I would feel more comfortable if he lost one or two thousand of his men," Gavin replied.

"One at the minimum," Hans agreed.

"Very well," Valerian replied. "One or two thousand it is."

How can a single man wield such power? Gavin thought. He would not *want* to have such power—to be able to casually destroy a thousand lives at a whim.

Valerian could win this war alone, Gavin realized. He was only using them to avoid showing himself.

"Carry on," Valerian told them. "I have things to which I must attend."

"Yes, Lord," they replied, as Valerian rose and left the council chamber.

"*All* of them?" Valther shouted. He couldn't believe what Locke, captain of the garrison at Heathton, had just told him.

"Yes, m'lord," Captain Locke replied. "All of my militia have taken with fever."

"Was there any warning?"

"No, m'lord. Last night, the men just started coming down with the fever, one after another."

"Was there any word of fever in Heathton?" Valther asked. This was not good. Those fifteen hundred men would be sorely missed once Valther breached Foxmire's walls.

"Not that I had heard," Locke told him.

"Separate them from the rest of the men," Valther ordered. If this fever swept through the rest of his army, Gavin would have won this war without lifting a sword. "Set up hospices in the empty inns near the castle. Report back to me with Talhaern when you have finished."

"Yes, m'lord," Locke replied. He turned and left Valther's tent.

Valther shook his head. The fortunes of this entire war had been against them from the start. First the freak blizzards had imprisoned the garrisons in their strongholds, allowing Gavin to march to Foxmire unopposed. Now pestilence was threatening to wipe out the force that had finally managed to challenge him. It was almost unnatural.

Valther blinked in surprise at an unexpected thought. What if it wasn't just *almost* unnatural? He seemed to recall a rumor about a practitioner of the Forbidden Arts in the court at Reykvid. Captain Locke would know more about that—Heathton was their garrison closest to Reykvid.

Would Gavin actually have allied with a man of the Black Arts? Gavin had once spent a summer in Marik's hall. The young man that Valther had observed then would not have done such a thing. But then, neither would he have burned the village of Foxshire to the ground. There were more questions here than answers. Far more.

"Two hundred cavalry ride with the train," Arik said. "As well as two hundred militia."

"*Two* hundred cavalry?" Ivanel asked.

"Yes, your grace," Arik replied. Ivanel frowned. When he last knew, Foxdale only held a hundred cavalry in its garrison. Apparently Marik had been expanding his forces in his lesser holdings as well.

If things had not changed, Marik's brother Valther was the captain of the Foxdale garrison. Unlike the captains of Foxwood and Heathton, Valther had placed his siege train under heavy guard.

"Terrain?" Ivanel asked.

"Flat as a board," Arik replied. "All the way between."

"Somehow, I am not surprised," Ivanel said. This was one

caravan he was not going to take by ambush with crossbows. If Ivanel dismounted his men, Foxdale's cavalry would simply roll over them once the initial volley had passed.

Ivanel could not hope to defeat this force. However, the priority was not to defeat them—Ivanel's mission was to destroy those engines. The question was, how, when they were under such heavy guard?

"Any farmhouses?"

"A few," Arik replied, shrugging. "They are not large enough to hide our force, however."

"Hiding is not my intention," Ivanel assured his chief scout. "Find me an abandoned farmhouse we can reach well ahead of the siege train. We're going to outfox the Foxes."

"Yes, your grace," Arik replied. His face betrayed his curiosity.

Ivanel inspected the farmhouse Arik had selected for him. It would do. Up close, it was obvious that the farmhouse had been abandoned for some time. That would not be at all obvious from a distance, however.

"I want every man by his horse, ready to leap into the saddle and ride!" Ivanel told his men. "Make it look good. We want them angry!"

"Yes, your grace," the men acknowledged.

"Does every man have his waterskin?" Ivanel asked. They did. He turned at the sound of a galloping horse. It was Arik.

"The train is just over the horizon," Arik said. "A little less than an hour away."

"Good," Ivanel said. "Where are my cows?"

Arik gestured behind him. Two more scouts were leading a cow each.

"There," Arik replied. "Although I can't imagine why you want them."

"Setting the stage," Ivanel replied, drawing his sword. "Bring them over by the old barn, but where they can be seen from the road."

"Hold her still," Ivanel ordered the scout. He gently placed the point of his sword against the cow's side. Then, with all his weight, he drove the blade in to the hilt, through the animal's heart. The animal grunted once and collapsed. Ivanel pulled his sword free and walked over to the other cow.

Ivanel walked away from the dead animals, wiping his sword. Foxdale's men would eat well tonight. Ivanel smiled—he doubted they would thank him for the meal.

"Fire the buildings!" Ivanel ordered, mounting his steed. "And the fields!" He turned and rode away, leading his half of the force northwest.

Gods, he thought, *please watch over my men. They know not who they serve.*

"Scouts!" the cavalry captain shouted when he saw the column of smoke lift from the horizon. Without waiting for orders, his scouts broke in full gallop from the train. *Good men, those,* Malcolm thought.

Scarcely the quarter part of an hour had passed when the scouts returned.

"Lord," the lead scout reported, "a hundred men, on horse, are sacking a farm."

"Did you see the farmers?"

"No, lord," the scout replied. "We saw a couple of dead cows. Any people may be in the farmhouse. The pigs are burning the farm."

"Were you seen?" Malcolm asked.

"No, Lord," the scouts replied. Malcolm clenched his jaw. They were still two days from Foxmire at the pace of the siege train. Captain Valther and the other garrison commanders had Foxmire under siege, so these could not be Gavin's troops out foraging. These were likely common bandits, taking advantage of the chaos of war to do a little looting.

"Cavalry!" Malcolm shouted. "Form up!" Foxdale's cavalry would show these vermin the depth of their mistake.

"Move out!" Malcolm ordered, slashing forward through the air with his sword.

"The enemy cavalry has moved out, your grace," Arik reported.

"About now, Jarl should be leading them a merry chase to the southeast," Ivanel mused.

"Yes, your grace," Arik replied, smiling. "They fell for it."

"That they did."

The bandits took to horse and fled as soon as Malcolm's cavalry came into view. The farmhouse was as the scouts had described. Malcolm gestured at the rider to his left, holding up five fingers and pointing to the farmhouse.

The man nodded and peeled away from the charge, culling other riders to go with him and inspect the farmhouse. If there were any of his clansmen left alive to save, Malcolm had to try. Five cavalrymen less would make little difference once they caught these swine.

Ivanel led his men up the road at a canter. Let the train think, until the last minute, that it was their own cavalry returning. Ivanel fingered the wineskin full of oil at his hip. A hundred of these ought to get a good fire going.

The arms of the catapults climbed above the horizon. Soon now. Ivanel unhooked the crossbow from his saddle. Around him, his men did the same. Soon now.

Malcolm's men had gained little ground on the bandits. They rode well, and their animals seemed in good condition.

He hated to let these scoundrels get away, but soon he would have to turn back to rejoin the siege train. Malcolm's men should have overtaken these scum by now. Something was not right here.

Then he heard the distant sound of horns from behind them. . . .

Ivanel ordered the charge as soon as the caravan sounded the alarm. The militia charged forward to defend the wagons, but faltered when they saw a hundred horse charging them.

"Fire!" Ivanel ordered, letting his own quarrel fly. Perhaps a score of men in the front ranks fell. It was enough.

The militia routed. The cavalrymen shouted in triumph. Ivanel replaced the crossbow on its hook on his saddle and pulled the waterskin from his belt.

With the militia in flight, the drovers did likewise. Ivanel watched as the men leaped from their wagons to take flight across the fields of wheat. When the cavalry charged through the caravan, there was no one left to oppose them.

Ivanel hurled his waterskin at a catapult. The small bag of oil burst on impact, soaking a patch of wood on the engine. Other skins followed. Ivanel set flint to a bundle of straw and leisurely tossed it onto the catapult.

Flames quickly licked up the arms of the engines. With no one to stop them, the men began torching the wagons as well—using Foxdale's own supplies of oil to soak them thoroughly. Soon heavy, black smoke was climbing into the sky.

"That cavalry's going to be on its way back here!" Ivanel finally shouted. "Let's not be here when that happens!"

Malcolm led his cavalry back into the remains of the siege train. The enemy was long departed. A mere handful of bodies dotted the area—obviously the militia and the drovers had routed rather than fight.

Malcolm couldn't blame them. From the tracks, it was obvious that at least a hundred horsemen had attacked the caravan. No, the blame for this debacle rested solely with him.

The wagons would burn for the rest of the day. The catapults would likely continue to burn throughout the night. There was nothing left to salvage here. Now, Malcolm's priority was to report. Captain Valther was going to have him hung for this.

"We can be in Foxmire by dawn," he said. "Let's move out."

"It seems pretty far-fetched to me, m'lord," Talhaern said. "I mean—a MageLord? If that were true, wouldn't we all be dead by now?"

"We don't know," Valther replied. "But look at what Locke heard from Reykvid. First the Lord Chancellor was accused of being just that. King Magnus dies, Gavin goes chasing off after this Valerian. Then they return together, and it turns out that this hunt master was some type of hedge wizard and it was all his fault. And now, Gavin rides to war *with* his Lord Chancellor. You don't take a castellan onto the field."

"I don't know what to make of all these rumors of magical towers and earthquakes and such," Locke added.

"I haven't heard of too many hedge wizards who can pull that off," Valther agreed. "Sound familiar? Unseasonably early blizzards? Sudden outbreaks of fever among the men? It is not Gavin's army we are fighting here."

"I think the first rumor was the true one," Valther concluded. "This poor hunt master was just a convenient dupe for Valerian. I also think he has Gavin's mind as he supposedly held Magnus's."

"It would explain much," Locke grudgingly admitted.

"All right," Talhaern said, shaking his head. "Suppose we entertain that this man *is* a MageLord? What do we do?"

"For now, nothing," Valther said. "We keep our eyes open for more signs. If we suffer too many more reversals, we may be forced to withdraw."

"To Foxdale?" Talhaern asked.

"From Fox clan lands," Valther said. "We can seek sanctuary with the Bear clan. Tell them what we suspect and, hopefully, enlist their aid."

"I hope we do not have to do that," Talhaern said.

"Neither do I," Valther agreed.

"Ivanel has destroyed the last of the siege engines en route toward us," Valerian told them. "He is en route to meet the occupational forces at Heathton. Also, the militia from Heathton, one thousand five hundred men, have .... taken ill. The fever is still spreading among our enemies."

Great gods! Gavin thought. *Fifteen hundred men removed from battle by one man.*

"Our occupational forces are within a day of Heathton," Valerian added. "How long will it take to secure the stronghold?"

"Most of Heathton's garrison is here, Lord," General Hans replied. "If the stronghold is undermanned enough, they will assault it and likely take it within two or three days. If they are forced to lay siege, it could take over a month."

"I take it their orders are to assault?" Valerian said.

"Only if they outnumber the garrison by twenty or more to one, Lord," Gavin said. "I suspect they do."

"By a large margin," Valerian confirmed.

"It should take them another three days to reach Foxwood," Hans added. "Foxwood is no stronger than Heathton. Two or three days and they should have the fortress."

"Then another day's march and they should arrive here," Gavin concluded.

"Now that Valther has fifteen hundred fewer men, are they a match for his forces?" Valerian asked.

"Barely, Lord," Gavin replied. "However, if the fever is still spreading, that should help."

"Good. I want to be back in Reykvid before winter hits."

"Yes, Lord," Gavin replied.

"Were all of the supplies destroyed as well?" Valther asked.

"Yes, m'lord," Malcolm replied quietly.

"Malcolm, protecting that siege train was your sole responsibility," Valther said. "Policing the countryside was not."

"No, m'lord," Malcolm agreed. "I should not have assumed that all of the enemy were contained in Foxmire. The loss of the engines and supplies is my fault alone."

"You will be flogged in front of the men," Valther said. "Twenty lashes."

"My lord, that is . . . not sufficient," Malcolm objected.

"Very well," Valther replied. "Twenty-five."

"My lord," Malcolm began.

"Malcolm," Valther interrupted. "I know what you were thinking. I could very well have fallen for that lure myself. Twenty-five and not one stroke more—is that clear?"

"Yes, m'lord," Malcolm replied.

"You are dismissed," Valther said. "Report back here in one hour."

"Yes, m'lord."

Valther watched as Malcolm left. A good man. He drove his men almost as hard as he drove himself. The lashes were more for absolution than punishment. Valther did not doubt that Malcolm's own sense of honor would punish him far worse without them.

Had the other engines been destroyed as well? The train from Foxwood was almost a day late at this point. Without those engines it would be near to impossible to retake

Foxmire. In addition, there was a cavalry force of undetermined size loose on the countryside.

Withdrawal was beginning to look more necessary. Another three hundred militia, two hundred from Foxdale and a hundred from Foxwood, had been taken by the fever since its outbreak. A handful of the infantry and cavalry had also been affected. The spread was slowing, but it had already taken its toll on his forces.

He would wait a few more days and see if the engines from Foxwood and Heathton arrived. Without them, he would be forced to withdraw.

"I'm sorry, brother," he whispered.

Three days later, runners came from Heathton with word of an army, five thousand strong, laying siege to the castle.

"We can safely assume that Heathton has fallen by now," Valther told Locke and Talhaern. "I have dispatched riders to Foxwood. We cannot hope to reach the fortress before Gavin's forces arrive there. Therefore, I have sent orders for the men to abandon the fortress and join us here."

"To what end, lord?" Talhaern asked.

"We are going to withdraw to Foxdale," Valther replied. "There we will gather the rest of the garrison and supplies from Foxdale and strike out for the lands of the Bear clan. From there, perhaps we can one day reclaim our own lands."

Gavin watched as the besieging forces withdrew. The siege had not quite lasted a fortnight. Valther was leading his troops out a scant day ahead of the occupational army. From the courtyard below, Gavin could hear the excited babble of the men.

Unlike them, Gavin could take no joy in this victory. This war had been won with blizzards and plagues—foul sorcery of the vilest kind. There was no honor in this.

Valther would enjoy a one day lead over them. Unencumbered by engines or supplies, he would reach Foxdale by the end of that time. Gavin's force, encumbered by the siege engines, would take four times that long to reach the fortress. However, they would need those engines at Foxdale. With two thousand men defending it, the fortress would not be an easy victory.

Unless Valerian lent a hand.

Valther supervised the scavenging of the fortress. Not one wagon would be left behind. Nothing that Gavin could use.

"Move it there!" he shouted to a group of men idling about. "We move out within the hour!"

His army now enjoyed a three-day lead over Gavin's forces. That would get him almost to the lands of the Bear clan before Gavin discovered that Foxdale was empty.

The crash of stone sounded by the outer wall. Valther's own engines were destroying the new outer wall. What was left would be put to the torch when they left. He would make certain that Gavin did not get so much as a usable fortress out of Foxdale.

Soon they were ready. The catapults were soaked with oil and set afire. Men dumped barrels of oil throughout the stronghold and set whole rooms ablaze. Within moments Foxdale was burning violently. Filthy black smoke soiled the sky.

The fires that danced in Valther's eyes were not reflections— they were flames of hatred.

"Let's move out," he said quietly.

"Foxdale has been destroyed, majesty," Arik reported.

"Destroyed?" Gavin asked. "By whom?"

"There are no signs of battle, majesty," Arik replied. "No bodies, save for animals. The tracks of a large force lead westward. I would suggest that they destroyed it themselves."

"Why?" Valerian asked.

"To keep us from having it, Chancellor," Gavin replied. "Valther is probably already in Chief Urall's hall."

"The Bear clan?" Valerian asked.

"Yes," Gavin said. "How long ago was the fortress destroyed?"

"Five, maybe six days," Arik replied.

"What do we do now, majesty?" Ivanel asked.

"Nothing," Gavin replied. "His lead is far too great for us to overtake him. Arik, track him. Make certain he *left* the Fox clan. We shall proceed on to Foxdale and wait for you there."

"Yes, majesty," Arik replied.

"Why are we going to Foxdale?" Valerian asked.

"To start rebuilding it," Gavin said. "With Valther and his army among the Bear clan, that fortress is vital to this region's defense."

Thank the gods it's over, Gavin thought.

Chapter
-------- Thirteen ------------

BJORN FLAILED THE reins to his new team of reindeer. The toboggan was loaded with as much hay as his team of three deer could carry—which wasn't much. This hay would go between the inner and outer planking of the cabin walls for warmth.

Driving the sled wasn't much different from driving a wagon. Keep the deer moving, steer with the reins and hang on. The main difference was that the reindeer were not actually hitched to the sled. The driver's hold on the reins was their only connection to the sled.

Rolf and the others would be surprised to see the sled. All three reindeer, the sled and a load of hay had cost Bjorn only two dozen rabbit pelts. He still had more pelts with which to pick up other supplies, but this hay was the current priority.

The Circle would be glad to know that the nearest lodge was a friendly lot, as well. They had been cautious at first, but Bjorn's tale of being driven from their home to the south by bandits had softened their hearts. They had gladly taken Bjorn's pelts, shown him how to drive the team and helped him load the sled. Bjorn suspected that they were glad to have someone who was willing to buy this year's surplus of straw.

If it weren't for the shadow of Valerian hanging over him, Bjorn could probably enjoy life up here. There were fewer people and, apparently, bandits were not much of a problem. The winters were harsh, but game was plentiful. Not a bad life at all.

As long as I don't mind being a prisoner in my own body for the rest of my life, Bjorn thought. *Or the nightmares.*

Bjorn was still plagued by dreams of being devoured alive by small, needle-fanged rats. Every two or three nights, the dream would return and he would awaken, drenched in sweat, listening intently for the sounds of scurrying in the darkness. Even the memory chilled him.

The just rising sun helped him drive the memory away. The trip that had taken him over a day to walk was going to take half that time in the sled. The deer were fast and tireless, more so than horses even. So the team was already going to earn its price by saving him half a day of travel.

Last night's snow was just starting to melt when Bjorn turned the team to the left, into the copse of trees around the cabin. He reached out with his mind and touched those of his friends. It wouldn't do to have Theodr meet him at sword-point when he arrived early.

Theodr was waiting outside when he arrived. The outer walls were almost up, and the roof beams had been set. Theodr was obviously surprised when Bjorn drove the sled up to the cabin.

"Where did you get *that*?" he asked.

"Traded for it at the lodge," Bjorn replied. "Saved me half a day's travel. This is how everyone gets around up here during the winter."

He laughed as one of the deer tried to nuzzle Theodr's side. The older man backed away indignantly.

"They're very affectionate," Bjorn told him.

"So I see," Theodr noted. "I also see that you got the hay we need."

"Yes, and some suggestions on roofing our cabin," Bjorn replied.

"*That* is good news," Theodr said.

"I'll head back to the lodge for more hay in the morning," Bjorn said. "With the team, I can be back tomorrow night."

"This should be enough hay for the walls . . . ," Theodr said.

"Yes, but we need ten times this much for the loft," Bjorn replied.

"Loft?" Theodr asked.

"I'll explain once we get inside," Bjorn replied. "Help me get the harnesses off of these deer."

*   *   *

The cheers of the people rang hollowly in Gavin's ears. He led his honor guard through the streets of Reykvid as they cheered his victorious return. Most of the army had been left behind to maintain order in Reykvid's new lands. Gavin smiled and waved to the people—Valerian's loyal puppet in every detail.

Never before had Reykvid annexed land by conquest. Even when the Star clan had attacked them, Magnus had only gone forth to reclaim his own lands. He had pushed far into the Star clan lands and sacked Chief Harold's hall, but he had withdrawn and left the land to its people. The next chief had been much more receptive to Magnus's offer of peacefully joining the kingdom.

Now, however, they had violated another clan's lands on trumped up excuses and taken it from them. This would not bode well for Reykvid. Now the other clans would begin to fear them—especially now that Valther had taken sanctuary with the Bear clan. Sometime soon they could very well be facing a war against several clans united against them.

Chief Urall was well suited to his clan. His clansmen affectionately referred to him as the "Great Bear." He was easily as tall as Marik, but much broader of girth, with dark brown hair and beard. Now that beard was beginning to gray, but Valther pitied the man who underestimated Urall.

"A MageLord?" Chief Urall asked. "Are you serious?"

"I am," Valther replied. "Freak blizzards locked us in our strongholds while Gavin marched, unopposed to Foxmire. My men were stricken with a sudden fever while we laid siege to retake Foxmire. One and a half thousand men in one night!"

"Gods!" Urall said.

"No fever spreads that fast," Valther continued. "Have you not heard the rumors from Reykvid?"

"I had," Urall replied. "But I had paid them little heed. What you tell me, though . . ."

"I am convinced those rumors were the truth," Valther said. "Do you take your castellan on the field when you go to war?"

"Certainly not," Urall agreed.

"Gavin did," Valther said. "His chancellor, Valerian, is the very same man who was accused of being a MageLord in Gavin's court."

"I thought the news of Reykvid's attack on your clan was grave enough," Urall said, "but this . . . Valther, if this is true . . ."

"We must unite the clans against Reykvid, Urall," Valther said. "Will you grant my troops sanctuary in your lands?"

"Yes," Urall replied. "Even without this news I would do that. Reykvid has become too dangerous. Do I have your oath of loyalty?"

"Yes, my lord," Valther replied.

"Give it," Urall insisted. Valther knelt before the chief of the Bear clan.

"I swear to follow you as my chieftain," he said, "to serve and defend you so long as I reside in your lands."

"Good. There is a farming village, Burton, near the border between our lands."

"I am familiar with it," Valther said, again rising to his feet.

"Take your men there. I will send supplies and engineers. You will conscript the local farmers and supervise the construction of a new stronghold there. When it is finished, your men will garrison it."

"That is very generous, my lord," Valther said.

"No," Urall replied. "I want my new border with Reykvid *well* defended."

"Yes. However, it is almost winter, my lord," Valther noted.

"Yes, you will not be able to begin the fortifications until spring," Urall agreed. "However, you can have the foundations dug and some of the outbuildings erected before then."

"Yes, my lord. What of the other clans?"

"I will send messengers to Chief Skald," Urall said. "If the Griffon clan will join with us, other clans will follow."

"Yes, that is true," Valther agreed.

"We will not be able to accomplish much more until spring," Urall said. "If we do march against Reykvid, I doubt it will be before next fall."

"A traitor?" Gavin asked. "Chief Balder?"

"He has been very outspoken about our war against the Fox

clan," Valerian said. "His words regarding your majesty have not been at all favorable."

I don't blame him, Gavin thought. Balder was the chief of the former Star clan. He, of all men, knew how Magnus had refused to spread his kingdom with the sword. If anyone objected to Gavin's conquest, it would have been Balder.

"This is disturbing news," Gavin said. "What do you suggest I do?"

"Send agents to his hall secretly," Valerian suggested. "Have them determine whether or not these reports are true."

"Majesty!" Counselor Haggard objected. "Are we going to take to spying on our own people?"

"We have heard grave allegations regarding Chief Balder!" Valerian insisted. "I am not suggesting that we send agents to every chieftain's hall in the kingdom. Just to Star Hall. If Balder is innocent, then these men will serve to vindicate him."

"And if these reports *are* true?" Gavin asked.

"If they are, majesty, you will have to charge him with treason."

Why? Gavin thought. *Why don't you just take control of his mind as you have so many others?* Gavin found himself beginning to hope that Valerian was finally reaching the limits of his power.

Gavin lay awake staring up at the darkness in his chambers. Chief Balder was imprisoned in the castle dungeons, convicted of treason. Sadly, the chieftain truly was guilty, although Gavin thought, with good reason.

At his trial Balder had openly accused Gavin of destroying everything his father had worked to build, and he was right. Only it wasn't Gavin who was destroying it—it was Valerian.

Balder had not made *that* accusation, although Gavin had more than half hoped that he would. Anything to turn the people against that monster. And he *had* been told the truth about Valerian at one point.

This must have been how father felt, Gavin thought. *Helpless to stop him and praying that someone, anyone would notice.*

Gavin *had* noticed, and all that it had accomplished was to get his father killed and himself under the demon's control. Gavin had no son, thank Hrothgar, and, with Valerian's plans nearing fruition, never would.

Under the MageLord's orders, Gavin had sent agents into the halls of every chieftain in the kingdom. Those agents reported not to the king, but to the Lord Chancellor— Valerian. How many more of Gavin's chieftains would soon be occupying the royal dungeons? How much longer would it be before the MageLord had no more need of Reykvid's king?

Bjorn lifted the heavy bale that Theodr handed up through the trap door into the loft. He moved it over and wedged it into place next to the other bales. With the plank roof overhead to keep out the snow, the hay would serve as a blanket, trapping the heat of the house in the rooms below.

They had finished hauling hay from the lodge just in time. Tonight the first heavy snowfall was burying them. Bjorn hadn't understood what the locals meant when they said that the true snows hadn't started yet. Now he knew.

The roof, which had had the last planks laid on just this morning, was already under a foot of snow, and the storm had just begun a few hours ago. If this kept up, Bjorn was not certain they would be able to get out of the cabin in the morning.

The deer would be fine, though. There was plenty of hay in the little makeshift barn he and Theodr had built for them. If the snow buried them, they would just be that much warmer. Still, Bjorn had to check his traps tomorrow.

He lifted another bale into the loft and wedged it into place. He would worry about tomorrow when tomorrow got here. Tonight he needed to finish haying the loft so that he could enjoy his first night under his new roof.

The cabin was huge compared to the shack in Hunter's Glen in which he and his father had lived for so long. The common room was larger than their shack had been, in fact. A small room would serve as Rolf's bedroom. With a fireplace of its own, Bjorn hoped the warmth would help with the cough his father had begun to develop.

The three larger rooms would serve for Freida and Theodr,

Angus and Hilda and, eventually, for Bjorn and Helga. Until they were wed, though, Bjorn would be sleeping in the smaller room that shared the second fireplace with Angus and Hilda's room.

Theodr handed another bale up through the loft. With difficulty, Bjorn wedged it into the last gap.

"I need three more for the trap door and that'll be it!" Bjorn called down.

"I've got *eight bales* left down here!" Theodr exclaimed.

"Better too much than not enough," Bjorn heard Freida tell her husband.

"The reindeer will eat it!" Bjorn called down. "It won't go to waste! Three bales, Theodr!"

"Coming up!"

Bjorn wrestled all three bales up into the loft before closing the trap door. He set the three bales on top of the loft door and tied them down with cord. Then he lifted the door—it was a *lot* heavier with three bales of hay tied to it.

"I'm coming down!" he called.

"I've got the ladder," Theodr told him. Bjorn felt for the rung and then lowered himself onto the ladder. He carefully closed the loft door and climbed down.

"There," he said. "We're finished with the house until spring."

"We hope," Theodr added.

"Theodr," Bjorn said, "I never knew you were so . . . so . . ."

"Annoying?" Freida suggested.

"Pessimistic," Bjorn corrected. "Is dinner ready yet, Aunt Freida?" Freida just looked at him. Finally she shook her head.

"Men," she said, walking back into the common room.

"Anyone who can reduce Freida to one word will make a fine High Magus someday," Theodr noted.

"Come on," Bjorn said, "I'm starving."

"May Bairn send his blessings and his protection upon our home," Rolf said.

"And bless all who reside within," Bjorn and the other members of the Circle said in unison. Rolf had insisted on blessing the house before they took their first meal in it. The smell of rabbit on an empty stomach was driving Bjorn nuts.

"As it was in the Time of Madness, we survive now in hiding," Rolf said. "So, after today, let no work of Power occur within these walls lest its presence betray us to our enemies."

Too late! Bjorn thought.

"May the gods watch over us and protect us," the Circle replied.

"As it was in the Time of Madness, we are the healers and the seekers of mankind," Rolf said.

"Let all who enter here find peace and succor," the Circle replied.

"So be it, now and forever," Rolf concluded.

"So be it," the Circle replied.

"Let's eat," Rolf said.

"So be it," replied Bjorn. Rolf, Angus and Theodr chuckled while Freida simply shook her head.

Dinner was worth waiting for. The stew tasted like the best meal Bjorn had had in his entire life. The only thing that would have made it better was a table at which to eat it. Now that they had the house finished, they could get started on some furniture.

"Got the roof up just in time," Rolf noted. A mild coughing fit silenced him.

"Certainly did," Bjorn agreed. He frowned at his father's cough. It wasn't sounding any better. "I just hope we can get out of the house in the morning. Father, I want you to drink some tea later."

"What are you going to put in it?" Rolf asked.

"Comfrey, coltsfoot and mullein," Bjorn replied.

"Sounds wonderful," Rolf said, in a tone that did not sound wonderful at all. "I can hardly wait."

"You know you need it, so hush," Freida chided. "Bjorn wouldn't have to force it down you if you took proper care of yourself."

"Well, Bjorn, I think you will want to make certain that we can get out tomorrow," Rolf said, ignoring Freida's remark.

"Why?"

"I have a wedding to perform tomorrow night," he said,

smiling. Bjorn glanced over at Helga, who looked away and blushed, also smiling.

"Oh!" said Freida, setting her bowl on the floor. "Tomorrow? Oh, my! Helga, stop—you can't eat that! Oh! Oh, my! Theodr—put the large pot on to boil! Oh!" Freida scampered off to the room she and Theodr shared, presumably in search of something.

"Well," Theodr said, not stirring from his stew, "that certainly made her night."

The six of them laughed and, for a moment, Bjorn was actually happy.

"*What!*" Gavin shouted, rising to his feet.

"The Raven Clan has decided to withdraw from your protection, your majesty," the messenger repeated. "After witnessing your majesty's actions with the Fox clan and with our neighbor Chief Balder, my chieftain has decided that his agreement to join the kingdom last summer was ill considered."

So it begins, Gavin thought. Under Valerian's tyranny, the kingdom was beginning to collapse. How would the MageLord respond to this?

"This is treason!" Gavin shouted.

"Call it what you will, majesty," the messenger replied. "The Raven clan does not recognize you as our king."

"Tell Braun that this decision is not wise," Valerian began. "Tell him . . ."

"I am speaking with the king, not his toady," the messenger interrupted.

"You can most certainly tell Braun that this decision is unwise," Gavin said. "We will not stand by and allow treason to go unanswered."

"Then I shall tell my liege to expect your troops come spring," the messenger replied. "You will find us more difficult to conquer than the Fox clan."

Gavin did not doubt that. The Raven clan would be preparing for this war throughout the winter. Every able-bodied man in the clan would be prepared to fight against them. And Ravenhall was every bit as impregnable as Reykvid. More so, perhaps.

"We shall see," Valerian replied.

It was a small Circle. Aunt Freida and her husband Theodr, Helga and her parents and, of course, Bjorn and Rolf. Their breath frosted on the frigid winter air.

". . . freely and of your own will?" Rolf asked. "To be Helga Angusdotr no longer and to become Helga Bjornswyf?"

"I do," Helga replied.

Rolf wrapped the silk sash around their joined hands as Bjorn stared into Helga's green eyes. The shimmering, green curtains in the northern night sky paled in comparison.

Curse you, Valerian, Bjorn thought. He was not even free to enjoy his own wedding. It was almost like watching someone else marry his betrothed.

"The two have become one," Rolf said, in his role as head of the Circle. "Bjorn, Helga—you are man and wife. May Bairn bless your union."

Bjorn kissed Helga deeply.

"Good," Rolf said. "Now let's all get in out of this accursed cold!"

This far northern winter had proven hard on Bjorn's father. Over the last few days the old man had developed a cough that even comfrey, coltsfoot and mullein had not relieved.

"Have you had your tea tonight, father?" Bjorn asked as they all walked toward the house. Almost on cue, Rolf began coughing—a wet, bubbling cough that did not bode well.

"No," Rolf finally answered. "I will brew a cup when we get inside."

"I think you should add feverfew and camomile to the pot tonight, father," Bjorn suggested.

"Probably so," Rolf agreed.

They entered the relative warmth of the large cabin they had all built together. Even with the fire, though, it was still chill inside.

"Sit by the fire, father," Bjorn said. "I'll get your tea started."

"No, you won't," Aunt Freida said, removing her heavy fur

coat. "I will. You have . . . other concerns tonight." Her eyes smiled as she glanced over at Helga.

"But . . ." Bjorn began.

"Hush," Freida interrupted. "I will brew your father's tea. And I'll make certain he drinks it, even if I have to sit on him and pour it down myself."

"She will, too," Theodr assured him. That was true. Freida had done the same to Bjorn all through his childhood.

"Hush, Theodr," Freida said. "Go get a blanket for Rolf."

"Yes, dear," Theodr replied, hurrying to find a blanket.

Bjorn hugged Freida. She and Theodr had no children of their own. When Bjorn's own mother had died in childbirth, Freida had all but claimed him as her own.

"I am so happy for you, Bjorn," she said. "And you too, Helga."

She moved to hug Bjorn's new wife.

"I can hardly wait until we've little ones about," she said. Bjorn smiled. The old woman was all but crying.

"Now, off with both of you," she said, wiping at her eyes with her outer skirt. "I want little ones by morning." Bjorn laughed.

"I don't think we can manage that, Aunt Freida," he replied.

"Well, it had best not be for lack of trying," she quipped. "Now off with you. I have to fix your father's tea. Shoo!"

"Here's the blanket, dear," Theodr said, returning with a blanket from Rolf's bed.

"Took you long enough," she said. "Go get the fire laid in his room."

Bjorn closed the door of his room, closing out the homey scene. His father was in good hands—some of the best, in fact. Still, Bjorn could not help but worry. That cough was not good. . . .

"Bjorn?" Helga said, interrupting his thoughts.

Bjorn turned and stopped. Helga stood before him, her dress in a pile surrounding her ankles. She was statuesque— tall, young and strong. Bjorn had never seen her this way. Her golden hair framed her head like an aura, and her sea-green eyes flickered in the firelight.

"Freida will take good care of him," she assured him. "Come, my husband. It is time for bed."

"I love you, Helga," Bjorn said. She said nothing, just held out her arms and smiled. Bjorn walked over and lifted her into his arms, kissing her. Her smell was wonderful.

"And I love you," she said.

Bjorn placed her on the bed, and she lay there as he undressed. Finally he slipped beneath the blankets and took her in his arms.

Curse you, Valerian, he thought.

Bjorn hauled back on the reins. His team of reindeer slowed to a halt. He stepped from the short sled and tied them to a nearby tree before venturing off to check his traps in this area. Hopefully, there would be some good pelts—not to mention meat for the stewpot.

The pelts were the more pressing need—at the moment. Soon, he or Theodr would have to take a trip south to pick up more herbs to treat Rolf's cough. It would probably be best if Theodr went. Some good pelts to trade would give him something to purchase them with.

Bjorn took his spear. He might need it if he ran into wolves or a lynx. He wrapped his scarf around his face and trudged off into the snow.

The first few traps were empty. The fourth, however, had caught an arctic hare. That was good—pelt *and* meat. The next trap had caught a snow fox. Bjorn frowned. Ordinarily, he would not trap an animal simply for its pelt. They needed the pelts, however.

Someone was waiting by his sled when he got back. Bjorn stopped out of bowshot. The man had a single reindeer with a small dish sled. Who was it?

"Bjorn!" the figure called. "It's me, Theodr!"

Theodr? Bjorn thought. His heart leaped in his chest. *Something must be wrong.*

Bjorn hurried down the short slope back toward his sled. If Theodr had come to find him, something must be terribly wrong.

"What is it?" Bjorn heard himself ask.

"Your father has gotten worse," Theodr replied. "Much worse. Freida wants you home."

Without a word Bjorn affixed his prizes and his spear to his sled. Theodr did not wait. He took his deer's reins, sat down on his sled and started home. Theodr would beat Bjorn home—his little dish sled was faster than Bjorn's toboggan, even with Bjorn's team of three reindeer.

Bjorn drove his team hard, shouting and slapping them with the reins. He managed not to lose too much ground and was able to keep Theodr in sight all the way home.

Bjorn leaped from the sled before it had stopped. He ran to the front door of the cabin. The deer would not stray—they would wait until someone came to unhitch them.

Freida caught him as he burst through the front door.

"You stop right there!" she told him. "Your father doesn't need you in there all fired up. Get out of those cold clothes."

"But . . ." Bjorn objected.

"Bjorn!" Freida said. "Go to ground and center your balance before you go in there!"

"Yes, Aunt Freida," Bjorn replied. He took a deep breath, forcing himself to relax. Another—he could feel the Power surrounding him calm.

"Better," she said. "Theodr, go unhitch Bjorn's team."

"Yes, Freida," Theodr said as he headed out the front door. Apparently he had just come in from tending to his own deer.

Bjorn peeled off the several layers of outer clothes one had to wear just to stay alive outdoors in this region. He handed them all to Freida, who hung them near the fire. Then he hurried to his father's room. Helga was already there.

"Father?" Bjorn said softly, kneeling by his father's bed.

Curse you, Valerian! Bjorn thought. *Don't steal this from me, too. Let me say goodbye to my father myself!* Unfortunately, Bjorn knew that was not going to happen.

"Bjorn?" Rolf asked. A coughing fit threw his aged body into convulsions.

"Yes, father," Bjorn said once the fit had passed. "I'm here."

"I don't think . . . I'm going to beat this one, son," Rolf said. A few more coughs shook his tired body.

"Sure you are," Bjorn said shakily. "It's just a little chest cough. Theodr or I will go south for more herbs. You'll be fine, come spring."

"No, Bjorn," Rolf said. "I don't think I'll see spring this year."

"Don't say that, father," Bjorn objected.

"Will you put . . . a little catnip in my . . . tea tonight?" Rolf asked. "To help me sleep?"

"Certainly," Bjorn replied.

"And bundle me up and . . . take me out so that . . . I can see the . . . Northern Curtain for a little while?"

Before you die, Bjorn silently completed. Tears formed at his eyes. Even those weren't real, thanks to Valerian.

"Only for a little while," Bjorn heard himself say. "You don't need to get chilled."

"Thank you, Bjorn," Rolf said. "You're . . . a good son."

"I love you, father," Bjorn said.

"I know you do," Rolf said, feebly patting Bjorn's shoulder. "I'm proud . . . of you, and I . . . love you, too."

You wouldn't be proud if you knew the truth, Bjorn thought.

"He needs his rest," Freida said.

"Let me stay," Bjorn said. "I'll stay quiet."

"Leave him for a little while," Freida whispered. "Once he's asleep you can come back. He won't sleep while you're here."

"All right."

Bjorn looked up at the night sky. Of course, the sky was almost always night, now. The sun rose from the horizon for only a few hours before noon and set a few hours after noon, barely warming the world from its nighttime chill.

Overhead, a shimmering green curtain hung in the sky. Bjorn could close his eyes and still see it, shimmering in Power as well as in light. It was beautiful.

Rolf had not coughed for some time now. Bjorn looked down to check his father. Rolf smiled at him weakly.

"In the . . . belly of . . . fire," Rolf said softly, "surrounded by . . . ice beneath a . . . curtain of light, sleeps Arcalion . . . the Ravager."

"What, father?" Bjorn asked.

"An old . . . legend," Rolf croaked. "Beneath a curtain . . . of light, sleeps . . . Arcalion the Ravager."

"Oh," Bjorn said. He had heard the legend before. Arcalion

was supposedly the greatest of the dragons summoned during the Time of Madness. When their Power had fled, Arcalion had turned on the MageLords and slain dozens of them.

Supposedly, Arcalion had flown to the north, where he found a fiery home surrounded by ice beneath a shimmering curtain of light. The Northern Curtain? It could be.

"Old legends, old men," Rolf mused. "Seems appropriate." A coughing spell racked his body.

"We need to get you inside by the fire," Bjorn said, once the fit had passed.

"Yes," Rolf agreed. "By the fire. Will you sit with me, Bjorn?"

"Of course, father," Bjorn replied.

"Thank you, son," Rolf said. "Let's go in."

Chapter
-------- **Fourteen** ------------

". . . As WE HAVE all come from the Mother, so do we return to her," Bjorn said. Rolf had been right—he had not seen the spring. In fact, he had not seen the next morning.

"And so, we return our brother, Rolf Ericson, to her fertile bosom," Bjorn continued. "In the eternal cycle of life, our brother shall return to us by nurturing the future children of our Mother. So we meet, and so we part, and so we meet again."

"So we meet," echoed the others of the Circle, "and so we part, and so we meet again."

"Goodbye, father," Bjorn whispered.

Goodbye, father, Bjorn thought. *I hope you can forgive me.*

He, Theodr and Angus lowered Rolf's body into the frozen grave. It had taken them from before sunrise until after sunset of the short northern day to dig the grave in the frozen ground. Filling it was much faster. Eventually, they covered over the bare ground with snow and swept it until no one could tell the ground had been disturbed.

The true graves of the mages were always unmarked. Usually they were buried publicly and then moved later. But no outsider ever knew the true resting place of one of the Circle. Here, where no one knew them, that was not necessary. Rolf's first grave could be his last.

"Goodbye, father," Bjorn said again.

"Goodbye, brother," the other members of the Circle added. "So we part."

Valther cursed the falling snow. It slowed the workers, who must spend as much time digging the snow as they did the foundations for his stronghold.

The stables and storehouses were the only permanent structures completed. At least the horses were comfortable. His men, however, were camped all around the construction site, living through the winter in tents.

Soon, though, the inner barracks would be completed. Then Valther could move his cavalry into permanent quarters. A few weeks after that should see the completion of the outer barracks. Then Valther could move his entire force into the new billets. That should serve to improve the morale of the men.

Valther had chosen a low hill between Burton and the Fox clan's lands on which to construct his fortress. The keep would sit at the top, of course. The stables and the inner barracks would surround the keep, against the inside of the inner wall at the base of the hill. The outer barracks would surround all of that inside the outermost wall. It would be a grand fortress. To hold all of Valther's men it had to be.

Urall's generosity in giving him this land would not go unrewarded. Once the castle was completed, Reykvid would not be able to attack the Bear clan easily. Not with an entire army acting as the garrison of this massive fortress.

Valther spied a lone rider approaching from the west. Valther watched him for a moment. Whoever it was, he was definitely headed for the castle. One man—it was probably a messenger from Urall.

"Find Captains Locke and Talhaern and order them to meet me in my pavilion," Valther ordered a nearby soldier.

"At once, m'lord!" the man replied. He hurried off to find the garrison commanders.

Valther continued to watch the messenger approach. Shortly, a small band of cavalry rode out to meet the man. He stopped for a moment, and then Valther's cavalry began to escort him to the camp.

Locke and Talhaern were waiting in his pavilion when he got there.

"You called for us, m'lord?" Locke asked.

"Yes," Valther replied. "I believe we are about to receive a messenger from Chief Urall."

Soon, the guard outside Valther's tent announced the arrival of the messenger.

"Send him in," Valther ordered.

"Greetings, my lord," the messenger said when he entered. His clothes and beard were dusted in snow and his features were flushed with the cold. He had obviously been riding for some time.

"I bring word from Chief Urall," the man continued. "He wishes you to travel to Bear's Den at once."

"Did he say why?" Valther asked.

"No, m'lord," the messenger replied. "Only that you were to leave at once."

"May I bring my captains?"

"I was given no instructions on that, m'lord. I would recommend a small guard, though. I saw no sign of bandits on the way here, but . . ."

"Very well," Valther said. "I will be ready to leave shortly. If you will go to the mess tent, the cooks will give you a hot meal and some mulled wine before we depart."

The man smiled through his snow-crusted beard.

"That would be a welcome thing," he said. "Thank you, m'lord."

"What do you suppose he wants?" Locke asked after the messenger had left.

"We shall know that when we get there," Valther said. "I suspect that Urall either has some news of Reykvid, or of our alliance with the other clans. But now we must prepare for travel. We leave within the hour."

Bjorn drove his team to the lodge. The sentries did not so much challenge him as greet him, waving to him as he drove his team past. Bjorn waved back.

He wrapped the reins of his team around one of the posts near the main door of the hall. He picked up his brace of pelts and knocked on the heavy door. A small panel opened in the door, and a familiar pair of eyes looked out.

The panel shut and Bjorn could hear the bar being lifted away. Soon the door swung open.

"Hurry," the old man said. "You're letting in the cold." Bjorn stepped inside and lent his shoulder to the door. He helped Karl lift the heavy bar back into place.

"More pelts?" Karl asked needlessly.

"Yes," Bjorn replied. "We need vegetables and flour."

"Lars will be glad to see you," Karl added. "Come with me. I will tell him you are here."

Bjorn followed Karl into the lodge. From what little he had learned, the lodge was typical of this region. The walls were of stone, several feet thick. This was more to keep out the cold than any attackers, however. The peaked roof was fashioned of whole logs lashed together and sealed with pitch.

Most of the hall's residents lived in the large common room. Fire pits lined the floor at regular intervals both for cooking and to heat the vast interior of the hall. Thick smoke almost hid the high roof from view.

Hide curtains were the main source of privacy for the residents. A few private areas were walled off near the back of the hall. Even there, one could climb the wall and look over if one were of a mind to. There was little true privacy.

Karl led Bjorn to the high table from which Chief Lars ate his meals and ruled his small clan. Lars was a large man, with graying red-blond hair and piercing blue eyes.

"Bjorn!" he called pleasantly when he saw who Karl was bringing to him. "What have you brought for me, today?"

"Pelts, my lord," Bjorn replied. "Four hares and a snow fox. I was hoping to trade them for vegetables and flour."

"Hmmm," Lars said, examining the pelts Bjorn laid on the table before him. "I don't know. These *are* good pelts, but food is hard to come by in the winter. I'll give you two bushels each of snap beans, cabbage and onions and a stoneweight of flour."

"My lord," Bjorn objected. "The snow fox alone should be worth that. I would be willing to trade for three bushels each of snap beans, cabbage and onions and *two* stoneweight of flour."

"Three bushels each!" Lars exclaimed. "I may be getting old, but I still have my mind, trapper! Two bushels each of snap beans and onions, three of cabbage and a stone and a half of flour."

"I have traded with you enough to know that your mind is *quite* sharp, my lord," Bjorn said, smiling. "Three bushels each of snap beans and cabbage, two of onions and one stoneweight of flour."

"Done!" Lars said, slapping the table.

"Thank you, my lord," Bjorn said, beginning to rise. "If you will excuse me . . ."

"Wait," Lars said. "You have only just arrived. Stay for a moment and share a hot drink with me. It is a long trip back in the cold."

"Thank you, my lord," Bjorn said, sitting back down. One of Lars's daughters placed a mug in front of Bjorn. He took it and drank deeply of the hot, spiced cider. It *was* good after spending all morning out in the cold.

"Something is troubling you," Lars observed.

"My father died yesterday morning," Bjorn explained.

"Lad!" Lars exclaimed. "You should have told me. 'Twas his cough?"

"Yes."

"The winter is hard on the old, up here," Lars said, nodding. "Although I never met your father, I share your sorrow. He must have been a fine man to raise such a good son alone."

"Thank you, my lord," Bjorn replied. "I believe he was one of the best men I have ever known."

"You must come back tomorrow," Lars told him. "And bring your family. We shall have a feast in your father's honor."

"My lord!" Bjorn said in surprise. "I . . . I don't know what to say . . ." This could be a problem. There was no way he could refuse the invitation and keep the good will of the lodge. The magi would have to take care and not drink too much.

"Will you come?"

"I . . . would be honored," Bjorn replied. "Thank you."

Valther led his captains through the doors into Urall's audience hall. He walked up to the dais where Urall sat and knelt on one knee, bowing his head.

"My lord," he said. "I have come in answer to your summons."

"And promptly, too," Urall agreed. "Rise, Valther, I don't stand on such formalities, here. I have news that I think you will find interesting. Come, you and your captains can join me in my chambers."

Urall's sitting room was comfortable. Valther sipped at a goblet of wine as the steward filled both of his captains' goblets. Urall dismissed the man after taking the flagon from him.

"I have some very interesting news from Reykvid," Urall said. "It seems that King Gavin has imprisoned the chief of the Star clan, Balder I believe his name is, for treason."

"You can't be serious!" Valther said.

"There's more," Urall added. "As a result of this act and Gavin's invasion of your lands, the Raven clan has withdrawn from the kingdom."

"What of the Star clan?" Valther asked.

"I do not know," Urall replied. "They are very close to Reykvid itself. Their new chieftain would not even receive my messengers. Chief Braun of the Raven clan was more than happy to see them, however."

"What action is Gavin going to take against this rebellion?" Valther asked.

"Braun believes that Gavin will attack him as soon as the spring planting is finished," Urall replied. "He also believes that this Valerian is a MageLord. More importantly, he is willing to act in concert with us."

"If he is right, we will have to attack into my clan's lands in the spring."

"Exactly," Urall agreed. "Your army, my own forces and Chief Skald's army will move to retake the Fox clan as soon as Gavin marches against the Raven clan. I suspect that the Star clan will revolt as soon as our alliance becomes apparent."

"We could sweep all of the way to Reykvid itself," Valther mused.

"It will be a race," Urall said, "between us and the Ravens."

Most of the residents of the lodge had fallen asleep at their tables. Even Lars was threatening to nod off. Too much drink, Bjorn thought.

It had been a grand feast, Bjorn had to admit. Lars had roasted an entire cow for the occasion and spiced it with sour apples and onions. It had been good to taste beef again.

The women were half leading, half carrying the men away from the tables. The ale had flowed quite freely tonight. Bjorn imagined that not much work would be done around the lodge tomorrow. Lars's wife, Bris, nudged him awake.

"Hm?" he said. "I wasn't asleep."

"Of course not," she said. "But I am tired. May we retire, husband?"

"Well, if *you're* tired, of course we can," Lars answered.

"We should be leaving as well," Bjorn noted.

"What?" Lars said, coming more fully awake. "Leaving? Nonsense! You are our guests for the night. I'll not send people home in the middle of the night in *this* weather. Especially not when home is half a day away. Bris can find you some place to sleep. Room is one thing we have in plenty!"

"Yes," Bris agreed. "There is no need to travel in the cold at night. You can leave in the morning."

"Thank you," Bjorn said.

"Let me see my husband to bed and I shall find blankets for you."

"Wake up, Bjorn," someone was saying. A man's voice— familiar but not a friend.

"Wake up, Bjorn," the voice said again. Bjorn's eyes fluttered open. Valerian stood over him, looking down.

"Forgive me, Lord," Bjorn whispered. He struggled to his feet.

"No need to whisper," Valerian assured him.

"Yes, Lord," Bjorn replied. Valerian looked around at the large common room.

"So this is where you're living now," he said. "I don't understand how you people can stand to live like this. Like cattle in a pen."

"No, Lord," Bjorn replied.

Valerian looked down at Helga's sleeping form.

"Still, you haven't done too badly," the MageLord said. He nudged the blanket off Helga with his foot and looked down at her.

"Not too badly at all," he said.

Leave her alone! Bjorn thought. *Damn you, Valerian!* Valerian looked back around the common room.

"Do you mate with her here?" he asked. "In front of everybody?"

"No, Lord," Bjorn replied.

You pig! he thought. *Gods, I wish I could kill you!*

"I should hope not," he said. "At least you're not completely animals." Valerian glanced around at the people sleeping near them and frowned.

"Where is your father?" he asked.

"He died two days ago, Lord," Bjorn replied.

"Oh," Valerian replied. "My condolences to the grieving son."

To Hell with you! Bjorn thought. *It's because of you that he's dead!*

"Thank you, Lord," he said.

"I suppose you lead the Circle now, then," Valerian noted.

"Not yet, Lord," Bjorn replied. "I will be initiated tomorrow night. Or killed."

"Killed?"

"If I fail the tests, Theodr will kill me, Lord," Bjorn replied.

"And you accept this?" Valerian asked.

"To do otherwise would draw suspicion, Lord."

"I mean, if I did not control you, you would place your life in this man's hands willingly?"

"Yes, Lord," Bjorn replied.

"Savages," Valerian spat.

"Yes, Lord," Bjorn replied.

"Do not worry, Bjorn," Valerian assured him. "This worm will not see any sign of my control of you. You *will* pass the tests."

"Yes, Lord," Bjorn replied.

"Go back to sleep, Bjorn," Valerian said. "You don't even interest me any longer."

"Yes, Lord," Bjorn replied. He lay down on the straw mat and drew the blanket back over Helga and himself. When he looked back up, the MageLord was gone.

The lodge awoke long before sunrise. Of course, sunrise was almost noon this far north. Men groaned and stumbled about, trying to go about their daily chores. As Bjorn had suspected, they were not making much progress.

"Safe journey to all of you," Lars said.

"Thank you, my lord," Bjorn replied.

"You know, you could come to live with us here in the lodge," Lars suggested. "Three more strong men are always welcome."

"Thank you, my lord," Bjorn said. "I am honored by your offer. But we just finished the cabin, and after working so hard on it . . ."

"I understand," Lars said, nodding. "When you've built something with your own hands, it is a hard thing to walk away from."

"I may not live under your roof," Bjorn added, "but I have come to think of you as my chief. All of us have."

Lars reached out and clasped Bjorn's forearms. Bjorn returned the gesture.

"If you have need of us, call, Bjorn Rolfson," Lars told him.

"And likewise you of us, my chieftain," Bjorn replied.

"I will see you off, trapper," Lars said.

They stepped out of the lodge. Lars's men already had their sleds ready. The women climbed aboard the toboggan. Angus, Theodr and Bjorn would ride the dish sleds.

Bjorn glanced up at the Northern Curtain. Soon the sun would rise and wash it out of the sky for a few hours.

"In the belly of fire, surrounded by ice beneath a curtain of light, sleeps Arcalion the Ravager," Bjorn said.

"He does not always sleep," Lars grumbled.

"What?" Bjorn said, turning to the old chieftain. "You've *seen* him?" Lars shook his head.

"Not I," Lars replied. "When my grandfather ruled this hall and my father was but a boy, he saw him. Longer than the hall itself, he was. He swooped out of the sky and carried off four of my grandfather's cattle—one in each claw. He returned three times. It was a hungry winter for the clan."

"I thought that Arcalion was merely a legend," Bjorn said. The chill that seeped into his bones had little to do with the cold.

"What stole six and ten of my grandfather's cattle that year was no legend," Lars said.

"Did your grandfather try to drive him off?" Bjorn asked.

"No," Lars replied. "The demon took no interest in the lodge, and my grandfather wanted it to stay that way. There was no fighting this thing."

"But enough of an old man's stories," Lars added. "The beast has not been seen since, and I pray it stays that way. Your women are waiting for you. Safe journey, Bjorn."

"Thank you, my lord," Bjorn replied. As he turned to leave, he glanced up at the Northern Curtain. It seemed more ominous than it had a few moments ago.

The Northern Curtain shed an eerie light on the snow-covered plains. Bjorn approached the small Circle where Theodr, Freida, Helga, Angus and Hilda waited.

Physically, there weren't enough to form the Circle. Angus stood to the north, Helga to the east and Hilda to the west. Freida stood just north of the center of the Circle, facing south. Theodr stood to her left, and a little in front of her. In his hands he held the sword that was both his badge of office and the last defense of the Circle.

Bjorn approached from the south. He stopped outside the invisible yet shimmering wall of Power that formed the Circle. Theodr stepped forward, stopping just inside the Circle. The tip of his extended sword touched Bjorn's chest between the third and fourth ribs. Bjorn felt Theodr's mind touch his own.

"How do you come?" Theodr asked.

"In peace and trust," Bjorn responded. "With malice toward none and love for all." The sword pressed against his chest with a little more force.

"Even for Gavin, king of Reykvid?" Theodr asked. "Even for the one who tried to slay you for his own gain?"

"Even for him," Bjorn replied. Bjorn felt Theodr's mind probing his own, testing the truth of his answer.

See it, Theodr! he thought. *See the taint that Valerian's Power has placed on me and drive your sword home!*

Instead the sword of the guardian left his chest.

"You may enter the Circle," Theodr said.

Bjorn stepped into the center of the Circle, carefully

stepping over the two lines that marked the boundary. He walked to the center of the Circle and stepped into the smaller Circle drawn there.

Freida's Power rose about him and Bjorn knelt, bowing his head in submission. Theodr stepped to his left and laid the sword across the back of Bjorn's neck.

Surely, he could not pass the tests. Not with the taint of Valerian's Power on his soul. Valerian had thought otherwise, however.

"Who are you?" Freida asked.

"I am Bjorn, son of Rolf," Bjorn replied. "I am of the Circle."

"Why do you come?" she asked.

"To serve."

"By what right do you come?"

"By right of Power."

"Do you seek to hold this Power over us?"

"No," Bjorn replied. "I place it in the service of the Circle." Theodr's sword shifted on the back of Bjorn's neck.

Yes! Bjorn thought. *He sees!* Bjorn waited for the sword to lift and strike his head from his shoulders.

But Theodr did not see. He was merely shifting his position. Thus far, the taint had gone undetected.

"I have here the medallion of the High Magus," Freida said. "This circle of gold has been passed down to us by Bairn himself from the Time of Madness and is scribed with his symbol. Will you take the burden of it about your neck?"

"I will," Bjorn said.

"Then rise," Freida commanded. Bjorn rose to his feet once Theodr had removed the sword. Theodr resumed his place behind Freida. Valerian had been correct. They did not see the taint, and now he would be made High Magus of the Circle.

Freida placed the medallion about his neck. Bjorn opened his garments against the freezing cold, allowing the frigid metal to touch his bare flesh.

All five members of the Circle stepped forward around the smaller circle surrounding Bjorn. They joined hands and closed their eyes. In the rite of bonding, they poured their combined Power into the medallion.

Bjorn cried out as the amulet seared his chest. The other

members of the Circle gasped in surprise, their concentration broken. Bjorn fell to his knees as the metal began to glow, first a dull yellow climbing through bright yellow to almost blinding white.

He toppled forward into the snow as the heat from the golden circle burned him.

I may have passed Theodr's tests, Bjorn thought, *but I did not pass Bairn's.*

And then the fire passed. Bjorn gasped as the medallion cooled against his chest. His breath came in heaving gulps.

"Bjorn!" Helga called to him, kneeling in the snow beside him. "Are you all right?"

"No!" he shouted. "None of us are!"

"What?" Helga said, confusion plain in her tone. She was not alone—Bjorn was also astonished. Had he just said that?

"None of us are all right!" he insisted. Yes! He was in command of his own mind again. Somehow his father's badge of office had broken the MageLord's hold on him.

"None of what I have told you since my return was true," Bjorn explained. "I have been Valerian's puppet. He *is* a MageLord!"

"The medallion . . ." Freida said.

"Yes," Bjorn agreed. "It broke his hold over me. But you must all flee! Valerian will come for me now that his Power over me has been broken."

"No," Theodr said.

"But you must!" Bjorn said.

"No," Theodr insisted. "We left our homes and followed Rolf. Now you are High Magus. We will abandon you no more than we abandoned your father. We stand together."

Bjorn thought for a moment. A strange tightness in his chest accompanied Theodr's announcement.

"Then we must all flee into hiding," Bjorn finally said.

"But where?" Helga asked. It was a good question. In the dead of winter, flight would not necessarily save them. They could either die at Valerian's hands or the cold's.

But wait—Valerian thought that they lived in Lars's hall. He would not know of the cabin. Still, the people at the lodge knew of it, and Bjorn knew too well how Valerian could draw knowledge from a person's mind.

"The cave!" Bjorn said. Lars and his people did not know about the cave. Valerian could not learn what they did not know.

"Valerian does not know of it!" he explained. "We can take refuge there for now. We have a few moments before Valerian learns where we are in which to pack, but we must hurry!"

Chapter
------- Fifteen -----------

BJORN WAITED IN the brush outside the cabin. They had packed quickly, taking only the essentials—food, fuel, clothing and Rolf's trunk. The others were waiting back at the cave, dissipating their Power into the earth lest it give them away.

Bjorn did likewise. Breathe in, hold, breathe out. With each outward breath, his Power dimmed and his magical senses and defenses faded. Still, as he knew all too well, those defenses were worthless against Valerian, and the aura of his Power could lead the MageLord to him like a beacon.

Of course, there was no guarantee that Valerian, with his vast Power, would not find him anyway. Bjorn hoped that the amulet he wore around his neck would help protect him from Valerian's senses just as it had broken the MageLord's hold on his mind.

The falling snow slowly tried to bury him. Bjorn did not brush it away. Nature's blanket would serve not only to keep him warm, it would also help to hide him from sight.

It had been several hours and no one had come. Bjorn was beginning to think that Valerian would not bother. What had the MageLord said?

You don't even interest me any longer, Bjorn thought. That was what he had said. Perhaps it was the truth. Perhaps Valerian found Bjorn so beneath contempt that he didn't *care* that Bjorn had broken his spell.

Bjorn glanced up at the Northern Curtain. No matter how many times he saw it, it was still a wonderful sight. It shimmered not only with light, but with Power. It was . . .

Something dark moved in front of the shimmering, green curtain. Bjorn's eyes widened as the object approached,

169

resolving into four figures on horseback. They glided through the air, motionless save for their flight.

They descended from the northeast toward the cabin. Bjorn watched as the four touched down in front of the cabin. In the dim light, he could recognize them. Valerian, Gavin, Ivanel, and William.

The three warriors dismounted and drew their weapons before entering the cabin. Valerian followed them inside. Bjorn watched, knowing full well that if he and the others had remained here they would have all been put to the sword.

Soon the four men emerged back into the night. Valerian stopped on the narrow porch. Slowly, he scanned the horizon. As his gaze swept past Bjorn's location, Bjorn felt the amulet on his neck grow warm. The MageLord did not pause.

"Find them!" he shouted, whirling toward the others.

"Yes, Lord," Gavin replied. "Ivanel, track them."

"Yes, majesty," Ivanel replied. The baron knelt on the porch just beyond the door. As Bjorn watched, Ivanel brushed at the snow with his fingers. Finally he stepped off the porch. He sifted through the snow in all directions.

Evidently he found nothing there, for he rose and walked over to the barn. There he found a trail beneath the fresh snow. Ivanel was *good*—Bjorn was impressed in spite of himself.

Bjorn smiled as Ivanel dutifully followed it back to the cabin. Once in front of the cabin, Ivanel again lost the trail. The women's brooms had been put to very good use, indeed, sweeping their trail clear behind them.

"Lord," Ivanel said, "they have covered their trail too well. I cannot track them."

"They cannot have gotten far," Valerian said. "Especially if they are taking time to cover their tracks."

"Perhaps not, Lord," Gavin said. "However, they travel in a straight line. We will have to search in all directions. Our chances of overtaking them are not good."

"Search!" Valerian commanded. "They must be found!"

"Yes, Lord," Gavin replied.

"They took a sled, Lord," Ivanel noted. "We can limit our search to the game trails."

Bjorn breathed a sigh of relief. If they only searched the

game trails, they would not find *his* hiding place in the brush.

"Do so," Valerian said. "Just *find* them!"

"Yes, Lord," Ivanel replied.

Bjorn watched as the three warriors left on foot to search the game trails. The cave was well over an hour from here and would be hidden by the snow. There was little chance of finding it.

Valerian waited at the cabin. As the minutes passed into hours, the Magelord became increasingly frustrated with Ivanel's reports.

"Enough!" he finally shouted. "We shall not find them this way."

"No, Lord," Ivanel agreed. "They are too well hidden."

"Then we will go back to the lodge!" Valerian said angrily. "And this time I will rip the knowledge from their minds!"

Bjorn's heart fell. Lars and his people could not betray them, for they did not know where the mages had fled. Still, Valerian would not be gentle with them. Bjorn had brought this down on them.

"Lord, the people at the lodge know nothing," Gavin argued.

"How do *you* know?" Valerian asked.

"I spoke with Bjorn at length, Lord," Gavin explained. "I know how the mages think. They would have told the people at the lodge *nothing*, so that there would be no one to point after them. They are quite good at hiding."

"Yes," Valerian agreed. "The vermin always have been. Come." The MageLord stepped off the porch and walked to the horses. Before mounting, however, he turned abruptly and faced the cabin. He raised his arms.

The cabin groaned and sagged, almost as if its own weight was too much for it. As Bjorn watched, the building shuddered, shutters popped open or broke. It seemed as though a giant hand were pressing down on the house.

Then, from the heavens, a streak of light began to fall, as though Valerian had just pulled a star from the sky. The falling star grew until it was visibly a ball of fire falling from the heavens. Bjorn watched, fascinated despite himself.

Then, as if it had been struck by a fiery mallet, the ground leaped. Bjorn briefly saw a ball of fire engulf the entire cabin before the impact sent him flying through the air.

A second impact as he struck the ground knocked the wind from his lungs. Then a rain of mud and snow buried him just before he lost consciousness.

Gods above! Gavin thought as he watched the very earth spew up like a fiery fountain before him. The ground jumped and bucked beneath his feet like a living thing as a wall of earth flew at them.

As Gavin fell to the ground, the rushing wall of earth parted around them. The horses screamed in terror, and Gavin heard his own screams echo in his ears.

In mere heartbeats it was over. Gavin struggled to his feet and stared in horror at the sight before him. A pit, twice as deep as the cabin had been tall and easily a hundred feet across, lay before him. The bottom of the pit glowed with molten heat. Of the cabin, there was no sign that it had ever been.

They stood on a peninsula jutting out twenty feet into the pit. For at least a hundred feet around the pit the area had been devastated. Trees were flattened and partially buried in debris. Gavin realized that if not for the MageLord's Power, they would all be dead.

How do you fight a man who can pull the stars from heaven to smite his foes? Gavin thought. Still, Bjorn was now free. If anyone had a prayer of opposing Valerian, it was he. As Gavin stared down into the fiery pit, however, that hope felt very small.

"We are finished here," Valerian said. "It is time to leave."

"Yes, Lord," they replied. Gavin turned and mounted his horse. The animal was much calmer than it should have been. More of Valerian's sorcery, no doubt.

As the MageLord lifted them into the air, Gavin looked down once more at the pit that had been Bjorn's home. Little did he realize that he flew directly over Bjorn's unmarked grave.

Bjorn woke to total darkness and massive weight pressing down on him. Where was he?

Panic gripped him as he remembered. He was buried alive!

Buried beneath, the gods only knew, how many tons of earth and snow!

Calm yourself, Bjorn, he thought. *Calm . . . calm.* He tried to breathe deeply, but the earth surrounding him would only allow him shallow breaths.

Calm Bjorn, he thought. He tried to move but every limb was pinned, immobile beneath the crushing weight above him.

He was going to die. He would either suffocate down here or freeze as the frozen ground pulled the warmth from his body.

He closed his eyes. To all things there was an end. Helga bore his child. Tears filled his eyes, washing away some of the sand and grit that had filled them.

No—now was not the time for grief. Now he needed to know that the others still lived. Slowly, he began to regather his Power.

Bairn, give me the time! he pleaded.

Helga blinked back her tears. All that was left of their home was a blackened pit. Whatever force had destroyed it had also leveled the forest for a hundred feet in every direction. The impact had shaken the cave almost a mile away.

Bjorn was nowhere to be found. She could not even feel his mind, and that meant he was dead.

Her mother's arms circled her from behind. Helga turned and buried her face on her mother's shoulders, weeping bitterly.

Helga?

Helga gasped, lifting her face from her mother's shoulder. "What is it, child?" her mother asked.

Helga?

There it was again. That faint touch—so cold, so . . . distant.

"Bjorn!" she shouted. *"Bjorn!"*

Helga!

"He's alive!" she shrieked. "Oh, gods, he's *alive!*"

"Helga, calm yourself!" Freida said, stepping up beside her and pulling her from Hilda's arms.

"You must concentrate!" the old woman said. "Concentrate! Ground and center! *Where* is he?"

Helga slowed her frantic breathing, closing her eyes to concentrate.

Bjorn? she thought.

Helga, came the reply. But there was so much . . . sadness in his touch. She reached out to him with her mind.

"It's dark," she said. "So very dark. And he's so afraid and so sad. Can't . . . breathe. I . . . can't breathe. So . . . cold."

Helga's eyes snapped open and she screamed in terror. Freida drew back her arm and slapped the terrified girl across the face.

"He's buried!" Helga shrieked. "Buried alive! Oh, gods! Oh, gods!"

Freida slapped her again.

"Helga, *where*?" she shouted. "You have to tell us *where*! Only you can!"

The girl swallowed. Her breath came in little, short gasps as she cast about with her eyes.

"Not with your *eyes*!" Freida said. "With your heart! Find your husband! Find the man you *love*!"

Helga closed her eyes.

Bjorn? she thought.

. . . helga . . .

Helga rose to her feet, eyes closed. She could feel him—could feel the cold and the darkness. She could feel the massive weight crushing the breath from him.

She took a step, and another, then another. Finally she opened her eyes.

"Here!" she said. "He's here!"

"Angus!" Theodr shouted. "Find something to dig with. Hurry!" As Angus searched the area, Theodr began clawing through the mixed earth and snow with his bare hands.

Bjorn, Helga thought.

. . . hel . . . ga . . .

"He's dying!" she shrieked. "Oh, gods, he's dying! Hurry—please hurry." Her words degenerated into hysterical sobs.

Rage welled up inside Theodr. With a strength he did not truly possess, he lifted a stone larger than his head and hurled it from Bjorn's grave. He had lost one High Magus to this monster. He would be damned before he lost another.

He dug like a badger, clawing at the unyielding earth, heedless of his bleeding fingers. Bjorn would *not* die.

The blade of a shovel struck the ground in front of him. Where had Angus found . . . ?

It was not Angus. More than two score men from the lodge were here. Strong arms lifted him away from the shallow pit he had begun. The lodge was half a day from here. How had Lars gotten here so quickly?

"*Dig*, you miserable whoresons!" Lars shouted. "Our clansman is down there! *Dig!*"

Earth literally flew from the pit as twenty men set to work with shovels.

Bjorn? Helga thought.

. . . hel . . .

"Hurry!" she screamed. "Please, hurry!"

"Careful, lads!" Lars shouted. "Don't stave in his skull with a shovel. Quickly, not deeply!"

"I've got 'im!" one of the men in the pit shouted.

"Hands only!" Lars commanded needlessly. The shovels had already been discarded beside the pit. They lifted Bjorn's body from the pit, covered in mud and dirt. He was visibly blue from the cold.

"Lord, 'e's breathin'!"

"Bring me a sled!" Lars commanded. "And furs! Lots of them! Strip him!"

They laid Bjorn's naked body on a bed of furs in one of the toboggans.

"Woman!" Lars shouted, pointing at Helga. "You're his wife. Shuck your clothes and get in there with him! Cover them up, lads!"

Heedless of modesty, Helga removed her clothes and lay down next to Bjorn on the toboggan. He was so cold! Cold furs were laid over them. Then the two of them were lashed like a bundle to the sled. Helga shivered as Bjorn's body hungrily stole the warmth from her own.

She closed her eyes and summoned the Power. There was more than one way to keep warm. She turned the Power inward, forcing it to warm her body to an almost feverish level.

Don't worry, my love, she thought. *I won't* let *you die.*

"To the lodge!" Lars commanded. "Quickly!"

Gavin lay awake in his chambers, staring at the ceiling he could not see in the darkness.

Bjorn was free—*free*! Somehow, someway, he had managed to break Valerian's hold on his mind. Now there was someone out there who *knew*. For the first time in a very long time, Gavin felt a flicker of hope.

But hope was a terrible thing, for with the hope came fear. Gavin had seen the MageLord destroy Bjorn's cabin. That was the first true, unrestrained use of his Power that Valerian had displayed. And it had been a terrible display indeed. What hope did someone like Bjorn have against someone with that much power?

More hope than someone like Gavin did.

Chief Braun broke the wax seal on the letter his messenger had brought to him. He lifted a goblet of mulled wine to his lips as he read. Smiling, he set the goblet down.

This was excellent news. Chief Urall had convinced the conquered Badger and Elk clans to revolt when Gavin marched against Ravenhall. The rest of the letter detailed the forces that each would be able to muster for the attack.

Braun rose from his chair and walked back to the council room. A large map had been laid out on the council table. Braun studied it.

To the north of Reykvid, the Bear clan, the Griffon clan and the remnants of the Fox clan's army waited to strike. When Gavin marched eastward against the Raven clan in the spring, they would strike through the lands of the Fox clan, into the lands of the Fire Sword clan and on to Reykvid.

Now, there would be another thrust, from the south. Braun counted out the pieces corresponding to the forces promised by the Badgers and the Elks and set them in their respective lands. These forces would eventually strike through the lands of the Wolf clan and on into Reykvid.

Gavin would be forced to withdraw his troops before they

ever reached Raven lands, or lose Reykvid. Then Braun would march through the Star clan lands to Reykvid. In all likelihood, the Star clan would then rise against their king and join with him. After all, was not their chief a prisoner in Reykvid's dungeons?

Braun nodded, smiling. He would discuss this new development with his captains on the morrow. By this time next year, Reykvid would be nothing more than an unpleasant memory. Even Gavin's pet mage would not be able to stop them.

Bjorn slowly opened his eyes. He was warm—too warm, in fact. It felt wonderful.

His chest burned and his eyes refused to clear. Vague faces swam before his sight.

"He's awake!" someone said. The voice sounded familiar, but Bjorn was too tired to concentrate.

"Lift him up," another familiar voice said. Someone did so. A sudden pang in his chest made him wince. Someone placed a wooden cup to his lips.

"Drink!" a voice commanded. That voice he knew.

"Mama?" he croaked.

"Drink!" the voice commanded again. Bjorn drank. The hot liquid tasted bitter, but it warmed him inside and made the pain lessen.

He coughed on the last swallow. A hand wiped his face with a cloth, and he was laid back down. His eyes fluttered closed, and darkness embraced him once again.

Theodr put his arms around Freida as she wept. This ordeal had not been easy on her. Now, two days later, the tears had finally come.

"He called me 'mama'," she sobbed. "He hasn't called me that for so long . . ."

"I know, dear," Theodr said, rocking her in his arms.

Bjorn awoke again. It was cooler this time. Where was he? The sounds of sleeping people surrounded him.

He tried to raise up on his elbows, but the burning in his

chest became a raging fire when he tried. He gasped out in pain and fell back. Someone stirred next to him.

"Bjorn?" she said.

"Helga?" he asked.

"Yes, love," she replied.

"Where . . . are we?"

"The lodge," she said. "Lars's men dug you free and brought us here."

"We cannot . . . stay," Bjorn said. "Valerian will . . . kill all of . . . them if he . . . finds us . . . here."

"It has been two days," Helga told him. "He has not returned." Helga placed her arm behind his shoulders and lifted him up. Bjorn winced.

"Drink," she said, placing a cup to his lips. He did. The bitter draught was cider laced with belladonna.

"Sleep," Helga ordered.

"Yes, dear," Bjorn replied.

"So, you walk among the living again," Lars said. Bjorn was propped up in his bed eating some porridge. Lars took the chair next to him.

"I don't know about walking yet," Bjorn replied, "but I do live."

"You have been less than honest with me, Bjorn Rolfson," Lars accused. Bjorn bowed his head.

"Yes, my lord," Bjorn replied. What had Lars been told? How could Bjorn explain the events of three days ago without landing all of them in the fire?

"Bandits are one thing," Lars said. "That was what you told me, but I thought I knew better."

"What do you . . . ?" Bjorn started to ask, raising his gaze to Lars's. The old man had raised his hand, middle finger laid over the index finger in the Sign.

"You . . . ?" Bjorn whispered.

"Yes," Lars replied. "I am of the Circle. We all are."

"*All* of you?"

"Yes, the whole lodge," Lars said, with a twinkle in his eye. "Scandalous, isn't it?"

"When you came here, we believed that you fled the hunt," Lars told him. "We allowed you to build your cabin because, if you were found, you would not be traced to us. We could claim ignorance, yet still aid our brethren."

"But the hunt is nothing compared to what pursues you, Bjorn Rolfson," Lars added. "When I saw Valerian, I could scarce believe what I saw. When I saw what had happened to your cabin, I had no choice but to believe. He *is* a MageLord?"

"Yes," Bjorn replied.

"Yes," Lars agreed, "of course he is. Tell me—everything."

Bjorn told him about his first meeting with Gavin and the prince's preposterous story. He told Lars about travelling to Reykvid and seeing Valerian for himself and the horror of learning that this man truly *was* a MageLord.

Bjorn admitted to the failed attempt on Valerian's life that had, instead, cost the king's life and of the ensuing pursuit of the MageLord. He detailed the futile battle at the tower and their eventual enthrallment to Valerian's Power. He omitted nothing, including Valerian's one visit to the lodge.

"That is how he knew to come here," Lars said. "I am glad that he did."

"*Why*?" Bjorn asked.

"If they had not come here seeking you, I would not have known to come to you," Lars replied. "And, I would never have seen a MageLord with my own eyes. That is a greater thing even than seeing Arcalion steal our cattle."

"Arcalion . . . ," Bjorn whispered.

"Yes," Lars replied. "Great catastrophes are indeed catastrophes. But they are also wonders to behold."

"Now, I once again ask you to join our lodge," Lars said. "Only this time, I will not accept no as an answer."

"We would be honored, my liege," Bjorn replied.

The days passed with agonizing slowness as Bjorn healed. Now that their secret was out, the residents of the lodge did not bother to hide their Power. For the most part, their auras were weak, pale things with a few notable exceptions. Lars, the strongest among them, did not shine as brightly as Hilda, the weakest of Bjorn's family.

Bjorn spent the time struggling with the ancient language of the Silver Book. Of course, it was no longer silver, but that was still how he thought of it.

Only the first five pages held any text. The remaining pages were blank. That could not be right. When Valerian had looked through the book, over half of the tome had been legible. Perhaps it was fading?

Bjorn checked the blank pages carefully. There was no sign of any faded ink on the parchment. He flipped back to the first five pages. None of the text showed any signs of fading.

Interestingly enough, the first five pages seemed to be one lesson and exercise. No more, and no less. If the book had simply faded, Bjorn doubted that it would have done so at such a significant boundary. No—there was Power at work here.

"How are you today?" Lars asked, walking back into the private area Bjorn was sharing with Helga during his recovery.

"Bored," Bjorn replied.

"That is the normal state of things during the winters here," Lars observed.

"Not *this* bored," Bjorn said. "I want to go out checking my traps and such. Instead, I am imprisoned in my bed."

"If I had your wife, I would not complain about being imprisoned in bed," Lars noted.

"Well," Bjorn stammered, "I . . . suppose not."

"What is this book?" Lars asked.

"It is an ancient tome of my father's," Bjorn explained. "It was magically sealed until Valerian opened it recently. It was useless to him, but it is written in the ancient language of the MageLords. I am trying to translate it."

"May I?" Lars asked.

"Certainly," Bjorn replied.

Lars picked up the book and opened it. He slowly browsed through the first five pages. Then he began flipping through the pages carefully.

"It is mostly blank!" he said.

"It wasn't when Valerian held it," Bjorn replied. "There is some Power on it."

"Well, I cannot make any sense of it," Lars said, handing the book back to Bjorn. "I should leave you to your work."

"No, please," Bjorn said. "To tell you the truth, I'm sick of sifting through it. Would you tell me more about your grandfather and Arcalion?"

"There is little more to tell," Lars said, sitting back down. "What more do you want to know?"

"Which direction did the dragon arrive from?" Bjorn asked.

"From the north and east," Lars said. "And he departed in the same direction."

"And he returned every night?"

"For three nights afterwards, yes," Lars confirmed. "Why?"

"That means his lair must be only one day from here," Bjorn mused. Lars looked visibly disturbed.

"I had never thought of that," he said. "Still, how far can a dragon larger than my hall travel in a day?"

"Not too much further than a pigeon, I would guess," Bjorn said. "Probably no more than a fortnight by sled. Certainly not more than twice that."

Lars chuckled.

"You almost sound as if you were going to go out and *find* him," he said.

"I am," Bjorn replied.

Chapter
------- Sixteen ------------

"BJORN, YOU CAN'T be serious!" Helga said. Bjorn sat in Lars's council room at the back of the hall. Lars and the members of Bjorn's Circle sat at one end of the large table with Bjorn.

"I have never been more serious," Bjorn assured her.

"But *why*?" she asked. Helga was almost in tears.

"I almost lost you when you were buried alive by Valerian," she added. "You have not yet recovered from that, and you are already planning to chase after something even more dangerous."

"Exactly," Bjorn replied. "Helga, none of us are safe as long as Valerian is alive."

"But how can this *help*?"

"I mean to find a legend with which to fight a legend," Bjorn replied.

"Why do you believe," Theodr asked, "that Arcalion will want to oppose Valerian?"

"Arcalion was summoned by the MageLords to fight their wars for them," Bjorn replied. "He was enslaved to their Power as thoroughly as I was to Valerian's. If the legends are correct, as soon as that hold was broken, Arcalion turned on his masters and destroyed them. I suspect he will not be pleased to learn that one of his former masters has returned."

"Lad," Lars said, "this all assumes two things. First, that you can even find Arcalion's lair and second, that, if you do, you will *survive* long enough to explain why you've come."

"This also assumes that Arcalion is *able* to destroy Valerian," Theodr added. "You may wind up delivering Valerian's greatest weapon to him."

"I don't think that Valerian has his full Power available to him," Bjorn said. "If he did, if Valerian wielded all the legendary Power of the MageLords, why would he hide behind others to do his will? I think Arcalion can destroy him."

"Bjorn," Lars added, "the winters are harsh here, to say the least. However, if you go further north, you will enter a land that will not see the sun again until spring. Further north the winter is a full season of night, and the cold is so great that your breath will freeze in your lungs. Few have travelled there, and even fewer have returned."

"It is not important that I return," Bjorn said. "Only that I succeed."

"'Tis madness!" Lars objected.

"Yes, it is," Bjorn agreed. "But sanity has not defeated Valerian. It is time to resort to madness before Valerian brings a greater madness down on all of us. Never again!"

"Never again!" the others echoed before falling silent. Those two words summed up the entire philosophy of the mages regarding the MageLords. Each person here had been drilled in that phrase since birth. For a time, the council room was silent as each weighed the meaning of those words.

"Very well, lad," Lars finally said. "Go, with my blessing. And my prayers."

"Thank you," Bjorn replied.

"You know that you will almost certainly die," Theodr pointed out.

"Yes," Bjorn said. "I do."

Helga lay on her side, facing away from him. Quiet sobs shook her form. Bjorn reached around her and held her to him.

"How can you do this?" she asked.

"I have no choice . . ." Bjorn began.

"Yes, you *do*!" she cried. "We could be happy here. Valerian thinks that you're dead or gone."

"His ambition would bring him here eventually," Bjorn said. "It might not be in our lifetime, but do you want our children to have to fight him once he is secure in his Power?"

Helga was silent for a time.

"Why does it have to be *you*?" she asked.

"Because, by Bairn's will, it has fallen to me," Bjorn replied. Helga rolled over to face him.

"It's just . . . I can't bear to lose you so soon after almost losing you once before," she said.

"So we meet, and so we part," Bjorn said, "and we *will* meet again."

"I love you, Bjorn," Helga said.

"And I you," Bjorn assured her. Helga wrapped her arms around him and pressed her lips against his. She rolled onto her back, pulling Bjorn atop her.

Gods, I wish I didn't have to go, Bjorn thought.

"I still think you should wait for spring," Lars told him. "At least you would have light in which to travel."

"Time is short," Bjorn replied.

"Besides, I have all the light I need," he added, pointing up at the Northern Curtain.

"That light gives no warmth," Lars said.

"I have my blankets for that," Bjorn said. He had built a tent of blankets on the front of the sled. That, in addition to his winter clothing, should help to protect him from the cold.

"Take care, lad," Lars cautioned. "The winter will take you if you don't respect her."

"I know," Bjorn said.

"The wolves to the north do not fear men," Lars added. "And there are bears the color of the snow that are even more fierce than the grizzled ones. Very far to the north it is easy to mistake the sea for the land. Take care—there are creatures in the water that will come up through the ice to take you."

"There is a sea to the north?" Bjorn asked.

"Yes," Lars replied. "Avoid it."

"Are there any people living to the north?" Bjorn asked.

"None that I know of," Lars said. "There may be a lodge or two further north but, if there is, I have not heard of it. Man cannot make his home where you travel—he is not welcome."

"I shall be careful," Bjorn assured Lars.

"See that you are," Theodr interrupted. "Since you would not allow me to travel with you, I shall hold *you* responsible if you die."

"I'll be sure to keep that in mind," Bjorn laughed. The truth was that Theodr would hold *himself* responsible, and Bjorn did not want that to happen either.

"See that you do," Theodr replied. He stepped forward to embrace Bjorn.

"Take care, High Magus," Theodr said. "I shall await your return."

"I will, Theodr," Bjorn assured him. Then everyone joined in bidding him farewell: Freida tearfully—Angus and Hilda stoically, but sadly. Then Helga stepped up to him.

"Farewell, my husband," she said. She slipped into his arms for a long, parting kiss.

"I will come back," Bjorn whispered to her.

"I will wait," she promised in return.

Bjorn stepped out of her embrace and climbed aboard the sled. He travelled lightly. Six bales of hay for the three deer and enough food to last himself a fortnight. Both were strictly emergency supplies. Bjorn hoped to live off game and hoped that the deer would be able to forage. Probably the most important item he carried was the lodestone arrow Lars had given him. It hung by a cord from the lip of the toboggan and always pointed to the north.

He pulled the lashings on his makeshift tent until the blankets were snug around him. He sat cross-legged on the sled, a nondescript bundle of cloth and fur. Only his eyes were visible behind a tunnel of fur.

He gripped the reins inside his cabin and called out to the team. They pulled away, slowly at first, but quickly gaining speed until they were moving at a trot.

Bjorn glanced behind him. Helga and the others stood, watching him depart. Inside the blankets, he could not wave.

Farewell, my friends, he thought. Then he turned his eyes to the north.

Bjorn carefully peeled the pelts from the hares he had shot earlier. On the first day, the quest was off to a good start. His Art had enabled him to find game, and his shots had been true. Tonight he would enjoy fresh rabbit rather than jerked beef. The second rabbit would be allowed to freeze, and he could eat it tomorrow.

The hobbled reindeer nibbled at the thick, waxy leaves and needles of the trees and bushes surrounding Bjorn's camp. Bjorn set the pelts aside, spitted the first rabbit and laid it across the fire. He turned the spit slowly and glanced up at the Northern Curtain overhead as the rabbit cooked.

It was strange. A man could love this harsh, unforgiving land. As Lars had said, the winter would take you if you did not respect her. Still, there was something about sitting out beneath that shimmering curtain of green, feeling the cold in your breath and listening to the total and absolute *silence* of the night that pulled at a man's heart.

Helga was right. They could be happy here. For not the first time, Bjorn questioned what he was doing. He and Helga could live out the rest of their days in Lars's hall and never have to think of Valerian again.

As long as he didn't come looking for us, Bjorn thought. He could almost relive the memory of the falling star consuming their cabin for the sake of nothing more than a fit of pique. The ball of fire, the force that had sent him flying and the rain of mud that had buried him alive. All were still in his mind with crystal clarity.

No, Valerian could *not* be ignored. As long as the MageLord lived, Bjorn and his family would never be truly safe. This search might almost be suicide, but ignoring Valerian would be almost the same as murder. Bjorn did not want to enter his next life with the blood of Valerian's victims on his hands.

The smell of charring flesh reminded Bjorn of more immediate concerns. He hastily removed the overcooked rabbit from the fire. Fortunately, it was not too badly burned. He dipped the meat into the snow in front of him to cool it a bit.

Although the outside was burned, the inside was still tender. Bjorn finished his meal quickly as the cold threatened to numb his face. He wrapped a small portion of the cooked meat in a cloth for breakfast tomorrow, tucking the parcel inside his coat.

Once he had finished he got up and went over to the sled to get his bedding. First he laid out a heavy hide to protect the rest of his bedding from melting snow. Atop that he laid several blankets before himself lying down. Lying atop the blankets, he wrapped them around him like a cocoon.

Good night, Helga, he thought before drifting off to sleep.

The bright morning sunlight woke Bjorn. He rolled onto his side, and his eyes fluttered open. He found himself looking straight into the liquid, brown eye of an animal.

"Yaah!" Bjorn shouted in surprise, rolling away. Around him, the three deer quickly sat up, looking around for the source of his alarm. Bjorn laughed, spooking them further. They jumped up and hobbled a short distance away from him. Bjorn extricated himself from his blankets, still chuckling at himself, and began packing his bedding back onto the sled.

During the night, the deer had obviously included him in their huddle for warmth. Tomorrow he would be better prepared for that. His stiff fingers fumbled with the sled's lashes as he tied his bedding into place. It would be good to get back inside his blankets on the sled and warm up.

Bjorn clucked to the deer. One timidly approached him, and Bjorn stroked its nose. Soon all three were harnessed and unhobbled for the day's ride. Bjorn climbed into the tent on the sled and lashed it back into place around him. The blankets themselves were stiff from the cold, but they would warm up soon enough.

"Hyah!" he called to the deer as he snapped the reins.

Bjorn shook his head to clear the snow from his hood. The snowfall was so heavy now that he could barely see the lead deer.

He glanced down at the lodestone arrow hung from the lip of the toboggan. It spun wildly in the wind, telling him nothing. For all he knew, he was travelling in circles.

"Whoa!" he called, pulling back on the reins. He had hoped to find shelter from the storm before stopping. That was not going to happen—his only shelter would have to be the snow itself.

He called the deer back to him. They came to the sound of his voice, their fur white with snow. In this weather he would not be able to unharness them. Still, they could rest together.

"Come on, Flaxen," Bjorn called gently. "Here, Brazen, lie down. That's a good girl."

The deer huddled together on his windward side, tucking their noses under their forelegs as they laid on the snow. Once Bjorn was certain they had settled in, he pulled the blankets of the tent over his head and lashed them closed. He leaned back against the bales of hay and prepared to wait out the storm.

Damned fool, he thought. Even if Arcalion's lair was out here, what were his chances of finding it? Practically none. He had travelled for over a sevennight, he believed. It was difficult to tell for, as Lars had warned him, Bjorn had left the sun behind a day or two ago.

He had found no game for the last two days, and forage for the deer had been all but nonexistent for three. Soon, he would have to turn back for lack of supplies.

But not before then, Bjorn vowed. If he were to be beaten, he would have to be beaten—he would not surrender. He would not allow his own despair to defeat him. The winter would have to beat him herself.

Bjorn closed his eyes and drifted off to sleep as the snow slowly buried him.

Darkness. Darkness and the weight of earth crushing him down—making him fight for each breath.

Bjorn awoke with a start. He was buried alive! He could feel the weight of the earth pressing down on him. Panic gripped him, and he sat up against the weight pressing down on him.

He could move. He was wrapped in furs and he *could* move. Slowly, he remembered where he was.

"A dream," he told himself, taking a deep breath. "Just a dream."

But he *was* buried. And breathing *was* difficult, mainly because it was so hot inside the blankets. Bjorn shook like a dog climbing out of a stream, trying to dislodge some of the snow that had fallen on him before opening his tent. He had to check on the deer. The weight of snow that was pressing down on him lessened.

Bjorn untied the lashings that held his cocoon of blankets

in place. Cold, crisp air seeped in, helping to wake him further. Bjorn poked his head out and looked around.

The skies overhead were clear, and the light of the stars and the Northern Curtain illuminated the white plain for miles. Of the deer, the sled and even himself there was no sign except for his head poking out of a mound of snow.

"Flaxen, Brazen, Charger?" he called. Three mounds of snow stirred next to him. Three snow-covered heads popped up out of the snow and looked at him. Bjorn laughed.

The deer took their revenge, though. Struggling to their feet, they shook violently, sending clouds of snow flying at Bjorn.

"Hey!" Bjorn objected, still laughing. Brazen stepped forward and nuzzled at his face, sticking her nose into the tunnel of Bjorn's hood.

"Come on," Bjorn said to them, pulling away. "We've got to get this sled out. Hyah!" The deer lined up and began pulling against the sled. The foot of snow covering it made their job difficult but, eventually, the curved nose of the toboggan lifted out of the snow.

"Hyah!" Bjorn called, snapping the reins. The deer pulled harder, and the entire sled lifted out of its white grave and slid to the top of the new snow.

"Whoa!" Bjorn called, pulling back on the reins. The deer stopped and promptly laid down in place. Bjorn shook himself, to dislodge the remaining snow from his blankets. Then he untied the lashings.

He had just begun to fasten his snowshoes when the deer suddenly jumped up.

"What the . . . ?" Bjorn said as the deer began to run. He was reaching for the reins when he saw them.

White-furred wolves with gray mottling leaped to their feet. The animals had half circled them and had been in the process of closing in on their bellies when the deer had finally smelled them.

Bjorn had no time to string his bow. He ripped the spear from its lashings on the side of the sled as the first wolf attacked.

He rammed the spear through the leaping animal's chest.

As the blade penetrated, Bjorn twisted the spear to the left, throwing the dead wolf away from him.

Then the wolves were everywhere. Bjorn could feel their hunger—the ravenous emptiness that had driven them to this desperate attack. Apparently they had found game scarce, too.

Bjorn used the spear as a quarterstaff. There were too many wolves pressing him to give him the opportunity for a thrust.

He caught one animal across the throat with the shaft as it leaped at him. He twisted to the side, and the animal's momentum carried it past him. As it flew past he used the momentum of his twist to slam the butt of the staff into the side of another wolf's head as it ran toward him. The animal fell to the ground, dead or senseless.

Jaws clamped around his ankle. Multiple layers of fur over the leather boots underneath protected him briefly. Bjorn lifted his spear and slammed the butt down on the head of the wolf before it could chew through to his flesh. It fell, releasing its hold on his leg. Bjorn glanced toward the team.

Unable to flee, Charger tried to use his antlers to defend himself and the females. There were simply too many wolves, and all three deer were hampered by the harness.

A gray-furred body slammed into Bjorn, knocking him from the sled. He shoved the shaft of the spear sideways into the wolf's maw, pushing the animal away from him. He brought his knee up under the animal's ribs, knocking the wind from it. He rolled to his knees in time to thrust his spear into another wolf that was closing for the kill.

No more wolves threatened him. The remainder of the pack had circled the team and was in the process of bringing them down. Two wolves slunk away from the battle, badly gored by Charger's horns.

Bjorn cried out in rage and rammed his spear through the side of a wolf as it made to leap at the wounded buck. The wolf howled and snapped at the spear ineffectually. Bjorn ripped his spear from the animal and slammed the butt, like a quarterstaff, across the side of another wolf's head.

Then it was over. With over half the pack dead, the remaining wolves took flight into the night. Bjorn looked down at his team.

All three still lived, but that was a temporary thing.

Charger's neck and forequarters had been savagely wounded. He would be dead in moments. The does were not so lucky. They might live for quite a while longer before they died.

Bjorn knelt by Charger. The buck's eye looked up at him, filled with pain. Bjorn summoned the Power and reached into the animal's mind. Charger was frightened and in pain. Bjorn could feel the animal's trust in him and the hope that he would make it better. He wanted to cry.

Instead, he reached into the animal's mind and found the pain. He quieted it and, with it, the buck's fear. Then he willed the buck's weaker mind to sleep. Charger's eyes drifted closed. Once the animal was asleep, Bjorn drew the knife from his belt and sliced Charger's throat open. At least he would die free of pain.

Bjorn moved to Flaxen. Like Charger, she trusted Bjorn to help her. Bjorn put her to sleep as he had the buck and released her from pain and life as well.

Brazen was different. As Bjorn reached into her mind he could see that she not only trusted him, she loved him. His hand on her muzzle was enough to calm her fears. Bjorn reached into her mind and willed her to sleep before cutting her throat as he had the others.

Then, he wept.

Bjorn loaded the last of the deer meat and wolf pelts onto the sled. The wolves had returned while he was butchering his team, but had kept their distance. Perhaps the wolves up here did not fear men, but Bjorn knew of one pack that had learned to.

He had tried to string his bow and fire at them, but it had shattered when he made the attempt. The cold had weakened it. As it was, the beasts had kept their distance.

Bjorn pulled the straps of the harness over his shoulders and began to walk, dragging the sled behind him. It was still the best way for him to carry his supplies.

As he left the bloody scene behind, the wolves crept into his abandoned camp. The only meat they would find was that on the skinned carcasses of their brothers. Bjorn did not doubt that they would eat it. With their bellies full, they would not bother him again.

The question before him now was whether to press on or turn back. Without his team, it was tempting to turn back. He could be back in the hall within a fortnight. However, if he could travel back, he could travel on. There really was no question, after all.

Bjorn held up the arrow and waited for it to stop spinning. Then he set his course to the north and east.

Chapter
------- Seventeen -----------

BJORN COLLAPSED AT the top of the hill. The effort of dragging the large sled up the hill had exhausted him. He lay there for a moment, his breath rasping in the frigid air.

Once his breath had slowed, he climbed to his knees and began hauling the sled the rest of the way up the hill. He estimated that he had travelled another eight days since losing his team. It was difficult to be certain in the unending night. The only thing he knew for certain was that he had slept eight times.

The wind was stronger on the hilltop. It sucked the warmth from him as it blew past. Bjorn strained his eyes to see in the darkness.

The snowy hills stretched away from him. In the feeble light of the Northern Curtain they appeared to be green. Occasionally, copses of stunted trees filled the valleys.

This terrain had slowed him considerably today. Or was it tonight? Bjorn shook his head—it didn't matter. Day and night had no meaning in this land. It was winter. At least the valleys carried the promise of game, although without his bow, Bjorn had no idea how he might bag it.

Bjorn scanned the horizon. There was nothing. No clue whatsoever to what he sought.

This is hopeless, he thought. *It would be easier to find an ant in a haystack.*

But finding an ant in a haystack wouldn't defeat Valerian. Still, Bjorn had almost exhausted half of his supply of venison. Soon, he would be forced to turn back, whether he had found Arcalion or not.

Perhaps Lars had been right. In the spring, he would at least have light during the day. Not to mention that much of this land would be thawed and game would be much more plentiful. He could return and make another attempt in the spring.

But something told him that spring would be too late. Spring would come to Reykvid long before it came to this land and, with it, Reykvid's armies would begin to march. For now, Valerian would be trapped by the winter in Gavin's palace. With the spring, he would undoubtedly move back into his impregnable tower and even Arcalion might be hard-pressed to root him out of there.

Bjorn replaced the harness around his shoulders and started to back down the side of the hill toward the forest. Before, he had been hard pressed to drag the sled up the hill. Now he had to keep it from dragging him with it as they descended. For now, he would stick to the valleys and the saddles rather than mount the crests of the hills. That would ease his travel somewhat, although it would also lengthen his route.

The sled caught on something behind him. Bjorn turned to see what he had struck. The sled had run into a small snowbank.

Then the snowbank stood up.

Even in the dim light Bjorn could see that the bear's claws were longer than his arm was thick. It opened its mouth to display an impressive array of fangs framed by black lips as it roared a challenge at him.

Why aren't you hibernating? Bjorn thought, even as he hastily threw off the sled harness. The sled, freed of his support, spun and began to slide down the hill. It distracted the bear for a few seconds.

Bjorn ran.

Bears can't run uphill, he thought. He stumbled through the snow. His snowshoes impeded his progress, threatening to send him sprawling.

But then, neither can I, he added. He almost felt the impact when the bear dropped to all fours to pursue him.

Bjorn's heart pounded in his chest. He used the spear as a staff, vaulting himself up the hill. The bear, much better suited for winter travel, quickly gained on him.

Oh, gods! Bjorn thought. Bjorn reached the top of the hill and threw himself forward. He felt the bear's claws swipe just inches behind him before his face hit the snow. He began to slide down the other side of the hill, rapidly gaining speed. His spear made a better sled, though. It went down the hill ahead of him.

Bjorn's snowshoes were pulled from his feet by the dragging snow. He could hear the bear behind him. Bears could run downhill quite well. Fortunately, there were no trees on this side of this particular hill.

Bjorn grabbed his spear and used it to regain his feet. He turned to look behind him. The bear was almost on top of him again. In desperation, Bjorn hurled the spear at the charging bear and turned to run.

The bear roared in rage behind him, spurring Bjorn to run faster. Wonderful—now he had made it mad. The frigid air burned his lungs as his legs pumped through the foot of loose snow on the next hill. Somehow, he reached the top of the next hill ahead of the bear. Without looking back Bjorn hurled himself down the opposite side of the hill, using himself as a human sled again.

He had scrambled halfway up the next hill before he realized that the bear was no longer chasing him. Bjorn glanced back. There was no sign of the bear. He tried to listen over the rasping sound of his own panting. He heard nothing.

Timidly, Bjorn turned back and crawled back up the side of the hill. He reached the top of the hill and listened. Nothing. Cautiously, he peered over into the next shallow valley.

The bear lay at the bottom of the valley, motionless. Surely it wasn't dead? Bjorn watched for a moment longer, but the bear did not move. Cautiously, one step at a time, he made his way down the hill.

The bear was dead. A broken shaft of wood protruded from the bear's left eye. Bjorn's spear.

"I killed a bear," he said aloud. Bjorn grabbed the bloody stub and pulled. With difficulty, the spearhead came out, making a sucking noise as it pulled from the eye socket. The head was bent, but not badly.

"I killed a bear," he said again. "Gods, I hope there's not another one around here."

Well, this *did* solve the problem of finding game, he supposed. Now he had to find his sled, though. And his snowshoes. His clothes had filled with snow during his flight. Some shelter might not be a bad idea, either.

Bjorn sighed and started up the next hill to find his sled. At least there was wood in the next valley for a fire . . .

Bjorn fitted the spearhead onto the new pine shaft he had cut for it. It had taken him two days to butcher the bear, but now he had enough meat to last through most of the winter.

Bjorn peered through the hole he had bored through the side of the shaft to make certain that it lined up with the hole in the tang of the spearhead. It did. With the side of his hatchet, Bjorn drove a wooden peg through the hole. Then he lashed the head into place with leather thongs.

That should do it. The spear had saved his life twice now. Bjorn would hate to be without it in this harsh land.

Bjorn laid the spear on the floor of the snow cave he had dug into the side of the hill. He reached over and turned the spit over the fire. The chunks of bear meat on the spit were almost done.

It was unfortunate that he would have to leave most of the bear behind. He wasn't quite up to hauling the sled around with three score stone of bear meat on it, though. The mere ten stone he was taking with him would have to suffice.

Still, the delay had been nice in some ways. It had been good to be able to get out of his winter clothing in the large cave he had dug. Bjorn took the spit off the fire and laid another stick of pine on the fading flames.

Bjorn pulled a piece of meat off the spit and bit into it. Tomorrow, he would set off again. His prospects were starting to look brighter.

Bjorn stared at the range of mountains ahead of him. Lars hadn't mentioned this. Probably because he hadn't known.

This certainly explained why the hills had been getting progressively steeper and rougher over the last five days. Bjorn had suspected this—he just hadn't been prepared for the sheer . . . immensity of the range. Further south the mountains were . . . gentler. These sharp, craggy monoliths looked completely impassable.

He could follow the range rather than try to cross it. He

would be travelling more north than east if he did so, but Bjorn doubted he could cross the range in the winter. With luck, he would find an obvious pass further north.

With luck.

"Dear, the sentries will call us if they see him," Hilda told her daughter. "Please come inside."

Helga turned to face her mother.

"I'm not cold," she replied.

"Do as your mother says, child," Angus told her sternly.

"I am 'child' no longer," Helga replied. "I am Helga Bjornswyf and I wait for my husband." Angus started to say something, but stammered to silence.

"Angus," Lars interrupted, "I know you're looking through a father's eyes, but take a closer look. Helga is no child."

"You're . . . right," Angus agreed.

"Helga," Lars said, "you may not be a child, but you are now of my hall. There are things to be done, so get back inside and get to work."

Helga looked at him for a moment.

"Yes, my lord," she finally said. Hilda took her by the arm and began to lead her into the lodge.

"What do you think his chances are?" Theodr asked quietly once the women were away.

"Ungh," Lars said. "It has been almost two moons. No one who has been gone this long in the winter has ever returned."

Helga turned back at the door.

"You are wrong, my lord," she called. Theodr and Lars both turned to her in surprise. How had she heard them?

"He lives," she added. "I can tell—here." She held a hand to her bosom. Then she turned and followed Hilda and Freida into the lodge.

"She speaks with the hope of youth," Theodr said once she had entered the lodge.

"Ungh," Lars said again. "She felt him and found him when he was buried twenty feet in earth and snow. I believe her. If anyone could survive out there, Bjorn could."

The wind literally howled through the hills like the spirits that heralded the coming of death. They would herald *his* death if Bjorn could not find shelter soon. There was no lee in any of the hills to protect him. The wind swirled around them and sought him out wherever he tried to find protection.

His hands and feet were already numb. The wind literally tore the warmth from his body. He had to find shelter soon or he would freeze to death.

Or make shelter. But he had been unable to dig in the freezing wind. The blowing snow filled in anything he tried to dig as fast as he could clear it away.

He was almost too weak to pull the sled. He leaned his weight against it, but the wind tried to drive him back as if determined to stop him. He couldn't abandon it.

The sled. He could use the sled. Bjorn slipped the harness from his shoulders. He couldn't feel his hands—he had to work quickly.

With numb fingers he fumbled at the lashes holding his supplies onto the sled. They finally came loose and Bjorn dumped the sled over, spilling everything onto the snow. He could find his supplies later when the storm passed.

Fighting the wind, he lifted the sled sideways over his head and rammed it into the snow. He was able to drive the sled more than a foot into the snow, but that wouldn't hold, not against this wind.

He picked up a large piece of frozen bear meat and used it as a hammer, driving the sled into the ground as he braced it up with his body. It was working. A few inches at a time, the sled sank into the packed snow. Soon, only a foot of the sled remained above the ground.

It didn't protect him from the wind, but now he could dig. Bjorn frantically hurled snow away from the leeward side of the sled. He left either end buried to hold his barrier up against the wind.

He made headway, first a foot, then two, then three into the snow. He stopped at four feet. That would have to do. Bjorn hurled the wolf pelts into the hole, fur side down. His blankets went on top of that. He crawled into the blankets, dragging the bear skin over all of that.

At last, protected from the wind, he could concentrate. Bjorn wrapped the blankets around himself in a cocoon. He knew the blankets were freezing cold, but they almost felt warm after the bitter cold of the wind.

Bjorn pulled off his gloves and opened his coat. His hands were completely numb. He slipped his hands into his coat and under his arms. He shivered uncontrollably.

Focus! he thought. He steadied his breathing and, slowly, his body followed suit. The uncontrollable shivering calmed somewhat. Bjorn tried to raise the Power.

It came, reluctantly. Bjorn turned it inward as warmth. Gradually, ever so gradually, he warmed. As he did, his control improved, yielding still more warmth.

His fingers began to burn as warmth returned to them. Bjorn gasped—the pain was almost unbelievable. Bjorn turned his mind away from it. The pain was only in his mind. It lessened.

Hope I haven't lost any fingers, he thought. *Or toes, for that matter.*

His feet also began to burn. That was good. He hadn't found shelter too late. After a while the pain passed from his fingers. Bjorn pulled his hands out of his coat and began wriggling out of his clothes. Now that the blankets had warmed up, he would be warmer without them.

He examined his fingers and toes by touch. He couldn't feel any severe blistering, and he could move all of them. Thank the gods!

His cocoon was now warm and comfortable. Once again he had beaten the winter.

Bjorn was not certain how long the storm lasted. He knew only that he was ravenously hungry by the time it passed and that he had been forced to leave his shelter to relieve himself several times during the storm. He had been able to stave off thirst by eating the incredibly cold snow of the walls of his pit.

Finally it did end, however. Bjorn emerged from his gravelike prison to find the air calm and the sky clear. The Northern Curtain beckoned to him, reminding him of his quest.

He could not continue now, however. First he would have to regather his supplies, expand his cave and spend a few days recovering from this ordeal. He would need a few good meals behind him before he was ready to press on.

Bjorn turned to haul the sled up another saddle between hills. He had not seen a tree, or been able to build a fire, for days. He had taken to eating the bear meat raw, allowing it to thaw inside his coat. It was not exactly appetizing, but it kept him from starving.

Something about the southern sky caught his attention. Bjorn looked up but couldn't see anything unusual, until he realized that the stars were washing out with the dawn.

Dawn! Bjorn almost wept. He had not realized how much he missed the sun. The sight of dawn breaking over the southern horizon was almost the most beautiful sight he had ever seen.

Bjorn looked around. Shadows filled the valleys between the hills. Shadows! Bjorn dropped the harness and scrambled to the top of the hill. He could see for miles beyond the hills to the flat, icy plains.

He looked northeast to the mountains. In the early morning light, they looked even more imposing than their dimly illuminated silhouettes had suggested. Bjorn turned to face the south and waited to greet the sun.

But dawn never broke. Within an hour, the sky was again fading to black—dawn and twilight rolled into the same event. This was only the first harbinger of spring in this frozen land.

Spring! If spring was arriving here, then the first thaws might well be occurring in Reykvid! Bjorn was almost out of time!

He hurried down the slope to his sled. He had to find the lair soon!

"How soon will we be able to march on Braun?" Valerian asked.

"We should see the first thaw within a moon," Gavin replied. "After that, it will be another moon before the spring planting is over."

"Who cares when the damned planting is over?" Valerian said.

"Lord, if we intend to use militia, we have to wait for the spring planting," Gavin explained.

"And we must use militia," Hans confirmed.

"Why?" Valerian asked.

"Lord, we do not have enough regular forces to take the Raven lands," Gavin began.

"I *know* why we have to use the militia!" Valerian shouted. "Why do we have to wait until the dirt grubbers plant their damned crops?"

You monster! Gavin thought. Valerian would rather let the entire kingdom starve than be inconvenienced by a few sevennights.

"If we move out before the planting, our desertion rate among the militia will be . . . total," Hans explained.

"We have to allow the people their lives, Lord," Gavin added. "Without a base of more or less contented population, we have no power base for future expansion."

Valerian thought for a while.

"I suppose you are right," he finally conceded. "Especially since I am not quite ready to reveal myself."

"Yes, Lord," Gavin replied.

"Two moons, then?" Valerian said.

"At the most, Lord," Gavin assured him.

The days were lengthening, although Bjorn had yet to actually *see* the sun. Even so, it was amazing how just the return of a few hours of twilight added such continuity to his life. Once again, he could count the days.

He debated leaving the hills and travelling on the icy plain. If he did that, however, he would risk missing a break in the mountain range during the long hours of darkness.

Movement out on the plain caught his eye. Bjorn looked out. A herd of deerlike animals moved out on the horizon of the icy plain. What did these creatures live on? There was no forage within days of here.

They were fairly large for Bjorn to be able to see them at this distance. The herd was heading in his direction, generally speaking. No—they were stampeding in his direction. Bjorn tried to catch some sign of what they fled from, but it was too far.

Suddenly the ice erupted underneath the herd. Bjorn saw a huge black-and-white form rise up through the ice in a spray of water. Even from this distance, Bjorn could tell that it was some type of great fish, black on the top and white on the belly.

"Gods above!" Bjorn cried. The monster carried one of the animals aloft in its maw. It rose straight in the air until Bjorn could see its massive flippers and then slid straight back down into the water underneath the ice. The only sign of its passage was a massive hole in the ice to the frothing sea beneath.

Bjorn had considered moving out onto the plain for swifter travel. Now he felt very comforted by the presence of solid earth beneath him. As long as he travelled through the hills, he knew he was still on the land.

Take care, Lars had said. *There are creatures in the water that will come up through the ice to take you.* Now Bjorn knew what the old man had been talking about.

The herd was still headed his way, if anything even faster than before. Bjorn began his descent into the next valley. He did not want to be in their way when they got here.

Bjorn checked his supplies. He had gone through well over half the bear meat. He should turn back now if he wanted to be certain of making it back to the hall.

Bjorn shook his head. To have made it this far only to be forced back now?

"No," he said aloud. He would not turn back. There had to be a pass further north. Either that, or an end to this range. He would press on until he only had one stoneweight of meat remaining.

With the coming of spring, game would be more plentiful. The large deer he had seen over a sevennight ago were proof of that. One of those would feed him as long as the bear had.

He set the harness over his shoulders and followed the range north.

Bjorn finally saw the sun. Ever so briefly, it crept over the tops of the mountains to the south before dipping back down.

He was down to his last two stone of bear meat. This was

close enough to the point at which he had said he would turn back. He had enough meat left to get him back to where he had seen the herd. Hopefully, they would still be near there. If he could kill one of them, he could continue on.

Bjorn cast one last, longing glance toward the north. If only . . .

Something climbed above the mountains beyond the horizon to the north. Bjorn squinted. It looked like a black cloud rising into the sky. Another storm?

No, it looked more like . . . smoke. And where there was smoke, there was fire.

"In the belly of fire," Bjorn whispered. He would *not* turn back. Either he had just found the lair, or he had, perhaps, found some sign of human habitation. In either case, it could be the end of his quest.

Chapter
------- Eighteen ------------

"LORD CHANCELLOR, WE are ready," Gavin informed Valerian.

"Excellent, your majesty," Valerian replied.

The armies were huge. Gavin and Hans jointly commanded a force of five hundred cavalry and archers, two thousand regular infantry and four thousand trained militia.

Ivanel and William would each command a force of two hundred fifty cavalry and archers, one thousand infantry and two thousand five hundred militia. The total combined forces numbered fifteen thousand. Reykvid had never before, in its short history, fielded a force this large.

Behind these forces another thousand infantry and militia would escort a siege train containing twelve large catapults. The combined forces and their supply trains filled the plains north of Reykvid. Unfortunately, assembling this force had left garrison posts throughout the kingdom undermanned.

As Gavin examined his force in the early dawn light, he felt an odd mixture of shame and pride. He was shamed at leading this force in so unjust a cause. He was proud, however, of the army itself. No clan chieftain in the world had ever been able to field such an overwhelming force of arms as the one that now lay under his command.

"Barons," Gavin ordered William and Ivanel, "take command of your forces and begin the march."

"Yes, majesty!" Ivanel and William replied. They turned their mounts and galloped off in opposite directions to join their forces. Ivanel would march his force northeast for half a day before turning east. William would march to the southeast for half a day before doing the same. After half a day's wait, Gavin's army and the siege train would begin the march eastward.

If all went according to plan, Ivanel would bottle up the garrison at Ravenwood while William laid siege to Crowton. This would free Gavin to march between the two strongholds straight to Ravenhall. In four to five days, he would cross the border into Raven lands. Another two days would see him at the gates of Chief Braun's hall. If all went well, the war could be over a moon or two after that, depending on Ravenhall's supplies.

If all went according to plan. With Valerian's Power, there was no reason that it shouldn't. Still, for some reason, Gavin had a feeling that things would not go smoothly for Reykvid this time.

Mavik stepped through the open door of the tavern. This early, there were few patrons, which suited him. A few travellers, such as himself, were enjoying the tavern's less than modest breakfast of buns and wine. Mavik was not here to eat.

He climbed the stairs that led to his room on the top floor. He had been charged a small fortune for those rooms, but the privacy the added expense had granted him had been well worth it. Mavik had brought a few women here to help foster illusions as to the reason he desired such privacy.

He checked the hair that he had wrapped around the door handle and then wedged between the doorjamb and the door. It was undisturbed. He placed his key in the lock and turned, forcing the door open.

The room was austere, worth nowhere near the full Reykvid sovereign a sevennight he was paying for it. One bed, one plain wardrobe and a small, rickety table with a single chair.

A heavy blanket covered what appeared to be a trunk at the foot of his bed. Mavik lifted the blanket to reveal five tall, square cages instead. The birds inside cooed and fluttered their wings as the morning light was finally allowed into their cages.

"Good morning, my pretty birds," he said. "I hope you slept well." Mavik stuck a finger into each of the cages, allowing the pigeons to nibble at his finger, scratching each gently behind the head. Then he opened one of the cages and carefully removed the bird, cooing and clucking at it as he carried it to the room's small table.

Mavik wrote a short message on a small piece of parchment. He carefully rolled the parchment and slid it into a small, leather case. Mavik carefully lashed the case to the bird's leg. He carried the bird to the window and opened the shutter. With a practiced motion, he tossed the bird out the window. It spread its wings and immediately took flight to the east.

Mavik released the other birds with similar, short messages. He closed the cages and laid the blanket back over them. Now he would have to hurry and book passage on the first ship bound for Bruin Cove. It would not be a good thing to still be in Reykvid a fortnight or two from now.

Chief Urall was eating dinner when a guard brought the parchment to him. He wiped his hands and carefully unrolled the tiny message.

"Gavin marches" was all it said. That and a date identifying that the message had been sent today.

"Send messengers to my captains at once!" Urall ordered. "We march in the morning!"

Valther inspected the construction. The outer walls of the keep had reached a full five feet in only one month. The innermost curtain wall had reached almost two feet. It was amazing what could be accomplished when one had almost two thousand men with nothing else to do.

"Rider approaches!" a sentry called. Valther turned to the west. A lone rider approached across the plain. At last! A messenger from Urall!

"My horse!" Valther commanded.

By the time he made it to the stables, his horse was ready. Valther swung up into the saddle and kicked his mount into motion.

"Hyah!" he shouted, spurring the animal to a gallop. Valther galloped down the low hill toward the messenger.

Please, gods, he thought, *let it be the order to march!*

"Lord Valther?" the man asked when Valther rode up to him.

"I am he," Valther acknowledged, reining his mount to a halt. "What word do you bring me?"

"Chief Urall is on his way here," the messenger replied. "He has sent me with orders that you are to have your men ready to march by tomorrow night."

"We will be ready!" Valther assured the messenger. "You may give him my response and my wishes for a swift journey."

"Yes, my lord," the messenger replied.

Valther turned his mount and raced back to the fortress. It was almost a pity—now Valther would never see it completed.

Urall arrived before sunset the next day. He brought two hundred fifty cavalry, a hundred archers, a thousand infantry and two thousand militia. Valther had expected more.

"My lord," Valther said: "Do you think we will be able to liberate my clan with this force?"

"Do not forget the Griffon clan, Valther," Urall replied. "Skald brings forces equal to mine. Besides, I should hope that your clansmen will rise up to aid us. If they are not willing to liberate their own land, why should we force it on them?"

"You are right, my lord," Valther agreed.

"Good," Urall said. "We are to meet Chief Skald at Foxdale. I believe that Gavin's forces have been attempting to refortify it."

"They will not have had much luck with that," Valther noted.

"No," Urall agreed. "You did a fair job of destroying the fortress before you abandoned it."

"The men of Foxdale will join with us," Valther assured Urall. "We should be able to drive Gavin's forces from it with ease."

"Good, because after that, we shall have to take Foxmire," Urall said. "I am not at all confident as to how *that* battle will fare. I understand that Gavin has posted a large garrison there."

"He would have to," Valther said.

"Come," Urall said. "We shall retire to your chambers and discuss our strategy . . . Chief Valther."

Gavin's army had spent the night at Star Hall last night. The capital city of Balder's clan had seemed less than hospitable to his men. Of course, that was to be expected, considering that Balder himself languished in Gavin's dungeons.

For that matter, during their entire march through the Star clan's lands, Gavin had felt more like he marched through an occupied territory than his own kingdom. People avoided them or, when they could not, greeted them with sullen, angry looks.

This was not good. The Raven clan had already withdrawn from the kingdom. If Gavin and Hans were not careful, they would find the Star clan's army at their backs while they were sieging Ravenhall.

In another day, they would be nearing the site of Valerian's tower. Gavin would have to keep the scouts from examining that area too closely, although he wished he could do otherwise. Then at least *someone* would know what was truly happening here.

He was beginning to give up hope on Bjorn. For a time, Gavin had taken heart knowing that Bjorn was alive and free with his knowledge of Valerian. Now it was obvious that the mage had simply gone into hiding. Not that Gavin could blame him. They had all tried to defeat Valerian and failed. What would Bjorn gain from another attempt save for his own death?

Gavin wondered where the hedge mage had gone to ground. In spite of his own disappointment, he hoped that Bjorn was safe . . .

The bitter wind howled outside Bjorn's small cave. Now that spring was beginning to arrive, the storms were becoming more frequent. Bjorn chewed idly at a small piece of raw bear meat. This storm had already lasted two full days and showed no signs of letting up soon.

Now that he had sighted something that could very well be the end of his quest, the delay was maddening. Still, there was little he could do about it—he might as well take advantage of the opportunity to rest.

Rest did not come easy, however. The delay was frustrating not only because he was so close to his goal, but also because he knew that while he sat here, Valerian was advancing his own plans. If only there were some way that Bjorn could know what was happening in Reykvid.

"Men of Foxdale!" Valther shouted to the assembled crowd. "This day we have taken back our homes!"

A cheer rose from the crowd. Valther waited for it to die down. The battle for Foxdale had been an easy one. With its outer walls destroyed and the keep gutted, Gavin's forces had been hard-pressed to defend the ruin. Outnumbered by more than ten to one, the garrison had been defeated quickly.

"But we are not finished!" Valther added. "These invaders still hold our clansmen and our chief's hall. We have powerful allies—Urall of the Bear clan and Skald of the Griffon clan. But we cannot reclaim our land unless all of us are willing to rise up and drive these invaders from our homes!"

Another cheer rose from the crowd, tinged with anger.

"Will you march to Foxmire with me?" Valther shouted.

"YES!" hundreds of throats shouted in unison.

"Will you march to Reykvid with me?" Valther shouted.

"YES!" came the response.

"Will we burn Gavin's castle to the ground?"

"YES!"

"Will we carry his head back to Foxmire on a spear?"

"YES!"

"Then we march at dawn!" Valther shouted.

"Hail Chief Valther!" someone among the militia shouted.

"Valther!" other voices shouted, rapidly growing in number. "Valther! Valther! VALTHER!" Even his regular troops joined in the chant.

"Get the militia organized," Valther told his captains. "I want them armed, bivouacked and counted by sunset."

"Yes, my lord," Locke and Talhaern replied. Valther turned back to the multitude shouting his name. With the spirit of the people this strong, the Fox clan would be free within a fortnight.

The storm had finally broken after three days. Bjorn searched the horizon—there! The column of smoke still stretched into the sky. The smoke seemed no closer, even though Bjorn had travelled for a full day before the storm had hit.

Watch it be somebody's campfire who is also travelling north, Bjorn thought.

That wasn't very likely, though. Bjorn had seen no signs of human habitation since he had left the lodge. Even if there were people up here, Bjorn had found precious little wood with which to build a fire.

If the source of the smoke *was* stationary, and it seemed no closer after a day's travel, then it had to be *very* far away. That also meant that for Bjorn to see it at this distance, it was much too large to be from a chimney or other human source.

No—it was the lair. It *had* to be!

On the morning of the seventh day, Gavin's army crossed the border into the lands of the Raven clan. Messengers had arrived during the night from Ivanel and William. The garrisons at Ravenwood and Crowton were occupied.

With no forces to oppose them, Gavin's army could be at Ravenhall in two days to begin the siege. The siege engines would arrive another eight days after that. Hopefully, by then, Braun would be ready to surrender. Gavin was still sick of bloodshed from the last war.

The walls of Foxmire rose into view as they approached the city. Valther had privately sworn, when he had been forced to withdraw and surrender the city to Gavin's forces, that he would return within the year. He had done so.

The city was barred against him. Valther scanned the walls. Armored men manned the towers and the walls. Gavin must have left a large garrison here indeed.

"Scouts!" Valther ordered. "I want a perimeter sweep around the city and a troop count within the hour!"

"Urall, if you would lead your forces north of Foxmire, and

Skald, if you would lead your forces to the east, we can seal these vermin in," Valther added.

"As you wish," Urall replied.

"With pleasure," Skald added.

The two chieftains rode off to command their forces. Valther turned to his captains.

"Locke, lead half the men to the south," Valther ordered. "Talhaern, you take the other half and seal this gate."

"At once, my lord," his captains replied.

Valther watched as his men made camp around the city. In three more days the catapults would arrive. At that time, they could begin the siege in earnest. Until then, none of Gavin's forces would get out to harass them.

"Malcolm, organize mounted patrols," Valther added. "I don't want to be surprised by any forces they may have hidden out here."

"Yes, my lord," Malcolm replied. Valther's cavalry commander had experienced that problem firsthand. Valther had no doubt he would be thorough in his patrol schedule.

"Station the cavalry between the infantry camps," Valther said. "And have my pavilion set up with the cavalry."

"Yes, my lord," Malcolm replied.

Satisfied with the proceedings here, Valther rode to join Locke at the southern gate. Locke was busily settling his men into position outside the southern gate.

Each captain was now in command of a force of over six hundred regular infantry and one thousand five hundred militia. The two hundred archers had also been split between the two captains, leaving Valther in direct command of only the four hundred cavalry.

Their combined forces numbered almost eleven thousand men. Still, this siege would be costly in time. If they were to meet with the other clans at Reykvid, Valther would have to find some means of shortening the siege. But how?

The scouts rode up to him, interrupting his musings.

"Sir, we count a thousand men on the walls of the city," the lead scout reported.

"Any sign of forces outside the city?" Valther asked.

"Not that we have been able to find."

"Thank you," Valther said. "Lord Malcolm is organizing mounted patrols—report to him."

"Yes, my lord," the scouts replied.

A thousand men on the walls. There were probably half that many that the scouts had not seen, and another five or six hundred in the castle itself. Gavin *had* left a large garrison in Foxmire.

That would only delay him. This was a garrison without support—which gave Valther an idea . . .

Valther rode to the southern gate of the city. Two standard-bearers rode behind him. One carried a white flag of truce, while the other carried the standard of the Fox clan. Urall and Skald rode alongside him with their standard-bearers following behind.

"Hail Foxmire!" Valther called, stopping outside of crossbow range.

"What do you want?" someone shouted back from atop the gate.

"We wish to parley!" Valther shouted back. "Will you send someone out with the authority to treat with us?"

"Wait!" came the reply.

They waited. Valther spent the time examining the repairs to the wall. Gavin had done a passable job of repairing the town wall. From this side, one could hardly tell that it had ever been breached. He wondered if it had been completely repaired, however. Once the engines arrived, this would be the location to attack.

The gate opened and a man rode out with half a dozen mounted guards. One guard carried the standard of Reykvid—the golden eagle on a flag of purple. Another guard carried a plain white flag of truce.

"I am Heinrich, captain of his majesty's guard at Foxmire," the man said. "Who are you and what do you want?"

"I want my city back," Valther replied. "And you know very well who I am."

"Yes, Lord Valther, I do," Captain Heinrich agreed. "However, I am neither prepared nor empowered to surrender Foxmire to you."

"Look around you man," Valther said. "You've got what?

Two thousand men in there? We have eleven thousand against you! If you surrender your forces to me, I give you my word that you, and your men, will be granted safe passage home. Without your armor and weapons, of course. If you refuse to accept my offer, we will not be so gracious when we retake the city."

"We are prepared to hold the city against you," Heinrich replied. "You do not have sufficient force to retake it."

"Perhaps you believe that your king will march to your defense," Valther said. "I assure you, Captain Heinrich—that is a false hope. Your king has already marched against Ravenhall with his entire army. There will be no reinforcements. You are alone."

Heinrich seemed unruffled by Valther's pronouncement. His dark eyes did not blink. Valther would not want to sit across a negotiating table with this man.

"Word has been sent," Heinrich replied flatly. "Until such time as I receive orders otherwise, I intend to hold Foxmire."

Heinrich's standard-bearers were less stoic about the news that their monarch had taken the forces that might have reinforced them on yet another war. They covertly exchanged nervous glances between themselves. Valther imagined that the rumors would spread through Heinrich's forces very quickly tonight.

"As you wish, Captain," Valther conceded. "My engines will arrive in a few days. You have until then to reconsider."

"Until then," Heinrich agreed calmly. Gavin's captain turned his chestnut mare and rode back through the gates of Foxmire. Valther and the other chieftains turned and rode away from the city.

"Good man," Urall noted. "'Tis a shame that he serves that pig, Gavin."

"Yes," Valther agreed. "It is."

The blaring of alarm trumpets jolted Valther from his sleep. What in Hrothgar's name was going on? If Heinrich had led his men from behind the walls to attack a force five times his size, he was a fool!

Valther bolted from his tent, naked. He did not bother taking the time to cover himself.

"What's the alarm?" he asked.

"I don't know, m'lord," the guard replied. Valther turned to his page, who had just emerged behind him.

"My armor!" he shouted.

"Yes, m'lord," the frightened boy replied, hurrying back into the tent. As Valther waited, a messenger ran up.

"My lord!" he said, panting for breath. "There is combat within the city. The southern gate has been opened!"

"Rouse the cavalry!" Valther ordered. The people of Foxmire would not be able to hold that gate open for long.

"Quickly! We ride at once!"

"Yes, my lord," the messenger replied. He ran off to relay Valther's orders. Valther's page arrived with his armor.

Valther quickly donned the leather underlining. As his page tied the thongs behind him, Valther slipped his breastplate over his head with the aid of the guard. The thick, leather coif slipped easily over his head, followed by the heavy padded roll that he wore like a crown beneath his helmet.

The page finished lacing the leathers and began strapping Valther's bronze greaves onto his shins. Valther settled his helmet onto his head and sat down so that the page could put his boots on his feet.

He rose to his feet as a guard led his horse up. Valther buckled his sword belt around his waist and climbed into the saddle. His page handed Valther's shield to him, and Valther turned and rode to the perimeter of the camp.

The first light of dawn was just beginning to illuminate the horizon. Throughout the cavalry camp, men were running to mount their steeds. Quickly, the cavalry formed up.

"To the southern gate!" Valther shouted once they had all formed. He spurred his mount forward, toward Locke's position outside the southern gate.

The hooves of four hundred charging horses churned the earth into a cloud of dust behind them. Despite the speed of their charge, the wall of Foxmire seemed to slip past them far too slowly. How much longer could the men of Foxmire hold that gate?

Locke's camp finally came into view. Locke's men were already roused and formed. In the brightening dawn, Valther could see a flight of arrows arch toward the gate. Locke had ordered his archers to give support to the townsmen. Good thinking—the archers could form and attack faster than any of the other troops.

"Horns!" Valther ordered. He did not want Locke's archers to fire once the cavalry were between them and the gate. Malcolm lifted his hunting horn to his lips and blew. The note echoed across the field.

Valther turned his mount to the left, cutting in toward the wall. With the townsmen attacking the gate, and the archers firing on the walls, Valther was willing to gamble that they would not fall under fire from the defenders. It would enable them to reach the gate much faster.

The rhythm of his mount's pounding hooves almost matched the pounding of his own heart. Valther felt it through his bones and in every fiber of his being as the animal beneath him devoured the distance between him and his goal. The blood that raced through his veins as fast as the ground passed beneath his horse's hooves was more intoxicating than wine.

The gate was still open when they finally caught sight of it. Valther threw his head back and let out a cry of victory—of sheer blood lust. His cry, and his fervor, were taken up by the men around him. Even the beast beneath him seemed to sense the fire in his soul, and redoubled its efforts to reach the gate.

The knot of men battling in the gateway scattered as the charging horses approached. In heartbeats, they were through the gate and in battle.

Valther smashed his sword down onto the helmet of a fleeing man as he rode past. The man flew forward, landed on his face and did not rise. Again, Valther cried out in battle lust. He spurred his horse forward, directly into a knot of almost a hundred men who were attempting to rally against the townsmen's sudden reinforcements.

Their ranks scattered as Valther and over a hundred charging cavalry slammed into them. Valther's mount smashed a man's skull with its hooves as it leaped into the press. His sword drove through another man's chest as Valther raced past. The impact almost pulled him from the saddle, but Valther barely noticed in the heat of his madness.

Within minutes the small group of defenders were either

dead or fleeing. Valther wheeled his horse about, looking for targets.

There were none. This gate had fallen. The townsmen looted weapons from the bodies of Gavin's fallen soldiers. Valther's breath rasped in his chest as he slowly became aware of the toll the battle had taken on him. Locke's infantry were marching through the gate.

"Captain Locke, secure this gate!" Valther ordered. Then he turned and shouted to the cavalry. "We ride! We ride to the west gate!" He wheeled his mount and spurred it down the streets toward the western gate.

It was almost noon by the time the battle was over. Smoke drifted through the streets from the many fires that had raged unchecked throughout the city. The city of Foxmire had been retaken. The surviving defenders had retreated to Foxmire Castle. Valther's forces, along with the men of Foxmire, now surrounded the castle.

Valther collapsed into a chair at a table in a nearby inn. His bronze armor was covered in blood and filth. The innkeeper sat a tankard of ale in front of him. Valther merely nodded to the man before taking a long drink from the tankard.

"The city is retaken?" Urall asked.

"Yes," Valther replied. "All resistance has been crushed. Foxmire is free again."

"Almost," Skald said. "There is still the castle."

"That will fall quickly," Valther assured the other chieftains. "With luck, Heinrich will surrender now that we have destroyed most of his garrison."

"And then we can march on Foxwood and Heathton," Urall said.

"No," Valther said.

"No?" Skald asked. "Are you just going to leave Gavin's forces in your strongholds?"

"I most certainly am not!" Valther replied. "We cannot wait until Foxmire is retaken, however. You and Urall need to march on to Foxwood and Heathton. I can take Foxmire Castle with my own forces. Otherwise, we shall be late for the feasting at Reykvid."

"We have no engines," Skald pointed out. "They will be

stopping here and will not move on until you have taken Foxmire."

"True," Valther agreed, "but you can at least lay siege and force Gavin's men to start using up their supplies. If we do that, then once the catapults arrive, the garrisons will fall quickly."

"Aye," Urall agreed. "Besides, they may surrender as well once they know that Foxmire has fallen."

"I will march to Heathton," Skald said.

"And I will march to Foxwood," Urall said.

"You have my thanks," Valther said. "I could not have liberated my homeland without your aid, my friends."

"Aye, we have forged a powerful alliance," Skald agreed.

"Powerful enough to defy Reykvid," Urall added.

"Yes," Valther replied. "Perhaps it is time for another kingdom to rise in Reykvid's absence." Skald and Urall fell silent. For a moment no one spoke, the three chiefs simply looking at one another carefully.

"Who would . . . *lead* this . . . kingdom?" Urall finally asked.

"I do not know," Valther admitted. "But I know where the palace would be. The foundations for it have already been laid."

"Burton," Urall mused aloud.

"It is more or less centrally located to our three clans," Valther pointed out.

"We plan too far ahead," Skald said. "We are too drunk on battle and ale to speak of such things."

"Aye," Urall agreed. "We should concern ourselves with this war before we consider other, larger tasks." The glance that Urall and Valther exchanged said that this discussion was far from over, however.

"When shall we march?" Skald asked.

"In the morning," Valther replied.

Chapter
------- Nineteen -----------

RAVENHALL WAS A forbidding sight. The fortress sat atop a sheer stone pillar that looked as if some subterranean giant had thrust it up through the earth itself. Snow still clung stubbornly to some of the upper, shaded slopes of the crag.

In the past, by some massive undertaking, a narrow road had been carved up the side of the bluff, snaking back and forth across its face as it climbed upward. The outer wall of the fortress was a good fifty feet below the top of the bluff. The wall followed the uneven contours of the bluff, snaking up and down, in and out like the world serpent itself. Its battlements loomed out over that treacherous road, guaranteeing that an approaching enemy would never make it to the top.

The inner wall and the keep sat atop the bluff. These structures were, in themselves, not that imposing. It was their location that made them impregnable, not their design. Overhead, the black birds that gave the fortress its name dove and circled. Gavin had heard that to kill a crow in Ravenhall was punishable by death.

The city that hugged the base of the crag was another story. Only a low outer wall surrounded it. The farmhouses that dotted the rolling hills surrounding the city were abandoned. Presumably, the local farmers had fled to the city for safety.

Even as lightly defended as the city itself was, assault was out of the question. Gavin had no doubt that Braun's catapults, from their lofty vantage, could strike any point in the city below. From that height, a few bowlfuls of iron darts would decimate any force attacking the city. There was only one tactic that could possibly work here—starvation.

"Have the men begin the earthworks around the city,"

Gavin said. "I want the inner rampart just within our engine range from the wall. Order the cavalry to begin mounted patrols."

"Yes, majesty," Hans replied.

"Is this the only way, majesty?" Valerian asked.

"I fear so, Lord Chancellor," Gavin replied. "If we assault the city, Braun can fire his engines against us."

"How long will it take to starve them into surrender?" Valerian asked.

"That depends on many things," Gavin said. "How many supplies they have, how many people are behind those walls and how strong their will is. If they force us to starve them all to death, this siege could last until midsummer."

"So, their supplies are the key point?" Valerian asked.

"Yes," Gavin replied.

What are you planning now, you monster? Gavin wondered.

Braun watched from the highest tower of the keep. He had had no idea that Gavin could raise such an enormous army. Gavin's army on the hills below numbered seven thousand strong.

If the reports from Ravenwood and Crowton were accurate, another force of four thousand men sat at each of those strongholds. That made Gavin's army fifteen thousand strong— more warriors than the city had men.

As Braun watched, Gavin's men began entrenching around the city. Gavin had wisely decided not to press an assault against the city. That was unfortunate. Braun's catapults could fire just outside the wall from this height. A few volleys could have done severe damage to any force assaulting the walls.

But no, Gavin was going to lay siege and probably maraud the countryside for supplies. Given their supplies, the city could hold out for three fortnights and the castle for twice that long. Braun smiled.

Gavin did not have that long. Within a fortnight, more likely within a sevennight, Gavin should receive word that Valther, Urall and Skald had invaded his holdings in the Fox clan. Raising this force *must* have taxed Gavin's resources.

Chances were that his kingdom was not defended heavily enough to withstand a united attack from three clans to the west and two from the east.

Gavin would be forced to withdraw in order to march to Reykvid's defense. When he did, the Raven clan would follow—from a cautious distance. On the field, Gavin's army could destroy Braun's entire garrison in a single battle. At Reykvid, however, there would be five other clans to aid them. Six if the Star clan rose against the tyrant. Gavin could not stand against all of them.

This siege was going to cost Gavin more than it cost Braun. Much more.

Gavin rode what would eventually be the safe zone between the two trenches, inspecting the work of his men. The ditch and rampart on the inside would defend against sorties from Ravenhall. The ditch and rampart on the outside would defend against any forces that might come to Braun's aid.

With the work force available to him, namely four thousand militia, it would take two fortnights or longer to finish the earthworks. Gavin would have to conscript additional labor from the local populace in order to speed up the work. He would talk to Hans about sending out the cavalry to gather additional labor.

As yet, the trenches were only a little over two feet deep and the ramparts only a foot high. At this depth they afforded little to no defense. Once they were finished, however, nothing would be able to enter or leave Ravenhall. At that point, Braun's fate would be sealed.

Just as my own is, Gavin thought. He stopped. The two guardsmen who rode the perimeter with him stopped as well. Gavin turned and looked to the east as the sun climbed above the horizon.

Gavin's fate had been sealed the moment Valerian had been found in that crypt. All of their fates had been.

But Bjorn had escaped his fate—had broken free of Valerian's hold. Gavin could not hope for that. He had no power with which to combat Valerian's sorcery. He could only obey.

Gavin thought of Bjorn often these days. Even now, three months after Bjorn had escaped Valerian's hold, Gavin still hoped that he was out there, somewhere, working to overthrow the MageLord.

Rationally, he knew that Bjorn had probably fled for his life. After all, Valerian had thoroughly demonstrated the futility of their opposition of him. Still, that hope stubbornly persisted, and Gavin could not help but cling to it. After all, it was all he had left.

I need you, my friend, he thought. *Do not forget us.*

Another five days of travel through the frozen hills had brought Bjorn noticeably closer to the pillar of smoke. It was definitely much too large to be a campfire.

Today, however, something else had joined the pillar of smoke on the horizon. Another bank of storm clouds swept in from the north. No doubt the storm brought even colder weather with it, as well as wind and snow. The spring storms in this region were bitter hell.

Bjorn guessed that the storm would hit before noon. He had best start preparing shelter now. Bjorn walked to the bottom of the hill, leaning back against the weight of the sled as it tried to pull him down too quickly.

At the bottom, he dropped the harness and took his axe and shovel from the sled. The wind would come mainly from the north, so he began to dig his cave into the southern side of the next hill.

Bjorn supposed that he should be grateful. He had enjoyed five unbroken days of good, almost warm, weather. However, winter still had a few more victories to claim before spring truly arrived here. Bjorn should not begrudge her her reluctance to retreat.

Even so, each storm gave Valerian that much more time to solidify his position. Made it that much more difficult to destroy him.

But he *would* be destroyed. Bjorn swore to that. No matter how firmly entrenched Valerian became, Arcalion *would* be powerful enough to destroy him. For if he wasn't, then there was no hope left.

Valther rode up to the gates of Foxmire Castle with his standard-bearer. The siege of the castle had lasted four days now. He had sent Skald's and Urall's engines on to Foxwood and Heathton, as they were too small to reach the outer wall of Foxmire without coming under fire themselves.

"Halt!" a guard called from atop the gate. Valther reined his mount to a stop.

"I wish to speak with Heinrich!" Valther shouted.

"Wait!" the guard replied.

After a moment, Heinrich appeared at the top of the gatehouse.

"What do you want, Valther?" Gavin's captain asked.

"I have come to give you one final opportunity to surrender," Valther replied. "You must realize by now that your king is not coming to your aid. Foxwood and Heathton have fallen. Surrender to me and you will be granted safe passage from my lands."

Foxwood and Heathton had not yet fallen, but Heinrich had no way of knowing that. Even so, those strongholds would fall quickly as soon as the engines arrived, so it was almost true.

"I cannot accept," Heinrich said.

"Captain," Valther said, "I have over five thousand men. You cannot hope for victory or rescue. Do not throw the lives of your men away for naught. The Fox clan has already retaken its lands. Holding this castle accomplishes nothing."

"I will not surrender," Heinrich repeated.

"So be it," Valther replied. He turned and rode away from the gate.

"Rats?" Braun asked.

"Yes, m'lord," Oslaf, Braun's castellan, replied. "Somehow, a plague of rats has managed to gain access to the storerooms."

Braun frowned. Those storerooms were buried deep in the catacombs beneath the castle. They had been carved from solid rock and fitted with tightly sealed doors.

"How?" Braun asked.

"I do not know, my lord," Oslaf replied. "I have guards

working in the storerooms to salvage what supplies have not been fouled. Once the supplies have been moved, we should be able to find out how they've gotten in."

"How much have we lost?" Braun asked.

"It is difficult to say . . ." Oslaf began.

"*How much?*" Braun shouted, slamming his hand on the table and rising to his feet. Oslaf recoiled back a step.

"A-at least half, my lord," Oslaf stammered.

Half! Braun thought. He sat down. Half of his supplies—gone.

"I . . . am sorry, my friend," he said to Oslaf. "'Tis not your fault."

"I understand, m'lord," Oslaf replied. "All of our lives depend on those supplies."

"No," Braun said. "Our lives depend on our allies now. They have to draw Gavin away before he starves us into submission."

"Yes, m'lord. I am sorry, m'lord. This *is* my fault."

"No, Oslaf," Braun assured him. "I suspect the blame for this lies with Gavin's new master."

"You mean . . . ?"

"Aye," Braun replied.

Valther watched as the massive engine was rolled into place. It had taken the city's craftsmen three days to build this device. Still, if it had the range Valther needed, it was worth the wait.

A massive arm rose straight up twenty feet from the pivot to a tiny bowl. The bowl was actually as large as that on any of the engines Valther had seen before, but it looked small against the bulk of this enormous engine.

Below the pivot, on a shorter arm, sat a counterweight of almost two hundred stone. A crossbar across the pivot supports would act as a stop, as would heavy timbers behind the counterweight.

When the long arm was winched back, the heavy counterweight would rise on the shorter arm. When the chains were released, the missile should be fired with more force than any engine Valther had ever seen. Assuming that the whole thing didn't simply tear itself apart.

If it did work, this engine would also be useful at Smithton, when Valther invaded the lands of the Fire Sword clan on the way to Reykvid. At Reykvid itself, it could be invaluable.

Finally the catapult was in position. The engineers inserted handles into the two winches on the back of the engine. Three men manned each winch and began lowering the arm of the engine. With agonizing slowness, the bowl lowered.

"How long is this thing going to take to load?" Valther asked.

"Quite some time, apparently," Locke replied.

"Quite some time" turned out to be an understatement. It took the engineers more than the second part of an hour to completely lower the bowl. The handles were removed from the winches, and four stout men lifted a stone into the bowl.

Everyone moved away from the engine except the lead engineer and two men with hammers. As Valther watched, the engineer raised his hand and the two men raised their hammers. The engineer dropped his hand, signaling the hammermen.

The catapult bar slammed up against the stop so fast that Valther barely saw it move. The entire back of the engine jumped like a spooked horse, throwing flat the three men standing on it.

Valther looked toward the wall in time to see the missile sail neatly over the wall and slam into the keep behind it. From here it was difficult to tell if there had been any damage, but Valther did not see how there could not be.

"I . . . think we . . . overshot a little," Locke said quietly.

"Aye," Valther agreed. He looked back to the engine. Men had gathered around the back of the engine, talking animatedly. Valther spurred his horse and rode over to the engineers.

"What is it?" he asked.

"We've busted one of the wheels, m'lord," the lead engineer replied.

"Get the wheel replaced and then get some more weight on the back of this thing," Valther ordered.

"Yes, m'lord," the engineer replied.

"How long will it take to repair?"

"The rest of the day, m'lord," the engineer told him. "We can try it again tomorrow."

"I want it fixed by sunset! We will try it again *tonight*!"

"Y-yes, m'lord," the engineer stammered.

Valther rode back to where his captains waited.

"We might as well return to the inn," he told them. "The engine will not be able to fire again before sunset—they broke a wheel."

"Is that the only damage?" Talhaern asked.

"It would seem so," Valther replied.

"I would say that our new engine is a success," Locke observed.

"Yes," Valther agreed. "Have the craftsmen start on another one immediately."

Gavin rode along the perimeter of the entrenchment, studying the work. The cavalry had gathered up almost a thousand locals to supplement Gavin's work force. Now the trench on each side of the safe zone was over five feet deep. The ramparts inside those trenches had each climbed to almost three feet in height.

At that height, the earthworks provided some measure of defense. That was good. After what Valerian had told them in council this morning, they would probably be needing that defense much sooner than they had expected.

The MageLord had conjured forth a swarm of rats to destroy Ravenhall's supplies. According to Valerian, over half of Braun's food supplies had been destroyed in the last three days.

Driven to hunger twice as fast as expected, there was no doubt that Braun's forces would soon be desperate enough to attack Gavin's position. If Gavin could not hold them here, they would escape into the countryside and take to banditry against him. Once that happened, it could take years to ferret them all out, if ever.

Almost as if in echo to his thoughts, the sound of horns reached him from the southern camp. Gavin wheeled his mount and sank his spurs into the animal's sides. The horse leaped forward into a gallop.

The horns sounded again. Surely Braun was not attacking

already? Perhaps he had decided to break out now, before Gavin's earthworks were complete? Braun had not struck Gavin as being that easily cowed when he and his father had negotiated the Raven clan's entry into the kingdom last year.

Gavin and his guards finally rode into the large circular area of the southern camp. There was no sign of attack. Gavin rode up to his pavilion and dismounted. He barely noticed the pages who took his horse as he dismounted and hurried inside.

"What is the alarm?" Gavin asked.

"A messenger has arrived from Foxdale," Hans replied.

"Foxdale?" Gavin asked.

"Aye," Valerian replied gravely. The MageLord seemed filled with cold fury.

"Valther," Gavin stated, turning to the messenger.

"Yes, my lord," the messenger replied. "Chief Valther has retaken Foxdale."

"There wasn't much there to retake," Gavin replied. "He'll not have an easy time holding it against Heinrich."

"He is not alone, majesty," the man replied. "Chief Urall and Chief Skald have also led forces into Fox clan lands in his support. Their numbers are estimated at eight thousand men in all."

Gavin collapsed into a camp chair at the council table. It had begun. The Fox, Bear and Griffon clans had never been overly close. Yet now they had united against a common enemy—Reykvid.

"Is that all?" Hans asked when Gavin remained silent.

"Yes, general," the messenger replied.

"You may go," Hans told him. The messenger bowed to Gavin, turned and left.

"Eight thousand men," Gavin said quietly.

"How can we salvage this situation?" Valerian asked.

"The first thing we must do is return to Reykvid," Hans replied.

"No!" Valerian shouted.

"Lord, we must!" Gavin insisted. "We left Reykvid virtually undefended to assemble this army. Valther could almost march unopposed straight to the palace!"

"This news is nine days old," Hans pointed out. "Foxmire itself could have fallen by now."

"Not likely," Gavin replied. "I'm certain that Heinrich could hold out against Valther for longer than a sevennight."

"True," Hans agreed.

"If we retreat, Braun will attack us from behind!" Valerian said.

"I hope he is that stupid," Hans replied.

"I beg your pardon, general?" Valerian said coldly.

"Lord," Gavin said, "Braun has only two thousand men in that fortress, at most. We have enough *infantry* to defeat him without considering the rest of our force. If he attacks us, we simply have to turn long enough to destroy him. I agree with Hans. I would hope that he is stupid enough to attack us if we retreat."

"What of Ivanel and William?" Valerian asked.

"They cannot hold their positions with Braun free to attack them," Gavin replied. "They shall have to retreat as well."

"So we have to pull out completely," Valerian grumbled. He sounded for all the world like a spoiled child robbed of some treat.

"Otherwise we stand to lose everything, Lord," Hans assured him.

"Very well," Valerian said quietly. "See to it."

"Yes, Lord," Gavin replied.

Gods, help us, he thought. It would take a miracle to save Reykvid now. Or a MageLord.

"My lord!" Oslaf said, rushing into Braun's chambers. "My lord, the invader retreats!"

"Gavin is withdrawing?" Braun asked, hardly daring to believe it.

"Yes, my lord!" Oslaf assured him. "His men are breaking camp even as we speak."

Braun breathed a sigh of relief. Word had finally reached Gavin of the peril his kingdom faced—long before Ravenhall's supplies had started to run low.

"Shall I have the men prepare to march?" Oslaf asked.

"No," Braun replied. "I do not want to set foot outside this fortress until Gavin leaves my lands. His force could crush my army like an egg. We shall wait for two days before we march."

"Yes, my lord."

"I want a feast tonight, Oslaf," Braun ordered. "Let the men know that we are through with lean rations for a while."

"Yes, my lord!" Oslaf replied, smiling. Braun smiled too, as Oslaf turned to leave, but it was a cold, vicious smile. Gavin's troubles were just beginning. . . .

The army was ready to move out two hours before sunset. Gavin turned once more to look upon Ravenhall. If the clans were rising against them, Gavin had no doubt that he would be facing Braun again very soon.

Gavin spared another look at the concentric ramparts that stretched around the city. It was an impressive sight. No doubt the next time Gavin saw Ravenhall, Braun would have started another wall there, now that Gavin had dug the foundations for him.

Assuming Gavin lived long enough to see Ravenhall again.

"The men are ready to march, majesty," Hans told him. Gavin turned away from Ravenhall and looked south, toward Reykvid.

"Give the order," he said.

Chapter
-------- Twenty -------------

BJORN STUDIED THE mountain. Due to the storms, it had taken him a fortnight to reach this point. However, he was now certain that he had found Arcalion's lair.

Unlike the jagged peaks which it sat among, the volcano was an almost perfectly round cone. From its crater a thin wisp of smoke rose into the air. Smoke also rose from various vents on the slope itself, rising to merge with the larger column. Despite its obvious activity, the slopes of the volcano were covered in snow and ice.

"In the belly of fire, surrounded by ice," Bjorn mused. This place certainly fit that description.

The only problem now was how to reach it. There were two lesser peaks between him and the volcano. There was no way he could pull the sled up the slopes that led to the saddles between the peaks.

So he would have to abandon the sled. If this *was* the lair, he would either leave here with Arcalion or not at all. If it was not, he could come back for the sled. It certainly wasn't as if someone was going to steal it, after all.

He would have to fashion a pack from the wolf pelts in which to carry his supplies. He could use the sled harness for straps and the lashes from his tent for stitching. That would enable him to at least carry *some* food. Then he could try to scale the saddles on foot.

First, though, he would have to make shelter for the night. The sun was just kissing the peaks of the range on its way down. When it was gone, the temperature would plummet. He had best have his cave finished by then.

With a sigh, Bjorn retrieved his axe from the sled.

*   *   *

The messenger arrived just after midnight. Ivanel lit the lantern and sipped a goblet of mulled wine, blinking the sleep from his eyes.

"Send him in," he told the guard.

The man stepped into the tent and handed Ivanel a letter, sealed with Gavin's signet. This had the feel of grave news. Ivanel broke the wax seal and unfolded the parchment as the messenger bowed and left his tent.

Indeed, this *was* grave news. Urall and Skald had joined forces with Valther and had retaken Foxdale. No doubt they were, even now, besieging Foxmire. According to Gavin, their force numbered eight thousand men.

Gavin's orders were quite clear. Ivanel was to withdraw from Ravenwood tomorrow afternoon and rendezvous with Gavin at the border. Gavin would meet the siege train tonight and destroy the remaining engines before continuing on. Ivanel was to destroy the engines in his camp before withdrawing. Ivanel set the missive on his small council table.

Gavin was right. With eight thousand men, Valther could conceivably march straight to Reykvid unopposed. This was of grave concern to Ivanel. Valther would have to march through Ivanel's lands to do so.

"Guard!" he shouted.

"My lord!" the guard replied, stepping into the tent.

"Rouse the camp and summon my captains," he ordered. "I want the men ready for combat within the quarter hour!"

"Yes, my lord!" the guard replied, hurrying to carry out his orders. Soon trumpets were blaring throughout the camp. Ivanel rose from the table and began to prepare as well.

He did not doubt that Braun would join Valther at Reykvid. If that were so, this garrison would not be among those besieging the palace. Ivanel had until noon to destroy it.

Bjorn tied the last leather thong and examined his handiwork. It had taken him almost the entire day to fashion the pack. He slipped it on over his shoulders. It felt comfortable.

Good. Now all that was left was to pack it. He removed the pack and placed his last stoneweight of bear meat into it.

Beside the meat, he placed a small bag of gold—a gift for Arcalion. On top of all that went two of his remaining wolf pelts—he might need them to line his shelters.

He laced the flap of the pack shut and slipped the handle of his axe through a small loop of thong he had left for that purpose. Then he slipped the pack back over his shoulders. It still felt comfortable. The weight settled easily onto his shoulders.

Bjorn took his spear and crawled from his snow cave. The volcano looked exactly as it had yesterday. A gust of cold wind pushed at Bjorn from the north. He turned to look behind him.

Silver-black clouds rolled in from the north, more menacing than any he had seen yet. Bjorn looked back to the saddle and back to the storm clouds. They were almost upon him.

"No!" Bjorn shouted. This could not happen—not when he was within sight of the lair! Not after everything he had gone through to get here. It could not! He hurled his spear to the ground.

"No!" Bjorn shouted again. "Nooo!"

Ivanel watched as the two remaining engines fired. One hurled stones at the outer wall of the fortress. The other hurled barrels of flaming oil over the wall itself. The third catapult had been destroyed before Ivanel's engineers had managed to silence Ravenwood's engines.

Black smoke rose from behind the wall. Ivanel's forces waited to storm the breach as soon as Ivanel's engines brought down the wall.

The engineers were doing well. Not even a quarter hour had passed before the engines fired again. More oil sailed over the wall.

"Have number two switch to stones and target the wall," Ivanel ordered. "There's nothing left to burn behind it."

"Yes, my lord," Captain Eadgil replied. Soon the engines fired again. The wall was weakening, but not quickly enough. The sun had risen over an hour ago. In less than another three they would have to withdraw to meet Gavin at the border. Ivanel spurred his mount and rode over to the engines.

"Is this the best you miserable whoresons can do?" he

shouted. "Put your backs into those winches or I'll stake you to the engines myself when we leave!"

"I want fresh crews," he told Eadgil. "Switch them out on the next firing. Make certain that they understand the urgency of their work and what I will do to them if they fail me."

"Y-yes, my lord," Eadgil replied.

"Is the supply train ready to march?"

"Yes, my lord," Eadgil assured him.

The next shots were fired much more quickly. The two missiles slammed into the outer wall. A portion of the battlements crumbled and fell to the ground. Excellent; another few shots would breach the wall.

More of the upper wall crumbled away on the next firing. Still, the wall was not yet breached. The time between volleys seemed to crawl, but Ivanel knew that was merely his own anxiousness.

"Strike lower on the wall," Ivanel ordered. "Maybe now we can shake it down."

"Yes, my lord," Eadgil replied. He personally rode to deliver Ivanel's orders.

The missiles flew, striking much lower on the wall. As Ivanel watched, the top of the wall swayed and crumbled. With a sound of crumbling stonework and splintering wood, the top five feet of the wall crashed to the ground. It was still not enough, but the next volley should do it.

"Archers!" Ivanel shouted. "Advance and lay down covering fire!"

His orders were relayed, and the archers advanced forward behind their mantlets. Soon they were assailing the wall with wave after wave of arrows.

The catapults fired again. Ivanel dared not breathe as the missiles sailed toward the wall. Would they breach this time?

They did. The missiles struck, and the entire remaining section of wall groaned and began to lean back. With a groan, at first, like a wounded bear, and then with a roar of crashing masonry, the entire section of wall collapsed back into the courtyard.

"Charge!" Ivanel shouted. Trumpets relayed the command, and his entire force of infantry and militia charged the breach.

It was no contest. A garrison of three hundred against over

three thousand men. Within the hour, the garrison had been slaughtered and the castle was in flames.

Ivanel had lost fewer than a hundred men in the assault.

"Captain, get the men ready to march," Ivanel ordered.

"Yes, my lord," Eadgil replied.

Valther rode through the open gate of Foxmire Castle. Less than an hour ago, his new engine had breached the outer wall of the castle. No sooner had he done so than Heinrich had taken down Gavin's flag, replacing it with the white flag of surrender.

Part of him was angry over that deception. Captain Heinrich had planned to surrender all along. He was only delaying Valther here as long as possible before bowing to the inevitable.

Another part of him had to respect the man. Despite the fact that Valther would be completely within his rights to have the man executed, Heinrich had defied him to the end, buying every moment that he could for his king. It was a pity that a man of such honor should serve a king with so little.

"Lord Valther," Heinrich said when Valther and his guard rode through the gate. "We surrender Foxmire Castle to you and . . . place ourselves at your mercy."

Valther could see how difficult the words were for the captain. Heinrich lifted his scabbarded sword flat in both hands up to Valther. Valther reached down and took the sword from Gavin's captain.

"I accept your surrender, captain," he said. "As I promised, you and your men shall be given safe passage from my lands. That is, any of you who want it."

"Lord?" Heinrich said.

"You heard right, Captain," Valther replied. He wheeled his horse and rode out where the defenders could see him.

"Men of Reykvid!" he shouted. "I have accepted your captain's surrender! Any of you who wish it shall be granted safe passage from my lands."

"However, this war has taken a toll on my clan," he continued. "Any of you who will take up arms and join with me shall be accepted as a full member of my clan."

"What?" Heinrich shouted. "No! Any man who accepts this offer will be guilty of treason against Reykvid!"

"Treason?" Valther asked. "Is it treason to oppose a man who murders his father with the help of a MageLord to take his throne? Is it treason to oppose a man who conquers by the strength of black sorcery? Valerian used his foul Art to spread plague and pestilence among my men."

"Men of Reykvid, it is not your king I am asking you to turn on—it is this monster, Valerian. Who among you wants to serve a MageLord?"

Valther turned back to Heinrich.

"Will you join with me, captain?" he asked.

"Never!" Heinrich replied.

"Were you at Foxshire, captain?" Valther asked. Heinrich looked away.

"Were you!" Valther asked.

"No!" Heinrich replied. "No. I . . . was not."

"But you know of it?"

"Aye," Heinrich replied quietly.

"Would Magnus have ordered that slaughter?" Valther asked.

"No," Heinrich said. "He would not."

"Would the Gavin you thought you knew have ordered that?"

"No."

"It was not Gavin's order," Valther assured him. "It was Valerian's. Will you join me?"

Heinrich looked back to Valther. The pain in the captain's eyes was not surprising. Valther knew he was a man of honor. That honor now tore him in two directions.

"Yes," Heinrich replied. "I will."

The sun was beginning to sink toward the horizon. Gavin looked to the north and south. Soon they should rendezvous with Ivanel and William, but he could see no sign of them as yet.

One of the cavalry rode toward them. Beside him rode a messenger.

More bad news, Gavin thought.

"Majesty," the messenger said. "I have grave news . . ."

"Hold," Gavin ordered. He turned to the knight.

"Thank you," he told the man. "You may go."

"Yes, majesty," the man replied. He turned and rode away.

"Your news?" Gavin asked. He did not want rumors flying through his camp.

"I have ridden from Foxmire, almost nine days hence," the man said. "Chief Valther has laid siege to the city."

Gavin nodded. That was no surprise, given yesterday's news.

"Urall and Skald were with him?" he asked.

"Yes, majesty," the messenger replied. "Their force is almost ten thousand strong."

"Ten thousand?" Valerian asked. "Last night, we heard he had only eight thousand men."

"I imagine he is gathering militia from among his clansmen," Gavin said. "Still, this news comes as no surprise. We knew that he intended to retake Foxmire."

"Yes, majesty," Valerian replied.

Arik, Gavin's chief scout, rode up to them.

"Majesty!" he said. "We have sighted Baron William and his army."

"Good; we shall make camp here," Gavin said. "Has there been any sign of my uncle?"

"Not yet, majesty," Arik replied. "Ravenwood is a bit further than Crowton, however."

"True," Gavin agreed. "He should arrive soon. Have the scouts range out to find him."

"Yes, majesty," Arik replied. The scout rode away to carry out Gavin's orders.

"Ravenwood has been destroyed, majesty," Ivanel reported.

"Destroyed?" Gavin asked. Ivanel had joined them shortly after sunset. His men had looked weary. Now Gavin knew why.

"Yes, majesty," Ivanel replied. "I received your orders last night and immediately began an assault on the fortress. We shall not have to worry about facing *that* garrison in Reykvid."

"What were your losses?" Gavin asked.

"Fewer than a hundred men, majesty," Ivanel replied.

"Excellent," Gavin said. "Well done, uncle."

"Yes," Valerian agreed. "If only the same had happened at Crowton."

"Forgive me, Lord," William said.

"No matter," Valerian assured him. "You were not ordered to assault the fortress."

"Yes, Lord," William replied.

"Has there been any further word?" Ivanel asked.

"Yes," Gavin replied. "Valther laid siege to Foxmire nine days ago. He has levied militia from among his clansmen. His force, combined with Urall and Skald, now numbers ten thousand."

"I warned that the clans would unite against us if we were not careful," Hans said. "If Braun marches against us as well, that will be another three or four thousand men against us."

"It does not matter if they march against us with twice that," Valerian said. "Once they have all gathered at Reykvid, they will die for this outrage."

"Yes, Lord," Hans replied.

Gods, help us, Gavin thought.

Gavin was uneasy as he led the army back to Reykvid. If Valther had laid siege to Foxmire nine days ago, he would be almost ready to march on the Fire Sword clan by the time Gavin could reach Reykvid. Once the city of Foxmire had fallen, which it might have already, Valther could split his force to attack Foxwood and Heathton while still retaining enough men to besiege Foxmire Castle.

The question would be whether or not Valther felt confident enough to attack Reykvid itself. Ten thousand men was a sizeable force. It just might give him the confidence he needed to consider such a thing.

Then there was the matter of timing. It could have merely been coincidence that Valther had attacked at a time when it would take nine days for word to reach Gavin. He suspected otherwise. Valther almost certainly had spies in Reykvid that had informed him of Gavin's absence. It was even possible that he and Braun had been in communication. If he had been assured of Braun's support, he would almost certainly invade.

"Majesty," a guard said, riding up to Gavin's entourage. "A messenger has arrived from Wolfden."

"Wolfden?" William asked. He and Gavin exchanged anxious glances. If Wolfden had fallen under attack . . .

"Yes, your grace," the guard replied.

"Send him to us," Gavin ordered.

"Yes, majesty."

"Wiglaf?" William said when the messenger arrived.

"Greetings, your grace," Wiglaf replied. "Majesty, I bear the gravest news."

"Tell us," Gavin ordered.

"Seven days hence Wolfshire was attacked by the clan Badger," Wiglaf reported. "At the same time, Pelton fell under siege by the forces of the clan Elk. Each force numbered over four thousand men."

"Four thousand!" William exclaimed.

"Yes, your grace," Wiglaf replied. "I fear they are almost certainly at Wolfden by now. Our garrisons are weak and unable to repel them."

And you blame me for that, Gavin thought. And rightly so. It was this campaign against Ravenhall that had left the kingdom so defenseless that clans thought safely subdued could not only wrest free from Reykvid's control, but could then turn and attack. And, once again, the timing was too perfect. For the Elk and Badger clans to already be in William's lands, they must have risen up within days of Gavin's departure for Ravenhall.

"This is no coincidence," General Hans said, echoing Gavin's thoughts.

"Indeed not," Gavin said. "There must be coordination here. That puts almost twenty thousand men against us."

"Until Braun marches with them," Hans pointed out.

"Wiglaf, I wish you to take orders back to Reykvid for me," Gavin said. "I will send a small cavalry escort with you."

"Of course, majesty," Wiglaf replied.

"We will make our best speed to Reykvid, but I fear we will arrive too late to aid Wolfden," Gavin added. "However, we shall liberate your lands at the first opportunity."

"Yes, majesty," Wiglaf replied.

"Hans, order a halt," Gavin ordered. "Have the men

prepare their noonday meal while I pen the orders Wiglaf is to carry."

"Yes, majesty," Hans acknowledged.

Valther's scouts returned with the good news that Urall and Skald both awaited him at Heathton. Heathton had been liberated and, if Urall was at Heathton, it could only mean that Foxwood had been retaken as well. It would still be two hours before the army reached Heathton.

"Captain Locke, you are in command," Valther said. "March the army to its rendezvous with our allies. I am going to ride ahead."

"Yes, m'lord," Locke replied. "Will you take an escort, m'lord?"

"No," Valther replied. "I intend to savor the ability to ride alone in my own lands safely." Locke smiled.

"I understand, m'lord," he said. "I shall try not to lose the army between here and there." Valther smiled back.

"See that you don't," Valther said, smiling. He spurred his mount into a gallop.

The afternoon was pleasant, with just a hint of chill in the air. The rhythmic pounding of his horse's hooves on the road echoed in his bones. Valther galloped until he was out of sight of the army and then slowed his mount to a trot.

Like most of his lands, the terrain here was flat, with few trees, most of the land having been put to the plow. People looked up from their fields as he rode past. Valther waved to them, knowing they did not know who he was. Perhaps he should have accepted Locke's offer of an escort. It would be unfortunate if he were mistaken for the enemy and shot by a farmer. Still, he wore the emblem of the Fox clan, and the people waved back.

Nothing untoward happened and, within an hour, Valther caught his first sight of the towers of Heathton. As he approached, Valther could see only minor damage. Good— work crews should have the castle repaired before winter.

"Who goes there?" a sentry challenged. Three men on horseback rode up to him.

"Chief Valther of Foxmire," Valther replied.

"Where is your army, m'lord?" the sentry asked.

"Close behind," Valther told him. "I rode ahead to confer with your chieftain."

"We will lead you to the command pavilion, m'lord," the sentry offered.

"No need," Valther replied. "Stay at your post—I'm certain I can find it."

"Yes, m'lord."

As Valther approached, it became obvious that the only appreciable damage was to the gate itself. That should be able to be repaired before the harvest. Excellent.

"Valther!" Urall's voice called to him. Valther dismounted and handed the reins of his horse to a page who ran up to him.

"Greetings, Urall," he said.

"Greetings," Urall replied. "Where is your army? Did you lose it in a ditch somewhere?"

"Hardly," Valther replied. "It is an hour or so behind me. I rode ahead so that we could confer."

"Without an escort?" Urall said. "Is that wise?"

"I have faith that my allies have cleared this area," Valther replied, smiling. Urall nodded.

"Indeed," he said. "Come, then—Skald is waiting in my pavilion."

Gavin sat alone in his pavilion. Five clans currently stood against Reykvid. If Braun marched, and he almost certainly would, that would be six.

Another possibility, the one that now troubled him, was that the former Star clan would rally with Braun when he marched through. On their way to Ravenhall, Gavin had noticed the almost open hostility with which his troops were received here. Now, on their way back, the reactions were the same. Reykvid was not loved here in what was once one of its loyal holdings.

Valerian had destroyed everything. Everything Gavin's father had spent a lifetime building was in ruins. Even if Valerian used his power to save the kingdom from this attack, the Reykvid that Magnus had built was dead. Instead of a kingdom fashioned of trust and honor, Reykvid was now a tyranny of fear and oppression.

"Majesty," the guard said, stepping into the pavilion. "A messenger has arrived from Reykvid."

"Send him in," Gavin said quietly.

"Your majesty," the messenger said, entering the tent and kneeling before Gavin.

"You may rise," Gavin said. "What news have you brought me?"

"Majesty, Foxwood and Heathton have fallen under attack," the man replied, rising to his feet.

"When?"

"Six days ago, majesty."

"Is that all you have for me?" Gavin asked.

"I fear so," the man said.

"You may go," Gavin replied.

So, Foxmire had fallen and Valther had split his forces as Gavin had anticipated. The city must have fallen in only a few days. Certainly the castle had not yet fallen. Heinrich was more capable than that.

Not that it mattered. Gavin was beyond hope. What little hope he had clung to was dying. And soon, when Valerian had no more use for him, he would die as well.

He found that thought oddly comforting.

Chapter
------- **Twenty-One** -----------

BRAUN SURVEYED THE force at his command. He had spent all winter training and equipping the militia for this war. Now he was able to field an army of a size unprecedented for his clan. Over five thousand men in all—less than a third of what Gavin had brought against him.

That had been a sobering experience. He had expected Gavin to march against him with a force of ten thousand or so—not almost twenty. Reykvid was *too* powerful.

That would change soon enough. The united clans would see to that.

"Captain," he said, "give the order to march."

"We are not going to attack Foxguard?" Urall asked, questioning Valther's decision to simply march past Ivanel's first border fort.

"It would delay us too much," Valther replied.

"I agree with Urall," Skald said. "I like not the thought of leaving an enemy behind us."

Valther laughed.

"What are they going to do?" he asked. "Attack us from behind? With two hundred men? If they do, we shall turn and crush them."

"They could attack the siege train," Urall pointed out.

"That is why my cavalry and a thousand militia ride with the train," Valther replied. "Two hundred infantry will be no threat to our engines."

"My lords," he assured them, "the border forts are of no concern to us. We must hasten to join our other allies at Reykvid. After we sack Smithton, we will march directly to Gavin's palace."

"Very well," Urall grudgingly agreed.

"Aye," Skald echoed. "We would not want to miss the battle at Reykvid."

"Indeed we would not," Valther agreed.

Bjorn pushed through the snow covering the entrance of his shelter. The first storm had passed this morning but had been followed immediately by another. He made his way to the smaller cave he had fashioned for a latrine.

The first storm had lasted three days. He had no idea how long this second would last. Every day—every hour grated on his nerves. Bjorn looked to the east. He could not see the lair through the blowing snow—could not even see the first of the mountains he would have to pass to get to it. If he tried to climb the saddles in this, he would either die or become hopelessly lost.

No, he would simply have to wait and trust that the gods knew what they were about.

The army was up at dawn, breaking camp. Despite Gavin's efforts, the rumors of the attacks had spread throughout the camp. The men knew that the kingdom was falling.

By the end of the day they would pass out of the lands of the Star clan and into what used to be the lands of the Golden Eagle clan—Gavin's father's clan. Those lands had been apportioned between Ivanel and William as inducement to form the initial core of Reykvid.

That clan was no more. In its place had risen the kingdom of Reykvid. The three united clans had gone forth and petitioned their neighbors to unite with them. After much negotiation two clans had agreed to join—the Hare and Lynx clans.

Magnus had built forts and garrisons throughout the kingdom with the taxes he collected from his new subjects. Roads that had been questionable at best were patrolled and cleared of bandits, and trade flourished within the kingdom.

And then Chief Harold of the Star clan had attacked the new kingdom. Magnus had marched his armies straight to Star Hall, the heart of Harold's clan. There he had exacted his vengeance, hanging Harold from the battlements of his own castle.

Then he had departed, leaving the people of the Star clan to rebuild their clan. When Balder became chief, Magnus had approached him with open arms and taken the Star clan in as willing, loyal subjects. Finally, Ravenhall had been persuaded to swear loyalty to Magnus. Reykvid had seemed unstoppable. It had been a golden age.

And it was over. In less than three years, Valerian had destroyed it all. One clan had revolted, another was likely to do so and five other clans marched against them.

"Majesty!" his guard told him. "A messenger from Wolfden wishes to see you."

"Send him in," Gavin replied. He doubted that it was good news.

"Majesty," the messenger said, kneeling as he entered Gavin's tent.

"Rise," Gavin said wearily. "What news do you have?"

"Majesty," the messenger replied, "Wolfden has fallen under siege."

"When?" Gavin asked.

"Four days hence, majesty," the messenger replied. "The Badger clan has attacked us with a force of almost four thousand men. The Elk clan was supposedly a day's march away with just as many."

Gavin nodded. Wolfshire and Pelton had fallen quickly. Under attack by both clans, Wolfden would not hold out much longer.

"Thank you," Gavin said. "You may go. Guard!"

"Yes, majesty?" the guard asked in reply, stepping into Gavin's tent.

"Summon Baron William," Gavin said. "I have news for him."

"We approach Star Hall, my lord," Braun's chief captain told him.

"Thank you, Guthlaf," Braun said. "Is there any sign of resistance?"

"The city is barred against us," Guthlaf replied. "A sizeable force of militia is gathered on the city wall. Perhaps a thousand men."

"Let us hope we do not have to fight them," Braun said. Braun's men could take the city, but not without suffering heavy casualties, and each man lost was one man less at the siege of Reykvid.

"Yes, lord," Guthlaf agreed.

Braun rode up to the gate of Star Hall under a flag of truce. Guthlaf rode nervously beside him.

"Hail, Star Hall!" Braun called.

"What do you want, Raven?" a man in bronze called down to him. This must be the captain of the militia. He was too old to be a regular.

"I wish to parley with your chieftain!" Braun replied. "I am Braun, chief of the Raven clan. Will he come and treat with me?"

"I will send a messenger to the hall," the militia captain replied. "That is all I can do."

"We shall wait," Braun said. "Who is your chieftain now that Balder rots in Gavin's dungeon?"

"Wulfgar!" the captain replied. There was a trace of contempt in his voice.

"But is not Ingeld Balder's brother?" Braun asked.

"Gavin named Balder's cousin chieftain," the captain replied.

"Does Gavin now determine the lineage of the Star clan?" Braun asked.

"I will send the messenger," the captain replied. He turned away from Braun.

Braun smiled. He had known very well whom Gavin had named chieftain. He also knew that Wulfgar was not a popular man. No doubt Ingeld yearned to avenge his brother.

After quite some time, the militia captain returned.

"Wulfgar will meet with you," the captain told him.

"Excellent!" Braun replied. Before he could engage him in any further conversation, the captain withdrew.

Braun waited for what seemed like forever. He glanced over to Guthlaf, who frowned back in reply. What was taking this upstart chieftain so long?

Finally the gates opened just enough to allow a portly man and four guards to emerge from the city. The gates remained open behind them. Obviously Wulfgar was more concerned with his own avenue of retreat than the safety of his city.

"What is the meaning of this?" Wulfgar demanded. "How dare you invade my lands?" Braun looked the chieftain over, wondering how the man's horse could bear to support him.

"We march against Gavin," Braun replied. "I have no quarrel with the Star clan. Will you march with us against the tyrant?"

"Never!" Wulfgar said. "The Star clan is loyal to the crown! We will not side with traitors!"

Braun frowned. What Wulfgar really meant was that he wanted to hold his power, and Gavin was the only way he could do that. Still, he was not actually speaking to Wulfgar. It was Wulfgar's men whom Braun wanted to overhear.

"Will you side with a MageLord instead?" Braun asked. "While your chieftain rots in Gavin's dungeon?"

"Balder is a traitor!" Wulfgar replied angrily. "*I* am chieftain now! And the Star clan will not side with traitors while I am."

"I do not recognize you as chieftain," Braun challenged. Wulfgar's mouth fell open, and he began to flush with rage.

"Ingeld," Braun continued, "Balder's brother is the rightful chieftain of the Star clan until Balder returns. You are nothing more than Gavin's boot-licking toady."

"Y-you," Wulfgar stammered, "I . . . how . . . Guards! Kill them!"

Braun backed his horse away a step and drew his sword. Guthlaf and the standard-bearers did likewise.

"Kill them!" Wulfgar shouted.

"My lord," one of the guards said, "we are under truce."

"I am your chieftain!" Wulfgar shouted. "Kill them!"

"No, my lord," the same guard, presumably the commander, replied.

"Go back behind your walls, Wulfgar!" Braun said. "Reconsider your decision. At dawn tomorrow I will sack your city and hang you from the battlements of Star Hall like a slab of pork!"

Wulfgar practically fled back toward the gate.

"I apologize, Chief Braun," the guard commander said before he turned to leave.

"If you are truly men of honor, put your true chieftain in his hall," Braun said. "Then we will speak again!" The guardsman said nothing in reply as he rode away.

Braun turned his mount and also rode away. He would not want to be Wulfgar tonight. . . .

Gavin's spirits did not rise at the sight of Reykvid. Today he did not even ride back in hollow victory—today he returned in defeat.

"Hans," he said, "take the militia and billet them in the city. We will need them to defend the city when Valther and his allies arrive."

"Yes, majesty," Hans replied.

Gavin looked up at the towers of his palace. For some reason the thought entered his mind that he would not see them standing so proudly again.

Of course not, he thought. *After this battle Valerian will have no more need of me.* Once he had demonstrated his power by destroying the armies of seven neighboring clans, no one would dare to oppose him. Then he would be free to dispose of Gavin and the others.

"William, Ivanel," Gavin ordered, "begin assigning the regulars to posts within the palace. I doubt that we have a sevennight before our foes arrive."

"Yes, majesty," they acknowledged.

"Come, Lord Chancellor," he said. "Let us ride ahead and see how the preparations for the siege are progressing."

"Of course, majesty," Valerian replied.

Gavin spurred his horse forward, anxious to inspect the preparations. The palace was a beehive of activity. From here Gavin could see that supplies flowed in from the city below via a steady stream of mules as the occupants prepared for the coming siege. Obviously Wiglaf had arrived safely with Gavin's orders.

The guards at the gate brought their pikes up to salute as Gavin and Valerian rode through the gate. Gavin turned to the left, passing the stream of mules that led to the inner gate.

Barrels and crates filled the inner bailey. Gavin nodded—

the preparations were going well. There looked to be enough supplies here to keep the defenders of the castle alive for several fortnights.

Gavin dismounted, and the pages hurried to take his and Valerian's mounts. People parted to allow them to pass.

"I am going to change out of my armor," Gavin said. "Join me in the throne room within the hour, Lord Chancellor."

"Yes, majesty," Valerian said.

Gavin turned and walked to his quarters. A hot bath would be a welcome thing before attending to matters in court.

The throne room was filled with Gavin's officers, sergeants and the higher-ranking castle staff. Slate-haired old Sigmund, the castellan, had served Gavin's father for years. Now he briefed Gavin on the preparations for the siege.

"Majesty, how many men will be bivouacked between the walls?" Sigmund asked.

"Seven thousand," Gavin replied. "One thousand of those are cavalry."

"Do you mean to feed the horses as well, majesty?" he asked.

"Yes," Gavin replied.

"Majesty!" the castellan objected. "That will tax our supplies severely."

"We can rethink that later, Sigmund," Gavin replied. "If the siege lasts longer than a sevennight, we will most likely butcher the horses."

"Yes, majesty," Sigmund said.

"How long will the supplies you have gathered last a force of that size?" Gavin asked. Sigmund consulted his papers and muttered to himself for a moment.

"Three fortnights, majesty," he replied. "If we butcher the horses after a sevennight, we can add another two fortnights to our time."

"Very good," Gavin said. "I have a full two fortnights of supplies with me, courtesy of the Raven clan."

"That will add another fortnight to our time," Sigmund replied.

"Three full moons," Gavin noted.

"Yes, majesty," Sigmund replied. "A full season."

"Excellent," Gavin said. "They'll not starve us out, then."

"Not likely," Sigmund agreed.

"Majesty!" a guardsman interrupted, walking up to stand beside Sigmund. "A messenger has arrived from Smithton."

"Bring him in," Gavin replied. Gavin and Ivanel exchanged glances of concern. Smithton was the chief city of the Fire Sword clan—Ivanel's lands. So, Valther had arrived at Smithton.

"Majesty," the messenger said, kneeling before the throne. He was very young, still a boy really. His beard had not yet come in.

"Rise and report," Gavin ordered.

"Majesty, the Fox, Bear and Griffon clans laid siege to Smithton three days ago," the messenger reported, confirming Gavin's and Ivanel's fears.

"Majesty," the messenger continued, "they number almost ten thousand. We do not have the strength to repel them. We beg for your aid!"

"We have no aid to give," Gavin replied.

"But, majesty!" the messenger began.

"What is your name, lad?" Ivanel asked, interrupting the messenger.

"Finn, lord," the boy replied.

"Finn," Ivanel said, "the king has no aid to give. The clans Elk and Badger even now lay siege to Wolfden on their way here. Valther, with the aid of the Bear and Griffon clans, marches against us from the north. The Raven clan, and possibly the Star clan, march on Reykvid from the east. If we ride out to fight any one, the others will cut us off from the palace. We must face them all here, where we are strongest. I promise you, we will take our lands back."

"Y-yes, lord," Finn agreed. There was a quaver to his voice.

"Who is your father, son?" Ivanel asked.

"Unferth, lord," Finn replied.

"*You* are Unferth's boy?" Ivanel asked. "I am getting old too quickly. Captain Eadgil?"

"Yes, lord?"

"Take young Finn here and see that he is outfitted and assigned to the infantry," Ivanel said. "We will give him the chance to avenge his countrymen."

"Yes, lord!" Eadgil replied. "Come, lad—we'll get you a sword and some armor."

Gavin watched as Ivanel's captain led young Finn away. In all likelihood, the boy would never see his father again. Suddenly, Gavin felt very tired and the weight of the crown on his head seemed to double.

"I am weary from our march," Gavin announced. "We will convene again on the morrow."

"Yes, majesty," Sigmund acknowledged. The entire room rose and knelt as Gavin descended from the throne.

Forgive me, Finn, Gavin thought. *I have no hope to give you.*

"Lord," Guthlaf said, stepping into Braun's pavilion. "There are sounds of combat coming from the city."

"I know, Guthlaf," Braun replied. "I have been watching."

"Shall we attack?"

"Certainly not," Braun replied. "We could wind up battling the very people we want in power. No, we shall let our neighbors sort this out for themselves."

"Yes, lord," Guthlaf said.

"Rouse the camp, however," Braun ordered. "If Wulfgar's forces emerge from the city, I want to be prepared to defend ourselves."

"Yes, lord," Guthlaf acknowledged.

Braun followed Guthlaf out of the tent. He stopped and turned to face the city of Star Hall. The sounds of shouting and the clash of arms had receded for the moment.

It had been a strange battle. There were no fires and few, if any, women's screams to be heard.

A man who battles in his own home strives not to damage it, he thought. Both sides fought in their own home tonight. One careless fire could rage throughout the entire city.

Braun waited. The sounds of battle rose and ebbed as the combatants fought through the city. Around him, the camp rose to battle readiness. Guthlaf returned shortly.

"The men are ready, lord," he reported.

"Good; prepare my steed and the flag of truce," Braun replied. "We may be going forth to parley instead of to battle."

"Yes, lord." Guthlaf departed to carry out his orders. The sounds of battle ebbed again. After a time, they did not return. The city had fallen as silent as death.

Guthlaf returned with Braun's horse and two standard-bearers. Braun lifted himself into the saddle. From the back of his steed, he surveyed the battlements.

A scant hour after the initial sounds of battle had woken him, Braun saw men return to the walls around the city. Now they would find out who had prevailed.

Soon the sound of trumpets came from the gate, and a large white flag of truce could be seen waving from the battlements.

"Come, Guthlaf," Braun ordered. "Let us see if the Star clan's new chieftain is more reasonable."

"Yes, lord," Guthlaf replied.

They rode up to the gate. As they approached, Braun saw a small object hurled toward them from the battlements. He reined his mount to a halt as the object bounced and rolled to a stop in front of him. Wulfgar's head.

"Gavin's puppet fouls our hall no longer!" a tall, slender man shouted from atop the gate.

"Are you Ingeld?" Braun asked.

"I am," the man replied. "Rightful chief of the Star clan until my brother's return."

"Will you march with us against Gavin?" Braun asked.

"I will!" Ingeld shouted back. "I shall either free my brother, or avenge him! Will you join me in my hall tonight, Braun?"

"I would be honored," Braun replied, smiling.

Another stone has just been added to Gavin's crypt, Braun thought as he rode toward the opening gate of Star Hall.

"It will take some time to gather our forces," Ingeld explained. "I have already sent messengers to the border forts with my orders."

"How many men do you think you can field?" Braun asked.

"Perhaps a little over five hundred regulars," Ingeld replied. "And another two hundred cavalry. In a couple of days I should be able to levy about two thousand militia."

Braun took a drink of his wine. He had hoped for more, but

Gavin had pulled heavily from all his subjects to form the army that had invaded Braun's lands.

"How many of your men are in Reykvid?" Braun asked.

"About five hundred regular infantry and a thousand militia," Ingeld said. "No cavalry."

"Will they turn on Gavin when we arrive?"

"Almost certainly not," Ingeld replied. "They will be under his thumb, obviously. However, once we clear the wall, they will almost certainly join with us."

"Good," Braun replied. "We will wait two days. After that, we must march on. Can you be ready by then?"

"Yes," Ingeld replied. "How large will the combined force of the allied clans be?"

"Over twenty-five thousand men," Braun replied, allowing for casualties.

"Twenty-five thousand!" Ingeld exclaimed.

"Aye," Braun replied. "Enough to do the job!"

"Let us hope so," Ingeld replied. "If Gavin *is* in league with a MageLord, an army ten times that size might not be enough to 'do the job.'"

"Then we can only hope," Braun replied, "and pray."

"Hrothgar help us," Ingeld said.

Chapter
-------- Twenty-Two ------------

THE WIND BLEW harder the closer Bjorn climbed to the saddle. It sucked the warmth from his body—made his joints stiff and his hands numb. He desperately wanted to stop and rest.

Keep moving, he thought. *Keep moving, you fool, or you'll freeze! You're almost there.*

He was almost there. The saddle between the peaks was less than a hundred feet above him now. It would be stupid to stop and die so close to the top. Bjorn forced his legs and arms to carry him further. The slope was steep, but by crawling on his belly and using his axe in the packed snow, he was able to make progress fairly easily, if slowly.

Besides, lying down gave the wind less opportunity to steal his warmth. Bjorn used his axe to cut another handhold in the snow. With his legs and his free hand he pushed and pulled himself up another foot closer to the top. Handholds above became footholds below.

It had become a routine. Chop, grab, lift; chop, grab, lift—one painful foot at a time.

It will be easier going down, he promised himself. It had to be. *Chop, grab, lift.*

It had taken him almost two days to climb this one saddle. *Chop, grab, lift.* He had at least one more such climb to make before he reached Arcalion's mountain lair. *Chop, grab, lift.* At least the lair itself seemed to be a fairly gentle slope all the way to the top. *Chop, grab, lift.*

Bjorn's breath burned in his lungs. *Chop, grab, lift.* For some reason, the slightest exertion seemed to tax his wind. *Chop, grab, lift.*

Finally, he reached the top of the saddle. Bjorn pulled himself over the top to the relatively flat crest. The wind

252

howled past him like a demon. Still, Bjorn sat there for a moment, looking across at the lair. Yes, he had one more saddle to climb, but only one, thank the gods. Then he would come face to face with Arcalion—with death.

No. He had already seen the face of death. Death was not a fiery maw, large enough to swallow a man whole. Death was dozens of tiny mouths with needle-sharp fangs. Death was slowly suffocating beneath tons of earth and snow. What Arcalion could do to him was nothing by comparison.

"Death is freezing to death on top of a damned mountain!" Bjorn added aloud. He looked down at the slope below him. Now he just had to figure out how to get down. . . .

Gavin startled awake and sat bolt upright in his bed. Someone was knocking very loudly on his chamber door. The knocking stopped.

"Majesty!" a guard called through the door.

"Enter!" Gavin called back. This had best be important to awaken him in such a rude manner. Unfortunately, it probably was.

"Majesty," the guard said, opening the door and kneeling before Gavin's bed. "Forgive me for waking you, but Arik has arrived from Starwatch. He says that he bears news which you must hear right away."

So, Braun had reached Starwatch. If he had reached Starwatch this quickly, then the Star clan had not attempted to hinder him. Chances were that Wulfgar had been deposed and that Ingeld now led his clan against Gavin alongside Braun's forces.

"Give me a moment and then send him in," Gavin told the guard.

"Yes, majesty," the guard replied. Gavin rose from his bed after the guard had left. He dressed quickly, throwing on a simple tunic and leggings.

"Send him in!" Gavin called. "And get my page in here!"

The door opened and Arik entered, kneeling before Gavin.

"Forgive this intrusion, majesty," he began.

"Forget the apologies," Gavin interrupted. "Just tell me why you are here."

"Majesty, Braun and Ingeld arrived at Starwatch yesterday

morning," Arik replied. "They lead a combined force of seven thousand men."

"Sit," Gavin said, seating himself in a chair by the garden window. His page had arrived and was busy drawing the curtains and setting out breakfast.

"Is Starwatch under siege?" Gavin asked.

"No, majesty," Arik replied, taking the chair opposite his king. "They marched past Starwatch without so much as slowing down. It was all that I could do to stay ahead of their advance riders."

Gavin nodded. As depleted as the garrisons were, it was no surprise that Braun ignored them. Seven thousand men had nothing to fear from a garrison of two hundred. Gavin should have pulled that force back to Reykvid when he marched past Starwatch himself.

"When will they arrive here?" Gavin asked.

"Possibly by nightfall, majesty," Arik replied.

"Thank you," Gavin said. "I shall alert the barons and . . ."

"Majesty," a guard interrupted, stepping into the room.

"Yes?" Gavin replied.

"A messenger has arrived from Wolfden," the guard said. "He insists on speaking with you at once."

Gavin closed his eyes and sighed. More bad news, almost certainly. He opened his eyes.

"Send him in," Gavin ordered.

"Yes, majesty."

"Majesty," the messenger said, kneeling before Gavin, "Wolfden has fallen. Chief Offa and Chief Hengest now march toward Reykvid with a force of almost eight thousand!"

"When will they arrive?" Gavin asked.

"Within three days, majesty," the messenger replied. "Also, Captain Eomund of Wolfpeak sends word that he is bringing his force to Reykvid to aid in your majesty's defense."

Gavin glanced at Arik. If the Raven and Star clans arrived before Eomund, the force from Wolfpeak would be annihilated.

"When will they arrive?" Gavin asked, turning back to the messenger.

"By nightfall, majesty," the messenger replied.

"Is that all?" Gavin asked.

"Yes, majesty."

"You may go," Gavin said. "Thank you."

"Yes, majesty." The messenger rose and left Gavin's chambers.

"Arik," Gavin began.

"I shall ride to meet Eomund," Arik said, guessing Gavin's unspoken request. "I shall inform him to hasten his march."

"Thank you," Gavin said. "I know you have already ridden long."

"These are bad times, majesty," Arik replied. "I hope that a little rest is all I have to fear losing."

"Hrothgar protect us," Gavin said. Arik rose, bowed and left.

Hrothgar is more likely to destroy us, Gavin thought.

"Guard!" Gavin called.

"Yes, majesty?" the guard said.

"Summon the barons, General Hans, the castellan and the Lord Chancellor," Gavin ordered.

"Yes, majesty!" the guard replied, closing the door to Gavin's chambers.

Gavin rose from his chair. He glanced down at the breakfast the page had set out for him and turned away from it. He was not hungry.

Gavin stood on the battlements looking to the east as if he could see the army still two hours away. The garrison from Wolfpeak had just arrived a few moments ago. Arik had gotten word to them in time.

They were a weary-looking lot. They had brought no supplies when they had fled from Wolfpeak. The enemy behind them had forced them to travel lightly to stay ahead of it. Instead, with no rations, they had force marched all the way from Wolfpeak. Fortunately, they would have time to rest and recover before any actual attack came.

"We are ready," Ivanel said, walking up behind Gavin.

"In another hour, drive them out," Gavin ordered. He had ordered Ivanel and William to strip the soldiers from the Star clan of their armor and weapons. Now the disarmed warriors waited inside the outer gate. Once their clansmen had arrived, they would be driven out to join them. Gavin wanted no traitors inside the palace to open the gates.

"Yes, majesty," Ivanel replied.

"Should we not simply kill them?" Valerian asked. "Why give the enemy another five hundred men?"

"That would turn our own troops against us, Lord," Gavin explained.

"How bothersome," Valerian replied.

You pig! Gavin thought. *All of this is your fault!*

"Yes, Lord," Gavin agreed.

"No matter," Valerian said. "Once all of the armies have gathered together, they can die with their clansmen."

Gavin remembered the destruction of Bjorn's cabin in the Wastes. He had no doubt of Valerian's ability to carry out his intent. Nothing could stop him.

"I believe it is time for dinner," Valerian announced. "Shall we?"

"I am not hungry, Lord," Gavin replied.

"Nonsense. You must keep up your strength, majesty," Valerian chided. From the MageLord, it was the same as a command.

"Yes, Lord," Gavin agreed. Valerian and Ivanel left the battlements. Gavin looked once more to the east before turning to follow them. Soon the clans united against them would be destroyed, and nothing would be left to stop Valerian. Then Gavin would die.

Hrothgar, let it be soon, he thought. *There is no hope left.*

Bjorn looked up at the ominous slopes of the volcano in the last light of day. Smoke and steam rose from its ice-crusted surface.

It had taken him six days to climb through the range to this point, but he had made it. Now, in his heart, there was no doubt that this was the lair. Here, ice and fire lived together beneath the Northern Curtain. No other place could be the lair.

Still, it would have to wait. Bjorn looked to the north. Another bank of storm clouds loomed over the horizon. By morning it would be impossible to climb the relatively gentle slopes of the volcano. Arcalion would have to wait.

Bjorn turned back to his task of digging his shelter. The gods only knew how long this storm would last. . . .

The snows from a late winter storm floated down onto the burning fortress of Smithton. The battle here had been fierce, but ultimately futile for the defenders. In less than a fortnight the hall of the Fire Sword clan had fallen.

"Do we march, Valther?" Urall asked.

"No," Valther replied. "Let us tend to our wounded and bury our dead for the rest of the day. We can march in the morning. We will need wagons to transport the wounded."

"We should be able to salvage plenty of wagons from the city," Skald noted.

"Good," Valther said. "We will march on the morrow. Let us meet in my pavilion to celebrate and plan our strategy."

Gavin stood atop what was commonly called the king's tower. To the north he could see down to Reykvid itself. To the east he could see out across the plains where the combined armies of four clans waited to do battle.

A late winter storm was moving in from the north. Only time would tell whether it brought rain or snow, but a chill in the air told Gavin that it might be snow. That would be good. It would be nice to see another snowfall before he died. He only wished that he could have seen summer again.

"Gods, forgive me," he said aloud. Alone, with no one to see or hear, he could voice his sorrow.

"At least allow me to see my father again before I join Hela to pay for my crimes," he added. Of course, no answers came—no assurances were given.

After a time, Gavin turned and descended down the tower stairs toward his chambers.

Bjorn stepped out of his small cave into the clean winter air. The storm had passed after three days, leaving everything, even the volcano, with a pure coat of white.

Today! Bjorn thought. *Today I reach the end of my search.*

The slopes of the volcano were much gentler than the surrounding mountains. Even so, Bjorn was panting for breath minutes after beginning his climb. His goal was the nearest column of smoke issuing from the side of the mountain.

It took him over an hour to reach that point. The slopes of the volcano might be gentle in comparison to the rest of the range, but it was still difficult going. Bjorn finally caught sight of the vent.

The opening was only half as tall as a man. Noxious-smelling fumes trickled from the hole in the mountain. This was *not* the entrance to the lair. Not unless Arcalion was smaller than a calf.

From where he was, Bjorn could see two other columns of smoke flowing from the mountain. One was almost on the same level, and the other was a good quarter way up the mountain.

He could reach the one at this height faster, but the higher openings were more likely to be the lair. Arcalion would undoubtedly lair high on the mountain, like an eagle.

Doggedly, Bjorn began to climb. Long before he reached the vent, he could tell that it was no wider than a man's head. Likewise, the lower vent, while fairly wide, was not even tall enough for Bjorn to wedge his arm into.

By the end of the day, Bjorn had explored almost a dozen vents, only to find that none of them was large enough to be a bear's lair, let alone Arcalion's. Tomorrow Bjorn would make for the peak. Hopefully there he would find the entrance to the lair.

Bjorn climbed into the narrow, inactive vent that he had found earlier today. This would save him the trouble of digging a cave for the night.

Tomorrow, he thought. *Tomorrow I will find him. If he's here.*

But Arcalion was here. He *had* to be.

Bjorn stood in the mouth of the vent. This was by far the largest vent he had yet found. If he reached above him, his fingers would just barely touch the top of the entrance. This *must* be it.

Bjorn dug into his pack. He had eaten the last of the bear meat last night. All that was left in the pack was the gold he had brought and two wolf pelts. Bjorn knelt down and carefully laid the gold coins out on the floor of the vent. Hopefully the gold would make Arcalion wait long enough to hear what Bjorn had to say.

Bjorn rose from his knees and looked down the vent. He could only see about thirty feet. No doubt he would hear the dragon coming before he saw it.

"Arcalion!" he shouted into the tunnel.

". . . arcalion . . . arcalion," his own voice said back to him mockingly. There was no other response.

"Arcalion!" Bjorn shouted again. "Arcalion, hear me! The MageLords have returned!"

". . . returned . . . returned" echoed back. Bjorn waited, but again there was no response.

"Arcalion!" Bjorn shouted.

". . . arcalion . . . arcalion . . ." After a moment, Bjorn turned away. Arcalion wasn't here. This was not the lair. The disappointment was too much to bear.

The mountain shuddered beneath his feet. Bjorn grabbed wildly for the side of the tunnel.

Oh, gods! he thought. *My shouts must have caused an avalanche!*

Bjorn looked up toward the peak of the mountain. There was no sign of an avalanche. The mountain shuddered again. Before Bjorn could turn to flee down the mountain, something erupted from the mouth of the volcano.

Leathery wings the length of Lars's hall and the color of pitch spread out to catch the wind. Bjorn's first impression was that the dragon was all wings, neck, and tail. It reached the peak of its upward soar and turned to dive back toward the earth.

Straight at Bjorn.

Reason fled as primal instincts seized control of his mind. He dove for the mouth of the vent, which he now knew was far, far too small for Arcalion. He screamed as a massive gout of flame blasted the ground where he had stood scant heartbeats before.

Bjorn fled down the tunnel, escape his only thought. He spied a narrow crack in the wall of the tunnel. He forced himself into it. It led several feet back from the tunnel and stopped.

The tunnel shook. Small, sharp bits of gravel rained down on Bjorn.

The night-black tunnel in front of him suddenly filled with a brilliant light. Bjorn could feel the searing heat as the dragon's flame filled the tunnel in front of him.

"Oh, gods!" he shouted. "Bairn! Save me!"

The flame stopped. Bjorn waited, trembling in his crevice in the side of the tunnel. The next blast he feared never came.

Who comes to me in the name of Bairn? asked a deep, resonant voice. There was no echo.

Bjorn blinked. Had that voice been in his mind? Or had he simply imagined it?

Who comes? the disembodied voice said again.

"Bjorn!" Bjorn shouted. "Bjorn Rolfson!" His own words echoed in the tunnel.

Come to me, Bjorn Rolfson, the voice commanded. *I shall not kill you—for now.*

Bjorn wriggled out of the crevice toward the tunnel. He cautiously peered around the corner toward the mouth of the tunnel. There was no sign of the dragon.

Come, puny ape, the disembodied voice commanded. It sounded irritated. *The word of Arcalion is forged of gold.*

Bjorn walked toward the mouth of the tunnel. He glanced down where he had placed his gift and then knelt down in astonishment.

Bjorn had laid the coins out roughly in the symbol of Bairn. Now that symbol was perfectly scribed in the floor, cast in solid gold.

That is all that has saved you, the voice told him. *Come forth.*

Bjorn swallowed and rose to his feet. Arcalion waited below the entrance to the vent. Bjorn's breath caught in his throat at the sight of the immense creature.

Arcalion's head alone was taller than Bjorn. His mouth was stretched into a permanent, reptilian smile with teeth as long as Bjorn's arm. His color, which at first seemed black as night, was truly all of the colors of the rainbow, dotted with flecks of gold. The dragon was easily the most beautiful creature that Bjorn had ever seen. And the most terrifying.

Yes, the voice said in his mind. *I am magnificent, am I not?*

"Yes," Bjorn breathed. "Even if you slay me, it will have been worth it simply to see you."

The dragon's eyes opened, and his head raised aloft on his massive, sinuous neck to study Bjorn.

Your words are not empty flattery, the voice finally pronounced. *Why have you come?*

"Great Arcalion," Bjorn began, "a MageLord once again walks the earth."

WHAT? the voice thundered in his mind. Bjorn literally fell to the ground from the impact within his mind.

"Y-yes," Bjorn said. "Even now he seizes power over all those around him. It will not be much longer before he seeks to control you as well."

Who is this MageLord? the voice asked. *What house does he claim?*

"His name is Valerian," Bjorn replied, climbing back to his feet. "He claims to have been the lord of the House of Rylur."

He is an impostor, Arcalion said.

"No!" Bjorn insisted. "He *is* a MageLord! I have felt his Power—seen his aura."

Rylur was Lord of the House of Rylur, Arcalion explained. *Valerian would have been Lord of the House of Valerian, had it existed.*

"Great Arcalion," Bjorn said, "the man held my mind and those of three other men as puppets. He put an entire room of people to sleep. He flies through the air on horseback. He called a star from heaven to destroy my home! If he is not a MageLord, then *what* is he?"

Open your mind to me, Bjorn Rolfson, Arcalion commanded. *Release your puny wards that I may see what you have seen without destroying your mind.*

Bjorn took a deep breath and then exhaled, banishing with it as much of the Power as he could. With a mental shrug he scattered his wards away from him.

Very good, Arcalion said. *Be still.*

Bjorn felt Arcalion enter his mind, much as Valerian had when he had sifted through Bjorn's memories. Valerian had been human, however. The touch of Arcalion's mind was completely alien. Thoughts and feelings, concepts that Bjorn could never hope to understand, crossed through his mind as Arcalion sifted through Bjorn's mind.

Finally, after reviewing all of Bjorn's memories concerning Valerian, Arcalion withdrew. As he did so, Bjorn experienced a feeling that he *did* comprehend. Amusement.

"Is . . . something funny?" Bjorn asked.

Valerian is no MageLord, Arcalion replied. Bjorn still sensed amusement in the dragon's mental touch.

"But how is that possible?" Bjorn asked. "I have never seen such Power!"

Indeed you have not, Arcalion agreed. *Valerian was an* apprentice *MageLord—probably of only the second rank, although almost ready to receive his third.*

"An *apprentice*!" Bjorn exclaimed. "Valerian is nothing but an apprentice?"

Yes, Arcalion said. *You will guide me to him.*

"Then . . . you will help us?" Bjorn asked.

No, Arcalion replied. *I shall help myself. Valerian is, even so, a possible threat to me.*

"Thank you," Bjorn replied.

Do not thank me, little mage, Arcalion said. *I promise, you and your kind will regret disturbing my slumber.*

Chapter
------- Twenty-Three ------------

HELGA WATCHED TO the north. Bjorn still lived—that she knew. Something was different, however. His touch had grown fainter over time, but now it grew stronger with each passing moment. And he was afraid. Excited and afraid.

Spring had finally come to Lars's hall. The snows were beginning to melt, and some shoots of green had already ventured forth to greet the sun.

Her eyes lifted to the sky. For some reason her gaze was drawn to the northern sky.

A bird lazily flapped its wings in the distance. Helga's eyes narrowed. That was no bird—its movements were wrong. More like a bat's.

And then she saw the aura that surrounded it like a faint haze. To feel the Power from this distance . . .

"Arcalion!" she shouted—almost shrieked.

"Arcalion!" she cried again. "Bjorn found him! 'Tis Arcalion! Arcalion approaches!"

People ran to her at the sound of her cries. Frightened eyes followed her pointing finger to the batlike shape above the horizon. In the short amount of time that she had seen it, the figure had grown as large as a hawk. It's long neck and snake-like tail were clearly visible.

"Arcalion!" others shouted. "'Tis Arcalion!"

"Is Bjorn with him?" Lars asked, pushing his way through the crowd to stand beside her.

"Yes!" she replied, laughing. "Bjorn rides the dragon!"

"Gods," Lars breathed. "To fly through the air on dragon-back . . ." For a moment he just stared in wonder. Then he shook his head violently.

"To the barns!" he shouted. "Quickly, drive out the

livestock! We don't want the dragon to stop and rip out the roofs for his meal! Spare those with calf! Hurry, you miserable whoresons!"

Men raced to comply with his orders. Soon, panicked cattle were charging across the fields. Just in time, too. Helga watched as the dragon swooped down toward the cattle like an owl chasing mice. . . .

"You're going to eat again?" Bjorn asked.

Be thankful that I will only claim four of your cattle— today, Arcalion replied. *Although this is the first time that a meal has been freely offered to me.*

Bjorn hung on to the harness that lashed him to the dragon as Arcalion dove toward the largest body of the herd. The dragon had made Bjorn wait at the lair while he flew off to take four of the large deerlike animals that Bjorn had seen. On their way here, Arcalion had taken another four. Now he was about to claim four cattle.

Bjorn felt an impact as Arcalion took the first cow in his foreclaw. Another impact soon followed, and then two more as the rear claws also seized prey. The dragon beat his massive wings and lifted himself back into the air. The cattle hung lifeless beneath them.

Arcalion banked to the right, away from the lodge. Soon the dragon was heading west, not south toward Hunter's Glen and Reykvid.

"Where are you going?" Bjorn asked.

To the place where your cabin once stood, the dragon replied. *So that I may eat my prey in peace and see the damage for myself.*

"A MageLord and now Arcalion," Lars whispered. "Nothing else I live to see will ever compare to these."

"One thing shall for me," Helga disagreed. "The sight of my husband safely home."

Bjorn tried not to watch as Arcalion devoured his meal. The dragon ripped the cattle apart with its teeth, devouring whole cows in three quick bites. Blood stained the snow for yards around the massive maw.

Climb onto my back, little mage, Arcalion commanded.

"I thought you wanted to look over the damage to the cabin," Bjorn said.

I have seen enough, Arcalion replied. *Valerian is powerful—he may even be of the third rank. He must die.*

Bjorn climbed up Arcalion's foreleg and onto the dragon's back. The body that had, at a distance, been dwarfed by the wings, neck and tail of the dragon was easily the size of the cabin that had once stood here. Bjorn made his way to the base of the dragon's neck.

Walking on the dragon's back was somewhat like walking on the cobblestone streets of Reykvid. The scales were hard and unyielding, and Bjorn doubted that Arcalion even felt his footsteps. He sat down at the base of the dragon's neck and lashed himself into the harness that Arcalion had allowed him to put there.

No sooner had Bjorn fastened the last strap than Arcalion bounded into the air, higher than the surrounding trees. Bjorn could not fathom how the dragon's legs, tiny in comparison to the rest of his body, could hurl him so high into the air.

The massive wings snapped out and beat the air mightily as Arcalion once again lifted himself into flight.

Which way? Arcalion asked.

"South," Bjorn replied, looking around. Everything looked so different from the air. It was difficult to orient himself.

Due south to Reykvid? Arcalion asked.

"Uh, I doubt it," Bjorn said.

Remember! Arcalion commanded. Bjorn felt the dragon probe his mind and quickly discarded his wards. Arcalion searched Bjorn's memories of the trip to Reykvid and the trip here from Hunter's Glen. Finally, the dragon's mind withdrew from his own. Bjorn could feel a trace of disgust in the dragon's withdrawing presence.

Do you not even know your own world? the dragon asked, contemptuously.

"I'm . . . sorry," Bjorn replied.

No matter, Arcalion said, turning slightly to the west. *We will retrace your landbound journey. It will lengthen our trip.*

"Do you know when we will arrive?" Bjorn asked.

By nightfall, Arcalion replied.

Nightfall! Bjorn thought. It had taken him two or three sevennights to travel from Reykvid back to Hunter's Glen. Then it had taken all of them another fortnight to travel this far north. Arcalion would travel this in a mere half day?

I am no crawling, landbound ape, Arcalion replied to Bjorn's unspoken thoughts. Bjorn said nothing. He simply watched in wonder as the ground rolled past beneath them.

"My lord," the scout said to Valther as he rode up, "we have met scouts from the Raven clan." Another man rode next to the scout. From his colors, black on black, Valther guessed that he was one of those scouts.

"How unfortunate," Valther said pleasantly. "The ball has started without us." The other man smiled.

"No, my lord," he said. "We have been eagerly awaiting your arrival."

"How many now surround Reykvid?" Valther asked.

"Fourteen thousand," Braun's scout replied. "The clans have surrounded the palace and cut off all land routes to the city."

"Where shall we position our troops?" Valther asked.

"My lord," the scout replied, "your army is still several hours' march from Reykvid. If you will return with me, you may discuss that with Chief Braun and the others long before your troops arrive."

"Very well," Valther agreed.

"My lords," he said, turning to Skald and Urall, "will you allow me to represent you to the other clans, or do you wish to come along as well?"

"Uh," Skald began hesitantly.

"You may speak for me, Valther," Urall replied. "I trust you to keep my interests in mind."

"As do I," Skald agreed.

"Good," Valther said. "I shall leave Captain Locke in command of my force during my absence. He is at your disposal."

"I think we can handle the march," Urall replied, smiling.

"Then let us be off," Valther said to Braun's scout.

"At once, my lord," the scout replied. Valther spurred his horse forward, leaving the slower moving army behind.

Today! he thought. *Today we meet again, little prince! Only this time it is* your *castle which is surrounded.*

The army surrounded Reykvid as no castle ever before. The camps stretched for hundreds of yards out from the palace. Once Valther added his forces to this army, nothing could save Gavin.

Even so, Valther noted four distinct camps. There was enough room between the camps to march a supply train. Each camp boasted its own ditch and rampart. There were no earthworks surrounding Reykvid itself.

Valther shook his head. This was not unity—it was distrust. He, Urall and Skald had abandoned separate camps, and separate commands, after Foxmire. When Smithton had been sieged, one earthwork had surrounded the entire city, manned by all of their troops together.

Valther raised his eyes to the palace. It was formidable. Valther did not understand, however, why Magnus's father had built his palace outside the city. Doing so had robbed it of its first line of defense—the city. Here, instead of first fighting through the town militia, the army could assault the palace directly.

"Braun's camp is the second to the north," the scout told Valther.

"Lead on," Valther replied.

Braun's camp was the largest of the four. It was easy to see why he was the nominal commander of this siege. He had the most strength. The scout led him to Braun's pavilion.

"We should attack the palace!" someone was saying too loudly. "Now that your engines have arrived . . ."

Conversation fell silent as Valther entered the tent. One chieftain, Braun if the black raven on his purple tabard was any indication, rose from behind the table.

"Greetings, Valther!" he said, recognizing the clan markings on Valther's armor. "Are Urall and Skald with you?"

"No," Valther replied. "They remained behind with the army. I rode ahead to discuss our strategy and to find where we should make our camp."

"I wish they had come," Braun said. "We could use their voices here tonight."

"I speak for Urall and Skald as well," Valther replied. "My words are their words."

"What . . . ?" Braun asked. He looked beyond Valther to the scout who had escorted him here.

"It is true, my lord," the scout told his chieftain. "I myself heard them give him the right to speak for them."

The room fell silent. Valther scanned each face at the table. Braun's dark, lean features looked puzzled and surprised. Ingeld, Valther already knew. He nodded pleasantly at Valther as the Fox clan chieftain's gaze met his. Valther smiled and nodded back in reply.

The other two men in the room were presumably the chieftains of the Elk and Badger clans. Valther could not tell which was which, as they bore no clan markings. They both looked at Valther warily. These men would be new to their seats, and not experienced in dealings of this level.

"I believe you already know Ingeld," Braun said, breaking the silence.

"I do," Valther replied.

"This is Chief Offa of the Elk clan," Braun said, indicating the large, blond, bearded man to his left.

"And this is Chief Hengest of the Badger clan," Braun added, gesturing toward the smallish, dark-haired man who sat next to Offa.

"A pleasure, my lords," Valther said, taking a seat at the end of the table opposite Braun. "Now, what was this I heard about attacking the palace?"

"My engines have arrived today," Braun explained. "It was my intention to use them to begin assaulting the city from above with oil and stones."

"The city is no threat to us!" Offa objected loudly. "They cannot lead a strong enough force up those narrow trails to attack us. We should begin to besiege the palace!"

"We would simply lose the few engines we now have," Braun said. "Gavin's engines on the wall will destroy them before our third volley."

"How many engines do you have?" Valther asked.

"Six catapults," Braun replied.

"Braun is right," Valther said. "Gavin's engines would destroy ours long before any serious damage could be done."

"Shall we just sit here and grow old?" Offa asked.

"Offa," Valther said, "it will not inspire confidence if the men hear us bickering like old women. I cast my three lots against an attack on the palace. With Braun's lot, that settles the issue."

"And mine," Ingeld added.

"Good," Braun replied. "Then we proceed with the attack on the city."

"No," Valther said.

"What?"

"Offa is right," he said. "The city is no threat to us—unless we make them desperate. Our quarrel is not with the people of Reykvid, it is with their king. Or rather, the man behind their king. I cast my three lots *against* an attack on the city. We do not need to give them a reason to attack us."

"And my lot settles *that* argument," Offa added.

"I . . . see," Braun noted. He did not seem pleased. It was obvious that he had just lost his tenuous command of the siege.

"Are there any other engines on their way?" Valther asked.

"Yes," Offa said, much more calmly. "Hengest and I have two catapults each, which should arrive tomorrow. We lost four in the siege of Wolfden."

Valther wasn't surprised, considering Offa's eagerness to attack the palace with only six engines. It was a wonder that he and Hengest had any engines left at all.

"In two days, my own siege train should arrive," Valther added.

"How many engines?" Braun asked.

"Ten," Valther replied. "Two of which I built for the siege of Foxmire. Those two have a range of over five hundred yards on flat ground."

"Five hundred!" Braun exclaimed.

"Yes," Valther replied. "They do not fire quickly, but their reach is far. When they arrive, we can attack the palace with impunity. We will use them to destroy Gavin's engines, and then our other catapults will tear down his walls. In two days, Reykvid will fall!"

"It would seem that the battle has been planned," Braun said.

"There are more details to work out," Valther said. "Those can wait until Urall and Skald arrive, however. Now—where shall we camp?"

The farming town of Nalur's Ridge came into view beneath them. Arcalion dropped into a long glide, dropping quickly toward the small village. Bjorn could see a herd of cattle ahead of them.

How many cows does he eat in a day? Bjorn wondered. The dragon had struck the herds in Hunter's Glen as well. Bjorn hoped that none of his former neighbors had seen him.

When I am awake, I eat much, Arcalion's voice said in Bjorn's mind. The dragon was skimming along the ground toward the fleeing herd. Herdsmen fled in all directions. The ground flew past in a blur.

Four impacts in quick succession heralded Arcalion's capture of more cattle. Arcalion began to beat his massive wings again, lifting them into the air and away from the village.

"Will we still make it by nightfall?" Bjorn asked.

Before, Arcalion replied.

This time, as he had at Hunter's Glen, the dragon ate in flight. His long, snakelike neck was able to reach all four of his talons. Bjorn watched as the ground fell away beneath them. This would be a story to tell his children someday.

If he lived.

Gavin watched. The sun was nearing the horizon, and the last of the forces to be arrayed against them had arrived. Ten thousand men strong, Valther had come to claim his revenge.

Unfortunately for Valther, that claim was going to be challenged by a MageLord.

"Is this the last of them?" Valerian asked.

"Yes, Lord," Gavin replied.

"Do your guards watch the tower entrance, majesty?" Valerian asked.

"Yes, Lord," Gavin said again.

"Then it is time," Valerian said. "These worms will rue the day they challenged *me*!"

Gavin looked away. He could not bear to watch the carnage that was about to occur.

Hrothgar forgive me, he thought.

The wind sprang up without warning. At first the evening was calm, with only the faintest hint of an evening breeze. Then the winds were ripping through the camp strong enough to rip the tents from the ground.

Valther saw his half-erected pavilion ripped from its poles and carried inland on the wind. He turned to the west to face into the wind, and froze.

Over the sea, clouds boiled like a kitchen caldron. A black wall of rain swept toward them from the sea. Lightning flashed among the night-black clouds, illuminating them briefly with white and silver.

This was no natural storm. The clouds boiled and rolled like a thing alive. Valther felt the icy grip of terror clutch at his heart and weaken his knees. How did one battle the wind?

"Gods help us!" he shouted.

Gavin watched the storm roll over the palace. As he had at Bjorn's cabin, Valerian protected them from the forces he was unleashing. The wind, which had shifted from the west to the south, seemed to blow past the castle without touching it.

The city was protected from the worst of the storm by the walls of the fjord. Even so, the docks and longships had been destroyed before the wind had shifted.

Valerian did not care about the people of Reykvid, however. His attention was wholly focused on the enemy camp. The wind and the driving rain had all but destroyed the camps. Gavin watched as one of Braun's siege engines was ripped apart and carried away on the wind.

Men lay helplessly upon the ground, clinging to the earth for life itself. The siege was over. Then Valerian lifted his arms, and the first bolt of white fire descended from the sky. The earth erupted where it struck, and men and corpses alike were carried away to the north.

Gods help us! Gavin thought, closing his eyes.

                         *   *   *

"What is *that*?" Bjorn said. To the south, in the dying light
of day, a wall of frothing clouds and rain flashed with vicious
lightning.

Valerian's work, Arcalion replied. *Can you not feel the
Power?*

Bjorn could. The entire storm was filled with it. Could
even Arcalion battle someone capable of this?

Yes, came the reply. Arcalion was beating his wings wildly,
climbing in the air. Bjorn's ears threatened to pop.

The dragon made no attempt to evade the storm. He simply
folded his wings across his back and flew into the wall of
wind-driven rain. Bjorn lay down as the massive wings
covered him. He felt the dragon begin to fall. Bjorn's heart
beat wildly in fear. What was Arcalion doing?

Bjorn felt the impact of the wind when Arcalion passed
into the storm. Beneath the heavy wings he could see nothing,
but his stomach told him they were still falling.

They seemed to fall for an eternity as the winds buffeted
them about. After the initial impact, however, the force of the
wind seemed to diminish. On they fell.

Suddenly, Arcalion's wings unfolded and caught the wind.
There was a lurch as their fall came to an abrupt end. Bjorn
fought to control his stomach.

In an instant, he was soaked to the skin. There was the taste
of salt on his mouth. Below them, he could see the white-
capped, choppy waves of the sea. The wind ripped the tops of
the waves and mixed it into the driving rain.

There was another lurch as a sudden updraft caught the
dragon's wings. The sea quickly fell out of sight below them,
lost in the endless gray of rain. Bjorn hugged against the
dragon's neck, lest the changing winds pluck him from
Arcalion's back despite the harness.

"Why did you do *that*?" Bjorn shouted, but the wind tore
the words away so that even he did not hear them.

To match the wind, Arcalion replied. *Be silent!*

Without warning, the dragon rolled to the left. A white-hot
bolt of lightning cracked past them on the right. Bjorn heard
a sizzle and then a clap of thunder so loud it deafened him. He

cried out in pain—it felt as though someone had driven knives into his ears. How had Arcalion known?

The winds continually tore at them. Even the great dragon was not immune to nature's fury. Arcalion beat his wings, trying to navigate through the winds like a sailor trying to navigate a region of maelstroms. He was not entirely unsuccessful.

The dragon dodged the fires of the sky thrice more before they suddenly left the storm behind. Bjorn's breath caught in his throat.

All around them the storm raged. Here, in this place, the winds spun around them like a god's top. Green and rose-tinted clouds drifted lazily as if, a mere arrowshot away, the storm did not exist. It was the most beautiful thing Bjorn had ever seen.

"Where . . . *are* we?" he asked.

The eye of the storm, Arcalion replied. *Its beauty burns your soul, does it not?*

"Yes . . ." Bjorn replied.

There is dragon in you, Bjorn Rolfson, Arcalion said. *But we must hurry.*

"Yes," Bjorn agreed.

Arcalion crossed the eye of the storm quickly. Soon they were diving into another wall of rain. This time, Bjorn was prepared when the dragon folded its wings over him. Now he knew why.

If Arcalion flew into that wall with his wings spread, even he was not strong enough to keep them from being ripped behind him. This way, the wind would sweep them up as they fell and Arcalion could open his wings *with* the wind.

Again Arcalion flew through the insanity of the storm. Again he narrowly dodged the bolts of fire that struck down from above. Again they were drenched in more water than Bjorn would have ever thought could be held aloft in the air.

Ahead of them, Bjorn could barely see a cliff looming at them through the rain. One stroke of Arcalion's wings lifted them above it, and Bjorn saw a mighty castle. Reykvid!

Even over the wind, Bjorn could hear Arcalion's roar of challenge. The castle, unlike the surrounding area, seemed untouched by the storm. At Arcalion's roar, the defenders turned. Men fled as Arcalion lifted his wings and dropped toward the palace.

Bjorn almost fell from Arcalion's back when the dragon's hind legs grabbed onto the battlements of the inner wall. The wall groaned beneath the weight of the dragon. Bjorn quickly unlashed the harness that held him to the dragon and jumped.

The ground beneath the wall had been softened by the heavy rain of the storm. Still, the fall knocked the wind from his lungs, although the pelting rain would not let him black out.

Above him, Arcalion reached toward Valerian with his massive maw. . . .

Gavin turned at the sound of the strange, savage cry behind him. The sight of the dragon robbed him of what little hope he hadn't realized was left.

Oh, gods! he thought. *Valerian has called on a dragon of old!*

"What in hell?" Valerian exclaimed. Gavin looked at the MageLord in surprise. *This was not his doing?*

A massive impact shook the palace. Gavin turned back to the dragon. The dragon had landed on its hind legs on the inner wall. The stone battlements crumbled and fell to the ground. As Gavin watched, a human figure tumbled ignominiously from the dragon's back to the ground below. A rider?

"Bjorn!" Valerian cursed.

Bjorn? Gavin thought. Bjorn had brought this monster against them? How?

The dragon hunched on the wall like a dog standing on its hind legs and stretched its neck out toward them. That maw looked as though it could swallow a horse whole, let alone a man.

Gavin breathed a sigh of relief when it became obvious that the dragon could not reach them. Then the flame came boiling out from the dragon's throat.

Gavin cried out and dropped behind the battlements. He needn't have bothered. The flames stopped against an invisible barrier just beyond the battlements. Even this monster was not proof against a MageLord. Gavin peered out from behind the battlements.

~With a cry of rage, the dragon leaped from the inner wall. A single beat of its massive wings carried it across the bailey to the tower. Gavin looked up at a hundred feet of scaled death and fell to the tower roof, screaming unabashedly.

Talons longer than his forearm sank into the stone as the dragon sought purchase, like a bird on a tree branch. The huge maw dove at them. Gavin instinctively threw up his arm in an ineffective gesture of panic and screamed.

Valerian fell back against the battlements and raised his arms, then pulled his hands down viciously into fists. White fire shot from the sky, striking the dragon squarely between the shoulders.

The bulk of the dragon fell across the tower battlements before it toppled from the wall. The tower itself crumbled beneath the impact. Amid blocks of stone larger than himself, Gavin fell.

Something soft, yet hard as stone broke his fall. Gavin opened his eyes to find himself lying on the scaled belly of the dragon. Was it dead?

The dragon's eyes opened. It was *not* dead. Without thinking, or looking, Gavin jumped from the monster's belly. Where was Valerian?

With a deafening cry of rage, the dragon rolled to its feet. Gavin dove under a portion of the collapsed tower for shelter. Cautiously, he peered out from underneath the rubble.

Everywhere, he could see people running. Most ran for the gate—the army outside was nothing compared to what battled within the palace. All of them ran from the dragon.

Gavin needn't have bothered hiding. The dragon had no interest in him or any of the others that scurried like mice at its feet. Its attention was completely focused on the figure hovering over the palace.

The dragon exhaled another column of flame as it leaped from the ground toward Valerian. The flame flowed around the MageLord, outlining an invisible ball around him.

The dragon's fire must have concealed its movement, because another bolt of lightning struck the ground where it had been. The flame stopped and the massive jaws closed around Valerian's invisible ball.

Before those jaws could close, a bright flash gleamed from between them, followed by a thunderclap. The dragon's head was thrown backwards and it toppled onto the roof of the palace. The dragon plummeted through the roof, crushing the entire west wing of the palace. How many people had been in there?

Gavin saw the inner wall of the palace crumble. Soon flames were raging in the garden and throughout the palace. More screams echoed horribly in Gavin's ears.

Valerian rose into the air above the palace. Apparently he had sought refuge in the garden. Gavin saw the dragon's head shoot up after him, propelled atop its snakelike neck and followed by its massive torso. Once again, the jaws clamped around an invisible barrier.

This time, the dragon breathed fire as soon as it had seized the MageLord. Gavin watched as the jaws slowly closed together.

Suddenly, a bolt of white lightning sizzled down from the sky, striking the dragon between its massive eyes. The dragon's flame abruptly died. It stood for a moment before toppling into the north wing of the palace. There was no sign of Valerian.

"Majesty!" a voice shouted. Gavin could barely hear it above the howl of the storm.

"Here!" Gavin shouted as loudly as he could. He crawled from underneath the tower. Ivanel ran toward him. Blood ran from several cuts on his brow, and his tunic was torn and bloody in many places.

"Do I look as bad as you?" Gavin asked.

"I fear so," Ivanel replied. "We have to get you out of here, majesty!"

"Not before I kill that spawn of Hell!" Gavin exclaimed. As soon as the words came out of his mouth he and Ivanel both fell silent, staring at one another in shock.

"We're free!" Gavin finally said.

"Let's go find him!" Ivanel said. They drew their swords and walked toward the palace. The amount of damage was staggering. They were able to enter the palace through a breach in the wall of the west wing.

The west wing was completely destroyed. Rubble and bodies lay everywhere, and flames were beginning to lick at the ruins. He and Ivanel crossed quickly to the burning garden.

The vegetation in the garden was fairly light, so most of the fire had already burned itself out. Gavin walked to the body of the dragon and turned toward the head. If Valerian was here, he would be near there.

They found him, lying by the dragon's head. One side of his face was badly burned. His chest labored with breathing. He was still alive.

Gavin reached down and grabbed the MageLord's hair. He drew back his sword and half lifted Valerian's unconscious form. The MageLord's eyes fluttered open.

"I beg your pardon, *Lord*," Gavin said as he brought his sword down across the MageLord's neck.

"Majesty," Ivanel said. Gavin looked at his uncle and then to where he was pointing.

A barbarous-looking figure approached them. His blond hair and beard had obviously seen neither comb nor knife in some time. The man was wrapped in unsewn furs and hides which he had obviously taken himself. Bjorn.

"How," Gavin asked, pointing at the dragon with his sword, "do you explain *this*? You never told me you had such power!"

"Power?" Bjorn asked. "The only Power I used was my reason. I convinced Arcalion that Valerian was as great a threat to him as to us. He came willingly."

"Arcalion . . ." Ivanel breathed. Gavin said nothing for a time.

"I suppose I should thank you," Gavin finally said.

"Majesty," Bjorn said, "I had no idea that . . ." He allowed the words to trail off as Gavin fixed him with a cold glare.

"I know," Gavin said. "These deaths are not your doing, but his." He raised Valerian's lifeless head in emphasis.

"Still . . ." Bjorn began.

Little mage, Arcalion's mental voice whispered in their minds.

"Arcalion?" Bjorn said, hurrying to the dragon's side. "You still live?"

Yes, the dragon said, *although not for much longer.*

"What can I do?" For a moment there was no reply. The dragon's glazed eyes simply studied him for a time. Bjorn feared that the great dragon had already perished.

"Arcalion?" he said.

You would, the dragon's weakening voice finally said. *You would . . . save me if you could.*

"I would," Bjorn agreed.

You cannot. Heed my final warning, little mage. One apprentice almost claimed your world. What shall you do when a true MageLord returns?

Bjorn felt Arcalion's touch fade from his mind for the last time as the dragon's eyes clouded over.

"What we can," he answered.

Chapter
-------- Twenty-Four -----------

GAVIN WAITED TO ride out with his barons to meet with the chieftains north of what was left of Reykvid. At least Valerian had reduced their forces to the point where they were no longer a threat. The forces that remained in the city were enough to defend against them.

Ironically, Balder, deep in the dungeons, had survived the destruction of the palace. He also waited to ride out and meet his brother. All about the palace, workers sifted through the rubble, removing the dead and attempting to restore order to the chaos that had once been Gavin's home. Even so, no one had yet devised a plan to remove the dragon from the garden.

"Are we ready?" Gavin asked, turning from the gruesome sight.

"Yes, majesty," Ivanel replied.

"Then we ride," Gavin said.

His father's grand pavilion had been erected on the plains east of the palace where the enemy camps had once stood. Once Gavin's party left the palace, another party rode toward the pavilion from the east. The enemy chieftains.

Both arrived at the pavilion together.

"Brother!" Ingeld said, when he sighted Balder.

"Ingeld," Balder acknowledged. "It is good to see you."

"Aye," Ingeld agreed, dismounting to embrace his brother.

"I return the clan to you, brother," Ingeld said.

"Thank you."

"Shall we gather inside?" Gavin asked.

"After you, majesty," Valther replied. For a moment the two men studied each other.

"I shall go first, majesty," Balder finally volunteered.

"Thank you, Balder," Gavin replied. Balder went inside. Several tense moments passed before he emerged.

"The pavilion is clear," he announced. Gavin dismounted and went inside, taking a small package from his saddlebags.

They all followed, taking seats opposite one another. Ingeld showed surprise when Balder sat with Gavin's party. Balder motioned for his brother to join him.

"Let us begin," Gavin said, "with my humblest apologies for the wrongs done to your clans in the name of Reykvid." He unwrapped the package—Valerian's head.

"And my assurances that they will never occur again," he added.

It was almost nightfall by the time Gavin returned to what was left of the palace. The workers had accomplished much in one day, although he noted that the dragon still lay in his garden.

The same could be said of the negotiations. Much had been settled in one day, but there was still much to be done. Gavin longed for bed, but there was one more task to be attended to.

He made his way down the steps in the back of the throne room to the dungeons.

"Leave us," he said to the single guard as he held out his hand for the keys.

"Yes, majesty," the guard replied. Gavin waited until he had left before turning the key and lifting the bar from the heavy oaken door.

Bjorn sat on a straw pallet in the cell.

"I liked my quarters the last time I visited better," the mage quipped as Gavin entered.

"I don't doubt that," Gavin said. "But it would not be safe for you to be at large. Here I need not fear a knife in your back."

"Save for yours," Bjorn retorted.

"It will be dark soon," Gavin replied, ignoring Bjorn's comment. "A horse will be waiting for you outside the east gate. I shall leave the door unbarred and unguarded. I think you can manage from there."

"I take it I am to trust you," Bjorn mused.

"You do not have much choice, I fear," Gavin replied. "In

three days, if you are found within my kingdom, you will be put to death, as will any mage we discover."

"Is this the thanks I get?" Bjorn asked. "After I have saved your kingdom and all the other clans? Imprisonment for myself and persecution for my kinsmen?"

"I have no choice," Gavin replied, looking away.

"There is *always* a choice," Bjorn disagreed.

"No," Gavin said. "Not always. You said it yourself—there are those who turn from your teachings and strive for the power of the MageLords. Valerian was not even a Lord, simply an apprentice. All it takes is one of you to turn and succeed for all of us to suffer. Goodbye, Bjorn. If you ever can, please forgive me."

The horse was waiting as Gavin had promised. Bjorn breathed a sigh of relief. As Gavin had said, Bjorn had little choice but to trust him. He walked up to the animal and prepared to unhitch it from the post it had been tied to.

"Bjorn Rolfson," a familiar voice said to him.

"So, it is a trap after all," Bjorn said without turning.

"No," Ivanel replied. "I am alone. I only wished to speak with you."

"About what?" Bjorn said, turning to the baron.

"Mainly to offer my thanks," he said, "and my apologies. It was I who convinced Gavin and William to release you."

"Thank you," Bjorn said. "It is nice to know that *someone* is grateful."

"Gavin is as well, but he does not understand."

"And you do?" Bjorn retorted derisively. Ivanel lifted his hand in the Sign.

"Yes," he said. "I do."

"You?" Bjorn asked incredulously. "But . . . how?" Ivanel had no aura whatsoever. Never had one clue to his identity slipped while Bjorn had known him.

"I have nothing of the Talent," Ivanel explained. "But my mother was of the Circle. Please try to forgive Gavin. His methods are wrong, but in his heart he strives for the same thing we do. Never again."

"Never again," Bjorn agreed.

"We will speak again, Bjorn Rolfson," Ivanel said. "In the

days ahead, many of the Circle will have to flee these lands. Will you help me?"

"I will," Bjorn said.

"So we part," Ivanel said. The words sounded strange coming from Gavin's uncle.

"So we part," Bjorn echoed. Bjorn mounted his steed and turned to the northeast. He had a long trip ahead of him.

Helga waited, watching to the south. Spring had passed into summer and now summer was half over. Still, she was certain that Bjorn yet lived and that he was near.

A single rider appeared at the edge of the forest. Helga peered out the narrow window. Was it?

It was! Bjorn was home!

"Bjorn!" she shouted. "Bjorn has returned!" She ran to the door, where the men on night watch pulled the heavy bar back. As the doors opened, she slipped between them to run and greet her husband.

Bjorn saw Helga running out to meet him and dismounted. She ran into his arms and Bjorn pulled her to him for a long kiss.

"Bjorn, lad!" Lars's voice said. "Welcome home! Although I see someone has beaten me to the welcome. And doing a better job of it than I am minded to, as well."

"I told you he would return, my lord," Helga said.

"That you did, lass," Lars agreed. "So, has the MageLord perished?"

"He has," Bjorn replied. "Unfortunately, Arcalion perished with him."

"Ah, but it sounds like you've the tale to tell," Lars said.

"Lars!" Bris admonished. "Tomorrow! He has other things on his mind tonight."

"No," Bjorn said, "you shall have your tale tonight, my lord. But I must warn you—it does not have a happy ending. And I fear it is not yet over."